ANNE STUART
THE Devil's WALTZ

MIRA®

ISBN 0-7783-2273-4

THE DEVIL'S WALTZ

For Gackt—the most delicious 450-year-old Norwegian vampire/Japanese rock star/Georgian rake alive today. Exquisitely beautiful, he's the best inspiration around.

Arigato, Gackt-san.

1

The Honorable Miss Annelise Kempton did not suffer fools gladly. Unfortunately it was her lot in life to suffer them far too often, and to maintain a relatively polite mien in the face of idiocy. It came from being penniless, almost thirty years old, unmarried, not a beauty and far too bright for a woman.

She'd accepted that lot long ago, with her usual lack of self-pity. Her profligate father hadn't been able to arrange any chance of marriage, but her godmother, Lady Prentice, had managed to provide her with a season when she was seventeen. Which, as her astringent older sister, Eugenia, had pointed out, was a total waste of money, since Annelise was hardly the type to attract many suitors. Eugenia herself had refused the offer of a season, knowing her own limitations, and married a vicar in Devon, where she happily ran her household, her husband, the church and the village.

But no offers had appeared for Annelise, who was taller than most of the indolent young men of society and unfortunately blunt, and her godmother chose to sponsor her younger sister, Diana, the next time around. Diana at last had succeeded, marrying a plump, pompous widower with three children and then promptly presenting him with four more.

And Annelise stayed at home, watching her father lose everything, including, eventually, his life in a drunken riding accident.

Lady Prentice stepped in once more, but there hadn't been much she could do. Diana would have welcomed her into her home, but Diana's husband was a toad, the children were spoiled, and she would do nothing more than take care of the litter as it yearly increased.

Eugenia would have taken her—she was a woman who knew her duty, but two strong-minded women could hardly share the same household, and besides, Joseph's vicarage was barely large enough for their two children and three servants. There was no room for a spinster aunt.

And the Honorable Miss Kempton could hardly work for a living in any of the posts suitable to one of a slightly lesser station. She might have been a companion or a governess, but her bloodlines went back to the Magna Carta, and no Kempton could accept money for services rendered.

They could, however, accept hospitality. And in the five years since her father's death, Annelise had lived with the Duke and Duchess of Warwick, proving a good friend to the dying duchess and keeping news of her husband's infidelities away from her fading eyes. Once the duchess passed away there was no place for her, and she moved to the Merediths in Yorkshire, where she spent her time entertaining a half-senile old lady, speaking French with the passably well-behaved grandchildren and growing older.

But the old lady died, as old ladies tend to do, and the children grew and had no interest in French since their countries were, as usual, at war, and once more Annelise moved on, this time to the London home of one Mr. Josiah Chipple and his exquisitely beautiful daughter, Hetty. Lady Prentice, the architect behind these living arrangements, had manufactured a lifelong friendship between Annelise's mother and Hetty Chipple's grandmother, ignoring the fact that one of Hetty Chipple's grandmothers was a barmaid and the other a farm girl. Not that it mattered. No one was going to bother to check the gentle fiction, and Hetty Chipple was about to make her debut in a society that would fall upon her like a pack of wolves. She was young, she was beautiful and what she lacked in breeding and background she more than made up for in fortune. There were dozens of young men willing to overlook the smell of the shop for the needed influx of money, and that sort of thing bred itself out in a generation or two, while the sort of money Miss Chipple had could last much, much longer if carefully tended.

The first sight of the town house was not reassuring to the Honorable Miss Annelise Kempton. Chipple House had been carved into the marble plaque beside the commanding front door, and the front hallway was so littered with marble statues that one had to move very carefully to avoid knocking into one. The effect, clearly meant to be tasteful and pleasing, was instead over-blown and chaotic.

She was shown into a drawing room decorated in just the wrong shade of blue, and the furniture was all very new, very shiny and very uncomfortable. She sat on the cerulean sofa, her back ramrod straight, her long, gloved hands folded in her lap, and considered taking off her glasses so as to dull the effect of the rococo trim on the walls. She glanced upward, as if seeking heavenly gui-dance, only to find a painted ceiling that was a far cry from the Italian masters who had perfected the art. She lowered her eyes to her lap again, looked at the gray kid gloves that lay against her gray wool skirt and sighed.

She hadn't a vain bone in her body, but surely a new dress now and then shouldn't be too much to ask. Except, of course, that her visitations were that of a guest, not an employee, and one could not accept anything so personal as a gift. Lady Prentice had paid for her wardrobe when her father died, mourning and demi-mourning, all of the best cloth that lasted forever and would never wear out, so Annelise went through her drab life in drab colors, and probably would until she died.

She'd considered eating huge amounts of food so that the clothes would no longer fit her, but unfortu-nately her constitution was such that she could never put any extra weight on her spare body. When she did, it went straight to her already full breasts, and that was not a part of her anatomy that she cared to have straining at the dull gray cloth.

She reached up and moved her spectacles up a bit. She needed them more for reading than anything else, but felt they gave her a distinguished air that went well with her narrow, plain face and severe hair. She looked like what she was: a well-bred virgin of no attraction and therefore worthy of no untoward attention.

She dropped her glasses back down on her straight nose and sighed again. A lesser woman would have relaxed her backbone, at least while no one was there, but the Honorable Miss Annelise Kempton was no such laggard. She sat, and she waited, until she heard the sound of voices and laughter from the hall beyond the closed doors.

It was late morning—prime visiting time, but she had been told—no, requested—to arrive then, and so she had. Her clothes had already been taken to a guest bedroom, and all that was needed was to meet her host and his young daughter so she could decide just how much work lay ahead of her.

It was always difficult for people to assess her position in their households. Sometimes she was put in one of the better guest rooms, other times she was put in a place little better than a maid's room. Having had a good look at the decor in Chipple House, she was rather hoping for the latter this time around. Mr. Chipple's propensity for bright colors would be hard to live with, and few people bothered to do more than was absolutely necessary with the rooms the servants inhabited. As long as she had her own room she would be content. She had an aversion to sharing a bed with a stranger, particularly since most people she knew didn't share her affection for frequent bathing. It was the one thing she insisted on, and she usually got her way.

She heard the sounds of a man's voice—low, beguiling and too quiet for her to make out the words, but the timbre of it was doubtless irresistible. Not her host. It could only be her young charge who shrieked with unseemly laughter, and there was no missing the booming jocularity of another man, one who must be her host. Josiah Chipple was a self-made man, and his origins showed in his speech. She wondered if she'd be required to work on that, as well.

She was up to any task they asked of her, but that didn't mean she had to like it. She would smile, nod and behave herself unless pushed too far, and then Miss Chipple would marry gloriously and the Honorable Miss Annelise Kempton would move on to her next station on the road of life.

She was getting disgustingly maudlin, Annelise thought to herself, dismissing the morbid thought. She was in London, the most fascinating city in the world; she would doubtless be warm, comfortable and well fed. There would be books aplenty in this house to keep her occupied when she wasn't making certain Miss Hetty was behaving herself. And this way she was dependent on no one's charity, always a boon.

She could hear the heavy thud of the front door, the sounds of footsteps as they moved back toward the reception room she sat in, and she waited, half expecting to hear the crash of one of those huge statues. Instead she heard voices. Miss Hetty Chipple was not happy to have her here.

"Why do I have to do this, Father?" she asked in a plaintive tone. Even muffled through the thick doors it was not an unattractive voice, despite the faint whine. She had the proper, classless diction of a well-brought-up young lady—at least Annelise wouldn't be charged with a sow's ear.

The rumbling voice of her father was far less genteel. "Because I say you do, pet," he said. "You'll be moving into a new life, far grander than any one you've ever known, and there are all sorts of tricks and rules an old sea dog like me would never know. I want the best for you, Hetty, and I intend to pay for it. Besides, the Honorable Miss Kempton is doing this out of the kindness of her heart."

"Ha!" said Miss Hetty.

"Ha!" thought Miss Kempton, grimacing. And then rose gracefully as the door opened and she caught her first glimpse of the young lady.

To call Hetty Chipple a pretty young lady would be an understatement of the grossest order. She was breath-taking, from the top of her golden curls to the slippers on her tiny feet. Her waist was tiny, her breasts were pleasing, her eyes a bright, cerulean blue (obviously her doting father had been trying to match their hue when he'd had this room painted), her mouth a Cupid's bow. She moved into the room with a consummate grace that made the usually elegant Annelise feel awkward, and when she smiled politely she exposed perfect white teeth.

Josiah Chipple was just as she'd imagined him, a plain, no-nonsense sort of man in a plain coat of brown superfine. He had big, hamlike hands, a nose that had been broken at least once, beetling brows and a stubborn jaw. "My dear Miss Kempton!" he said with his thick, Lancashire accent. "You do honor to our poor household. We are both so sorry we kept you waiting, when you've been so kind as to accept our invitation. We had an unexpected visitor—"

"My future husband," Hetty interrupted.

Her father cast her a reproving look. "Now, now, Hetty, we're not rushing into anything. You can have your pick of almost anyone on the marriage mart—no sense jumping at the first stallion who wanders into the pasture."

"He's not the first—but he's the prettiest," Hetty said defiantly.

"We'll see. The season has just begun. Why don't you show Miss Kempton to her rooms? She must be exhausted from her travels."

Annelise hadn't had a chance to say a word yet, an unusual occurrence in her voluble life. "I came from my godmother's," she said, "in Kensington. It wasn't far at all. I'm delighted to meet you, Mr. Chipple." If he wasn't going to do the honors then she'd have to gently coax him in the right direction. "I'm so happy you've invited me to stay. And this must be Miss Hetty."

"Who else would I be?" Hetty responded.

Annelise kept her smile firmly planted on her face, disguising her clenched teeth. "Indeed, and quite charming you are," she said in dulcet tones. "But you'll find that proper introductions tend to take up a fair amount of time in polite society. A bore, but necessary."

Josiah Chipple beamed, unabashed at his own error. "You see, Hetty. She'll show you just how to get on. Should have done introductions first, of course. Why don't you two girls go on up and get Miss Kempton settled in? I'm sure you'll have a lot in common."

Thirteen years separated the two *girls,* Annelise thought, and probably the only thing they had in common was their nationality and their gender. And most young men would probably take issue with the latter. "That would be most agreeable," she said. "I'd like to freshen up a bit."

"I was going to go for a ride in the park," Hetty protested.

"You can do that later. I expected Miss Kempton would enjoy a ride, as well."

"I don't ride," Annelise said. It was both true and untrue. She hadn't been on the back of a horse since her father had been thrown to his death, and she had no intention of ever doing so again.

Josiah frowned. "You don't ride?" he echoed. "You'll have to learn. We'll see to it, won't we, Hetty?"

"I don't see why we should bother. She's not going to be here that long and I can go riding with one of the stable hands."

Rude, as well, Annelise thought. "I appreciate the kindness," she said, gently directing that sentiment toward Josiah, "but I have a fear of horses and I've never been able to overcome it." That was an out-and-out lie. She still loved them, even the black stallion who'd thrown her father. It hadn't been his fault—he'd carried her father a hundred times when he was that drunk. But in the end his luck had run out.

"Miss Hetty and I can go for a walk in the park later," she added. "In the meantime I would love the chance to improve our acquaintance."

It was going to need some improving. Miss Hetty was about to open that perfect mouth of hers to argue some more, when her father spoke.

"Go upstairs with Miss Kempton, Hetty," he said, and there was a note of steel beneath the rough voice. One that his daughter was wise enough not to disobey.

She flounced out of the room, not even bothering to glance over her pretty little shoulder to see if Annelise was following her.

"She's a high-spirited filly," Mr. Chipple said fondly, "but she's a good lass. I'm sure the two of you will be best friends in no time."

"I'm sure you're right," Annelise said faintly, and started after the obstreperous young creature.

Indeed, it was a shame she was too well bred to earn a living, Annelise thought as she slowly climbed the wide marble stairs. Hetty was waiting at the top of the flight, tapping her tiny foot impatiently, and Annelise had the fleeting notion that the little brat might try to shove her back down those stairs.

If she tried, she'd be going with her, she thought grimly. She reached the landing and gave the girl her coolest smile. The chit came only to her shoulders—making Annelise feel like a hulking giant.

Hetty looked up at her with her wide blue eyes. "My, you are a big one, aren't you?"

Hetty's comment had the opposite effect from what she'd intended. At least the girl was smart enough to know where to twist the knife. Very few people knew she was self-conscious about her height, but Hetty had homed in on it immediately. She was going to be a worthy challenge.

"Quite large, in fact," Annelise said briefly. "But I trust you have enough sense not to make personal remarks to strangers. I'm more than aware that you are none too happy with my arrival, and plan to demonstrate just that in any way you can. However, in polite society one does not comment on another's physical attributes. A general compliment usually suffices."

Hetty stared at her. "I don't have to be polite to you. You're a mere hireling."

"In fact, I am not. People of my station do not work for a living. I am merely helping out as a favor to my godmother. I consider you my charity work."

Hetty blinked, and Annelise wisely moved farther from the treacherous marble staircase. "You dare…" Hetty sputtered.

"My dear child, I am the Honorable Miss Annelise Kempton, daughter of a baronet, granddaughter of an earl, with my family's name emblazoned in the Domesday Book long before anyone in your family learned to read. I would suggest you consider carefully what *you* dare. I don't expect your father would be pleased to hear that you insulted your guest. He went to a great deal of trouble to arrange this visit."

Hetty's lower lip trembled, and Annelise remembered that for all her arrogance, Hetty was just seventeen, and far less sure of herself than she appeared.

"Pax," she said gently. "I only want to be of assistance, and I promise you I'm neither a governess nor an ogre. My task is to help you attract the right sort of attention, secure the marriage you deserve. Your fortune is astonishing, particularly considering you are your father's only heir, and of course it's unentailed. Beyond that, you know perfectly well that you are very pretty."

Hetty was rousing herself to fight back. "I'm not pretty, I'm beautiful! One of the greatest beauties of all time, better than the Gunning sisters, better than—"

"You don't need to be more beautiful than the Gunning sisters—they had no money to lure a well-bred husband. With your face and your circumstances you should do very well indeed, once I've given you a little polish."

"I don't need—"

"Even a rare diamond needs a bit of polish," Annelise said firmly. "Now show me to my room and you can tell me about the young men you've met, who might be a good prospect. I don't need to ask who has fallen at your feet—I'm certain they all have. But you can afford to be very picky when it comes to a mate. He needn't have money, but your father would prefer a title, and he must be of good character."

"I've already chosen," Miss Hetty said firmly. "And no one is going to tell me I can't have him!"

That was what she'd heard them arguing about earlier, she thought. "Has the gentleman made known his intentions?"

"He doesn't need to. You said it yourself, every man in London is at my feet. I can choose whomever I please, and I choose him."

"And who, exactly, is this paragon who has captured your heart?" she inquired, following her charge down the wide, unfortunately-papered hallway until they came to a bedroom door. Hetty flung it open with a dramatic gesture that was entirely wasted, since there was nothing dramatic about the large room she was being offered.

"He's a viscount," Hetty said. "Or at least he will be once his uncle dies. And he doesn't have a penny, but he does very well at cards. Besides, I'll have enough money for the both of us."

"True enough."

"And he's absolutely beautiful. I deserve a beautiful husband, do I not?"

"There is no reason why you shouldn't have one," Annelise replied, wondering how she was going to broach the possibility that extremely beautiful men were often not particularly interested in women.

"So I'll have him."

"Who?"

"Christian Montcalm."

And if Annelise had been the type to swoon, she

would be flat on the garish carpet at that very moment, dead to the world.

Fortunately Annelise had never swooned in her life, so she simply shut the door, leaned back against it to look at the defiant Miss Hetty and said, "No."

2

"I beg your pardon?" Miss Hetty said in a frosty voice that would have done Annelise justice.

"Christian Montcalm is out of the question. His reputation is notorious, and he is no sort of match for an innocent young girl like yourself," she said. "I know he's a very handsome man—I've seen him. He's also a shallow, degenerate wastrel, a gambler, a seducer, a charlatan, and if even half the stories that are spread about him are true then you'd be better off dead than married to such a depraved monster."

"Don't be ridiculous—he's not a monster at all. He's absolutely charming."

"That's what's so dangerous about him," Annelise said grimly. "His face and his charm lure people into trusting him. Much to their misfortune."

"What in the world did he ever do to you?" Hetty demanded.

"Not a thing," Annelise replied truthfully. "We have never been formally introduced, and I hope never to be. He's a man who doesn't belong in the kind of circles your father aspires to. I'm astonished he would even countenance such a match…"

"Oh, he says I can't have him," Hetty said airily, tossing herself onto the damask-covered bed with a total lack of decorum. "But I know my father. I'm his only child—of course he'll want me to be happy, as long as I manage to secure someone with a title. If I want to marry Christian Montcalm then I shall. After all, I'd be a viscountess—not quite as nice as a duchess but all the dukes I've met have been old and ugly. Besides, I expect all Christian needs is the love of a good woman."

Annelise laughed. "I'm afraid Mr. Montcalm has availed himself of the love of a great many good women, leaving them the worse for it. You'll find someone else just as charming and far less dangerous."

The moment the word was out of her mouth she could have bit her tongue. *Dangerous.* What impressionable, romantic, headstrong young girl wouldn't be fascinated by a dangerous man? Annelise had never been that young or that stupid, but Hetty Chipple was ripe for trouble, and clearly she was not going to be listening to common sense for the time being.

She would just have to make certain Hetty wasn't in Montcalm's company until she came up with a suitable alternative to distract her. Girls Hetty's age fell in and out of love quite easily. London society was certain to be able to produce at least one attractive contender to distract her from Montcalm's dubious charms.

A demure expression crossed Hetty's lovely face. "I suppose you're right," she said with a soulful sigh that

Annelise didn't believe for a moment. "I'll just leave you to get settled in, shall I? I need a bit of a rest myself—have to be beautiful for tonight."

"Tonight?"

"We're going to Lady Bellwhite's. I'm sure you'll enjoy it."

"I've always enjoyed her gardens," said Annelise, remembering the opportunities for mischief that ran rampant in the place. "I'm certain I'll appreciate it even more with your company."

Hetty almost made a face but she stopped herself in time, clearly remembering that she was trying another tack with her unwanted friend. "I shall, as well," she said sweetly.

Annelise waited until the door closed behind her to sit down on the now-rumpled bed. It was a good, solid mattress—at least there were some advantages that money could buy. She pulled off her bonnet and set it down beside her, catching a glimpse of her reflection in the mirror.

Having spent the better part of an hour staring at the perfection of Hetty Chipple, the vision was even more disheartening.

She glanced down at her feet. It was really unfair that she be cursed with big feet, particularly when compared to Hetty's tiny ones. Of course, her feet were in proportion to her ridiculously long legs, but even so, fate could have been kind enough to make at least something out of proportion.

But fate had been busy elsewhere. She had long legs,

long arms, a long neck and a long face. She knew her physical attributes far too well—she had fine gray eyes, but they were usually covered by her spectacles. Her hair was an indeterminate shade—a mixture of brown, blond and red hues, and the only thing she could do was pin it tightly to the base of her neck and hope no one would notice its odd color. At one point she'd tried to wear lace caps to further disguise it, which also had the benefit of proclaiming her old-maid status, but the caps tended to flap in her face and itch, or catch on the rims of her spectacles, and she'd given them up regretfully.

The cut of the dress was suitably shapeless, disguising her small waist as well as her large chest. Indeed, she wouldn't attract attention from anyone, which was just as she wanted it... Unlike Hetty Chipple, who would draw trouble to her like a magnet.

On impulse Annelise stood up and went to the window, looking across at the rambling downs of Green Park. In time to see Miss Chipple, totally without chaperon, disappear into the shrubbery.

Annelise didn't waste time with her hat. She raced out the door, grabbed the first maid she saw and tore down the steep marble stairs and into the street, dragging the poor girl behind her. Fortunately Josiah Chipple was nowhere to be seen. While Annelise was there as a favor to the shipping magnate, she still had a strong sense of responsibility, and letting a young girl run through a park unchaperoned was not going to happen while she was a member of the household.

It was a cool day, and there were doubtless strange

looks being cast their way, but Annelise was too determined to catch Hetty before she caused a complete scandal to even notice. She plunged into the bushes where she'd last seen Hetty, dragging the hapless maid with her.

She could see Hetty up ahead, alone, seemingly waiting for someone in the shelter of one of the overgrown bushes. There was no doubt who she was waiting for, and no doubt that Annelise would have to move fast.

She sped up, just as Hetty started to step through a narrow break in the hedge, and caught her by the back of her gown, hauling her backward.

Hetty was too astonished to let out more than a little squeak, but when she saw who'd grabbed her, her bright blue eyes filled with a murderous rage.

"You!" she said, her voice rich with bile. "Leave me alone."

There was one advantage to being almost a foot taller than Hetty—they were no even match. Annelise turned her around and shoved her at the maid. "Get back to the house, now!" she said. "And perhaps I won't tell your father that you're out to ruin all his careful plans."

Hetty opened her mouth to protest, then shut it again. So there was something that still had power over Hetty. "I'll never forgive you for this!" she hissed, and then flounced off, the maid rushing to keep up with her.

Annelise stood there in the chilly air, watching the pair of them, and she sighed. Challenges were all well and good, but her godmother had failed to tell her what a handful the girl was going to be. She might have to go to Mr. Chipple with her concerns, but not before she tried to talk Hetty out of her infatuation. Chipple might not know of the depth of Montcalm's depravity—he wouldn't have traveled in circles where Montcalm's unsavory reputation was bandied about, but Annelise had heard more than enough tales of the absolute perfidy—

"I take it that's Miss Chipple being dragged away?" a voice, rich with amusement, sounded in her ear. It was a warm voice, the same voice she'd heard earlier at the Chipples', but Annelise froze. She considered her options. She could ignore the voice, follow the two women and never look back. Or she could turn and face the cause of all this trouble and put him in his place.

She had never been a coward and she wasn't about to start now. Even though some small, sneaking part of her felt like someone turning to face a Gorgon, she knew perfectly well she wasn't going to be turned to stone, or a pillar of salt, or anything at all. But when she turned, she felt herself stiffen like one of Chipple's marble statues.

She had never been so close to him before. Her previous acquaintance, such as it was, had been across crowded ballroom floors, where she'd heard whispers about the women he danced with, the women he flirted with. She was well out of her league with someone like Christian Montcalm, and he would have been totally unaware of her existence—just another awkward wallflower. She had watched him, fascinated, and told herself "pretty is as pretty does" with a deprecating sniff.

But, oh my heavens, he was pretty! His dark hair was long, tied back simply, but one lock fell forward to caress his high cheekbone. She'd always had a weakness for well-defined cheekbones. His faintly tilted eyes were a deep, fascinating green—she'd never been close enough to see them before, but they held a hint of laughter that was undeniably appealing. And his mouth, his lips... It was no wonder he seduced every woman he met, talking them into doing unspeakable things. His rich, full mouth alone could seduce a nun.

And he was taller than she was. She'd expected he probably would be, since he towered over most of his dance partners, but that his height made her feel suddenly delicate was simply one more unfortunate circumstance. The man was well-nigh irresistible, particularly as he looked at her steadily out of those laughing eyes.

But Annelise was made of sterner stuff than that. She swallowed, then found her voice, grateful that it came out calm and cool. "That was Miss Chipple," she said. "And she had no business being out here meeting a gentleman without a chaperon. Though no gentleman would have ever agreed to such a meeting in the first place."

He appeared unruffled. "And what business is that of yours? Hetty didn't mention she had an ogre spying on her every move. I would have been more discreet."

"I doubt you know what discretion is," she said. "—and I'm a friend of the family, keeping her company while she makes her debut."

"No, you're not," he said, tilting his head to survey her more closely. "The Chipples know very few members of society as yet, and you're clearly not of their world. You're not a governess—you're not meek enough. If I guess right, you're a woman of breeding who's fallen on hard times. So exactly who are you?"

A number of retorts came to her, most of them originating from the stable. She had learned a very colorful vocabulary of curses from her father's stable lads, but she tried to keep them to herself. It was a cold spring day, but he was radiating heat, and those exotic eyes of his were very…disturbing.

"I'm someone who is going to make your designs on Miss Chipple impossible to carry out," she said. "So cast your lures elsewhere."

He laughed. Like everything about him, his laugh was enticing. "That sounds like a challenge. And a gentleman never resists a challenge."

"But I thought we'd already ascertained that you're no gentleman."

He didn't even blink after so heinous an insult. "I'd kill a man for saying that," he said mildly.

"Then it's fortunate for me that you have some standards, despite all rumors to the contrary. Goodbye, Mr. Montcalm."

Another figure stumbled through the bushes, this time a shorter, slender man, with his hair askew and a faintly bleary expression on his face that signaled either dim wit or too much wine at such an early hour. Annelise didn't care to find out.

"Who's this Long Meg, Christian?" the man demanded. "And where's the pretty little chit? I was going to keep watch for you but demme, I think I'd prefer to go inside and get something to warm me up."

"Go right ahead, Crosby," Montcalm murmured without moving his gaze from Annelise's. "I still have some business to conduct."

"Not with her, old man!" Crosby protested. "The woman's a dragon. And a bit long in the tooth. Not your type at all."

"I'm open to all possibilities," Montcalm murmured in a silken voice. "She's not that old, and if I can get her to remove those spectacles she might be quite entertaining."

"There'll be no getting beneath her skirts, old man. I know the type—too starched to even bend at the waist."

Annelise had had enough. Bravery was all very well and good but standing so close to Christian Montcalm and listening to his friend insult her was more than she cared to endure.

"Good day, gentlemen," she said, letting a lingering, ironic emphasis on the word *gentlemen* make her point. It sailed straight past Crosby, but Montcalm simply laughed that dangerously seductive laugh.

"You may be sure we'll meet again, dragon," he said, and for some reason the term sounded more affectionate than insulting. No wonder the man was so dangerous— even she was not totally impervious to his wicked charm.

"I doubt it." She wheeled around and took off, back stiff, shoulders straight, as dignified as she could manage, being outside without a coat or a hat. She wouldn't look back—they were probably laughing at her—and she wouldn't run. Though it would take forever, she would walk back up the hill to the street and across to the Chipple mansion; she would not let him see that for the first time in what seemed like years, she was unaccountably close to tears.

"Bastard," she muttered under her breath, liking the sound of the curse. "Goddamned rutting bastard." Even better. Now she was feeling better. The tears had vanished, the house was in sight, and the next time they met she'd be better prepared.

But she was going to make every effort to ensure that there was not going to be a next time.

"Who the hell was that?" Crosby demanded. "You told me you were meeting the heiress."

Christian Montcalm turned to look down at his slightly inebriated friend. Crosby had never been the most reliable of his cronies, but then, Christian didn't tend to consort with reliable people. "The dragon got in the way. Don't worry—there'll be other chances."

"You're the one who should be worried. If you don't come up with some money soon you'll be in the river tick."

"Nonsense." He shoved the loose strand of hair away from his face. "There'll be cards tonight, and I can make more than enough to tide me over until the engagement can be announced."

"But you can't always count on the cards, old man. They don't always fall your way."

Christian smiled. He wasn't about to point out to Crosby that not only was he absurdly lucky when it came to cards, he was also skilled and unscrupulous enough to do something about it if the cards misbehaved. "I don't expect to have any problem." He turned his gaze back to the tall figure of the woman marching away from them. She was almost out of sight, which was a pity. She was really quite diverting—more interesting than the tiresome beauty was. His conversation with Miss Chipple, when he wasn't stopping her mouth with temptingly chaste kisses, consisted of an unending line of compliments. For such a beauty she demanded constant reminders that she was, indeed, unmatchable. It was very tedious.

The dragon was far more interesting. True, she was no young maiden, but he'd had mistresses far older than she and enjoyed them tremendously. She couldn't be much more than thirty, making her younger than he was, a thought that amused him. She spoke to him like a maiden aunt, scolding a naughty boy.

Ah, but he was a naughty boy. And he had every intention of becoming a great deal naughtier. And the dragon was just the sort of woman he could make mischief with.

He wouldn't, of course. He was a pragmatic man, and he'd set his sights quite clearly on Miss Hetty Chipple, the underbred, over-rich, delectable morsel who'd just been snatched from him. Marriage to a compliant young heiress was just the thing to smooth his way for the time being, and even if Hetty seemed to have a mind of her own he had little doubt that he could control her. He had enough tricks up his sleeve to keep her docile and well behaved—sex always had the most interesting effect on virgins, and there were any number of ways he could manage to throw her off balance. And it would be most pleasant, given that trim little body of hers.

Then, when she grew tiresome, as they always did, he could further his acquaintance with the dragon, which he suspected would be far more interesting and a much greater challenge.

How would she look without her spectacles? How would she look without her clothes? She would have long legs to wrap around him, and he was connoisseur enough to see that despite her general skinniness she had a decent bosom. Yes, she'd strip quite nicely.

As soon as he could talk her into it.

But first things first. "We'll go play cards, Crosby," he said pleasantly. "And then perhaps I'll decide to attend Lady Bellwhite's soiree so I can further my suit."

"With the heiress? Or the dragon?"

Christian glanced down at him. Crosby was never the brightest of men, but every now and then he was surprisingly astute. Or perhaps Christian had been too transparent. No, that was impossible. He'd spent years perfecting his charming, impassive facade.

"How well do you know me, Crosby?"

"Well enough."

"Then you know I am, in all things, a practical man. Miss Chipple will become the future Viscountess Montcalm, and if the dragon gets tumbled somewhere along the way, then so much the better."

"You're an inspiration," Crosby said fervently.

"Indeed," Montcalm murmured as the dragon disappeared from sight. "I know."

3

The last thing Annelise was in the mood for was a formal soiree at Lady Bellwhite's, particularly after her unpleasant encounter in the park. Hetty was nowhere to be seen when Annelise returned to the house, and even the maid had disappeared. At that point she didn't know which room belonged to her young charge, and she had no intention of asking. She'd been busy enough for one morning. Presumably Hetty had locked herself in her room, sulking. If she'd managed to slip out the back way and go off chasing after Montcalm again, so be it. For the time being she was on her own.

Lady Prentice had been less enthusiastic about this little visit than she had the previous ones. "I don't like sending you to someone who smells of the shop," she'd said archly, "but Mr. Chipple has so much money it could sweeten even the rankest odor. He seems a pleasant enough man, and while his daughter is undoubtedly pert and ill mannered, I have every confidence that you can help marry her off to someone suitable, thereby putting yourself in Mr. Chipple's

debt. He's known to be a generous man when someone does him a boon, and if you're able to turn his
daughter into a titled young lady he might be persuaded to secure a small income for you. It would
mean nothing to a man like him, and while living in
London would be ruinously expensive, you've always
said you prefer the countryside, and his generosity
might even run to a small cottage on one of his hold-
ings." She shook her head briskly. "Heaven knows, I'd
love to have you here with me, but I can barely scrape
by with the little portion I have left. These men of ours,
dear Annelise. Gambling ruinously, leaving their
women bereft of both a man's protection and the security of a comfortable income. Your father should
have been horsewhipped."

"I imagine he was, on occasion," Annelise had replied, not bothering to rise to her father's defense. She
had loved him dearly, but there was nothing she could
say that would make his misbehavior acceptable. Particularly when it ended in his death. "And I won't count
on anything until it happens. I may not be able to assist
Mr. Chipple in his paternal endeavors."

"Oh, I am certain you can. I have no idea what happened to the girl's mother, but apparently there's been no
sensible female presence in her life for many years. You
can fill that gap, explain to her the little details of society that are so terribly important, and who knows, you
might end up getting Chipple to marry you. I could wish
better for you, but the money covers a lot of drawbacks."

"I have no intention of marrying, Lady Prentice,"

she'd replied, scarcely hiding her shudder. "I don't care how much money he has."

"He'll doubtless be knighted before long. Maybe even a higher rank. Money like that can buy a lot of favor from the crown."

"No, thank you."

"Just a thought, my dear," Lady Prentice had said, signaling for the maid to remove the tea tray. "Keep it in the back of your mind."

The memory of that conversation was almost enough to make Annelise pack her bags and walk straight out of the house. She could take shelter with her sisters for at least a short period of time, and the day had gone from bad to worse. All the money in the world wouldn't make Josiah Chipple an appealing husband, Hetty was a brat, and as for her unsettling encounter with Christian Montcalm…

She could hope that was the only time she'd have to deal with him, but she was far too practical to entertain such a thought. He had his avaricious eyes set on Hetty, and he wasn't going to give up without a fight. One she was entirely ready to offer him.

No, if she left this garish house and its spoiled mistress it would be tantamount to handing her over to the man. A dedicated wastrel could go through even the most extraordinary sum of money, and all reports concluded that Montcalm was dedicated indeed. When he'd used up Miss Chipple's money and her beauty he'd have no choice but to move on to another conquest. He'd have the hindrance of a wife, tucked away in some country estate to interfere with his fortune hunting. But there were things that could be done about that, accidents that could be arranged, and she wouldn't put anything past the man with the cool, laughing eyes.

"Enough, Annelise!" she said out loud. She was a practical woman, full of common sense, accepting of her lot in life and embracing it without complaint. Her one failing was an excess of imagination. Few people knew she read lurid novels whenever she was alone or that she could embroider the most fantastic tales about total strangers in a matter of moments simply for her own amusement. At least she had the sense to know it was only a fantasy. Christian Montcalm might be a fortune hunter and a scoundrel, but that didn't make him a murderer.

She was blowing things out of proportion again, she reminded herself. There would be more than enough handsome young men at Lady Bellwhite's this evening, and with any luck at all Hetty would turn her sights elsewhere.

Or at least one could hope.

Annelise dressed for dinner in one of her two best gowns. It was black, of course, and very simple. The advantage to that was she could make it appear as if she had a veritable wardrobe, simply by the addition of lace and shawls and other gewgaws. The neckline was unfashionably high, and she could only be grateful for the extra coverage, the skirt narrow, and the waist loose enough that she could dress herself without needing a maid to lace her. Lady Prentice had been very practical when she had seen to Annelise's wardrobe. If only the clothes weren't so drab. But it had already been decided by the world in general that Annelise would never marry, and why waste money on flattering clothes when they still wouldn't be enough to attract a mate?

She joined Josiah and the rebellious Hetty in the library before dinner. Hetty was sitting by the fire, dressed in a perfect concoction of pink lace, and she tried to ignore Annelise's arrival, staring into the flames with fierce concentration.

"You look lovely tonight, Miss Kempton," Josiah said in his booming voice, and Annelise was uncomfortably aware of her godmother's matchmaking maneuvers. "Where are your manners, girl?" he demanded of Hetty. "Say good evening to Miss Kempton!"

"Good evening," Hetty muttered, still staring at the fire.

"And has my daughter been behaving herself? She's a bit headstrong, you know, and she thinks she knows what's best for her. I'm counting on you to keep an eye on her for me, make sure she meets the right kind of young gentlemen. I don't much care whether they've a fortune or not—I've more than enough money to keep my Hetty in style for the rest of her life, including whoever she chooses to marry. But she'll be wanting a title, don't you know, and I expect she'll insist on someone young and handsome. She's too flighty to recognize the worth of an older, more established gentleman. I'm sure you're not so unwise," he said with a knowing look that was far too familiar.

Oh, God, he was flirting with her, Annelise thought. She managed her best smile. "Oh, a girl with Miss Hetty's qualities can certainly expect to find someone of a compatible age and nature. In truth, I think she'd be best off with someone closer to her own age, perhaps in his early twenties." A good ten years younger than Christian Montcalm.

Neither of the Chipples looked pleased with that statement, though oddly enough Hetty seemed less disturbed than her father.

"She's marrying a title, and that's all there is to it," Josiah said flatly, and there was an ugly expression around his mouth that Annelise didn't quite like. "She's had enough of country living and local squires. She needs some town bronze, and then she can have her pick of anyone I deem suitable. She's moved way past childhood friends."

Who'd said anything about childhood friends? Hetty's pretty little mouth turned downward, but still she said nothing. So there was yet another unsuitable suitor in her life. Clearly someone young and rural had once caught her eye, and she hadn't yet dismissed him entirely.

Anyone would be better than a life with Montcalm and his cronies. She needed to find out more about this childhood suitor to see whether he might be a perfectly reasonable choice.

At least it showed that Hetty could be easily distracted. If she'd set her eyes on the exotic Christian Montcalm so quickly, then she could be gently urged in another direction without too much difficulty.

"If you're talking about William I assure you I've

completely forgotten him," Hetty grumbled. "I'm much more interested in Christian Montcalm."

"I'm not certain I like you seeing him, missy," Josiah said. "I've heard rumors that he's not quite the gentleman he should be, and I expect you can do better. Perhaps we don't have to aim as high as a viscountcy…"

"Titles are overvalued anyway," Hetty said with a suddenly hopeful look in her blue eyes that Annelise found interesting.

"Not to me," Josiah said flatly. "And if we don't go to dinner soon we'll be late for Lady Bellwhite's. I had to go to a great deal of trouble to get us an invitation, and it wouldn't do to arrive late."

"Actually," Annelise said gently, "it would be even worse form to arrive early. About an hour after the event is scheduled to begin is usually the optimum time to arrive. That way a great many people are already there to appreciate the lovely entrance your daughter makes, and yet it won't seem careless or rude."

"Not everyone follows your silly rules. Christian Montcalm often shows up at the very end of the evening," Hetty said.

Annelise smiled faintly. "My point exactly."

"Then we'll arrive precisely at ten o'clock," Mr. Chipple announced.

"And leave before the very end of the evening," Annelise added, only to catch Hetty's glare.

"And I'll be a lucky man, squiring two such pretty ladies," Josiah said gallantly.

The sound Hetty made was almost a snort, but her

father had already started toward the door. He paused to confer with the butler, and Hetty sidled up to Annelise. "You didn't tell him about the park, did you?"

"No."

"Are you planning to?"

"Not at this moment. I'm certain you saw the error of your ways. A young lady's reputation is of paramount importance."

"You are such an old maid!" Hetty said. "Do you spend your entire life lecturing? Don't you get tired of it?"

Indeed, she did. There was nothing more tedious than pointing out social lapses to a spoiled little girl, and lecturing always suggested an air of superiority, which Annelise never felt she could quite carry off. "I'm here to help," she said stiffly.

"And besides, my reputation doesn't matter. It'll be gone to the devil when I marry Christian Montcalm anyway," she said cheerfully.

"Your language, missy!" Josiah Chipple rumbled, with sharper ears than Annelise would have thought.

"Yes, Father." And she stuck out her tongue at Annelise as she sailed by, making her feel very old and tiresome indeed.

Josiah was a man of his word—they arrived at Lady Bellwhite's town house at precisely ten o'clock in the evening. The street was already crowded with carriages, the noise and the music from the elegant little mansion spilled out into the streets, and Annelise groaned at the thought of another crowd. At least there'd be suitors, she told herself, already less than enamored of this particular visit.

And she was right. By the time they reached the ballroom they'd passed by three rather weedy young men, four elderly widowers, an earl with a weak heart and a bad reputation, and a bevy of other possible contenders for Hetty's delicate hand. And no Christian Montcalm, to Annelise's relief.

At the last minute Annelise had donned one of her discarded lace caps. It flapped down around her face, and while it was irritating, at least it gave her a dubious sense of protection. A woman in a lace cap was proclaiming that she was beyond the age of marriage and that the only gentleman importunate enough to ask her to dance was Mr. Chipple.

He was easy enough to dissuade and Annelise settled back in her corner amidst the chaperons and widows, gossiping pleasantly as she sipped the glass of punch Mr. Chipple had thoughtfully provided before disappearing in the direction of the card tables.

She wasn't quite sure what to make of the man. Chipple looked relieved when she refused his offer of a dance, but the delivery of the punch was a courtesy that was a bit too marked. If he started getting romantic notions she would have to abandon Hetty to her fate after all.

But then, half the women there seemed to have a great interest in the bluff Josiah. As Lady Prentice had said, money would perfume the stink of the shop quite effectively, and there were any number of widowed ladies casting curious eyes in Chipple's direction. He

seemed unaware of it, but once the ladies knew that Annelise was a part of his household, at least for the time
being, she was besieged with questions.

Annelise nodded and murmured agreement and
passed on whatever encouraging information she could
think of. Yes, she'd answered numerous times, he was
a most devoted father. Yes, his house by Green Park was
quite large. No, he'd been widowed for a great many
years, she believed, and had yet to choose a new wife.
Yes, perhaps London was just the place for both Chipples to form new attachments. Shipping, was it? Not as
bad as it could be. Really, shipping was quite a respectable trade, if one must have a trade, and he did carry
himself quite well, didn't he?

There were at least half a dozen women there, no
more than ten years older than she was, who would love
to provide Josiah a new wife. He might even marry a
title himself, though of course he wouldn't benefit fi-
nancially from it. But he could say, "my wife, Lady Er-
mintrude," with great pride.

Clearly she needed to match make for the both of
them. His gratitude should be boundless if he managed
to secure his own happiness, as well, and perhaps she
might end up with that tiny cottage and a genteel income
to call her own after all. Anything was possible.

"You haven't seen Christian Montcalm, have you?"

The conversation wasn't addressed to her, and she
pretended to ignore it, but the sound of his name had her
immediate attention.

"You think he'd dare show his face here?" another

voice replied. "Surely not after that escapade with Lord Morton's wife!"

"Morton has taken her to the continent until the scandal dies down," the first woman said. "As for Montcalm, he sold his soul to the devil years ago. This latest scandal will make little difference, I expect."

"No, indeed," said the second woman, fanning herself vigorously. "We can only be thankful he is unlikely to try to show his face here tonight. If he does I think I might be tempted to give him the cut direct."

The first woman laughed. "No, you wouldn't, Lavinia. All he'd have to do is smile at you and you'd be at his feet. You should never have gotten involved with him in the first place. It was more than five years ago and you've yet to look at another man."

Annelise could stand it no longer. She turned to glance at the women. She recognized Lavinia Worthington. She was the same age as Annelise's older sister, but she'd aged far better. She was widowed several years ago, if she remembered correctly, and hadn't yet doffed her widows' weeds. Maybe she had the same financial problems Annelise did. Or maybe she just knew how stunning she was in black. The diamond necklace around her elegant neck was worth a hundred black dresses.

"I'm more than ready to look at another man. I think Mr. Chipple might suit me very well."

"You wouldn't!" her companion sputtered.

"I would," said Lavinia. "You're right—Christian has ruined me for anyone else. The things he does in bed are beyond sinful and so wickedly delicious that you'd want to die with pleasure. I'm not going to get that again, so I might at least settle for a comfortable amount of money."

"More than comfortable, if what I hear is true," the first woman said. "But take a glance across the room if you think you can really do it."

Annelise turned her head, to follow their gaze, only to see Christian Montcalm, a vision in satin, holding Hetty's hand in preparation for the next dance.

4

Annelise could cover a surprising amount of ground in no time at all, even weaving her way through the crowded dance floor. She was tall, but she had a certain grace, and was able to slip to the other side of the room without causing much notice, just in time to physically fling herself between Montcalm and Hetty.

It was perhaps not the best decision, since he'd been holding Hetty's hand in preparation for leading her out to dance, and when Annelise used her body to break them apart his arm brushed against her breasts. With any other man she would have thought it an accident. With this man, who was a known connoisseur of beauty, she wasn't quite sure.

She had to move fast and had always been good at thinking quickly, so at the last minute she'd grabbed young Mr. Reston by the hand, thrusting him forward. "Miss Chipple, may I introduce you to Mr. Reston? He's a great admirer of yours, and begs the favor of this dance."

"I…er…that is…" Mr. Reston had turned a bright

pink that didn't go well with his spots. "I mean, I would be honored if I could have this dance, Miss Chipple."

"Lovely," Annelise said cheerfully, putting Hetty's limp hand in Reston's gloved one and giving them a little shove toward the dance floor. "I'm certain Mr. Montcalm will understand."

Hetty would have lingered, but Mr. Reston finally understood his duty, and a moment later he was leading her through the paces of a country dance, and within moments Hetty was laughing.

"I'm certain Mr. Montcalm understands very well," Christian said, his low voice sending shivers down her spine. Too much imagination, she told herself, turning to look at him. *Up* at him. Such a novel experience. Why were all the men so short and she so tall? Except for someone like Montcalm, who was out of reach and unacceptable?

She dashed that thought out of her brain instantly. She'd been around matchmakers too long—why in the world was she thinking such thoughts in terms of herself? She was about to give him a look of smug triumph when she realized the cool green of his eyes did not appear particularly amused.

"Miss Chipple had promised me this dance," he said. "I don't like having my plans thwarted."

"I imagine you don't," she said sharply. "There are any number of women who would be more than happy to dance with you."

"And only one who'd hate it beyond belief," he said. And before she realized what he was doing he'd taken her hand and swung her onto the dance floor.

She hadn't danced in years. Certainly not since her father's death. She should have fumbled, tripped, but dancing had always been one of her few gifts and the steps came back to her by instinct. She should have pulled away, and indeed, she felt dozens of curious gazes in their direction, but the hand that held hers was very strong and Christian wasn't about to let her go. He wasn't the sort of man to give in and having a struggle on the dance floor would be undignified and unwinnable.

"Everybody is staring," she said in a whisper. "Let go of my hand."

"I wanted to dance. You robbed me of a partner—it's your duty to replace her—"

"Not with me!" she whispered, horrified. It couldn't have been a worse dance. It was one of the newer dances, one where the partners always remained with each other, always touching. If it had been a quadrille she could have easily slipped away, but his fingers gripped her tightly, and he wasn't about to release her.

At least they were on the edge of the dance floor and not in the middle, where Hetty was enjoying herself just a bit too noisily for all to see. She'd have to caution her about laughing too loudly, Annelise thought absently as she turned gracefully. She would do so as soon as she managed to get away from this awful man. At least they were moving back now, beyond the curtains toward the balcony, where no one would see them.

It wasn't until he'd swept her out into the chilly darkness of the terrace when she'd realized this was not a good idea after all. There were no witnesses to her embarrassment, but no witnesses to stop him, either. *Stop him from what?* Tossing her over the side, two flights down to the street below? They'd whispered of frightful things....

He came to a halt, but he still hadn't released her. "This is the second time you've gotten in my way, dragon," he said, his voice a drawling caress. "I don't like being frustrated."

"You'll have to get used to it as long as I'm around. I'm not letting you near Miss Hetty."

"Why not? Clearly the girl will be married for her money. With that background her pretty face won't be enough to lure much of a title, which must be her father's intention."

"True—" Annelise said, tugging her hand from his strong hold surreptitiously. His gloved hand was still on her arm and he didn't seem in any mood to let her go. "—but with the money then she can at least find a respectable suitor, and you, sir, do not qualify as such."

"Ah, but not everyone likes respectable. I'm convinced Miss Chipple is enjoying the consternation she causes when she flirts with me."

"I'm not enjoying it," Annelise said crossly. "Will you please let go of me?"

"Not yet," he drawled. "I came to this insufferably boring party for the sole purpose of furthering my suit with your flighty young heiress and you've botched that entirely. I think you and I have to come to an understanding."

"I consider that highly unlikely."

"I intend to marry your silly little charge. I need the

money, and I have little doubt that she'd choose me above all the men she's met so far in London. She has a fascination for danger, and anything you say to discourage her will have the opposite effect."

"I won't argue with that." Why wouldn't he release her? Why did the warmth of his hand spread through the thin kid gloves he was wearing so that it almost seared her skin? "You're quite dazzling in a tawdry, ne'er-do-well sort of way," she continued, "but it's not going to be her choice."

She'd managed to silence him. He stared at her in astonishment. "Tawdry?" he choked.

"Young girls are always attracted to rakes," Annelise stated in practical tones she was far from feeling. "Which is why wiser heads rule attachments of this sort. If her father doesn't realize how unsuitable you are I'll make certain he's informed of it. You'll have to look elsewhere for your fortune."

She didn't like that gleam in his eyes. Beautiful eyes, tinged with green and gold, and sly like a cat's. "I don't know of any other heiresses who've chosen to arrive in London this season," Montcalm said. "Unless you're possessed of a tidy income, dragon—"

"I haven't a penny."

"Too bad. I could have enjoyed making you eat your words," he murmured in a voice far too affectionate. He reached up and flicked the lace cap surrounding her face like a nun's wimple. "And what the devil is this? You weren't wearing it in the park this afternoon."

"I wasn't wearing anything at all in the park this afternoon." The moment the words were out of her mouth she could have bit them back, but he did no more than raise an eyebrow. "That is, I ran out without a hat or cloak. I am a lady of a certain age and this lace cap denotes my position…"

He ripped it off her head and sent it sailing over the side of the terrace. She watched it drop to the ground with mixed feelings. It was made of very fine lace. It made her feel eighty years old, and she was not yet thirty. "Exactly what color is your hair, dragon?"

Enough was enough. "Gray," she snapped, yanking her arm from his. He still didn't release her. She took a deep, calming breath, picturing herself as a starched and disapproving governess. "Mr. Montcalm, you have no interest in what color my hair is or whether or not I have a fortune. I am certain you have an innate sense of who is worthy prey for your schemes, and I hardly qualify. I realize I frustrated your plans for the evening, and while I can't apologize, you can surely see that this is getting us nowhere. Please let go of me and I'll return to the party."

There was an absolute stillness about his face that made her stomach tighten nervously. He was an astonishingly handsome man—there was no doubt of that whatsoever. With his high cheekbones, exotic green eyes and soft, beguiling lips, it was little wonder that he managed to enthrall an impressionable young thing like Hetty Chipple. Indeed, if Annelise were ten years younger and just a little more foolish she might be distracted, at least momentarily, by the laugh lines around his eyes, by the way he looked at a woman, which doubtless had to be dispensed to all women in his vicinity because he could hardly be looking at her in any particular way, could he? He had nothing to gain.

"Ah, dragon," he murmured. "You underestimate yourself. You do your best to convince the world that you're a stiff old maid, when I doubt you're much older than me."

"I beg your pardon! I'm twenty-nine!" she said, goaded. Deliberately, she realized belatedly.

"Not such a great age after all. Then think of me as a wise elder, dispensing advice. Don't enter into battles you can't win. You're outmanned and outgunned when it comes to Hetty Chipple. I will have her. I don't care what lengths I have to go to in order to marry her, but I've never been one to be squeamish. I'm afraid I can be quite ruthless."

She believed him and her own sense of certainty began to falter. She had never been a coward or a quitter, but this was starting to look like a fight she might lose. And indeed, what business was it of hers? Josiah Chipple wanted his child to marry well, but he wasn't thinking in terms of her happiness, only social success. And while Christian was a rake, he was from a family as old as hers, and would be a viscount before long. All she had to do was persuade Josiah that it would do and she could cease to worry. Cease to have anything to do with this difficult man except to nod politely when he visited his fiancée. Whether she'd be called upon to help guide her through a lavish society wedding was something she didn't care to consider. Someone else could come in and restrain Mr. Chipple's more exuberant lack of taste.

"Do you love her?" she asked, feeling a small amount of hope.

"Good God, woman, of course not!" he said, clearly appalled. "I don't believe in love. At the best there's affection and a certain carnal compatibility, but that hardly equals love. Do I strike you as some sort of romantic poet? I'm much too hardheaded for that."

"She needs to be loved," Annelise said in a small voice.

He stared down at her. "Does she indeed?" he said after a moment. "Maybe she just needs to be kissed."

She didn't even have time to let the words register. He hadn't released her arm, so it was a simple enough matter for him to sweep her unsuspecting body against his, pushing her farther into the shadows of the terrace, up against the cool stone wall, and kiss her.

Sheer astonishment kept her motionless, but then, he didn't appear to expect much participation from her. He still kept his iron grip on her arm, but his other hand cupped her chin gently as he pressed his lips against hers, the cool kid gloves strangely enticing against her face. But nothing as strange as the unexpected softness of his lips, brushing against hers, kissing with slow delicacy that left her in a trance, unable to move. Her eyes fluttered closed as she floated.

"Lesson one," he whispered against her lips. "Now time for lesson two." And he tilted her chin down, so that her mouth opened beneath his, and he kissed her that way, a deep, intimate kiss that should only be shared by lovers. She could feel her entire body react in shameful, unexpected ways, and she reached up her hands to try to push him away, but she was uncharacteristically weak, and she closed her eyes, letting her head drop back and allowing him to kiss her in the shadows of the moonlit terrace.

He was the one who broke the kiss. He was the one who looked down at her, suddenly breathless, but with the moon behind him she couldn't see his expression—she could only see the bright glitter of his eyes. "You're an eager pupil, dragon," he said softly.

"What's lesson three?" she asked in a strangled voice.

"You're not ready for that, love. I trust I'll be around when you are. In the meantime, though, we may as well work on lesson two. You're not as adept at kissing as Hetty might be, but with a little trial and error…"

This time when she shoved him he fell back, releasing his hold on her arm, moving out of her way so that her escape was clear. She didn't hesitate, pushing past him, and she would have left without a word if his faint laugh hadn't followed her.

She stopped at the French doors, whirling around to glare at him. "You ought to be gelded," she said, as harsh and as coarse an insult as she could come up with in the heat of the moment.

His laugh grew. "Oh, no, my dear. You really wouldn't like that at all."

The heat and noise of the ballroom was an assault on her shaken body as she walked back inside, shutting the doors behind her. Shutting him away. She had no idea whether people were staring at her—Montcalm had whisked her away from the party so quickly she didn't know whether anyone realized she'd disappeared with London's most notorious rake. At that moment she didn't particularly care.

She wanted to run, but at the last minute her back stiffened. She had survived many worse things than a stolen kiss on a terrace, and she would certainly survive this. First of all she must find Hetty amidst the dancers.

When she spotted her she breathed a sigh of relief. The young beauty had gone on to another unexceptional partner and was drinking in the admiration and flattery as any seventeen-year-old would.

For the moment she was safe. Annelise slipped from the ballroom to one of the retiring rooms, sinking down in front of a mirror to fiddle with her hair. The slight breeze on the terrace had loosened its strict knot, probably aided by Montcalm's random destruction of her lace cap, and as she tried to smooth it back into submission Lavinia Worthington sank down beside her.

"You're looking very well, Miss Kempton," she said, eyeing her far too closely. "I'm pleased that you decided to rejoin society."

Lavinia had always had an acid tongue, quite often used at Annelise's expense, referring to her as the Giant, and Madame Timbertrees. Annelise tried to summon a cool smile but her mouth felt stiff, strange.

"And obviously you're pleased, as well," Lavinia continued without waiting for an answer. "I wouldn't have thought you'd be the kind for clandestine flirtations, but perhaps I was wrong about you."

"Clandestine flirtations?" Oh, God, had Lavinia seen her dancing off with her former lover? The very thought made her physically ill. "Why should you think that?"

"I have eyes in my head, Annelise. I may call you that, mayn't I? You've just been thoroughly kissed—any fool could see it. The reddened, slightly swollen lips, the dazed expression in your eyes. Have I missed something? Are you engaged?"

Annelise surveyed her reflection with horrified fascination. Yes, she looked well kissed. And she'd been very well kissed indeed. Not that she had a great deal to compare it to—she'd never been kissed before. Not once. Starting with someone who was undoubtedly exceedingly skilled in the art of kissing was going to make her far too difficult to please in the future.

Start and stop, she reminded herself. He only kissed her to shock and fluster her, and he wasn't about to repeat the mistake. "I'm not engaged, Lavinia. I'm past the age of marriage—I enjoy a life of peaceful pleasures and the occasional delights of society."

"Then who kissed you?"

It was almost too tempting to tell her, Lavinia who was still pining for Montcalm five years after he ended their relationship. But temptation was something Annelise tended to resist, and she was going to have to stiffen her resolve still further, if Montcalm continued.

"No one at all," she said. "You're imagining things. I'm afraid I'm not the sort to attract admirers."

"Not even your eligible host?"

For a moment Annelise had no idea what she was talking about. And then she realized with astonishment that Lavinia was concerned she'd been kissed by Chipple, not the rakehell. She wanted to laugh in relief, but her wisdom kept her silent.

"Mr. Chipple holds absolutely no interest for me," she said, trying to ignore the deliciously well-kissed feeling that still lingered. "Feel free to pursue him yourself, Lavinia. It was a great pleasure to see you again." And she made her exit before Lavinia could summon another word.

After all the unfortunate tricks fate had played on her during this first day in the Chipple household, it must have decided she deserved some relief. Mr. Chipple and the relatively cheerful-looking Hetty were in sight, obviously searching for her.

"There you are, Miss Kempton," Josiah said in a voice loud enough to be heard in several rooms. "We've been looking for you. Time to go home, don't you think? My little girl needs her beauty sleep."

Hetty didn't look any too pleased at the notion, but she'd clearly enjoyed herself dancing so she wasn't as ill tempered as usual. "Where did you disappear to?" she demanded. "Last I saw, you were trying to get rid of Christian."

"And I did. I pushed him over the balcony. He should trouble you no more."

Hetty's china blue eyes widened in gullible horror, but Josiah simply chuckled. "She's teasing you, puss.

You're not going to throw yourself away on the first man who offers. Come now, Hetty, get your mind back onto important things. Were there any young gentlemen who caught your fancy?"

"Perhaps this conversation could wait until we're in the carriage," Annelise suggested softly, all too aware of the curious stares around them.

"This conversation can wait until the Thames freezes over," Hetty snapped. "Come along." She swept out the door, rather like she was the teacher and Annelise the recalcitrant pupil.

In fact, there were areas where Hetty was clearly far more experienced. Areas that Annelise had no interest in exploring any further.

And Miss Hetty Chipple was going to have to learn that kissing dangerous men could lead to nothing but trouble. Any self-respecting female would never let a man take that kind of advantage of her.

Unless that self-respecting female was addled enough to go out onto a darkened terrace with a man, engage in a battle of wits and then do nothing when she was thoroughly, lengthily kissed.

Oh my God, thought Annelise. Which one of us is the real fool?

By the time Christian Montcalm and his coterie of friends found themselves walking down the street past Lady Bellwhite's house a light mist had fallen. Crosby was complaining, as usual, and one of the others was suggesting a scenario at the Rakehells' Club that sounded only vaguely entertaining, when Christian halted. He was wearing a short dress sword, seemingly more for show than protection, and he unsheathed it and scooped a sodden piece of fabric from the street. He glanced up. The doors to the terrace were open now, and the music filtered down, and a faint smile curved his lips.

"What's that disgusting thing?" Crosby demanded. "Since when do you pick filthy rags up from the sidewalk?"

"When they're a souvenir, Crosby." He didn't care to explain himself, but Crosby was at the point in his nightly imbibing when he was most persistent and annoying. Christian concentrated instead on the scrap of lace in his hand. He'd thrown it farther than he thought—he would have expected it would end up stuck in the trees that surrounded the Bellwhites' house.

But instead it had shown up at his very feet, and even in its sodden condition he'd known exactly what it was. It was a sign. Of what, he had no idea, but he expected the future to prove interesting.

Anything to alleviate the tedium of his life.

The lace was very fine, delicate, and he stretched it out in his hand for a moment. *A net to catch a dragon,* he thought. And he tucked it into the inner pocket of his coat, eliciting shrieks of protest from Crosby.

"You'll ruin your clothes, demme!" he said.

"If we spend the rest of the evening doing as Godfrey suggests I expect they'll be in far worse shape," he murmured. "And if the coat is ruined I can always buy another."

"Not on your credit."

"Crosby, you are being astonishingly ill bred tonight. Behave yourself or go find other, less discerning people to annoy."

Crosby's face darkened with embarrassment or anger, Montcalm didn't know. Or care. And then Crosby laughed. "It's hers, isn't it? You dog."

He was startled enough to jerk his head around. "I beg your pardon, Crosby."

"Miss Chipple. She must be quite besotted with you, to be so indiscreet."

Montcalm smiled, unaccountably relieved. "What can I say? Miss Chipple was as obliging as always."

"Wonder if she'll be as obliging with the rest of us, once you're married," Godfrey said wistfully.

"Better to wonder how obliging I'm likely to be." The silken threat in Christian's voice was unmistakable.

"You've always shared in the past," Godfrey said, aggrieved.

Christian closed his eyes for a moment, summoning up the image of impish Hetty Chipple, with her sweet, rosebud mouth and her insatiable appetite for chaste kisses. But it wasn't Hetty who appeared in his mind—it was the still-nameless dragon, staring at him in shock after he'd kissed her. A shock he hadn't been entirely immune to.

"Things change," he said out loud. "It's one thing to share a willing whore—"

"Or unwilling," Crosby added with a snicker.

"—But another thing when it comes to my wife.

Once she's given me a couple of healthy sons she can do whatever she pleases, as long as she's discreet and careful."

"And if she's not?" Godfrey demanded.

"Then I'll simply have to make sure she understands the rules," Christian replied gently, striding down the rain-damp streets of London, his coterie following behind him.

5

There was no reason for Annelise to be quite so exhausted. She'd only danced once, and despite the stimulating encounter on the terrace had arrived home not far past midnight. She retired immediately, making it clear that Hetty should do the same, and she was undressed and in bed within half an hour.

It was a very nice bed, already warmed, with a fire blazing in the fireplace. Mr. Chipple's love of bright colors hadn't penetrated this far, and the room was a soft, soothing shade of rose. She should have fallen asleep the moment her head hit the pillow.

Should have. Even a steady-tempered, practical woman of twenty-nine would be understandably rattled by her first kiss. More so because it wasn't offered by an eager young man or an importunate suitor. She'd been kissed, quite thoroughly, by a man she despised, a man who called her "dragon" and mocked her and had wicked, nefarious plans for the innocent, though admittedly annoying, Miss Hetty Chipple.

Thank heavens those wicked plans had nothing to do

with her, other than it being her duty to thwart them. As far as she knew she'd managed to keep her wits about her when he kissed her—she hadn't kissed him back, or put her arms around him. She'd simply held still, like a virgin martyr at the stake, while the flames licked deliciously around her...

She rolled over in the bed, punching the pillow. It was shameful, yet, but in the end probably entirely normal. After all, it was human instinct to mate, and natural to enjoy kisses and caresses, wasn't it? Not that he'd caressed her. Or touched her inappropriately. Except with his mouth. No man should have that lovely a mouth— it was unfair to susceptible women everywhere. Not that she susceptible, of course. And even if she were, she was far too practical to imagine that she was anything but an annoyance and hindrance to Christian Montcalm. Like a cat with a helpless little mouse, he enjoyed playing with her, batting at her, while he waited for more important prey.

She threw back the covers, far too hot on a chilly spring night. She should read something. Something boring and familiar to put her to sleep, and that had nothing to do with kisses. She could go for Caesar in the original Latin, but that might be a little too punitive. Maybe some nice treatise on land management.

Actually that might be more interesting than she might expect. As she watched her father's last remaining property fall into rack and ruin she could only think of small things that could be done to salvage its value. The proper rotation of crops. Improvements to the surrounding tenant homes. Proper breeding of livestock for the maximum results when it—

No, she wasn't going to think about breeding. Or about the ramshackle old house and estate that were gone forever, sold off to repay some of her father's huge debts. It was gone, and her only hope was to eventually find a small cottage in the country where she could live out her days in peace. With spaniels and cats, since she wasn't going to have children.

A chill swept over her, and she dived back under the covers. It was a cold, dismal night, she thought, huddling deeper into the warm blanket. She was thinking like a woman of fifty, not one who hadn't even reached thirty. Not that she expected romance or marriage, or even had any interest in them. She'd learned to be self-sufficient. The only offers she'd be likely to attract would be widowers needing someone to keep rein on their children. She'd rather be a paid governess than be rewarded for her efforts by sharing a bed with some portly, ill-tempered man...

And why was she thinking of sharing a bed with any man at all? The Chipples were generous with their allotment of pillows, and she pulled one over her head, to shut out the light, shut out the thoughts that were plaguing her. Too much wine, she told herself, though she'd barely had a glass. Too much imagination—her besetting sin.

By tomorrow things would be in proper perspective. Montcalm's evil machinations would be clear, she would warn Mr. Chipple just how unsuitable he was, and with any luck he would no longer be allowed anywhere near Hetty. Then Annelise could hold her head high and forget all about the Unfortunate Incident on Lady Bellwhite's Terrace.

If only she could sleep.

When she awoke it was well past her usual time of rising, though the house seemed relatively still. The sun had risen, though the shutters were still closed against the light, and she slid out of bed to push them aside. It was a bright, sunny day, early enough that few people were out, and even the park looked empty. Most people waited until a more social hour—eleven or so, to make their grand promenade, to see and be seen. It hadn't been far off that hour when Annelise had been forced to go chasing after Hetty, and she wondered absently where her charge's rooms were. And whether they could be equipped with a lock.

She was already dressed when she heard the shriek, and while it sounded far from disastrous she bolted out of her room without her shoes on, wondering whether the nefarious rake had managed to sneak into the house. Or whether it was a more literal snake.

It was neither. It was easy enough to find Hetty's room—it was at the far end of the hall, the door was open and, while the excited shrieks had calmed, Miss Hetty was still in an obvious state.

Annelise halted in the open doorway, giving her a moment to take in the full splendor of Hetty's bower.

It looked as if a pink sugarplum had exploded, covering the room with dripping pink icing. The entire place was awash with pink lace and satin—from the bed coverings to the chairs to the discarded clothing that some maid had neglected to take care of. Hetty had probably banned her from the room.

The entire effect was that of a bordello for fairies. And then she caught the scent of roses, and realized what had excited Hetty's attention: pink roses, masses of them, overblown and gaudy, perfuming the room like a flower shop.

Apparently Miss Hetty was so delighted with the offering that she was inclined to be welcoming. "Aren't they gorgeous?" she demanded of Annelise. "He must have bought every pink rose in town!"

"There certainly are a lot of them," she agreed, but Hetty was too pleased to notice the reservation in Annelise's voice.

"Such a darling, extravagant man!" Hetty cooed, looking as if she wanted to embrace the wall of roses against her young bosom. She'd regret it if she did—that strain of roses had particularly nasty thorns, and while the flower seller would have done his best to remove most of them, it was an impossible task, making that type of rose more expensive than any other.

Annelise knew her roses—she missed the rose garden she'd tended so faithfully almost as much as she'd missed her father—and she wondered why Montcalm would have selected them. It could be no one but he— the rose was showy, just a wee bit gauche, and the sheer abundance of them was almost a mockery of a gesture. One that was totally lost on Hetty.

She was holding the card in her hand. "He says, 'These roses can't begin to do justice to your beauty.'" She turned to Annelise with a triumphant smile. "Didn't I tell you? I've managed to capture the most beautiful man in society in a matter of a few short weeks."

"He needs a wealthy wife," Annelise said gently, almost sorry to remind Hetty of the sordid realities of life.

But Hetty simply shrugged. "They all seem to. If I have to be married for my money I may as well pick someone beautiful."

"Beauty is only skin deep," Annelise said, sounding like her old nurse, sounding like she was a crotchety seventy-year-old.

"And everything he does is pretty," Hetty said dreamily.

She was thinking of his kisses, Annelise thought with a sudden flare of feeling that she refused to define. Christian Montcalm said Hetty was a far better kisser…the rat bastard! She'd only just remembered that part, having been too distracted by the actual event.

She couldn't bring herself to say anything else. She suddenly remembered she was standing there in her stocking feet with her hair still loose down her back, not a very ladylike way to appear.

"I'll see you at breakfast, my dear," she said, hoping the affectionate term might make her feel more dignified.

Hetty waved her away, barely noticing, and Annelise gritted her teeth as she started back down the hallway.

One of the maids waited outside her door. It was the same one she'd dragged to the park with her—Lizzie. She bobbed a polite little curtsy when Annelise approached her, and she felt an unpleasant sense of foreboding.

"I wondered if I could be of any assistance, miss. I have some experience as a lady's maid, and Mrs. Buxton said it was all right if I offered my services to such an honored guest."

It had been so long since she'd had a personal maid attend her that the notion was disconcerting. "That's very kind of you, Lizzie, but I'm used to looking after myself."

Lizzie looked disappointed. "As you wish, miss. But you've only to let me know if you change your mind."

"Thank you." She expected Lizzie to head back down the stairs, but still she lingered. "Did you want something else?"

"Miss Hetty isn't the only one who got flowers this morning, miss. I just put them in your room."

Oh, God, Annelise thought. What kind of insult had he come up with now? Weeds? Cattails?

No, it couldn't be Montcalm—he didn't even know her name. Oh, horrors, it couldn't be Chipple himself, could it? If she was going to have to fight off his advances she'd leave Hetty to the not so tender mercies of the rakehell, Montcalm.

But she didn't betray her agitation. "Thank you, Lizzie," she said. "That's all for now."

The poor girl wasn't happy with her dismissal, but Annelise was not about to give anyone the satisfaction of seeing her reaction. She waited until the maid had vanished down the hallway toward the servants' stairs and then went into her room. She managed to close the door behind her before she stopped still.

Beautiful spring flowers. Irises, daffodils, delicate tea roses, all in the softest pastel shades. Small, perfect, exquisite.

The card lay on the table beside them, and her name was written quite clearly in dark ink, an impatient, masculine hand. The Hon. Annelise Kempton. And she felt a sudden, wrenching disappointment. They couldn't be from *him*. Christian Montcalm didn't know her name.

And for heaven's sake, why would he be sending her flowers? She was a thorn in his side, far worse than the ones still adorning Hetty's pink roses, and he was hardly likely to be rewarding her. It had to be Chipple, except that she lived in his house, had seen his garish taste, and he couldn't have ordered such a perfect, delicate bouquet.

And then she saw the snapdragons amidst the flowers. She opened up the sealed envelope, gingerly, as if she expected spiders to pop out. The actual note was even worse—"Dragon—let me know when you're ready for lesson three."

She could feel color suffuse her body, and she was a woman who had trained herself not to blush. It was the same handwriting—he knew her name after all, even if he preferred to call her that awful term. Dragons were large, fire-breathing, scaly creatures, and besides, they were the ones who endangered the maidens, weren't they? He was getting his mythology all wrong.

If she had sense at all she'd open the windows and dump the flowers out into the garden below, so that one of Chipple's army of servants would take care of them. But there were times when beauty overruled her senses, and flowers were one of her weaknesses. She loved the scent of spring flowers, the hint of hope and new life, and especially the soft yellows and lavenders and pinks of their petals.

She was strong enough to ignore where these came from, wasn't she? She'd simply destroy the note so no one could see it.

Burning would be the only choice—servants tended to be curious about things, and who could blame them? But the coals had died down completely, leaving the fireplace cold.

Her shapeless brown-striped dress had no pockets, and she couldn't leave the note lying about. She folded it carefully and tucked it between her breasts, the only secure place she could think of. Shoving her hair into a hasty knot at the back of her head, she slipped into her shoes and left the room, closing the door behind her.

Christian Montcalm kept rooms on Upper Kilgrove Street. As a single gentleman he wasn't expected to have a town house, which was a damned good thing, because he was already six months in arrears on his rent, and only his charming smile kept him from being tossed out on the street. That and the fact that he had a plump, elderly landlady rather than a landlord, who fed him tea and cookies and treated him as an indulgent mother would treat her son.

There were times when he almost couldn't remember his beautiful mother, a part of a different world, it seemed. All that was long in the past, a time he'd just as soon forget, since there was no returning.

He'd been born in France, which to some people might make him French. Those people would be wrong.

The Montcalms were an old, proud family. His grandfather, the Viscount Montcalm, had been the brother of a duke, and he'd been a cold, heartless old man, more concerned about the family name than the actual members of it. Christian's own father, Godfrey, had been the younger son, with no title, and he'd made the grave error of falling in love with a Frenchwoman. Madeleine de Chambord was a great beauty, daughter of a marquis, with enough wealth that though Christian's grandfather railed against the match he couldn't actually stop it. When Geoffrey had chosen to make his home in France there was nothing the viscount could do about it—there was too little money left in the estate to use blackmail, and Madeleine was far wealthier than the Montcalms. The viscount had written off his younger son, and Geoffrey and Madeleine had made a very happy life in a small château in Normandy.

He was the second of five children—three boys and two girls. His older brother, Laurent, had always been a bit of a prig—he'd taken his role as eldest brother seriously, and tended to preach down to his four siblings. After Christian came Helene, and it was clear from the age of two on that she was going to rival her mother's great beauty. Then Jacqueline, plump and freckled and so mischievous that their father would toss her in the air and call her the spawn of the devil, to which she'd reply, "Then you must be the devil," much to the amusement of Geoffrey and Madeleine and the disapproval of Laurent.

And then there was baby Charles-Louis with golden curls, wide blue eyes and the sweetest disposition. While Laurent might have felt responsible for the rest of the children, with Christian it was his baby brother with whom he had the strongest connection. He'd had great plans—he would teach him to ride, fight, how to flirt with girls and not listen to little prigs like Laurent.

A happy family they'd been, the seven of them, with Madeleine's elderly grandmother joining them, and various cousins coming and going in a vast, casual open house.

He should never have left. No one talked about what was going on, as if such news was distasteful, but he should have known somehow. Laurent had been sent to England to meet his disapproving grandfather when he reached the age of fourteen, and had actually met with the old man's approval before returning to the family home. It was little wonder—they were both disapproving, self-righteous toads, young Christian had thought mutinously.

And then it had become his turn. He hadn't wanted to leave—he knew he would hardly meet with the same kind of fellow-feeling. Laurent (or Laurence, as the viscount referred to him) was the good son, obedient, respectful. Christian was the bad one, always getting into trouble, much to his father's amusement and his mother's despair. She would cry over him, sometimes. He could remember that. She cried when he got into a fight with three farm boys and they'd beat him to a bloody pulp. They hadn't looked so good afterward, but he'd refused to give their names. A peasant who laid a hand on the aristocracy was risking his life, even if he was only a child. And Christian had been ten years old and looking for a good dustup.

He did everything he could to keep from getting on the boat to England, including sneaking off one and walking all the way back to St. Matthieu while his mother wept with anxiety. It was the only time he remembered seeing his father angry with him, and the next time when they took him to the boat he stayed on it, mutinously. Not that they'd had any choice—they'd sent him with one of the burly footmen who deposited him at his grandfather's estate in England, turned around and headed straight back to France before Christian could manage to follow him.

He hated his cold, miserable grandfather almost as much as the old man hated him. Christian was too much like his mother, the old man told him. Pretty and useless and too French. And Christian had shouted back that he was much happier being a Frenchman than a stuffy, pale, stupid Englishman with too much pride and no heart.

The viscount had backhanded him across the face. The altercation had unfortunately taken place at the top of the stairs, and Christian had fallen, breaking both his arm and leg, keeping him from returning to France when it had been originally planned.

He always blamed his grandfather. Not for the slap,

not for the broken bones. But for keeping him away from France, just long enough that he couldn't go back. The Terror was sweeping over the nation, and it even reached the peaceful beauty of the Normandy countryside.

He knew how his family died, though he didn't like to think about it. He'd often wondered whether the guillotine would have been kinder—it was a swift death, but the long ride in the tumbrel would have filled his sisters with panic, knowing what awaited them.

And how would they manage to put a baby like Charles-Louis in such a contraption? Surely he was too small?

But burning to death in the château must have been worse. All of them, the servants, his family, his grandmother, the strong footman who'd brought him to England, the plump young housemaid who'd let him kiss her. All of them dead, while he was safe in England, doing nothing to save them.

He often wondered if the three boys who'd pummeled him had been in the crowds of blood-hungry animals. Most likely. There were rights and wrongs on both sides, he knew that. But he still hated the French with all his heart and soul, ignoring that half of him.

It was twenty years ago—he seldom thought of it anymore. He had no idea why he was thinking of it this morning. Perhaps because, despite the very Englishness of him, he couldn't bring himself to face sirloin and ale first thing in the morning. He drank chocolate, nibbled a brioche and stared out the window at the sky that was as blue as his baby brother's eyes.

By the time Crosby Pennington showed up at his doorstep, lamentably prompt as always despite the copious amounts of wine he imbibed, Christian was already bathed, dressed and ready to face the world, with nothing more on his mind than the far too easy challenge of Miss Hetty Chipple's substantial portion. And the far more interesting prospect of dealing with the fire-breathing dragon.

She'd probably thrown his flowers out the window, he thought. He knew who she was now—daughter of Sir James Kempton, who'd gone through his inheritance and killed himself with his reckless riding, leaving three daughters behind. Two married, one impoverished, unmarriageable, with only an Honorable to her name.

The dragon. She'd had a season, someone told him, but she hadn't taken. He'd probably seen her on some occasion or other, but despite her impressive height he hadn't noticed her. But then, he seldom noticed anything but astonishing beauties, and the dragon, though possessed of a certain charm, was no diamond.

The woman wore spectacles! Astonishing—he'd never met a woman under forty who wore them. They usually squinted at the world ingenuously, preferring to exist in a blur than ruin their looks—when most of them didn't have looks to ruin.

It wasn't that Miss Kempton was unattractive. She had lovely gray eyes behind those intrusive spectacles, and a surprisingly delectable mouth. Her beautiful creamy skin made him think of the rest of her body, and if she was a bit too stubborn looking for most men, then they would be missing a most interesting challenge.

Something he ought to skip, as well, he reminded himself. He needed to concentrate on securing Miss Chipple's hand in marriage and make sure the vows were said before something could put a stop to it…like her chaperon, who could see him far too well out of those soft gray eyes. She looked at him and saw the wretch that he was.

And as usual, it just made him want to behave even more wickedly.

She'd be his reward and his challenge. Once Hetty Chipple was wedded and bedded, though not necessarily in that order, then he could concentrate on the very proper Honorable Miss Annelise Kempton.

And he could find out if dragons really had claws.

6

Despite the folded note that seemed determined to burn its imprint onto her breasts, Annelise faced the day with equanimity. It was a lovely day, and she had no intention of spending it indoors, any more than she was going to allow Hetty out on her own. A refreshing walk in the park along public paths would be just the thing to put roses back in the cheeks of her young charge…er…friend…

Annelise scowled. She had always been most unfortunately outspoken—her elder sister had chided her for it, her father had laughed at it. She believed in facing things head-on, in calling things what they were and not prettying things up. Which, unfortunately, was not the way things were done in society. At the advanced age of twenty-nine she'd reluctantly learned to hold her tongue, but it still chafed.

She was Hetty's unpaid chaperon but Annelise had a job to do nevertheless, even though the details were unspoken. In return for a roof over her head, decent meals and the vague possibility of some help toward her future, she was little more than a governess shepherding her charge through the rough seas of society.

Except one didn't shepherd anything through seas, did they? The poor sheep would drown. She laughed at the notion. There was her imagination and her tendency to dramatize going awry again, tossing her into mixed metaphors that would have done her silly younger sister proud. She was spending far too much time thinking, and not enough time acting. Fresh air would clear her addled brain and sweep away any lingering thoughts about last night.

She found Hetty in her overripe bower, reading something. She quickly shoved it out of sight, but not before Annelise could recognize the look of it. It was a French novel, of the type Annelise favored. She hid them, too, knowing the kind of contempt they garnered from the rest of the world. She wondered if Hetty's was one she hadn't yet read.

She wasn't about to ask and lose her dignity completely. "I thought a walk in the park would do us both good," she said abruptly. "We both could benefit from the exercise."

Hetty glared at her. "I had plenty of exercise last night—I danced every dance while you sat in the corner. Take a walk by yourself."

Annelise was torn between relief that Hetty apparently didn't know she'd danced with Christian Montcalm and annoyance with her rudeness. Her temper won out.

"I had a very pleasant dance with a very handsome man," she said. At least half of that wasn't a lie. "And you need fresh air as much as I do."

"I'll open a window."

"You'll put your shoes, your hat and your cloak on and come with me, young lady," Annelise said sternly. "Or I'll inform your father who sent these gaudy flowers." Blackmail had always been an effective tool.

"He probably knows," Hetty said in a sour voice, but she moved off the chaise and reached for her discarded shoes. "And I told you, I can talk him into anything."

"Including marrying a murderer?"

She'd said it for shock value, but to her dismay Hetty simply shrugged. "Don't be ridiculous. I don't believe he killed anyone."

"He's killed at least three people in a duel."

"That's different. Though I'm going to have to change his ways…the crown frowns on dueling and I don't fancy having to go abroad until some scandal dies down."

"You're going to change him?" Annelise repeated, skeptical.

"Of course. Once he settles down I suspect he'll be just as tame and boring as all the husbands I've met. Domestic life tends to have that effect."

"So once he weds you he'll have no more interest in gaming, dueling and mistresses?"

"Why should he?" Hetty's blue eyes were guileless. "He'd have me."

Annelise couldn't argue with such dedicated self-approval, so she didn't bother. "How pleasant," she murmured, feeling the piece of paper burn against her skin. "But I have less faith in the redemptive powers of love."

"That's because you're a spinster," Hetty said with

no real malice. "No one wanted you, so you think that true love doesn't exist."

"And you think Christian Montcalm loves you?"

"Of course. How could he not? I'm beautiful, lively, graceful and very rich. I'm irresistible."

There was the trace of something in Hetty's voice that made Annelise listen a little closer. She kept underestimating the girl's intelligence—there was a note of cynicism in her voice that she wouldn't have wanted anyone to recognize. For some reason Annelise wanted to reassure her, but she resisted the impulse. Hetty might know her main allure was her dowry, but she had little doubt as to her own beauty, and that kept her very happy indeed.

It was a lovely day, just a bit cool, but the sky was bright blue and the park was crowded with strollers and riders. Annelise kept a wary eye out for a certain exceedingly tall gentleman, but he was mercifully absent. Besides, what was the likelihood of him appearing in the park at just the moment she brought her reluctant charge outside? He was hardly the type to lie in wait without a good idea that his efforts would be rewarded, and Hetty had had no interest in walking in the park.

They walked along the path in a surprisingly companionable silence. She should have spent the time with an improving lesson on sedate behavior when dancing, but then, given her own behavior last night, she was hardly the one to talk. Except that the trouble had begun when they'd stopped dancing.

Thank God Hetty hadn't seen her, she thought once more.

Annelise was so lost in her disturbing thoughts that she wasn't even aware of the voice. Only that Hetty had frozen in place with an unreadable reaction on her usually expressive face.

"Hetty! Miss Chipple!" A young man was calling her name, ignoring the neat pathways and moving toward them across the carefully manicured lawns. Annelise couldn't remember that voice from the night before, nor could she see him clearly. She pushed her spectacles up to her forehead and was able to focus on him as he hurried toward them. A perfect stranger wearing country clothes, his hair too long, his face too unguarded for anyone who'd spent time in town.

"Miss Chipple!" he called again, but the two of them had stopped, waiting for his approach, and he sped up, until he reached them, breathless.

To Annelise's astonishment the boy had manners. "I beg pardon, miss," he addressed her first. "I'm an old friend of Miss Chipple's, and my enthusiasm got the better of me. If you'd allow me to introduce myself I'd be most grateful."

Hetty was standing painfully still, her expression still unreadable, and Annelise nodded her permission, more curious than anything else. Who or what would turn Hetty into a white-faced, stone statue?

"I'm William Dickinson," the young man said. "An old friend of the Chipples. We grew up together, Hetty and I."

It was more than that, as any fool could see. Hetty finally broke her frozen pose. "What are you doing here,

Will?" she asked unhappily. "You know we weren't supposed to see each other."

Hetty wasn't supposed to see Christian Montcalm, as Annelise was tempted to point out, but she was much too fascinated with the drama going on in front of her.

"Can't an old friend check to see how another old friend is doing? I just happened to come up to London…"

"Just happened? You hate London. You hate cities, you told me. You want nothing more than to spend your entire life in Kent as the perfect country squire."

"I thought I could change," Will said in a quiet voice.

More and more interesting, Annelise thought. She should put a stop to this, invite the young man back to the house. If he were really persona non grata he'd come up with an excuse. But right now this was far too fascinating to interfere.

"It wouldn't matter," Hetty said. "You can't change your family, and their estate is not nearly old or illustrious enough to suit my father. And you can't suddenly come up with a title when your future clearly lies in being Squire Dickinson of Applewood. I'm destined for better things in this life than living a dreary existence in the country with nothing to do but have babies and grow fat. I'm very happy here. I have more than a dozen suitors, I go out every night and dance until I'm exhausted, I hear music and go to the theater and have stimulating discussions about books and such…"

William Dickinson snatched his hat off his head in frustration, crushing it between his big hands. "You haven't changed that much, Hetty," he said. "You never cared much for music, you don't like plays unless there's a murder in them, and your taste in literature isn't the sort of thing people sit around and discuss. Most people despise novels. Your father has put too many grand ideas in your head, when you know you'd be happiest back home with a man who loves you."

"A man?" Hetty's laugh was derisive—she must have been practicing, Annelise thought cynically. "A boy, I think. A childhood playmate, and perhaps my first sweetheart, but I can look much higher when it comes to marriage. I'll be a viscountess at least."

"And who's this viscount? Does he love you?"

"Of course. And he's handsome, not too old, and very witty. I've moved on, Will. It's time you did too. Go back to Kent. You don't belong here."

Annelise would have given the fortune she didn't have to see what Montcalm's reaction would be to being called "not too old," but then, life was never fair.

William Dickinson was a very handsome young man, in an honest, rawboned fashion—a far cry from Montcalm's faintly decadent elegance. His face was tanned by the sun, his strong jaw set with frustration, but the love in his blue eyes didn't waver. Their children would have the prettiest blue eyes, Annelise mused, before remembering her chaperon's duties.

"Mr. Dickinson," Annelise said. "Perhaps it would be best if you come back to the house for tea, so you can continue this discussion."

"I'm not welcome under Mr. Chipple's roof," he said in a stark, dramatic tone that was perfectly suited to Hetty's dramatic streak. "And I don't have much else to say. Except that you don't belong here either, Hetty. Come home with me. We don't need your father's money— we don't need the fancy city people and all this foolishness. Come back home and marry me."

"I already told you that was out of the question. As did my father, much more forcefully. I assure you, I'm where I belong and very happy about it. Go back home and forget about me, Will." She didn't sound nearly as certain about it as her words suggested. Her lovely blue eyes were looking suspiciously moist, her plump lower lip seemed close to trembling. Annelise retrieved a handkerchief from her sleeve and presented it to her.

"I don't need it," she said, grabbing it and dabbing at her eyes. "I'm just so angry. Why can't I make you understand, Will? It was one thing when we were young and foolish, but I'm grown up now, and I understand the way the world works. It wasn't to be."

Annelise wished she had a second handkerchief with her because Will Dickinson looked as if he was about to burst into tears himself.

Montcalm or Dickinson? No matter what Mr. Chipple's grand ambitions were, it was more than clear that happiness lay with this raw young man from the country, at least in Hetty's martyred eyes. And what was Annelise's role in all this? To further her host's ambitions—to ensure that Hetty married neither a scoundrel nor a nobody from the countryside.

And Annelise was a woman who knew her duty. And blithely chose to ignore it. "It's a beautiful day," she said in her calm voice. "Why don't the two of you walk down by the duck pond and sit. The benches there are empty—if I sit here I'll be able to keep an eye on you and you'll both be very well chaperoned but yet able to converse without restraint."

"Could we, miss?" Will said, some of the despair lifting from his eyes for a moment.

"Miss Kempton," Hetty muttered, finally remembering her manners. But she wasn't objecting to the notion. She glanced in the direction of the duck pond longingly.

"Of course," Annelise said, moving to the bench, wishing she still had her handkerchief to brush it off, but sitting anyway, giving them a serene, approving smile. "You need time to talk things out. I'll be right here."

Mr. Dickinson held out his arm with all the stateliness of a royal duke, and after a moment Hetty put her tiny gloved hand on his sleeve, looking up at him. And in a brief instance all was clear. Hetty was just as much in love with Will Dickinson as he was with her, and the bucolic life could make her blissfully happy. She was young enough to enjoy the admiration of all those around her, but smart enough to eventually need more in her life. Will Dickinson would be steadfast, loyal, protective and devoted. What more could a woman ask for?

She watched them as they made their way down to the pond, and felt a sentimental dampness in her eyes. She fumbled in her pockets, but the handkerchief was already with Hetty, so she sniffled bravely, only to find a snowy white handkerchief proffered from behind her, the hand holding it strong and gloved and dripping with lace.

Annelise had learned some excellent curses from the grooms in her father's stable, as well as a few from her father when he was in his cups and indiscreet, and "hells bells" just slipped out before she could silence herself.

Christian Montcalm took the seat beside her, laughing. "Now, that's hardly the language for a dragon," he said. "Does Mr. Chipple know that the Honorable Miss Kempton swears like a fishwife?"

"That wasn't my fishwife language," she said. "You haven't annoyed me enough to deserve it. Yet."

A man shouldn't be that handsome. The faint lines around his eyes had to be from dissipation, not laughter, but knowing their cause didn't lessen their appeal. It was no wonder an impressionable young thing like Hetty had succumbed to his charm. What woman wouldn't?

She wouldn't, Annelise reminded herself. She looked at him. "So I assume that Hetty's reluctance to come for a walk was because she'd already planned to slip out and meet you?"

"Not at all. This was pure happenstance. If she was planning to meet me she wouldn't be off with another young man, totally unchaperoned."

"She's not unchaperoned—I can see them very clearly from here, and besides, I'm the one who sent them down there so they could talk." Unfortunately they were sitting a bit too close, and Will's arm was around her. She should get up and intervene, but then Montcalm would follow her, and that was the last thing she wanted. It would make matters even more complicated than they already were.

"You sent her? Why am I not surprised? And what does this stalwart young swain have to offer that I do not?"

"He's a decent, honorable man. You're a wicked, wretched—"

"Hush now, Miss Kempton. You have better manners than that. I don't understand why you've taken me in such dislike—I'm a perfectly charming gentleman."

"A bit too charming," she said tartly.

"Merci du compliment," he murmured. "However, I must tell you that I don't like it when people interfere with my plans, even pretty little dragons like you."

Fury bubbled up inside her. "Let us be perfectly clear on this, Mr. Montcalm. I don't like being mocked. We both know I'm neither little nor pretty, and I don't need you reminding me."

The laughter left his eyes abruptly. "How very interesting," he said, half to himself. "I've found your weak spot. And such a misguided, silly one it is."

Annelise opened her mouth to deliver an even more effective curse but he simply put his gloved hand against her lips, silencing her. It shouldn't have been disturbing—the thin leather of his glove kept his skin from touching her mouth, but her stomach still knotted at the sudden memory from last night of another, much more intimate touch.

"Never mind," he said. "We'll work on that later. In the meantime, what am I to do about love's young dream down there?"

William had put his arm around Hetty's delicate shoulders, and their heads were resting together, and

Annelise suspected they weren't talking at all. "It's no concern of yours."

"Ah, but it is. My intentions are honorable matrimony—that's my future bride down there, behaving indiscreetly. So the question is, should I do nothing and let her tarnish her reputation, thereby making my less-than-stellar self more acceptable to her father? Or do I interfere, saving Miss Chipple from making a cake of herself, and thereby earn her father's undying gratitude?"

"You should go away and let me deal with it," Annelise said crossly. "They're young and in love but not totally lacking in morals. As some people are."

"By some people you mean me. Ah, Miss Kempton, you are so harsh in your judgments. And the young lovers do touch me. It will sadden me to break them apart, but I need Miss Chipple's fortune, and I fully intend to marry her, no matter what her young man or you or even her father say."

"Her father could cut her off without a penny."

"Unlikely. He seems very indulgent, and who else would he be spending his money on? Unless you're thinking of marrying him yourself and supplanting his daughter in his affections."

Annelise shuddered. "Perish the thought."

"Very good. You're not as practical as I thought you were, which gives me hope."

"Hope for what?"

He smiled mysteriously but didn't answer. "Besides, it would be a terrible waste to see you married to a man like Chipple."

"All that money out of your reach?" Annelise suggested.

"It isn't the money that I'd mind."

"Stop it!" Annelise said, reaching her limit. "You may flirt with everything on two legs, male or female, but I'm not susceptible to your meaningless, flattering lies. You can't charm me into supporting your pursuit of Miss Chipple. She deserves better."

"Perhaps," he said, "but she'll have me, whether she likes it or not. I will marry her—she's too choice a prize to let escape. You, however, are another matter entirely."

"Well, I know it," Annelise said unflinchingly. If he was about to catalog her deficiencies it would be nothing new to her. And she had already listed his. "But it is no concern of yours. Miss Chipple is a beautiful, wealthy heiress and I'm a very determined, strong-minded spinster who's not going to let Hetty throw her life away on a rake and a scoundrel and a…a…degenerate." The last insult came out a little desperately, and she had the sudden feeling she'd gone too far.

Apparently she hadn't. Mr. Montcalm merely smiled lazily, despite the darkness in his eyes. "And what do you know of degeneracy, Miss Kempton?"

"Nothing at all."

"Then leave it to me to instruct you. Once I marry Miss Chipple I'll have more than enough time for your education. You'd be surprised how…stimulating certain experiences can be."

Before she could gather her wits and reply he was

gone, strolling away from her and the duck pond, most likely dismissing all thought of her. And she would have given anything if she had been able to dismiss him and his words as easily.

7

Miss Kempton really was the most delicious creature, Christian thought as he ambled away. He couldn't remember meeting such a prickly, defensive, yet charmingly vulnerable woman in his life. Most of his female acquaintances were either great beauties or women of a certain…er…moral laxness, and the Honorable Miss Kempton was neither.

He'd touched a raw spot quite accidentally when he'd been flirting with her. She seemed to have no difficulty with him calling her "dragon," but "pretty" and "little" seemed to bring forth her rage.

Well, in truth, she wasn't little. At least not in height. But although her dull clothes were fairly shapeless, even the evening dress last night, he'd been able to ascertain that she was slender in the right places, full in the others.

The fact of the matter was, he considered her pretty. Not a great beauty, as was more his usual style. He loved her eyes, even when they flashed lightning at him, and he'd been wanting to taste her mouth since he'd first seen her using it to castigate him. It had been everything he'd wanted, and if her insults hadn't been so diverting he would have been tempted to kiss her again.

He wanted to see her with her hair loose around her shoulders and out of those wretched clothes. He was tempted to crush the spectacles beneath his boot heel— he suspected she used them more as a defense than a tool to aid her vision. When people were truly short-sighted the glass distorted their eyes. Annelise's eye-glasses seemed far too thin to be of much use.

But he was getting distracted from the main prize. He needed to secure the impressionable Hetty first, then he could concentrate on the far more challenging dragon. In the meantime things were moving along quite nicely. Josiah Chipple would be extremely displeased with the arrival of Hetty's childhood love, or so he assumed the young man to be. Once Christian had settled on the heiress he'd made it his business to discover everything he could about her and her family, though some information had been frustratingly hard to come by. Mrs. Chipple had died when Hetty was quite young, according to Hetty. Mr. Chipple had amassed his fortune through shipping, though how he had advanced from a simple importer to someone with the dazzling fortune he now possessed was shrouded in mystery. Christian didn't particularly care where the money came from, as long as he could get his hands on it.

Which he planned to. His debts were getting more pressing, and his luck at the cards last night had been less than usual. Probably because he'd been unduly dis-tracted by his encounter on the terrace and the damp piece of lace tucked in his coat. A weakness he couldn't afford.

For the next few weeks he would concentrate on his financial salvation. And then he'd allow himself to play.

She was still clutching the lacy handkerchief in her hand, Annelise realized. She should throw it on the ground, stomp on it to express her total rage and disgust with Christian Montcalm. But in the last few years economy had been drummed into her, and it was too fine a handkerchief to wantonly destroy, she told herself virtuously. She reached under her cloak and tucked it into her bodice, next to the folded note that still lay there. At this rate she was going to become quite top heavy, she thought with a trace of grim amusement. She could only hope Montcalm didn't take it into his head to present her with anything bulky.

He wasn't going to present her with anything at all. As soon as she got back to the house she was going to give the lovely handkerchief to one of the maids, burn the note and toss the flowers out the window. Well, perhaps she might leave the flowers—they were lovely, and not to blame that they'd come as a mocking salute from a wastrel.

She glanced down at the duck pond. They were sitting far too close together—Montcalm had been right about that. And perhaps Mr. Chipple wouldn't be pleased, but once she told him of the danger his daughter was courting he might be more amenable to the safe, reliable comfort of someone like William Dickinson.

They didn't even notice her approach. Hetty had been crying, the tears making her china blue eyes even more beguiling. She was one of those rare females who looked even lovelier when she cried. Her nose didn't drip and turn red, her eyes didn't swell, unlike Annelise's. It shouldn't come as a surprise and it wasn't the least rancorous—Hetty was simply everything Annelise was not.

They jumped up guiltily when she appeared in front of them, and Hetty fumbled in her lap for her discarded glove. It was a good thing no one had seen them but the ducks, Annelise thought, or Hetty might have done real damage to her reputation. And it was all Annelise's fault.

But it wasn't too late to mend. "I think you should come back to the house with us after all, Mr. Dickinson. It's almost teatime, and I'm certain you'll want to renew your acquaintance with Mr. Chipple. I expect Hetty will welcome the chance to restore amity between the two of you."

Hetty didn't look as if she welcomed anything. "He can't come home with us," she said flatly. "You don't know my father—he doesn't like to be thwarted."

"No one's thwarting him, my dear. And I suspect he would dislike subterfuge even more, and word will certainly get to him of this afternoon's accidental meeting."

"How would he know?"

"Because I would tell him. I have a certain responsibility, and it was my choice to allow you to have some time in relative privacy."

"You don't have to…" Hetty began, but Annelise continued smoothly.

"Besides, if I don't, you can be sure Christian Montcalm will. He saw the two of you, and he would find it to his advantage to inform your father."

"Who's Christian Montcalm?" William asked. His ruddy cheeks were the complete opposite of Montcalm's pale handsomeness, and Hetty's face flamed at the mention of her suitor.

"He was here?" Hetty said in a choked voice, clearly horrified.

Annelise didn't wait for Hetty to come up with an explanation. "He's simply one of her many suitors. The most determined and the least desirable of them. If he has the chance he'll cause trouble, and I need to circumvent that."

"He wouldn't do such a thing!" Hetty protested.

William looked down at her in surprise. "Hetty, are you in love with this man?"

"Of course not, Will!" she said in a cross voice. "I just want to marry him."

William looked tempted to bolt at this artless confidence, so Annelise simply took both their arms and herded them back up the path. Mr. Chipple could scarcely be as difficult as Hetty warned, but it wouldn't hurt to be as honest as possible. The sooner they faced him, the better.

"We'll have tea in the green salon," she informed the maid when they arrived back at the house. "And ask Mr. Chipple to join us if he's able."

In fact, the green salon was a bilious color designed to make any inhabitant look like a corpse, with the notable exception of Hetty. As far as Annelise could tell, nothing could lessen her incandescent beauty. Perhaps she was being too cynical—Christian Montcalm might have fallen desperately in love with the exquisite creature and her fortune was merely a happy adjunct, despite his crass avowals.

And the moon might be made of green cheese, she thought. If it were, it was probably the hideous color of Josiah Chipple's parlor. After all, if Montcalm was really in love with the heiress why had he kissed her on the terrace? He should be focusing all his efforts on winning his beloved, not tormenting her protectors.

William and Hetty seemed to have exhausted their entire conversation, though Annelise suspected the mention of Christian Montcalm had put a decided damper on things. Therefore it was up to her to keep matters going, and she prattled on like a total idiot, serving tea, discussing the weather, asking polite questions, which resulted in monosyllabic answers except when she happened on the topic of country living. William became almost voluble, and to her surprise Hetty joined in. Since Annelise herself preferred living in the country things loosened up for a bit, until Mr. Chipple appeared in the open door, glowering.

Hetty didn't help matters by looking nervous and guilty, but William jumped to his feet, instantly polite, and took the proverbial bull by the horns by starting up a conversation.

"Good afternoon, sir," he said, his voice betraying his nervousness only slightly. "I ran into Miss Chipple and

Miss Kempton in the park, and Miss Kempton was kind enough to invite me back for tea. I hope you don't mind that I trespassed on your hospitality, but I wanted to renew my acquaintance with both of you during my short time here in the city."

Annelise must have imagined the chill that had emanated from the door. Mr. Chipple stepped into the room, affable enough. "It's good to see you, Will. What brings you into the city? You're a country boy, born and bred. I wouldn't think the likes of society would suit you very well."

"I had a commission for my father," Will said with only a slight stutter. "I thought I would take advantage of the trip to acquire a bit of town bronze. I expect it's a lost cause."

"It's smart of you to recognize when a cause is lost," Chipple said with a pleasant smile that somehow failed to warm. "When are you going back home?"

"I'll be here for a week."

The obvious, polite response would have been to invite him to stay in the house, or at least proffer a dinner invitation. As titular hostess Annelise was about to do just that, something stopped her: the unspoken tension in the room. The usually friendly Mr. Chipple suddenly seemed a great deal less hospitable.

"Then perhaps we'll run into you again," Chipple said. "Though I doubt we'll travel in the same circles. Hetty, I think you should have a rest before Lady Helton's ball tonight. You'll be up all hours and you need your beauty sleep. Hetty has a great many suitors, William, and it's quite exhausting for the dear girl. Miss Kempton, could I see you in the library at your convenience?"

The dismissal was clear and abrupt, and there was nothing to be done. Even Hetty didn't argue. She merely murmured a listless farewell to her devoted swain and left the room, followed by her father.

There was nothing Annelise could do to redeem the situation, but she at least managed to put a softer sheen on Chipple's rudeness, forcing him to drink another cup of tea and discuss the merits of sheep versus cattle. He was obviously longing to unburden his heart to Annelise, but she was determined that he not. As long as she wasn't officially privy to their clandestine affair she could feel righteous in her social choices. Once she knew this unacceptable young man was a determined and ineligible suitor, at least to Mr. Chipple's eyes, then she would have no choice but to keep him away.

And she was still hoping for something, anything, to save Hetty from the dire mistake of a man like Christian Montcalm.

It was probably no more than half an hour later when Annelise presented herself at Mr. Chipple's study. If he was unhappy with her delay he failed to show it, or even to acknowledge her presence just inside the doorway as he pored over his books, leaving her to wait awkwardly.

But Annelise was not the sort to wait. She walked into the room and seated herself in one of the chairs opposite the desk and said, "You wished to see me, Mr. Chipple?"

There was no missing the astonishment in his small, dark eyes. He'd probably never had a woman fail to be cowed by him. Annelise had never been fond of bullies— when confronted they were usually full of harmless bluster, and she expected Josiah Chipple to be the same.

He slammed his book shut, leaning back in his chair. He hadn't risen since she'd appeared—a notable insult that was doubtless designed to express his unhappiness with her. She would have to find a tactful way to explain to the man that manners and displeasure could coexist, but at the moment she was beginning to understand some of Hetty's caution as far as her father was concerned. So she sat still and held her tongue, her hands folded in her lap, waiting.

"Will Dickinson is not welcome in this house," he said flatly.

"Indeed? I gather he's a childhood friend of Hetty's, and he certainly seemed quite unexceptional. I thought it might relieve some of her homesickness to spend time with an old friend."

"She's not homesick! This is her home now, and she loves being the center of attention." Annelise could scarcely dispute the latter, so she stayed silent. "Her affection for William was simply that of a child. She knows her duty and she's more than happy to fulfill it, as it benefits her as well as me."

"And what is her duty, Mr. Chipple?"

"I thought you were already clear on this, Miss Kempton. She is to marry well. A titled gentleman. His fortune is not important, but his standing will ensure that she and my descendants will be unquestioned members of society despite her working-class father. She has the face and the fortune for it, and I'm not about to be contravened at this point. There are any number of possibilities available, and I don't want Dickinson confusing her about who she should marry. Women are easily distracted, and she's not that bright to begin with. She has the sense to do as I tell her, but I need to make certain that there's no unfortunate temptation from her former life."

For a moment Annelise said nothing. Hetty was a great deal smarter than her father gave her credit for, but that was probably a lost argument. "Did Mr. Dickinson propose marriage?"

"He did indeed, the impudent boy! As if I'd let any treasure of mine go so easily. She'll have a title or my name isn't Josiah Chipple."

Unfortunately, she suspected it was, indeed—no man would choose such an undignified name. And there was no argument she could come up with at this point, except…perhaps one.

"He's at least a more respectable choice than Christian Montcalm," Annelise offered.

Mr. Chipple scowled. "Has that fellow been sniffing around her skirts?" he demanded crudely. "She can do better than him. I'm not saying he wouldn't do in a pinch—man's going to be a viscount, after all. That's nothing to sneeze at. He's a bit of a scoundrel, I gather, but a wife can change all that."

"Perhaps you don't quite understand the severity of

the situation. Christian Montcalm is more than a scoundrel—he's considered persona non grata at the best houses. His reputation is such that he is cut by some of the most influential high sticklers in society. His behavior in the past has been so questionable that it's unlikely to be salvaged, and marriage to your daughter wouldn't help her any. She'd be as ostracized as he is, perhaps more. People are more tolerant of men's bad behavior, but they'll have no reason to welcome your daughter into their houses."

Mr. Chipple stopped to consider this. "How very enlightening, Miss Kempton. I'm glad to see I didn't make a mistake in having you come join us for the season. You understand things that are quite beyond my experience. But if Montcalm is not accepted at the best houses then why do we keep running into him?"

She could hardly tell him that the nouveau riche Chipples were also unwelcome in the best houses. After all, there was only so much their sponsor, Lady Prentice, could do, and even Annelise's unexceptional presence in their household could only elevate their social standing one small notch. "He makes it his business to seek your daughter out. Mr. Montcalm's quite determined to marry her, and your daughter finds him very attractive. I've tried to warn him off but he pays no mind."

"Of course he doesn't—why would he listen to a woman?" Chipple replied. "So clearly I'll have to step in to make certain he receives the message that his attentions are unwelcome. Do you expect there will be a problem?"

Annelise remembered the cool mockery in Montcalm's laughing eyes. "I don't think he'll give up without a fight. As you've said, your daughter is both beautiful and possessed of a remarkable fortune. Most men wouldn't admit defeat lightly."

"Then I'll have to make sure Montcalm understands," Chipple said. "It's a shame, though. She did seem to fancy him, and it got her mind off young Will until the little bas—er…until he showed up again. And a viscountcy was the most promising so far—I'd hate to settle for anything less."

Again, Annelise thought, there was the problem of not being invited to the more exclusive gatherings. But with determination, that could change—despite Josiah's working-class drawbacks Hetty was really quite charming, and many society matrons would overlook the smell of the shop for such a well-endowed wife for one of their sons. "I think we need to be patient, sir," she said carefully. "As long as Christian Montcalm knows that he's wasting his efforts, and if it turns out that Mr. Dickinson is truly unacceptable, then we can move forward."

Indeed, it grieved her that the young lovers were going to be parted. Her sentimental streak was coming forth again—Will and Hetty had looked so sweet together.

But the undoubted blessing of involving Mr. Chipple would be that Christian Montcalm would no longer trouble be Annelise's responsibility. She had little doubt Chipple would make it very clear that any alliance was out of the question, and Montcalm would have no choice but to turn his attentions elsewhere, sparing Annelise from her very disordered feelings.

"Trust me, Miss Kempton. I'll take care of Mr. Montcalm. In the meantime, you distract my daughter from any romantic memories she might harbor for Dickinson. She's not marrying a farmer no matter how much she cries."

Had Hetty cried for Will Dickinson? Interesting, since she'd said her father would give her anything she wanted. Unless it interfered with his own ambitions, apparently.

"Certainly, Mr. Chipple. In the meantime perhaps we might miss the ball tonight—Christian Montcalm is certain to be there, and you won't have had time to discourage him effectively."

"Oh, I will most definitely have enough time, Miss Kempton. I'm an efficient man, and once I decide on a course it's as good as accomplished. I don't expect you'll be seeing Montcalm at Lady Helton's, or anywhere else for that matter. I'll make certain there's no room for misunderstanding in my message."

She thought she detected a faintly ominous edge to Chipple's hearty voice. Must be her wild imagination again. "In that case perhaps I should go and have a rest before the evening's festivities. Unless you had something else you wish to discuss?"

"Not at all, Miss Kempton," he said, rising this time like a gentleman. "You've been very helpful to me. Go get your rest while I attend to business. I want you to be fresh enough to keep an eye on my daughter."

No one was ever that fresh, Annelise thought with a trace of asperity, noting that Chipple hadn't suggested she might benefit from a beauty sleep. Like most men he would consider it a lost cause.

But indeed, she was unaccountably weary after the stimulating day. It was the time outdoors, not the company that had exhausted her, she decided. After all, Christian Montcalm had only subjected her to his unwanted presence for a few short minutes.

Annelise's room was still and quiet, and when she lay down on the bed, she felt the paper press against her breast. She reached inside her gown and pulled the note and handkerchief free. The small fire was burning in the grate to ward off the evening chill, but she was too tired to climb off the bed and toss the note in. She could accomplish that simple act eventually. There was no great rush.

She looked at the lacy handkerchief in her hand, then brought it to her face. It smelled of her scent, of course, the subtle rose that she favored. But it smelled of him as well—something spicier, foreign and mysterious.

She reached under the coverlet and shoved the offending handkerchief under her pillow, along with the note, then wrapped herself in the throw at the foot of the bed. Easy enough to dispose of later, she thought sleepily. There was no hurry to get rid of the things. Now that she'd managed to get rid of Montcalm himself.

8

Christian Montcalm knew quite a bit about women, and he knew when to advance and when to retreat. He'd been quite assiduous in his attentions to the silly Miss Chipple, and she'd jumped like a trout for a piece of bait. A night or two of absence would no doubt begin to eat away at her blithe certainty that he was hers for the taking—the chit was far too sure of herself.

He didn't have the slightest concern that the appearance of Hetty's childhood sweetheart would prove an obstacle in his plans. Miss Chipple was young and impressionable enough to be distracted quite easily, and she'd be married before she even realized she wanted someone else.

Tant pis, he thought. Too damned bad, he corrected himself. He hated it when he absently lapsed into the French that had been as familiar to him as English. He found himself doing it more so, in fact, since he'd lived in France with his family.

But that had been a lifetime ago, and there was nothing French about him. Not even his lovely mother would recognize him.

A night at the cards without the distraction of Miss Chipple and her dragon proved very pleasant. His luck held, and by the early hours of the morning he was pleasantly at peace with the world. Two bottles of wine had contributed to that mellowness and the plump size of his purse moved things along. Even though he'd turned down the generous offer of the beautiful Mrs. Hargate, he still strode home through the early-morning streets a comparatively well-pleased gentleman.

He managed to live in a decent part of town, but no area was safe at that early an hour. Not that Christian had any particular concern. He had a certain reputation, even on the streets, and most men of the criminal class gave him a wide berth. Perhaps it was respect for a fellow transgressor, he thought with some amusement.

So it was with some surprise that he turned the corner into the narrow street where he lived and realized he wasn't alone.

They were hiding in the shadows—at least two of them. He wondered whether they were waiting especially for him, or if they were looking for any victim who happened to wander into their path. He was about to find out.

He whistled an old country song as he made his way down the alley, stumbling slightly as a drunken man should, muttering to himself and giving the perfect impersonation of easy prey. They let him make it as far as his door before they emerged out of the darkness. Two of them, sailors by the look of them—big men—

neither as tall as he was but far bulkier. Which would give them more brute strength, but make them move slower, he thought as he deliberately fumbled with his key. They would be easy enough to take and a fight would be invigorating, but he wasn't certain he wanted to be bothered.

They thought they were creeping up on an oblivious, drunken gentleman. He rattled the keys once more, put his hand on his sword and said in a clear, distinct voice, "Let's not do this."

It stopped them cold. He turned to look at them. It was nearly dawn—he hadn't realized he'd been out that late, and the night was brisk. The men were shivering— obviously not used to England's climate.

He'd managed to totally confuse them. And then the larger one, whom he presumed was the brains of the operation, took a bullying step forward. "It ain't up to you. We've got a job to do and we aims to see we do it."

"But I'm afraid I don't agree. I'm not about to hand over my money without a fight. A fight, I'm afraid, that you'd lose."

The brains of the operation proved sadly lacking. "Two to one, and there's not much brawn to you. And we're not here for the money, though I imagine Smitty and I can help ourselves with no one the wiser."

"Really?" His tone held nothing but polite inquiry. "Then I can only presume you've come to kill me. An even more difficult task than robbing me, I'm afraid."

"We'll manage," growled Smitty.

"I doubt it. Is there any particular reason you chose

me to murder? Do my clothes annoy you? Are you revolutionaries from France trying to spread democracy?"

"Frenchies?" The first man spat on the ground in disdain. "We're being paid. Nothing personal, you understand—it's just a job."

"I shan't take it personally," Montcalm said gently. "And exactly who hired you? I can think of at least a dozen people who'd want me dead, and half of them would have the means to hire ruffians to come after me. But most of them would know I'm not easily taken down."

"All men die sooner or later," the first man said. "I've killed enough that I know how easy it really can be done."

Christian's faint smile would have chilled a smarter man, but his two assassins failed to notice the danger. He could dispatch the two of them at any time—he was graceful and unaccountably lethal with sword and knife—and equipped with both. But he was not about to use them before he found out who hired the two men.

"So who have I offended now, that he went to the docks to find thugs?" Then it dawned on him. "Oh, how naive of me. He already knew you, didn't he? You must be employed by Josiah Chipple."

Smitty looked disturbed. "Should he know that, Clemson?"

"It won't matter, idiot!" Clemson snapped. "He'll be dead." He turned back to Montcalm and grinned, exposing his blackened teeth. "And if you think we're simple sailors, then you don't know much. You can run as fast as you like and I'll catch you. I can take down a man in seconds."

"And why should I run?"

"For your life, man," Smitty broke in impatiently. "—like the blacks we chase in Africa…"

"Shut up, Smitty!"

"You said it doesn't matter what he knows," Smitty whined. "He'll be dead. We can cut his throat to make sure he can't talk."

"If he's dead he can't talk anyway. And I have every intention of cutting his throat. Too bad there's no market for someone like him—he'd fetch a pretty penny if we sold him to some stinking Arab. They like men, and this one's got such a pretty face. A nice arse too, I'll wager."

"Maybe we should—"

"We'll kill him, Smitty. Can't you see he's just trying to distract us? Prolong the inevitable?"

"That's delay, not prolong," Montcalm corrected in a polite voice. "Assuming you mean the inevitable is my gruesome death at your hands, then I'd want to delay it, not make sure the experience lasts."

"I don't have time for this," Clemson exploded, starting toward him, his knife drawn.

Montcalm sighed wearily, pulling out his own small, jeweled dagger, better suited for a gentleman's hand, half the size of Clemson's weapon.

Clemson looked at it and laughed. "You think you can cause any damage with that tiny pig-sticker? You're a bigger fool than you—"

He stopped speaking, because Montcalm had thrown the knife with deadly accuracy, and Clemson was down on the ground in a pool of blood.

He was making choking noises from the knife lodged in his throat, but he would die quickly. Montcalm turned his gaze to Smitty, arched an eyebrow and said, "Next?"

Smitty was a smarter man than Clemson, after all. He was backing away, nervously, and Montcalm let him go. In the end he wasn't in the mood for a chase.

Before Smitty could break into a run he called after him. "You might inform Mr. Chipple that I'm a harder man to kill than he thinks."

"I'm not going anywhere near the man," Smitty stammered. "You don't fail Josiah Chipple and then live to talk about it."

"But I need you to give him a message."

"Take it yourself," Smitty said in a panic, and he turned and ran down the alleyway.

Montcalm watched him go. Clemson was dead by now—no great loss to society, apparently. Christian walked over to the corpse and looked down, then pulled his dagger free. So Josiah Chipple was a slaver—what a fascinatingly useful piece of information. Most people preferred to ignore the fact that men made fortunes trafficking in human flesh, and so far Josiah had managed to keep the source of his success in shipping a secret.

Not anymore. It wouldn't matter how pretty Hetty Chipple was, how rich, how virtuous—which he certainly doubted—or how bright. If she was the daughter of a middle-class slaver there would be no respectable offers, certainly no titled ones.

Except, of course, for someone like Christian Montcalm, whose reputation was already in shreds.

It wasn't as if he intended to spend the rest of his life in London. He would inherit nothing from his elderly uncle but the title, but he already possessed Wynche End near the coast of Devon. It had belonged to Christian's great-aunt, and it was almost uninhabitable, though if his grandfather had found any way of depriving Christian of it he would have.

Christian had often considered selling it—the house was in shambles but the land was extensive and some of the finest farming plot in all of Devon. Fifty years of lying fallow had only improved the soil. He could have sold it to someone like Chipple, to whom money was no object, and whoever bought it would have torn down the rambling old house and put up something shiny and new. But he had a great affection for the house, even in its current state of disrepair, and Hetty's money would provide the perfect infusion the poor old place needed. And out in Devon it wouldn't matter where the money had come from—merely that the bills would be paid.

A shame for poor Hetty if the truth came out about her father. If she behaved herself he would have no problem allowing her to go off to London to visit her father and enjoy herself discreetly. As for him, once he left London he had no particular wish to return. He'd tasted all of its pleasures and vices, and while they'd been intoxicating, he'd had enough.

* * *

His rooms were cold. He could only afford a day servant, and Henry wouldn't be arriving for hours. The logical step was to go to bed and seek the respite of a good morning's sleep.

But he could build a fire as well as the next man, and he was in no particular mood to put off his duty. His hands were bloody from the knife, and it put him in a particularly foul mood. He would like to be more sanguine when he was forced to kill, to simply shrug it off as an unpleasant necessity.

But he hadn't been able to inure himself to it, not quite. And perhaps he was just as glad he hadn't.

He washed his hands and the knife in a basin of cool water, carefully drying the weapon and laying it back down on the counter. It had been a gift from his mother on his twelfth birthday. She would have had no idea when she gave it to him just how frequently he would use it over the years.

But then again, maybe she did. She was, after all, French.

He found himself smiling faintly—an unusual occurrence. Thinking of the French tended to put him in a foul mood, but thinking of his beautiful mother warmed him, and there was no denying that his mother was, indeed, a Frenchwoman. Born, raised and died at the hands of her murderous people.

It was interesting to see just how terrified Smitty had been at the thought of facing Josiah Chipple. Of course, it might have been simply the shock of seeing his partner in crime die so suddenly, but he doubted it. Slavers were an unsentimental lot, and death was an integral part of their trade, both for their cargo and for those who tried to interfere.

Unfortunately for the not very clever Smitty, if Josiah Chipple was as formidable as he thought he was, then he was already doomed. A man like Chipple wouldn't let even a small detail escape his attention, and Montcalm's botched murder was no small detail.

He was going to have to decide just the most effective and remunerative way to deal with Josiah Chipple. Something with finesse, something insulting, and definitely costly. No man set hired thugs on him without paying a very steep price indeed.

He would take Chipple's money, he would take his pride, and he would take his daughter. And enjoy every moment of it.

Annelise should have been in a much better mood. There had been no sign of Christian Montcalm at Lady Helton's party, no sign of him the following night, as well. Josiah Chipple's subtle warning must have been surprisingly efficient, and Annelise could rejoice that she would probably never come closer than the other side of a crowded ballroom again.

Unfortunately, she wasn't in the mood for rejoicing. It was probably the rain. It had been pouring steadily the last twenty-four hours, and even when she tried to open the window to let some air into her stuffy bedroom the rain lashed inside, and she had no choice but to shut it again. She felt smothered and stifled in the Chipples' opulent house, and even the monstrous Greek statues in the hallway seemed particularly glum.

Hetty was equally miserable, rising late with swollen eyes, moping around the house, alternately sighing noisily or snapping at anyone who crossed her path. Annelise was not about to put up with her charge's rudeness, but she couldn't help but wonder whether it was the absence of Mr. Montcalm or Mr. Dickinson that was breaking Hetty's heart.

It probably didn't help matters that the house was rife with tension. Mr. Chipple was holding a party that evening—dinner, cards and dancing for forty, and even the experienced London servants were in a tizzy trying to prepare for the event. Hetty had changed her mind about her gown at least seven times, several of them with Annelise's helpful prodding, since some of Hetty's gowns rivaled her father's taste in decor. Even Annelise was on edge—while most of the guests were from the lower echelons of high society, a few were coming simply out of respect to Lady Prentice and her goddaughter, and she cringed at the thought of Josiah Chipple meeting some of the starchiest of women with his faltering manners. The disapproving, formidable women who were above reproach, invulnerable, and never, ever wrong.

At one point Annelise had even thought to model her life on those women who always knew how to do the right thing, say the proper thing.

But the sad fact was that Annelise had been unfortunately lax in the last few days. The note lay hidden among her underthings, having yet to make it into the cleansing flames of her evening fire, and the handkerchief somehow found its way beneath her pillow, night after night. Every time she reached for the two items she promised that the next morning she would dispose of them. But for some reason she never did.

Not that she should castigate herself—they had only been in her possession three days. She was being absurd—she had just been too busy to deal with their disposal. Which only proved how little they mattered to her, she told herself, that she could forget so easily.

She glanced at her meager supply of evening dresses. She'd worn the muddy brown silk one twice already, which left the dull gray, which was a mixed blessing. The cut was a bit tighter—it delineated her narrow waist and, when she took off her spectacles, made her eyes appear even more gray. On the other hand, the cut was just a bit too low for Annelise's piece of mind, forcing her to wrap a fichu around her shoulders, which made her look as if she belonged to another generation. There was no help for it—she wasn't about to go around displaying her bosom for all to see. Not that Christian Montcalm would be there to see it, of course. The Chipples would be the very last place he was invited.

Not that he'd bother to look, either. But the question was irrelevant, since he wouldn't be there. She pinned the lace scarf around her shoulders, arranging it to cover the expanse of skin exposed by the dress, and reached for her beloved pearls.

They were the only thing of value she had left. Her

mother had given them to her when Annelise was thirteen, just before she died and Annelise's father had stopped making any effort at sobriety, and she treasured them. They were sumptuous pearls, large and perfectly matched, belonging to Annelise's great-grandmother, a notable beauty in the court of King James. Word had it that the pearls had come from the king himself, as a gift to an accommodating aristocrat, but Annelise didn't bother to think about that part. Even though she was no beauty herself the pearls made her feel that way, an odd connection with her ancestor. When she wore the priceless, dazzling pearls then she, too, could become a little bit dazzling to those who were discerning enough to see.

Not that anyone tonight would be looking at her, but the pearls, as always, gave her a warm feeling of being cherished. And even though the sale of them could have bought her the cottage and even the living she longed for, she wouldn't part with them.

As Mr. Chipple's titular hostess she had to be down early in time to greet their guests, with Hetty firmly by her side. She wasn't certain she could soften Mr. Chipple's noisy goodwill, but she would try. As more and more people arrived, crowding in among the marble statues, the warmer the room felt, and the hotter the fichu became. She tugged at it, then noticed the sudden tension in the air. There'd been no dip in conversation, no flurry of whispers, but she'd sensed immediately that something was wrong, and she looked up…up, into the mocking eyes of Christian Montcalm.

9

For a moment Annelise stood frozen in time, the noise of the guests muffled around her. She saw Mr. Chipple, veins bulging at his forehead, about to explode into a scene that would forever destroy any hopes he had of an eventual knighthood or his daughter marrying well, and there was nothing else she could do but step in.

"Christian!" she cried, putting a dazzling smile on her face. "You were able to come after all!" And she caught both his hands, leaning forward to kiss him on each cheek.

She should have known he'd take advantage of it. He should have barely brushed her skin, but the kiss he landed just below her spectacles was firm and warm, not the kiss of a casual acquaintance. And Annelise's mind was still racing, trying to avert disaster.

She pulled back, her smile still firmly planted on her face, hoping she wasn't blushing. She didn't blush easily, but the damned man hadn't let go of her hands, and between the two erratic men she had no idea how she was going to salvage the situation with half of society and Mr. Chipple's faux-Greek statues watching.

But she could try. She turned to the fuming Mr. Chipple. "This is my dear, dear friend Christian Montcalm," she said blithely. "It's been so long since we've had any time together that I knew you wouldn't mind if I invited him." Indeed, half the guest list was there at her invitation, but they were all people Chipple was determined to impress.

She'd given him enough time to calm down. He barely bowed in Christian's direction. "Montcalm," he said stiffly.

Hetty looked up, her blue eyes mystified but her good sense keeping her silent. "Good evening, sir," she said sweetly.

He still hadn't released Annelise's hands, and the last thing she wanted was to let him go cause mischief in the Chipples' ostentatious mansion. Fortunately fate, which had been wickedly capricious of late, decided to deliver her a boon in the form of her godmother, Lady Prentice.

Amelia Prentice summed up the situation in an instant and took charge. "Good evening, Josiah, Hetty," she said. "And my dear Annelise. Why don't you go renew your acquaintance with your old friend and I'll stand hostess in your place? After all, I am sponsoring Miss Hetty in her debut."

Annelise could have kissed her godmother, but first things first. "Bless you," she said, and deftly turning her hand in Christian's, she pulled him away from the crowded foyer.

He followed her, silently, willingly, as she led him

through the already crowded rooms. She had no idea where she was going to take him—outside was a terrible idea, given what had happened on the terrace—but she needed to make certain no one could hear them. In the end she dragged him out to the little side garden with its iron gate leading out onto the back alleyway. She could simply push him out and lock the gate behind him, but that wouldn't preclude his coming back in the front door.

In the center of the garden stood another one of Chipple's beloved Greek statues, this time a half-clothed woman, and Annelise immediately promised herself she would do a thorough tour of the house to find less embarrassing places to have a tête à tête.

Though Christian didn't seem the slightest bit interested in the perfect marble breast that was almost at eye level. He'd probably seen far too many of the real thing, she thought uncharitably.

"What the devil are you doing here?" she demanded, finally succeeding in yanking her hand free.

"Such language, my pet!" Christian murmured. "But then we're such old, close friends that you should feel comfortable expressing yourself so forcefully."

"You need to leave. Immediately. I barely averted a scene of horrifying proportions, and I can't count on Mr. Chipple being ruled by his good sense."

"Well, I'm not entirely sure I should thank you for that, dragon," he said. "If he'd made a scene he would have created a situation where Miss Hetty, despite her wealth and her beauty, was far less desirable, thereby making my own suit more favorable. On the other hand, since he had no choice but to welcome me into his house in front of half of society—though not the top half, I noticed—then from now on he'll be forced to tolerate me, giving me a chance to win him over."

Annelise looked at him, scandalized. "Was that your plan?"

He laughed. "No, my sweet. I doubt I could do anything at all to win Mr. Chipple over once you informed him just how ineligible I was. I do have you to thank for that, do I not?"

She wouldn't feel guilty. "Of course. I told you I would. I intend to make certain Hetty marries someone who will love and cherish her—"

"And who says I won't love and cherish the little baggage? Money makes me very affectionate."

"You're disgusting. I want you to leave!"

"But I'm not going to. I need to have a conversation with Mr. Chipple and I don't intend to depart until I've had it."

"If you think asking for Hetty's hand in marriage will get you anywhere then you must be mad."

"And we both know that I am not. I need to have a word with Mr. Chipple about his methods of discouraging suitors. He lacks finesse."

Annelise had been doing her best not to look at him, for the simple reason that looking at him caused a treacherous reaction in her body. But at that she did, into his undeniably beautiful face, and she saw the slow burn of a deep anger that had nothing to do with her.

Without thinking she reached up to touch his face, but he flinched, thank God, before her fingertips could graze his skin. She immediately crossed her arms, to make her hands behave. "Mr. Chipple is not used to the mores of polite society. If he sent someone to rough you up a little—"

"You might say that," Christian murmured.

"Then he was very wrong," Annelise continued, ignoring the interruption. "But then, you don't seem to take no for an answer."

"Only when I want to," he replied. "Do you know where your host's massive fortune comes from?"

"From shipping. Why should you ask?"

"Shipping what?"

"I have no idea, nor do I care. Spices, lumber, exotic animals. The further Mr. Chipple removes himself from the unfortunate associations of trade the better."

"I rather think you might care, dragon," he said, "but I'm not about to enlighten you. I'll have a brief word with Mr. Chipple and then I'll leave. Will that make you happy?"

"My own happiness is not your concern," she said in a stiff voice. "You cause trouble and distress wherever you go, and I intend to protect Hetty—"

"So you've said," he broke in. "But in truth I'm capable of causing great pleasure to those willing to sample it. But we're not here to discuss that, are we? I have no intention of ruffling your feathers again. Though I'm not sure I've ever seen a feathered dragon before. Tell me, do you have feathers instead of scales? I know you breathe fire, but you're actually quite soft in the right places."

She raised her hand to slap him but he caught her wrist before her hand could connect with his shadowed face. "You wouldn't want to do that, my pet," he murmured. "I've already been assaulted once today, and I'm not in the mood to let it happen again."

"And what would you do about it?" she shot back, furious.

"What I always do when you annoy me," he said, and kissed her.

It wasn't much more than a brief touch of his mouth on hers, but it made the blood sizzle in her veins, and she jumped back as if he'd bit her, wiping her mouth.

He shook his head, laughing, the darkness in his eyes vanishing. "My dear Miss Kempton, you are far too easy to play."

"Then find someone who's a better adversary! Go away and leave us alone!"

"I'm not about to leave any of you alone. Mr. Chipple and I need to come to a…an understanding, if you like. Miss Hetty is far too desirable a prize to ignore, and as for you, dragon…well, I find I have a certain irresistible fondness for you. I enjoy these little battles."

"Go away," she said through gritted teeth.

"Eventually," he said, his eyes running down her dress. "You really do have the most abominable clothing. And why you're covering up your breast with that fichu is beyond my comprehension. And the pearls, while quite lovely, are false, and you deserve better. If you would only wear better clothes, arrange your hair differently and lose the damned spectacles, you could be quite pretty."

This time she didn't try to slap him, though she desperately wanted to. "I'm not interested in being pretty," she said, "and the pearls are real."

"You're wrong on both counts, dragon. But we'll work on you later. As delightful as this little flirtation is, I need to find Mr. Chipple. We have some business to discuss, but I promise I'll come in search of you when I'm done."

"God give me strength," Annelise cried in exasperation. "The kindest thing you could do is to leave me alone."

"I know," he said touching her face gently, lifting the strand of pearls away from her neck and then letting them drop. "But I'm never kind."

Annelise made it a point of honor that she never shirked her duty, never ran from trouble, never failed to face the unfaceable. But some things were more than even a Kempton could bear. She was going to plead a miserable illness, and if anyone pushed her she would give them far too many details, and then she was going to lock herself in her bedroom, burn the damned note and tear the handkerchief into tiny pieces.

She was using stable language, at least in her own mind, and she ought to be ashamed. But she was trembling with so many emotions she couldn't begin to single them out, and didn't particularly want to. She just wanted to escape.

There were three directions she could go—back into the house with all those curious eyes, out into the main gardens where guests would doubtless be conducting their own little flirtations, or into the very alleyway itself. She had little choice—she could easily circle around the servants' entrance and escape up the back stairs to her room without having to run into anyone likely to question her. The servants would gossip, but that was their right, and it was certainly the least of her worries.

She closed the iron gate quietly and stepped out into the darkened alleyway. Perhaps not her smartest move, but she was beyond thinking clearly. She was moving toward the stables when she thought she saw a male figure slipping into the shadows.

If she had any sense she should have run. But the shadow looked familiar, and she was clearly showing no caution at all tonight, because she called out. "Who's there?"

The shadow froze, and then slowly, sheepishly, Mr. Dickinson emerged into the flickering light of the torches. "Good evening, Miss Kempton," he stammered.

"Good evening, Mr. Dickinson. Why aren't you inside enjoying yourself instead of skulking around out here like a criminal?"

He flushed. "I'm not welcome, Miss Kempton. I just wanted to see if I could catch a glimpse of Hetty through one of the windows. I've never seen her all decked out for a London party, and I wanted a picture in my head to carry with me as I live out my life alone."

Ah, the drama of youth, Annelise thought, hiding her smile. At least it was jolting her away from her own melodramas. "You're giving up so easily, Mr. Dickinson? I would have thought you'd be willing to fight for your true love."

"What can I do? Mr. Chipple has refused to allow me to court Hetty. He may seem like a jolly old gentleman to you, but let me tell you in the country he's not a man to cross. Bad things happen."

"Pish!" Annelise waved away his forebodings with an airy hand, weary of William's drama. "You're dressed well enough in case someone sees you. Come with me."

He didn't even ask where, the poor boy. He just followed, as she turned back to the iron gate that led to the side garden.

For a moment she was afraid it was locked, but all it took was a fierce jiggle and it opened again. Will followed her inside, docile as a lamb, and then stopped short at the exposed marble breast thrust in his view, and he turned bright red.

At least one of Hetty's suitors was properly abashed by the shameless statue. Unlike the dissolute Montcalm, who was probably causing trouble even now.

"I'll go find Hetty, and you can steal a few moments together," she said. "Stay right here and don't move."

"If Mr. Chipple were to find out—"

"I believe Mr. Chipple has other things to worry about this evening," Annelise replied. "And I have complete faith in your gentlemanly behavior, Mr. Dickinson."

"Of course, Miss Kempton!" He seemed even more

shocked at the thought that he might misbehave than he was at the undressed marble female.

"Very good. But don't take too long. This party is in honor of Hetty, and she'll be missed."

"Yes, ma'am."

She left him staring fixedly at the ground, rather than the anatomical marvels of whatever Greek goddess Chipple had commissioned. The party was in full swing when she slipped into the house—no one seemed to notice as she threaded her way through the chattering crowds. People were so busy enjoying themselves she could only assume that Chipple and Montcalm hadn't stabbed each other or fallen into a shouting match, but in any case, that was beyond her control. She found Hetty in the green salon, surrounded by three adoring young men.

All three would have been suitable for marriage. "Excuse me," Annelise said, taking Hetty's hand and drawing her aside for a moment, totally ignoring her duty.

"What do you want?" Hetty demanded in a sulky voice. "I was enjoying myself. There's nothing wrong with any of those gentlemen."

"Are you considering any of them?"

"No!" she said.

"Then you might be interested in a breath of fresh air, so to speak. In the side garden off the reading room."

"I know where the side garden is," she said crossly. "Why would I want to go there?"

Annelise mentally counted to ten. Her charge was not being as astute as she usually was. "You might find something more appealing than that oversize statue."

"Oh!" Dawning realization spread across Hetty's face, followed by suspicion. "But why should you…"

"I'm feeling sentimental," Annelise said. "And slightly ill. I'm retiring for the night, but I'm trusting you to behave yourself like a lady. Actually I'm not trusting you, but I expect Mr. Dickinson will make certain you comport yourself properly. Good night, Hetty."

She started to turn away, when Hetty put her tiny little hand on her arm, leaned forward and deposited a totally unexpected kiss of gratitude on her cheek. "Bless you, Miss Kempton," she breathed, and slid through the crowds so quickly that people scarcely noticed her passing.

People wouldn't notice her own passing, either, Annelise thought grumpily, but not for the same reasons. But in truth she was quite touched by Hetty's gratitude—perhaps the chit wasn't as shallow as she seemed. She definitely had the good sense to prefer William Dickinson's solid worth compared to the peacocks who surrounded her in London. Except, perhaps for the grandest peacock of all.

Her momentary calm brought on by her ill-advised matchmaking vanished with the memory of Christian Montcalm. He was nowhere to be seen. Neither was Mr. Chipple, which was either a good thing or a bad one. But tonight it was no longer her concern, and if she didn't get away from here in another minute she was going to burst into tears.

She closed her bedroom door behind her and leaned against it. Each time she was around the blasted man her reaction was worse. How dare he say such things to her? And how dare he lie about her precious pearls?

She went straight to the chest of drawers, shoved aside her undergarments and found the offending note. It was crumpled from resting against her breast and from being open and reread far too many times, since she had to make certain he was as shocking as she thought. She kept hoping that perhaps there'd be a clue to defeating him in the strong slant of his handwriting.

And tonight of all nights the fire had burned down in her grate and the room was cold. The servants were far too busy with the party, and they wouldn't expect anyone to retire for hours.

She considered ripping the note into tiny pieces, but even then it would still exist, and she needed it to go up in flames, to vanish entirely. She'd been a fool to wait so long.

The handkerchief was still under her pillow and she pulled it out, trying to rip the damned thing in half. It wouldn't tear—if was made of the finest linen weave, the Valenciennes lace was very strong, and she gave up, crumpling it into a little ball as she sat down on the bed.

A stomach complaint, she decided. That's what she would tell them, necessitating her absence for the rest of the evening. If Montcalm and Chipple decided to go at it then it was no longer her concern. In truth, if Chipple made a scene then Hetty would most likely be free to marry young William, which to Annelise seemed like a very good thing. Perhaps she'd overestimated Dickinson's sense of honor and right now the two might be eloping to Gretna Green.

In which case all she could do was rejoice. Keeping elderly women company was fine but herding a strong-willed young beauty through society was not the way she envisioned her future. Particularly if it brought her into the presence of people like Christian Montcalm.

Not that there very many men like Montcalm, thank God.

But if tonight became a debacle her godmother would have a difficult time finding another welcoming household. It didn't matter—if it came to that she could sell her priceless pearls and find some small cottage in the country, living out her days with cats and books and long walks and peace.

She slid the pearls off her neck and looked at them. They were the same as ever—luminous, beautiful, priceless. Montcalm made her doubt everything about herself, from her pearls to her very nature. And she wasn't going to let him do it again.

She slid the pearls into their soft, embroidered bag and tucked them back into her drawer, hidden among the sensible undergarments. Since there was no fire she had no choice but to shove the note back with the pearls, though it felt somehow traitorous to do so. She undressed quickly and climbed into bed, blowing out the candles so that she lay in perfect darkness in the cool, still room.

She could hear the noise from the party downstairs. The music from the ballroom, the sound of laughter and voices drifted upward to her second-floor bedroom. Apparently the party was going off without a hitch.

Annelise curled up and willed herself to sleep, the offending handkerchief still clutched in her hand.

10

Christian moved through the crowded house with his usual aplomb. The most demanding of society was nowhere in sight—Chipple's background made him as much a persona non grata as Christian's reputation—so he was greeted by most of the acquaintances that he passed. He stopped here and there for a short quip, a brief conversation, but then moved on to his eventual destination with single-minded determination.

Chipple's library wasn't that difficult to find. His brand-new house had been designed by Rotterdum, one of the architects used by new money, and Christian had already been in several. The layout was essentially the same, though when he slipped inside Josiah Chipple's study and closed the door he felt a momentary start before he realized the tall, shadowy figure was simply one more of Josiah's damned statues.

There was a fire going, but clearly no servant was going to be checking on it during the demands of a party, so he stoked it up himself until it came to a nice blaze, then helped himself to Chipple's brandy. It was cognac, and he had to resist the impulse to throw it into the fire. He avoided all things French when he could help it, limiting himself to canary and claret rather than the French stuff. For harder spirits he preferred whiskey, but he decided not to be picky, and he sat down in one of Chipple's comfortable leather chairs and propped his feet on the desk, admiring his elegant boots. They'd cost a pretty penny—maybe he'd even eventually pay the poor artisan who'd worked so hard on them. In the meantime, he could enjoy the wonderful sheen and wait for Chipple to make his appearance.

It didn't take as long as he'd expected, though he was on his second glass of cognac. The party was still going strong—the noise and the music filtered through the closed door, and he wondered briefly where the dragon was. Probably searching for him to give him another one of her lectures. Or perhaps she'd given up for the night. She'd looked a bit defeated when he'd left her in the garden.

A shame—both the leaving, and the defeating. He liked his dragon when she was breathing fire, and he would have been more than happy to see whether he could arouse her…ire…if he hadn't had business to attend to. No man hired assassins to kill him and got away without being sternly reprimanded. And made to pay a price.

Chipple didn't even notice he was there. His face was flushed with wine and good humor, and he was halfway toward the desk before he realized he wasn't alone. His expletive was suitably sailor-like, and impressive even to a man like Christian.

"Good evening, Chipple," Christian said, not bothering to rise, or even remove his feet from the vast mahogany desk. "Have a seat."

If he'd had any doubts as to Chipple's true calling the expression on his face made it vanish. The cheerful nouveau riche father was simply a facade. The man living behind it was capable of just about anything.

"I wouldn't make a fuss if I were you," Christian continued smoothly. "It's past time you and I came to an understanding, and I don't think you want any witnesses as to what I have to say."

"I don't know that I want witnesses as to what I'm going to do," Josiah grumbled, but his initial flash of rage had vanished, leaving him wary. "Take your boots off my desk, you whoring son of a bitch."

"Certainly, you soulless purveyor of human flesh," Christian replied in a mild tone, stretching his legs out in front of him. "Society is so interesting, don't you think? So many simply refuse to accept a man because his money is self-made, and those who do hold the most ridiculous standards. Trafficking in human beings is regarded in very low esteem, and of course illegal in this country. If the source of your money were to become public knowledge you wouldn't be invited anywhere, and your daughter could kiss a titled marriage goodbye. But you know that already, don't you? You've gone to great effort to cover up the fact that you make your money off the slave trade."

It was a telling blow. "You have no proof," Chipple said hoarsely, dropping down in the seat behind the desk.

Christian kept his triumphant smile to himself. It wouldn't do to underestimate someone like Josiah Chipple—he would have no qualms in simply cutting his throat and leaving the servants to clean it up. Then again, Christian wasn't easily bested, and he was on his guard.

"It would be easily obtained if I put my mind to it. At the moment I'm a bit perturbed. Two men attacked me this morning, and to my surprise they weren't simply out to rob me. They seemed quite determined to kill me."

"Imagine that," Chipple said with a sneer.

"Clearly they weren't properly warned as to who they might be dealing with. They seemed quite surprised when I put up a fight. So surprised that they were, perhaps, a bit too talkative."

"What happened to them?"

"I'm afraid I killed them both," he said blithely. The second man who'd run off was terrified of Josiah Chipple's wrath, and having seen the look in his host's eye, Christian could understand. Not that he should go to any trouble to save a man who was out to kill him, but he could afford to be generous in this circumstance, since he was about to get exactly what he wanted. "I suppose I could have spared one, dragged him before a magistrate and lodged a formal complaint, but I decided that dealing with you directly would be much more efficient."

"I had nothing to do with it."

"Of course you didn't. And I expect you are such a stalwart and law-abiding citizen that you would make it your duty to see that nothing like that ever happened again, at least to me."

"What do you want, Montcalm?"

Christian smiled sweetly. "Your daughter's hand in marriage, of course. I thought I made my most honorable intentions clear."

"You're only interested in her fortune!"

"Wouldn't you want a son-in-law who was eminently practical?"

"She can do better."

"Alas, I can't argue that," Christian said. "I must admit my reputation is a bit…shady. Unlike your own unblemished one. But I'm expecting marriage to make a new man out of me. A sober, devoted husband and father…"

"You aren't fathering my grandchildren!"

"Then I suppose we can always have a celibate relationship. And of course there are ways of preventing pregnancy, but I imagine you know them and would rather not think of them in terms of your daughter." He took another sip of the cognac. "I wouldn't do that if I were you," he added as Josiah made an involuntary move toward him. "If the poor girl were orphaned she'd have no one to look after her."

He halted, wisely. "The Honorable Miss Kempton—"

"Ah, yes, the Honorable Miss Kempton. She does try to be inflexible, does she not? I'm afraid if it came to a battle between us then I would undoubtedly win. She's not nearly as fierce as she would have one believe." He allowed himself a faint smile at the memory.

"I'll find someone else…"

"Accept the inevitable, Chipple."

Josiah sank down in his chair, a calculating expression on his face. It had taken him long enough, Christian thought lazily. He had to be a smart man to acquire the kind of fortune he had, but it was taking him a damnably long time to get down to business. Perhaps it was simply that he didn't want to admit defeat on any level.

"How much do you want?" Josiah demanded hoarsely.

"I beg your pardon?"

"You know what I'm talking about. I'll give you five thousand pounds to leave my daughter alone and to be silent about any speculations as to where I made my money."

"Sir, you insult me."

"Ten thousand pounds."

Christian was enjoying this. "What kind of gentleman do you think I am?"

"Twenty thousand pounds."

"A remarkable sum of money, indeed. But your daughter is your sole heir."

"Fifty thousand pounds and not a farthing more. Or I'll kill you myself and be damned to the consequences."

"You could try," Christian replied in a silken voice. "But I would hate to see such a thing happen. And it would be so hard on poor little Hetty. I suppose in good conscience I can only agree. After all, I would hate to see her abandoned with a father in the dock."

"I could always get away with making you disappear."

Christian smiled. "Believe me, you couldn't."

"I'll send someone over to your rooms with a banker's draft—"

"And a knife? I don't think so."

"Then how do you expect me to arrange this…?"

"You're not the sort of man who trusts anyone, even banks. I'm certain you can find at least that much hidden in this house."

"Do you think I'm a fool? I could be robbed."

Christian was tactful enough not to point out that that was exactly what was happening. "Most street thieves have the sense to steer clear of me, because my reputation precedes me. I imagine the same holds for you. The members of the criminal underground are very well informed, and only a dolt would think to rob you."

"Isn't that what you're doing?"

"We are simply two gentlemen—and I use that term with great affection—who have come to an agreement due to our mutual concern for your daughter. We both want what's best for her, and I would never be so bold as to think that I could aspire to her hand." Christian was enjoying himself. "I'm willing to relinquish her affection at great cost to myself, and it is only to be expected that it be at great cost to you, as well."

Josiah Chipple stared at him for a long moment. "All right," he said finally. "I accept."

"Of course you do," Christian murmured. It was a lie, of course. Chipple might hand over the cash, but he'd do everything within his power to get it back, and he'd choose his assassins a little more carefully next time.

On the other hand, Christian had absolutely no intention of relinquishing his hold on adoring little Hetty. Why should he, when he could have the fifty thousand pounds and her, as well? And once he had her, Chipple would definitely think twice about having her husband slaughtered. No, he'd have no choice but to accept him into the family. Though somehow Christian doubted they'd be spending much happy time together, even when the children came along.

She'd be a viscountess, which was what she wanted. He'd have enough money to live as he pleased, though he wasn't sure his young bride would find it as amenable. If she grew tiresome he could send her to live with her devoted father for long periods at a time, taking her noisy brats with her, while he concentrated on dragon baiting.

He was moving way too fast—he had to secure the lady first. And by the time they were married Annelise would be long gone, off to some other needy family.

"Stay here and I'll go get the money."

"I think I'll come with you. I feel the need to stretch my legs."

"You think I'm going to allow you to see where I keep my emergency funds?" Chipple demanded.

"And it is an emergency, is it not? I also know that you would change the location of your secret stash regularly, so you'll be giving away no secrets. Unless you have one of your black slaves chained with it to keep it safe."

"Don't be ridiculous," Josiah said stiffly. "And I'd appreciate it if you stopped mentioning that. If word of my former life reached society it could be devastating."

"Former? I gather it was an ongoing concern."

"I've retired," Chipple said.

"Of course you have," Christian replied, not believing a word. "Shall we go? Your guests must be wondering where their host is, and Miss Hetty might come to check on her dear father."

Josiah Chipple didn't like to lose. "There's a word for people like you," he said darkly.

"The word is blackmailer," Christian said. "Though I prefer businessman."

"We'll go through the garden," Josiah said.

"We'll go through the house," Christian corrected. "I imagine you have at least one man stationed outside the house at all times, and it would simply take a gesture from you to have him attack. And then we'd have another bloody corpse to deal with, and it still wouldn't be mine. Accept the inevitable and cut your losses."

Chipple glared at him. He rose and walked over to the fireplace, fiddling with the books. A small section of shelving swung out, revealing a tiny compartment filled with neat packages. Chipple reached his hand inside, and Christian spoke.

"I wouldn't go for that pistol if I were you. If it's been in there for long it will no longer be properly primed, and think of the noise it would make. And I think it should be quite clear that I'm not about to go quietly."

Chipple turned back with his hands full of neatly bundled sacks. "I accept defeat when I must. If this is what it takes to get rid of you then I consider the price small enough."

Now, that was a total lie on every account, Christian thought as Chipple counted out the sacks. He wasn't the sort of man who ever accepted defeat, and he wouldn't part with a penny unless he had no other choice. At the moment he realized that he had no choice, but Christian expected that to be only temporary. Which required him to act quickly.

"It's quite a bit to carry around—are you certain you're safe on the streets with it? I could send a link boy with you…"

"I'll be fine." It was a hefty sum of money, one that he couldn't very well tuck into his fashionable pockets, but he certainly wasn't about to have Chipple send someone with him, someone who'd doubtless try to relieve him of his bounty. "I'm afraid I'll have to beg the favor of a bag to carry it in, though. I'll be sure to have it returned."

Chipple made a low, growling noise, rather like that of a hungry polar bear, but he simply nodded, tossing a small embroidered sack across the desk. "Consider it my parting gift," he said. And there was no mistaking the murderous look in his small, dark eyes.

Christian rose, stretching lazily, and gave his future father-in-law his most fetching smile. "I'm pleased we've come to an understanding," he said. "I knew we would deal well together, as one businessman to another."

"Get out of here," Chipple snapped.

Christian Montcalm scooped up the money, placed it in the soft velvet bag and gave Chipple a mocking bow.

He could see Chipple's eyes dart back to the open panel, doubtless considering whether to risk using the gun, but he clearly thought better of it. He'd try something soon, though, and the quicker Christian put his plan into motion the better.

"Good evening, sir," he murmured.

"Goodbye," Chipple snarled. He stood there, motionless, as Christian Montcalm sauntered gracefully out of the room.

William Dickinson knew when a cause was lost. He'd known even before he'd traveled to London, but he'd risked everything for one last glimpse of her. He was from yeoman stock, an old family of impeccable lineage with no aspirations beyond the careful managing of his estate and the surrounding villages. His father was the local squire, a good man and one William hoped to emulate. And in truth, Hetty was too far above him to spend her life as the wife of a country gentleman—too beautiful and too wealthy for such a simple man. He knew it, accepted it. But he couldn't help dreaming.

If she really did come to meet him, as Miss Kempton said she would, then he could tell her goodbye. Give her up to a grander future than he could ever provide.

But not with someone like Christian Montcalm. He'd heard the rumors, and a man like that wasn't worthy of a treasure like Hetty. She'd be better off in the country than tied to a scoundrel like him.

Josiah Chipple wasn't going to let that happen, though. If he wouldn't let his only child throw herself away on a wealthy country family, he'd hardly let her go to an impoverished rakehell with a title that wasn't even his yet.

Will sat down on the marble bench, then turned to keep his eyesight away from the offending statue. For some reason Chipple thought these obscene Greek marbles made him refined. With Chipple it was a lost cause.

It was a wonder that Hetty was as sweet and delicate as she was, but she could thank her mother for that. The poor woman had always looked a little afraid of her mostly absent husband, but she had raised her daughter well until her sudden, unexpected death. Hetty could look almost as high as she wanted for a good marriage, and Will had long ago accepted that fact.

He just wanted to say goodbye. To wish her Godspeed. To tell her he'd accepted her decision gracefully, knew she didn't love him, and in fact, that he had moved on himself and would be marrying Miss Augusta Davies (or at least, as soon as he asked her, since she'd been chasing him for years now).

When he saw Hetty coming toward him his heart leaped in his throat. He rose, turning his back on the statue, straightening his already neat clothing, his graceful departing speech all prepared.

She slipped into the garden, closing the door behind her. She was a vision of pink and lace and glittering gems, her artful tangle of blond curls like a halo, her perfect rosebud lips pouting, and angelic blue eyes wide with love, and he melted.

"Oh, bloody Christ, Hetty!" he exploded. "I can't live without you!" And ignoring his promise to Miss Kempton, his vows to himself, his duty to his parents, and his sense of honor and decorum, he swept Hetty into his arms and planted his mouth on hers in one long, bracing kiss.

Her response was not what he would have expected. She tore herself out of his arms and burst into noisy tears.

Guilt swamped him. "Oh, Hetty, darling, I beg your pardon. I should have never…please forgive me. I thought I could control myself…I ought to be horse-whipped…I'm a wretched—"

She looked up, and her tear-filled eyes were smiling, and she put her hand against his lips, silencing his babbling apologies. "You do still love me, Will!" she breathed happily. And she flung her arms around his neck, kissing him back.

11

For Annelise, the day did not start in an auspicious manner. She hadn't slept well—tossing and turning with nightmares so vivid they should have woken her up. It would have been a blessing if they had—she simply would have lit the candles by her bed and read something improving until her mind settled. Well, perhaps not really. She would have read something thrilling and romantic (she was halfway through *The Dungeon's Bride*) with the assurance that it would distract her thoroughly. Unfortunately she drifted just below the surface of sleep, prey to the most disturbing imaginings.

It was very early when she awoke, barely light, and she expected the other members of the household would rise even later than usual, given that the party had gone on till the early-morning hours. She would have time to enjoy a solitary, peaceful breakfast and perhaps even a walk in the park before the Chipples straggled out of bed.

She dressed quickly, pushed open her shutters and dismissed the idea of a walk in the park. It was pouring rain— if she'd been halfway observant she would have heard it lashing against the windows. The streets below were awash, refuse floating by in the deep running puddles, and people picked their way carefully through the mess.

At least there'd be no Chipples. She could still have her peaceful meal, then find a nice quiet room to read and restore her disordered senses. The last few days had upset her equilibrium—she would simply insist on some time to herself.

Breakfast was laid out in the smaller dining room that had been painted an alarming shade of yellow. She ate quickly, then took her cup of hot chocolate with her as she went in search of more salubrious surroundings.

There were no servants around—clearly they were taking advantage of their master's laxness to enjoy a little peace themselves. Annelise wandered through the ground floor of the mansion, keeping as far away from the front hall as she could. Part of her dream the night before had been that the statues had moved, coming toward her with ominous intent. Even more disturbing, it had been the rakehell who had rescued her, when any sane woman would prefer possessed statues over the inherent danger of a man like Christian Montcalm.

She opened an unfamiliar door, and for a moment thought she had discovered the perfect retreat. It could only be Mr. Chipple's library, and the rows and rows of unread books drew her irresistibly forward, when she should have just closed the door and retreated.

She let out a little squeak as she saw the statue. This one was male, and completely unclothed, and after the first few moments of fascinated regard she turned her gaze away, determined to vacate the room immediately, when she saw the unexpected hole in the wall. She turned her back on the offensive statue and approached the mysterious crevice. Part of the book shelf had been cunningly designed to disguise it, but a hidden compartment lay in the midst of the books.

She did have a problem with curiosity as well as imagination, and while she knew she should just turn around and leave, she couldn't resist drawing closer to inspect the hole. There were no lights in the room and the gloom outside didn't do much to penetrate the shadows. She couldn't actually see inside the compartment, so she put a tentative hand in, wondering whether she'd touch something nasty.

She did. It was hard and cold and even before she drew it out she knew it was a pistol—but unlike any one she'd ever seen. Not a gentleman's pistol for the unspeakable practice of dueling. This one had no ornamentation, no delicacy. It was large, and heavy, and it looked as if it had no use in this world but to kill.

She shoved it back into the hole, terrified that it might go off, and slammed the door shut. A moment later she realized her mistake—she should have left things as she found them. She tried to reopen the hidden door, but it remained closed, and all the tricks she attempted did no good.

She was making a fuss for nothing, she told herself, stepping away from the desk. There was still a glass with a splash of cognac in it—clearly the servants hadn't been in yet. They could have closed the door—no one would even suspect the Honorable Miss Kempton had been snooping.

She stepped out into the empty hallway, then turned and closed the door silently behind her.

"May I help you, miss?"

The butler's voice made her jump, and she spun around, her hand pressed against her racing heart. "I was looking for a quiet place to read, Jameson."

"You don't want to go in there, Miss Kempton. That's the master's study, and we're none of us allowed inside except when he tells us. When the maids clean he stands right there watching. He wouldn't like it if he thought you were snooping around."

Annelise straightened her back and gave the impudent Jameson a haughty stare. "I don't snoop," she said. A complete lie, but it wasn't his place to point it out to her. "Find me a quiet room with decent light where I can read and I'll trouble you no more."

Jameson stared at her for a long moment. He was an odd sort of butler, and Annelise assumed he was merely typical of Chipple's mistaken notions of society. Most butlers managed a veneer of gentility so as not to offend their sensitive masters, but Jameson looked more like a pugilist than a valet. His uniform fit his bulky body perfectly, but he made Annelise think of an unpleasant wild animal, like a bear, just waiting to attack.

Imagination again, she chided herself. And she wasn't going to offer any more babbling excuses. Not that Jameson would tell on her, but it was demeaning to feel as if she'd been caught doing something naughty. As, in fact, she had.

"I'll escort you to the pink salon," Jameson said. "Miss Hetty never uses it, but it was designed for ladies to retire to. I'm certain you'll be quite comfortable."

"Thank you, Jameson." She was certain of no such thing. If the shade of pink was bilious enough she'd have no choice but to return to her room, or face the downpour herself. But the pink room was less ghastly than it could have been, the chaise was surprisingly comfortable, and within moments a servant had arrived to start a cozy fire. She curled up in the lounge and opened her book, ready to disappear into the fanciful dungeons herself.

The only problem with books, she thought dreamily, is that for some reason the heroes were always just a bit too perfect, almost to the point of tediousness. Their noble behavior would just as likely endanger the hapless heroine. And the heroines themselves showed little ingenuity or resilience. She would hope that if she were kidnapped by a scheming villain she'd be able to do more than weep and faint.

And as for the villains, it was easy enough to see that those disreputable characters were by far the most interesting aspect of the books. They were Machiavellian, monstrous, charming and evil, and it was with great satisfaction that Annelise read of their bloody demise. If only the same thing could happen to the real villain in her life.

The moment the thought popped into her head she

sat up, horrified at herself. She didn't wish ill on anyone, even Christian Montcalm. She didn't want him to die, she just wanted him to go away and set his sights on some other young heiress with a protector who was far less vulnerable than Annelise was.

Not that she ever would have thought herself vulnerable. She had always been excellent at setting things to right, curbing young men's mischievous behavior and keeping her father in one piece until his last, fateful ride. It was absurd that one overly handsome man would be able to disturb her so effectively.

In truth her state of unrest probably had absolutely nothing to do with Christian Montcalm and more to do with Annelise herself. She was facing the advanced age of thirty, the point of no return, and while part of her viewed her advancing spinsterhood with equanimity, a small, vain part of her cried out, "Why not me?" Silly, of course. Childbirth was painful and dangerous, men were ill behaved and annoying, and she liked not having to answer to anyone very well.

Except she did—to Mr. Chipple, Lady Prentice, her interfering sisters and all of society. Perhaps she should make the first steps to sell the pearls, she thought. Even if she succeeded and Hetty Chipple managed to marry wisely, it wasn't enough to give her a sense of accomplishment. She was tired of all this, and she wanted nothing more than to run away.

She couldn't run, of course. But she could walk, sedately, with enough money to set herself up. And as soon as Hetty was settled, that was exactly what she would do.

The rain had stopped and the sun had come out, sending sparkling diamond motes through the air. She put her book down and rose from the chaise. With the advent of the sun the room had grown stiflingly hot, and the latticed door leading to one of the gardens would let in a breath of fresh spring air…

She put her hand on the doorknob and then froze, staring through the glass. This side garden was a mirror image of the one where she'd met with Montcalm the night before—it lay on the other side of the main gardens and was presumably for the use of the ladies of the household. Early roses were blooming, their soft petals wet with rain, and standing in the middle of the garden, looking up at the house with a speculative expression on his face, was Christian Montcalm.

It was just past eight o'clock in the morning—no time for visits. He was up to something nefarious, as always, and she could simply ignore his mysterious presence and go back to her room, or she could confront him.

Confronting him would lead to nothing but trouble, she knew. But she opened the door and stepped out into the tiny garden.

"I wondered if you were going to join me, dragon," he murmured, still staring up at the house. "I saw you watching me for quite a while, and I couldn't believe you'd slink away without doing battle once more."

"What are you doing here? It's barely eight o'clock in the morning—I'm surprised you're already up."

He looked at her then, and smiled. "I didn't go to bed."

"Now, why doesn't that surprise me?"

"Because you're becoming far too familiar with my little ways, my pet. Which room belongs to your charge?"

"As if I would tell you! What were you going to do, serenade her with a French love ballad?"

"No!" There was a surprising harshness to his voice, one he immediately banished. "I have lamentably little musical talent—if I were to sing to her she'd run screaming from the house."

"Then feel perfectly free to do so. I can even have the servants drag a piano near the window so that I might accompany you."

"So helpful," he said. "But I will decline your kind offer. I merely came to bid a distant farewell to my lost love."

"Your lost love?"

"Yes—Miss Hetty. I have relinquished any claim I might have on her hand."

"You had no claim on her hand," Annelise snapped. "And I had no idea you possessed such good sense. What made you decide to be reasonable?"

"Oh, a number of very persuasive reasons," he said. "For one thing, I have an absolute terror that she might have inherited her father's decorating tastes, and I couldn't let her clutter up Wynche End with naked statues."

Indeed, the statue in this garden was entirely nude, and though she could only see it from the back, presumably male, due to the musculature and the arrangement of the hair. If Annelise never saw a marble statue again it would make her a very happy woman.

She felt a faint splotch of color rise to her cheeks, both at the sight of the marble buttocks and the memory of her fascinated survey of the male statue in Chipple's study. Would this one be the same in front, or was there a variation in men's…

"Why are you blushing, dragon? Surely you've been subjected to all these second-rate sculptures already."

"Most of them. I try not to look," she said firmly. "What is Wynche End?"

"Alas, the place I call home when I'm not in London. Which, admittedly, is seldom. My esteemed grandfather managed to make certain I inherited nothing from his estate but the eventual title, but Wynche End belonged to my mother's family, and since they're all dead it now belongs to me. It's in a state of total ruination—the roof leaks, the wood is rotting, the surrounding village and farmland lying fallow, but it's mine, and Miss Hetty's money would have enabled me to put it in good heart once more. However, I can't trust her taste in decoration, and Greek statues were too high a price to pay."

"Indeed. And where is this monumental ruin?"

"Were you thinking of taking her place, dragon? I'm certain your preferences would be an improvement, but I somehow doubt you'd be as enthusiastic about the other duties of connubial bliss. It's in Devon, near a tiny village called Hydesfield. The coast around there is none too welcoming— a stretch of land once peopled by wreckers, but in the last century they've resorted to simple smuggling. I could always join in if I have to resort to earning a living."

"Surely things couldn't be that bad." She let the irony hang heavy in her voice.

"I could always take you as a shining example. I could go on a series of well-disguised visits, teach young men the ways of society."

"God help them and society in general. One of you is more than enough."

"You wound me to the heart, Miss Kempton," he said with mock sorrow. There was a glint of devilry in his eyes. "You seem so wise—you always have the answer for everything. Perhaps you might help with a question that's been plaguing me."

"If you go away I'll help you with anything."

"I wouldn't be so rash in my promises if I were you, dragon. I have a habit of holding people to things."

"I'll be more than happy to answer whatever question you might have if you'll just leave."

His wicked smile widened. "It's this statue. How are you on your Greek mythology? I'm certain you're well versed in all manner of intellectual studies—what do you remember about this one?"

She was going to have to move around to the front and join him. That, or admit defeat and run, and she wasn't about to admit defeat to a man like Montcalm. At least she'd spent far too many moments examining the unmentionable parts of the male statue in the library. Marble-engraved...parts...wouldn't have to shock her.

"Which God is he?" she asked in a deliberately calm voice, moving around to the front of the statue and then freezing.

"Priapus. The very fertile son of Aphrodite and Dionysus. I've always wondered what the explanation for his condition was."

She couldn't move. She'd recognized all the other ancient Greek statues—she should have realized that Chipple wouldn't have the taste to keep this one out of sight.

There was most definitely a difference in the depiction of his marble genitals. The god Priapus was in an eternal state of excitement, and his marble phallus jutted out, almost at eye level.

She could do nothing to control the wash of color that swept over her. "I have no idea," she said in a hoarse voice, unable to move.

"Apart from exposure to you, I mean," he whispered. "Perhaps if you go back in the house he'll change to a more sedate fellow."

She couldn't keep her eyes off him, and she swallowed nervously. She managed to rally. "I believe you were in his presence first, Mr. Montcalm. If anyone has excited him it must be you."

She surprised a laugh out of him. "Still fighting, dragon? Perhaps you're right—those Greeks were odd fellows. I was just judging by the effect you tend to have on me."

She couldn't help it—her eyes dropped to a part of his body she never should have acknowledged, then darted away from him. She struggled for her vanished composure. "Unfortunately the sculptor was prone to exaggeration in this one's case. Such proportions are highly unlikely," she said. She was very proud of her cool, distant tone. She could have been discussing the artistic merits of a landscape.

Except that Christian Montcalm's beautiful mouth curved into a broader smile. "Ah, my precious, what an innocent you really are, even at such an advanced age. I should have realized you were simply an aging virgin. If anything, his cock is on the small side."

She jerked her head around, shocked. No one had ever used that word in her presence, though she'd overheard the stable boys bandy it about, and she knew perfectly well what it meant. But that a gentleman should use such a word in her presence was beyond belief.

"Don't faint, dragon," he murmured. "It's just a word. Words have only the power you give them."

"I want you to leave."

"And I will, my pet. I told you, this was just a farewell visit to the object of my twisted desires."

"She doesn't need you to say farewell. I'll convey your regrets."

"I wasn't talking about Hetty."

Annelise was a strong woman, but this was one assault too many. "Go away!" she cried, unaccountably near tears. "Stop mocking me and leave, or I'll have Jameson toss you out."

"Oh, my precious!" He pulled her into his arms, and she could only put up a token fight. The tears she'd been fighting for hours, seemingly for days, had broken through, and even though the last thing in the world she wanted to do was cry in front of him, it was already past her control.

He held her in his arms, against his body, and the strength and warmth were oddly soothing, considering he was the bane of her existence. She was afraid he was going to kiss her again, and afraid he wouldn't, but he simply held her, stroking her hair, murmuring soothing noises in her ear.

"You don't belong here, Annelise," he said, and she could hardly object to him using her name. He'd already used a number of offensive words, and in comparison her name seemed harmless enough. "Go back to Lady Prentice and stay there. This isn't a safe place for you."

She didn't bother to argue—the only danger to her was the man holding her. And he would soon be gone. "I can always sell my pearls…" she said with a hiccup.

He put his hands on her arms and drew her away, looking into her eyes. Her tears and his body heat had steamed up her spectacles, and she couldn't see him clearly, which was just as well. "Annelise, the pearls are fake," he said gently.

"They're not. They can't be! They've been in our family for hundreds of years and no one would ever…." She let her voice trail off.

He already knew the answer. "It must have been someone at the very end of their rope. When someone is that lost in rage and grief they do foolish things, forgetting when there are still people who love them."

She pulled herself out of his arms, letting denial and fury sweep over her. "What would you know about that?"

"About being lost in grief and rage? I know far too well. As for people who still love them—well, I'm afraid that's a mystery to me. Anyone who loved me died twenty years ago."

There was something in his voice that sounded harsh. Something she was afraid to question.

And then it was too late. He kissed her, hard and quick, as if he was afraid to linger. And then he was gone, with the side gate clanging shut behind him, leaving her standing there, alone, hopeless, and totally confused.

She looked up at the satyr-like statue. "You should be ashamed of yourself," she told him in a weak voice.

The statue said nothing, merely looking down at her impassively, as if to say, what should I be ashamed of? But by then Annelise was gone.

12

The Honorable Miss Annelise Kempton was not the kind of woman to pine over things that she could never have. At least, not for long. By the time she reached her room she had composed herself, and she only felt a slight need to slam the door behind her.

She went to her drawer and picked up the soft velvet bag that held the Kempton pearls. It, too, had been made by an ancestor—some ancient kinswoman, doubtless with higher morals than the one who'd bedded King James—and was stitched virtuously, a design of intricate beauty. The velvet was slightly rubbed in places, and she opened the drawstring, letting the pearls fall into her hand.

They were as beautiful as ever. Lustrous, warm. And fake. He was right, of course. A scoundrel would be certain to know when jewelry was fake—it would be part of his stock-in-trade. When had her father switched them? She couldn't really tell—he'd kept them for her, and she'd worn them once a year on her birthday. She'd never noticed any change, but then, her lack of vanity would have ensured that she didn't spend a great deal of time staring in mirrors.

Or perhaps it was an excess of vanity. She had never looked as she wanted—not a plump beauty like her younger sister, not a striking one like her elder, and not an adorable little cherub like Hetty Chipple. She was tall and plain and bespectacled, but she'd loved her pearls.

It must have happened when she was nineteen, she thought. Things had been growing more desperate. They were down to two servants, one of them in the stable to care for her father's beloved horses, and she'd begun to suspect the horses hadn't been eating well. Their coats and eyes were dull, they moved sluggishly, she couldn't even coax her beloved Gertie into a full gallop.

And then one day there had been three new servants, two of them in the stable. The horses began to look better, properly cared for, properly fed. The same wasn't true for Annelise and her father—their table was meager to the point of Lenten. And her father become less and less responsive.

But that sudden influx of money had to come from somewhere, and James Kempton would sit by and watch his house fall into ruin and his daughter starve into spinsterhood, but he'd rob his own mother to feed his horses. Or rob his own child.

It should have felt like the worst kind of betrayal. But it wasn't. She'd known what he was, quite clearly, known that he'd loved her despite his failings. Almost as much as he'd loved his own misery. The worst betrayal was that he had died.

She put the pearls back in their bag carefully, pulling the drawstring tight, and replaced them in her drawer. Next to Christian's scrawled note, promising her a third lesson in the art of love.

She wasn't going to burn it after all. He was leaving—it was doubtful she'd ever have to suffer his company again. She should get down on her knees and offer up a prayer of thanksgiving. Instead she tucked the note inside the velvet bag, along with his lacy handkerchief. She dashed the tears away from her eyes, the stupid things, tidied her already severe hair, and headed back downstairs, the very picture of calm self-possession. If she was going to ache inside, at least no one was going to know it.

Still no signs of the sluggard Chipples. The sun was out in full now, and the fallen rain sparkled like diamonds on the trees and the cobblestones. Of course, Jameson was nowhere to be seen when she really wanted him, but she hunted him down in the dining room.

He was as impassive as ever—perhaps she'd imagined that faint note of cunning in his flat eyes. "I'm going for a walk in the park, Jameson, if anyone asks where I am."

"I don't expect the Chipples to rise for quite some time, miss. The last guest didn't depart until three in the morning." There was nothing in his tone or expression to cause offense. And yet he made her uneasy.

"I should be back in an hour."

"Do you wish to have a maid accompany you? Or do you have business of a private nature to conduct?"

She wanted to slap the smirk off his face, but he was so big and ugly she was afraid he might hit her back, and one tap from those giant paws would send her flying across the room. He really was the strangest-looking butler, and so she ought to explain to Mr. Chipple, except that after her discovery earlier this morning she didn't particularly feel like discussing anything with her host.

"No business, and no need of a maid. I just want some time alone to clear my head."

"And your time in the garden wasn't private enough for you, miss?"

He'd known that Montcalm had been there. Known, and done nothing, except perhaps spy on them. He would have seen Montcalm kiss her, for the last time. At least it had clearly been a chaste kiss of goodbye. Well, not entirely chaste—she doubted that word could ever be applied to Christian Montcalm. But it had been brief, and decisive.

She wasn't about to dignify Jameson's question with an answer. How she conducted her life was none of his business. Who ventured on Chipple's property was, but he had chosen to do nothing about it.

"I should be back in an hour," she said. "Or two, if I feel like it."

"Yes, miss." He was immediately all propriety, but his insulting demeanor stayed with her as she walked the short distance to the park. There was definitely something very odd about the Chipple household, though Josiah Chipple did his best to hide it. His butler looked like a retired pugilist and had the manners, as well, the man kept a pistol in his library and there were times when she caught a certain expression on his face that was a far cry from the jovial shipping magnate.

But for the next hour she wasn't going to think about that. Wasn't going to think about Christian Montcalm, or her father, or any of the other men in her life who had clearly just been sent to plague her. She was going to enjoy the sunshine, the smell of the damp earth, and think about nothing at all but how nice it would be to be in the countryside, in a garden, with all of London so far away it might as well not exist. She would plant roses, she thought. And hollyhocks. And snapdragons…

"Miss Kempton."

Bloody hell, she thought as William Dickinson hailed her. Maybe she could pretend she hadn't heard him, maybe she could walk fast enough that she'd outpace him. She had long legs, and could cover ground quite rapidly, but she could hear him gaining on her, and the note of desperation in his voice. Unless she decided to break into a sprint, he was going to catch up with her, and trying to get away was an undignified waste of time. She halted, plastered a polite expression on her face and turned to face him.

The sight of William was a shock indeed. "Mr. Dickinson, are you all right? You look as if you've been set upon by Mohocks." The roving bands of street criminals had become bolder and bolder, and there seemed to be little anyone could do. First Montcalm, and then William Dickinson…

"A minor dustup, Miss Kempton. I'm fine," he said, clearly lying. He had a split lip, an eye that was blackened and swollen, and his clothes, though he'd made an attempt at righting them, had clearly seen something a bit more than a scuffle. "I have to return to Kent, and I wondered if I could prevail upon you to do me a huge favor."

"You're going back so soon? I thought you were planning to stay in London at least another week?"

"It's a…family issue," he stammered, clearly not a very good liar. "I wondered if you might take a note to Miss Chipple for me."

"Mr. Dickinson, you know I can't do that. I would never have let you see her last night but I was overset. It would be most improper, and her father has yet to approve your suit, but Mr. Montcalm has been persuaded to withdraw his offer, but in time—"

"He's not going to change his mind," William said bitterly. "Hetty and I were going to meet and approach him together, but I've…I've changed my mind. She's much too far above me to even hope. I should never have come to London, never have dared to approach her…"

"William, she loves you," Annelise broke in patiently. Lovelorn histrionics were tiresome, but at least they put her own silly longings in the right context. "You may have argued, and Mr. Chipple may have seemed obdurate, but I'm sure with time and diligence he can be persuaded to change his mind. Fortunately, Mr. Montcalm has chosen to relinquish any claim he might have to her affections and the way is clear for you. Your only drawback is that you lack a title, but I would think that Mr. Chipple would, in the end, prove reasonable if it's his daughter's happiness at stake."

"Mr. Chipple…" he began, and then stopped himself. "Mr. Chipple has made it very clear that I am foolish to hope."

"And you would accept defeat so easily? I would have thought better of you."

"I'd fight to the death for her," he said fiercely.

"Then why are you leaving?"

"My family…" he said, his voice harsh. "I need to ensure my family's well-being."

It was such an outrageous notion that she could scarcely bring herself to say it. "Has Mr. Chipple threatened you?"

William laughed. "I'm not worried about myself, miss."

"He's threatened your family? You must realize that he's full of bluster—even a man with his less-than-stellar background would never dare to touch any members of an old family…"

"He'd touch them. He'd have them killed. And he could do it. He's not the man you think he is, Miss Kempton. I've always suspected as much, and my parents have as little to do with him as they can, but when I told them I was in love they agreed to let me try. But he's a bad man."

"Surely you're exaggerating," Annelise said desperately. "He's just a gentleman with too much money and not enough manners who dotes on his only child."

"If Hetty ran away with me, it wouldn't be only my

family who would suffer. He would make Hetty pay, as well."

"But I gather you come from a solid family. Surely you will have enough income to provide for her if Mr. Chipple decided to cut her off without a penny."

"That's not what he'd do."

The words were ominous. "What do you mean?"

"He doesn't like being thwarted. He has plans for Hetty, and if she ruins those plans he'll see her destroyed. He wouldn't hesitate at murder." His voice broke.

Annelise felt cold inside. Surely this was all the wild imaginings of a lovesick young gentleman—it was far too bizarre to even countenance that there might be truth in it. But there was no doubt William believed it, and he was terrified. Not just for his family, but for his beloved.

Chipple had done an excellent job of convincing him that if he went near his daughter their lives were forfeit. It was ridiculous, of course. He probably thought Chipple was behind whoever had beaten him, as well. Annelise wasn't about to try to argue anymore—he was so firm in his belief that common sense wouldn't reach him.

The fact was, people simply didn't do things like that. At least, not people she knew. They didn't threaten and beat people, and they most certainly would never kill anyone. Particularly the one they loved most in the world.

Ridiculous. And so Dickinson would realize, once he got away from the city and recovered from his traumatic encounter with London street gangs. In fact, it was lucky he was even alive at this moment.

"I won't argue with you, Mr. Dickinson. Nor will I take a note to Miss Chipple. You may give me a verbal message and I will consider whether I'll apprise her of it."

He reached inside his rumpled coat, and for one wild moment she expected him to pull out a dueling pistol. When he withdrew a piece of paper she wanted to laugh. She was being as silly as he was, imagining conspiracies and danger where none existed.

Except that Chipple really did own a very ugly pistol.

"You may read it first, Miss Kempton. I labored for hours trying to say the right thing."

She opened the folded vellum reluctantly. It read:

My dear Miss Chipple,

I have belatedly realized the foolishness of our attachment, and accept the fact that wiser heads have prevailed. I am returning home to Kent, where I expect you shall soon want to wish me happiness in my forthcoming marriage to Miss Augusta Davies. I wish you all the joy and happiness you may find in your new life in London, and be assured that I will always remain your steadfast friend, William Dickinson.

Annelise lifted her gaze. "You're engaged?"

"I will be. As soon as I return home. It's the only thing I can do to protect her. Miss Davies has always shown a marked partiality toward me, and my parents approve the match. I'm certain we will deal very comfortably together."

"And what about Hetty? I suppose she'll just move on to the next handsome young man…"

"She's not like that!" he said hotly. "I'm hoping—rather, I'm certain—she'll see reason once she stops to think about it. A girl shouldn't go against her parents' wishes, no matter how…no matter whether she agrees or not. Her well-being depends on it." There was such heartbreak in his voice and in his face, coupled by real fear. The notion that Chipple would harm his daughter was far-fetched, totally ridiculous, and yet he believed every word. Which either meant that he was a lunatic and no fit match for Hetty, or that Annelise herself was in a very dangerous situation.

He must have read her mind. "And you can't desert her, Miss Kempton. It should be easy enough to find a suitable parti now that I'm gone and you've gotten rid of Montcalm. She needs someone to watch over her, make certain she's safe."

"From her own father?" Annelise scoffed.

"From her own father," William said. "Please, Miss Kempton, I beg of you. Promise me you won't abandon her."

Which was exactly what she'd been thinking of doing. But in the end, even in the unlikely event that William was right about Mr. Chipple, the biggest danger to Annelise's peace of mind had relinquished his plans. Christian Montcalm was out of her—their—lives, and she could face a hundred murderous Josiah Chipples without flinching.

"I'll give her your letter," she said finally. "And I'll

stay with her until she's safely, happily married to a gentleman of good character."

"One who can stand up to Chipple."

"Any more stipulations?" Annelise asked in a light tone.

William was not amused. "I'm leaving in the morning, but it would be better if Hetty believes I'm already gone. Our attachment has been long-standing but they say that first love mends easily enough."

But not true love, Annelise thought. At times she wasn't even sure if she believed in such a thing, but if it did exist, it was in William's shadowed eyes and Hetty's exuberant heart.

"I'll keep her safe."

"Bless you," William said. And he kissed her on the cheek.

13

Christian Montcalm was not in the very finest of moods that evening, and the fact that he wasn't only added to his irritation. All his plans were moving along swimmingly, he had more money than he'd ever had in his recent memory, and things were set in motion. He would have to relinquish his irrational attraction to Hetty's dragon, but there'd be other, prettier dragons to seduce. The problem was, the Honorable Miss Kempton's allure was nothing so simple as prettiness. She had character, something he'd been told he was sadly lacking, she had morals, she had a steely determination and an unexpected wit. She also had the most delectable mouth he'd ever tasted, and he would have given ten years off his life to strip her of her eyeglasses, her lace caps, her shapeless gowns and everything underneath them. She could wear her false pearls—they were actually rather good copies, and they looked quite nice on her. Though he'd much prefer to see her in real ones, glowing against her creamy skin.

He shook his head, to drive away the betraying

thoughts. Annelise Kempton was behind him. A splendidly remunerative future beckoned, and Hetty Chipple was gorgeous, energetic, and enjoyed kissing enough to assure him that she would enjoy the other, more intimate pleasures he intended to show her. Very soon. He was foolish to think of anything else.

Chipple's servants were not of the best character, and while they were uncharacteristically terrified of their middle-class master, they were still open to bribes. He didn't need much warning—just that Hetty was alone at the house, with her father and the dragon occupied elsewhere, and he could set to work. It was too much to hope it would happen tonight, but he was getting impatient. The longer he waited, the more he thought of things that shouldn't be tempting him, and the sooner he got Hetty off to the wilds of Devon the better.

Not that the land around Wynche End was particularly wild. Untended, unmowed, unploughed and unfarmed, but nothing that a good influx of money couldn't set to rights. It was the one thing his son-of-a-bitch grandfather couldn't keep from him, though he could withhold any of the funds necessary to maintain its upkeep. The roof leaked and there was dry rot in the library. Generations of mice had eaten through almost every mattress in the house, the few carpets that were left were ripped and faded, and the curtains had been shredded by the bright sunlight.

It was a disaster, all right. Fortunately he could count on the Brownes to keep an eye on it, and he'd already sent word. Bessie Browne would see that at least one bedroom was swept free of mouse dung and shavings, at least one large bed would be found in one piece, aired, and dressed in the least mended sheets. All in waiting for his virgin bride.

At least he assumed Hetty was a virgin, though he didn't particularly care one way or another. And she wasn't necessarily going to be his bride the first time he bedded her. He had the feeling she might balk at the last minute, and the only way around it was to effectively ruin her. Having her overnight would be enough to destroy her already fragile reputation, but actually claiming her energetic young body would make her unlikely to challenge her fate.

At least he could promise her pleasure. He was very good at pleasing women—he had devoted a great deal of time and energy into learning exactly what women liked. He knew how to charm the shy ones, amuse the proud ones, battle the feisty ones and overwhelm the jaded. He could be tender when needed, and he could be rough. He could discover exactly what each woman needed and provide it, and in doing so magnify his own intense pleasure.

Not that Hetty was going to be difficult. She was a healthy young thing, unashamed of her body and physical affections. She liked to kiss, she purred when he stroked her, and even if she thought she was in love with some country yokel from her childhood he could soon make her forget all about him.

Just as her lithe little body would wipe the thought

of anyone else out of his mind quite effectively. It was always wise to concentrate on one woman at a time, and it was about to be Hetty Chipple's lucky day.

He had three different invitations for the evening—one for a gentlemen's evening of mystical mumbo jumbo that was growing frankly tiresome, no matter how nubile the young ladies provided happened to be. Another for a musical soiree at Lady Prentice's, and he'd rather be flayed than subject himself to such a thing. He'd told Annelise that he hadn't a musical bone in his body. It had been a lie. He had such a strong affection for music, for the pianoforte in particular, that he couldn't bear the kind of indifferent performances he was usually subjected to.

The third option was a ball at Sir George and Lady Lockwood's town house. They were new money, as well, though more respectable than Chipple's dark source. Lockwood had made his fortune in banking, and he was accepted almost everywhere. And there was an excellent chance that the Chipples would be there.

He was tempted to stay away—make Hetty wonder where he was, make the dragon think he really meant it when he said he was done, make Josiah Chipple believe he'd really managed to buy him off. It would be the safe thing to do, but Christian had never been particularly interested in being safe. He was just about to leave for the ball when he heard someone pounding at the door.

His manservant, Henry, would get rid of them, but it was always possible it was his source from Chipple House. To his annoyance Crosby Pennington sauntered into the room.

"Have I interrupted something, old man?" Crosby inquired lazily. "It's rather late to be going out for the evening. Why don't you and I share a bottle and a few hands of cards."

"I have other plans, Crosby," he said. "And I think you've already had a few too many bottles. I wouldn't want to take advantage of you at the gaming table."

"Nonsense," Crosby said. "Even when I'm on the floor I can still play better than most, though I will admit you're a bit of a challenge. However, word has it around town that you've come into a very tidy sum of money. You've even paid off your tailor, for God's sake! Next thing I'll be hearing is that you've paid the greengrocer!" The very notion seemed to affront him.

"I have. I'm about to go out of town, Crosby. A bit of rustication will do wonders—society tends to sap one's strength after a while, and I long for a bit of fresh air, the songs of birds, the smell of growing things."

"How much have *you* been drinking?" Crosby said suspiciously. "The very thought of the countryside revolts one's tender sensibilities."

"I wasn't asking you to join me," Christian pointed out.

"And wild horses wouldn't drag me there. I still can't understand why you'd be going. You haven't killed anyone new, have you?"

"If I'd been dueling you would have heard."

"True. Still, dueling isn't the only way to kill a person," he said with great delicacy. "But I know you well enough to know that you've either done something that requires you to leave town immediately, or you've got some grand scheme in the works."

"A bit of both, as a matter of fact."

Crosby beamed at him. "Then I insist we share a bottle and a few hands of cards. If you're so flush you can afford to lose some to me, and my pockets, as always, are to let. I don't suppose you need any assistance in your little endeavor?"

He considered it. Crosby was bottle-brained and capable of great viciousness, but he was also oddly reliable. The smart thing would be to have him distract Annelise Kempton. He wouldn't get very far, but she might be so busy fighting him off that she wouldn't notice her charge was disappearing under her steely gaze.

"Not a thing you can do to help, but I thank you for offering," Christian said smoothly. "But a hand or two of cards would be a grand idea. Who knows when I'll be in town again?"

"Done," Crosby said, seating himself at the table. "And am I to wish you happy? A marriage in the offing?"

Christian smiled, saying nothing. He trusted Crosby as much as he trusted anyone, which was to say, not at all.

The cards weren't going Crosby's way, and Christian was feeling generous, so he played badly, enough so that Crosby was feeling quite smug in his earnings, when his manservant entered the room and whispered in his ear.

Christian set the cards down, pushed the tidy stack of coins in Crosby's direction and rose. "I'm afraid I have to call it a night, my friend," he said. "Apparently things are moving a bit faster than I expected."

Crosby didn't hesitate in scooping up the money—
he must have had another abysmal hand. "You're certain there's nothing I can do to help?"

"Not a thing. Except observe your usual discretion."

"Then I wish you happy, old man," Crosby said, rising and throwing his cards on the table, as well, face up.
As wretched as Christian had expected. "And I appreciate your skill tonight. You've always been a good
friend."

He should have known Crosby would see through his
deliberately sloppy playing. "A little country air would
do you some good, as well," Christian suggested lightly

Crosby shuddered. "The countryside? I think not.
I'm quite content with my cosmopolitan pleasures." He
held out his hand. "Good luck," he said.

"And you, as well, Crosby."

Henry had already packed his bag, and it didn't take
Christian long to change into uncharacteristically dark
and sober clothes. Perhaps he should have sent Crosby
in the dragon's direction, he thought belatedly. They'd
be well suited. She could lecture him and probably get
him away from too much wine, cards and wicked
women, and he could give her children and a respectable marriage away from the constraints of having to
live in other people's houses and do their bidding. Crosby's income was adequate if he weren't so addicted to
gaming, and Annelise would be the sort to manage a
household very carefully. He'd been a fool not to throw
them together and make everything nice and tidy.

Except that it wouldn't be tidy. Crosby might be the

closest thing he had to a friend, but he didn't completely trust him. And even if he did, he wasn't giving him Annelise. Too bad for her, but if he couldn't have her, then nobody could. He didn't expect anyone would really appreciate her. And he was selfish enough not to want anyone to have the chance.

Perhaps later. There was no hurry in settling Miss Kempton—no one else was going to come sniffing around her skirts in the meantime. In another year, once he was solidly married and Hetty had a child on the way, Christian's irrational interest in her mentor would have vanished, and he could happily match-make without feeling the slightest twinge of jealousy. His attraction to her was simply a momentary madness, soon to pass.

Chipple House was dark. Torches were burning at the front entrance but he had no intention of going in that way. He'd already made a thorough reconnoiter of the place, and he knew which doors were the easiest to open and the least likely to be watched. It was going to be almost laughingly easy—no dangerous father keeping guard, no dragon to defend their little princess. He could almost wish for more of a challenge.

He slipped past the unlocked gate, courtesy of his well-bribed assistant, and into the darkened garden. With no lights from the house or the streets it was pitch-black, but he was like a cat—he could see very well in the dark, and he knew exactly where he was going.

To the bower of his future bride. And if he was feeling a little bit less enthusiastic than he should have been, well, he would soon get over it and concentrate on the business at hand.

Annelise was not happy at being dragged out that night, but Josiah Chipple had insisted on her company. Hetty was home, refusing to leave her room and Chipple was not about to miss an evening at Lady Prentice's, even for a suspiciously ailing daughter who seemed more afflicted with tears than anything else.

It had been quite the scene, Annelise thought with a tiny shudder, sitting in the back of Lady Prentice's salon and sipping on a weak punch. At least she made certain Chipple was nowhere around when she gave Hetty the note from her first love, but indeed, though the affection between the two was clear, she had no idea that Hetty was capable of such extreme feelings. And it wasn't histrionics on her part. When she read the note she turned very pale and did her best to hold back the tears that sprung to her eyes.

"Where is he?" she'd demanded. "Is he downstairs?"

Annelise shook her head. "I met him in the park this morning, and he begged me to bring this to you. He's quite determined in his resolve, Hetty."

Hetty stood motionless, a tiny doll of a figure in her overstuffed pink bower. And then she burst into tears, and there was nothing Annelise could do but put her arms around her and try to soothe her.

The tale came out in disjointed gulps, and it was nothing more than Annelise had suspected, though perhaps a little further along. "He said he loved me," Hetty sobbed. "We were going to face my father together, and if he said no then we were simply going to run away… He wouldn't be able to stop us if we spent the night away from the house. He'd have to accept William. I don't understand how he could change his mind."

Annelise had little trouble following Hetty's pronouns. There was nothing she could do—she didn't want to believe that there was any real danger to anyone, but the sight of Will's bruised and swollen face told its own tale. If he'd truly threatened his own daughter it was simply to scare the unwanted suitor away, but Annelise was appalled that Josiah Chipple could even think of such a thing. She'd landed in a very bad place this time, despite Lady Prentice's care, but until Hetty was safely married she couldn't very well leave. She'd made a promise to Will, and even if she hadn't, she wouldn't abandon such a clearly unhappy girl. She was made of sterner stuff than that—she'd never run from a challenge.

She'd stroked Hetty's hair and soothed her tears and tucked her into bed with a tisane to help her sleep, and then she had no choice but to go out to her godmother's with her seemingly benevolent host, while his daughter wept her heart out.

But while she sat in the corner, listening to a truly dreadful soprano, she cast a mental eye over all the marriageable prospects. Few of them were in the room—most young men did their best to avoid an evening of culture, and if the woman singing Handel was any example she couldn't blame them.

But Annelise needed to get Hetty engaged quickly,

so she could escape. There was Sir Julian Hargreaves, handsome enough, though perhaps not overburdened with wit. The earl of Clonminster, though he was a widower and not known for his good temper, was still reasonably attractive for a man of his age. Lord Baldrick Abbott dabbled in science, something Hetty would find dreadfully boring, and he tended to look down his overlarge nose at women. Jasper Fenton, while lacking a title, might be the best prospect—he was a younger son from an excellent old family, and if Hetty was accepted by Lady Fenton she'd be accepted everywhere.

Indeed, London was lamentably short of qualified suitors this season, a dire shame, but there may have been someone she'd overlooked. With the glittering Christian Montcalm out of the picture, and childhood sweethearts abandoned, it shouldn't take long to find a suitable candidate. She was a trifle concerned that Hetty wouldn't bounce back from her latest heartbreak as quickly as she could wish, but then, she'd been ready to marry Christian Montcalm until William had shown up. She could be distracted again.

Except, in truth, Christian Montcalm could tempt a saint with his wicked charm, and a young girl would have little defense against it. Unlike a wiser, older woman like herself, Annelise mocked herself. At least he was no longer going to be a problem, and she could breathe a sigh of relief that she wouldn't have to encounter him again. Her heart should be bursting with joy, though she felt strangely heavy.

Time. In a day or two Annelise would be back to her

old self. In a day or two Hetty would be flirting and dancing, her first love forgotten.

In the meantime, the two of them were just going to have to suffer.

Chipple House was dark and silent, but Christian knew exactly where he was going. His well-paid confederate, an under-footman named Davey, took his coins and tucked them in his pocket.

"They're all in the servants' hall," he said. "Even Jameson. He's the one you'd have to watch out for, but he and the cook are otherwise occupied, and will be for at least another hour. Miss Hetty's room is the third door on the left, and it's far enough away that no one will hear her scream."

"She's not going to scream," Christian said coolly. "And what about you?"

"I'm getting out of here. Josiah Chipple ain't the kind of man to cross, and he'd find out it was me sooner or later. I don't fancy ending up in an alley with my throat cut."

Christian didn't bother to reason with him. In fact, he suspected Davey was quite right. An alley, or the Thames. Chipple was a dangerous enemy.

There was no sound coming from behind Hetty's closed door, but light seeped beneath it, and he didn't bother to knock. She'd have to get used to her husband walking in on her.

He pushed open the door. She was sitting in front of a mirror, a vision in pink, and while she'd clearly been crying she was a girl whose tears were simply an added embellishment, making her beautiful blue eyes glisten, and her rosebud lips tremble slightly. Ah, she was a rare treat, and he was going to enjoy teaching her about life and pleasure. Damn it.

Her tear-filled eyes opened wide with wonder. "What are you doing here?" she breathed.

He gave his most practiced, seductive smile, and she responded as she ought, melting a bit. Really, she was too easy. He did prefer a bit of a challenge, like...

He held out his hand. "Your father has rejected my honorable offer of marriage," he said. "So I thought we should reject his rejection and take care of it ourselves."

He'd managed to startle her. She glanced down at a piece of paper in her hand for a long moment, and then crumpled it angrily. She looked up at Christian with a brilliant smile. "I'm ready," she said.

And they were off.

14

It was later than Annelise would have wished when they arrived back at Chipple House. Mr. Chipple bade her a courteous good-night before heading in the direction of his library, and she did her best to shake off the feelings of mistrust. He'd been his usual, affable self all evening—slightly boisterous but not unacceptable, and William's wild tales seemed more and more unlikely. Except that she'd seen the pistol. And Jameson was not the sort of butler to put heart into one.

She was unaccountably tired, and she moved up the sweeping staircase slowly. She ought to go in and check on Hetty, but there was neither light nor sound coming from behind her closed door. The tisane must have worked particularly well—the poor child would have been exhausted from her tears. There'd be time enough in the morning to sort things out.

It was a fairly cool night, and a fire was burning in her hearth. She closed the door behind her, went straight for the dresser and took out the crumpled note. There would be no lesson three, and the sooner she got rid of any and all reminders of Christian Montcalm the better she'd be. She took the paper and crossed the room, resolutely throwing it on the fire.

And as soon as she saw the edge catch and flame orange, she instinctively snatched it out again, burning her hand, stomping the flames as they curled around the vellum.

It was only singed around the edges. Her hand was in slightly worse shape, but it would heal. She was an idiot, a fool, a cotton-brained romantic, but she wasn't going to destroy the token of the closest thing to a love affair that she'd ever had, whether he'd simply been toying with her or not. When she was seventy, living alone in her cottage in the country with her cats all around her, she could sit in her chair and reread the note and think fondly of her foolish youth.

Even though she wasn't accustomed to thinking of herself as foolish, in the case of Christian Montcalm she was a total blithering idiot. The one blessing was that no one would ever know she had a temporary weakness of resolve. Christian Montcalm was the only one even half-aware of her susceptibility, and she doubted he knew just how stupid she was capable of being. And given his profligate way of life, he'd probably be dead in ten years or so.

For some reason the notion failed to comfort her.

She slept poorly. There was no sound from Hetty's room to disturb her, but downstairs Mr. Chipple's voice bellowed upward once or twice, and there was a great commotion with servants running to and fro. She ought to get up and check, see if she was needed, but since the noise was coming from the area where Mr. Chipple's private rooms were located she consoled herself in thinking it was none of her business and simply put the pillow over her head to shut out the noise.

She heard the maid tapping at her door, and she opened one eye. It was bright daylight outside, peeping in between the shutters, and she groaned. Her head hurt; she hadn't slept well in days, and if Hetty could plead a fake illness then so could she. "I'm not feeling well, Jane. I'm going to rest for another hour." Or five, she thought to herself, closing her eyes again.

The knocking continued, a little louder, and Jane's plaintive voice came from behind the thick panel. "Please, miss," she said, and even muffled, her voice was clearly tearful. "There's been a bit of trouble."

Bloody hell, Annelise thought, enjoying the mental curse. She threw back her covers and climbed out of bed, just as Jane pushed open the door.

"What is it?" she asked, reaching for her plain woolen robe.

"It's Miss Hetty. She's gone."

Annelise froze. "Gone where?"

"No one knows, miss. I just went to bring her morning chocolate and there was no sign of her. Her bed's not been slept in, and some of her clothes are missing."

"Where is Mr. Chipple? Does he know?"

"That's the problem, miss. Mr. Chipple was called away last night due to a business problem. He said he wouldn't be back for a week or so, but that you were to keep a close watch on Miss Hetty."

"Oh, God," Annelise said weakly, sinking down on her bed. "Was anything else missing from Hetty's room?"

"Her jewelry, miss."

That answered her unspoken question. If she'd run off with William she'd have no use for her jewelry, though she was such a little magpie that she might very well have taken it anyway. But it was far more likely that a suitor of a more avaricious nature had run off with her, one who would make certain her very valuable jewels came along.

The question was, had she gone willingly? And where?

"Was there any sign of a struggle?" she forced herself to ask.

Jane looked even more shocked. "Certainly not, miss. Were you thinking she was abducted? We would have heard something in the servants' hall."

"And what has been done about this so far?"

"Nothing. Mr. Jameson accompanied Mr. Chipple, and the next in command is Mrs. Buxton, and she told me to ask you. Should we call in the Bow Street Runners? Try to find out where Mr. Chipple is? He'd want to know that his daughter has gone missing."

"I think it would be much better if he knew after the fact, once she was safely returned home," Annelise said firmly. "And there's no need for the runners. I expect she simply went to visit one of her female friends. Probably someone became ill and she felt she had to rush to her side. She was foolish to go out without an escort, but she was upset last evening, and wasn't thinking clearly. I expect she'll return, or we'll get a note explaining what has happened."

Jane didn't look as if she was going to believe this far-fetched explanation for one minute, but she was well trained enough not to voice her skepticism. "Yes, miss. In the meantime, what should we do?"

In the meantime, Annelise was half tempted to go down to Mr. Chipple's abandoned library and see if the pistol was still there, so she could fire a ball into Montcalm's black heart for running off with an innocent. She took a deep breath.

"There's nothing we can do at the moment, Jane. She'll return momentarily with a perfectly reasonable explanation, I'm certain of it. That, or she'll send a note."

"There've been no messengers this morning," Jane said darkly. "Oh, that is, except for the flowers."

"Someone sent Hetty flowers?"

"No, miss. You."

Damn and blast, she thought. "And where are these flowers?" she asked in a dangerous voice.

Jane looked even more nervous. "In all the excitement we forgot about them. I'll bring them right up."

"Never mind. It will only take me a moment to get dressed and I'll get them myself. What kind are they?"

"Pretty, yellow roses and blue irises, miss. And snapdragons."

She was still shoving her hair back into its usual bun as she raced down the stairs. The flowers sat at the bottom, a sweet profusion of color, and the note was prominently attached. She could have burned the other one, she thought, since she was about to receive a second.

Sorry to run off with the golden goose, dragon, but a man must be practical. I regret we'll never get to lesson three, but I'll dream of it at night. Christian.

"Bastard," she said out loud, between her teeth. "Son of a bitch, rutting bastard."

"Miss?" Jane was looking as horrified as if one of the ugly marble statues had spoken.

In a crisis the worst thing one could do was lose one's head, Annelise reminded herself as she crushed the letter in a fist. She needed help, and she needed it fast.

"Did Mr. Chipple take his carriage, or did he go on horseback? And is there another conveyance in his stables?"

"Sorry, miss. He only keeps the one carriage and he took it. There are a number of nice horses you could ride—"

"No!" Annelise said with a shudder. "I don't ride. Get me a hack. Who knows that Miss Chipple is missing?"

"You were the first person I've told."

"I'm the only person you'll tell," she said firmly. "You're to explain to everyone that Hetty and I have gone for a visit to my sister in the country. A little fresh air away from London seemed just the thing. I know where she is, and I'll simply go fetch her and take her away for a few days, so it won't be a lie. You can do that much, can't you? Even with Mr. Chipple?"

"Mr. Chipple frightens me," Jane admitted, her voice nervous.

"All the more reason to ensure that he doesn't worry. I'm responsible for Hetty, and I'll make certain she's safe. In the meantime, I need you to call me a hack while I throw a few clothes together. I don't expect to be back for a few days."

"Miss, are you sure…?"

"Quite sure," Annelise said firmly. "Now run along and do as I say, my girl. I promise you, all will be well."

Annelise only wished she felt so certain inside. She tossed a change of clothes in her valise, and at the last minute took her pearls. By the time she'd raced downstairs the carriage was waiting.

She drew her drab gray cape around her, putting the hood over her head. "Remember what I said, Jane," she called as the carriage drew away, leaving Jane alone on the front doorstep with a troubled expression on her face.

Annelise had never been alone in a hired carriage before, but she knew from her years of riding that showing nervousness was a major mistake. It really would have helped if she knew where she was going.

"I need to find a friend at a hotel, and I don't remember the name of the place."

"Can't help you there, miss," the driver replied.

"It's either the Albion or the Albemarle. Do you know either of them?"

"Yes, miss. Which one do you want to try first?"

"The nearest." If only she could remember where

William Dickinson said he was staying. If only he was still there. When she'd met him in the park he said he was leaving today, and he might have gotten an early start. In which case she wasn't sure what she would do.

She drummed her fingers on the leather seat beside her. She'd forgotten gloves and a hat, but at least the hood of the cape would provide both coverage and disguise. It seemed forever until the driver pulled to a stop, and he wasn't about to get down and open the door for her, a novel experience.

"You'll wait for me," Annelise said, a statement, not a request, as she wrestled with the door and the fold-down steps on her own.

"Who's to say you're going to return? How about some money up front?"

Oh, God, money! She'd been so shatter-brained she'd forgotten all about that little necessity of life. For all that she considered herself a self-reliant woman, in the end she was just as helpless as all the pretty young things on the marriage mart.

Don't show fear, she reminded herself. "You'll be paid when I find my friend," she said in a voice that no one would dare argue with. And she marched into the Albion Inn with her back ramrod straight.

It only took her a moment to find the owner. "Excuse me, sir, but I'm looking for a gentleman. My cousin, William Dickinson." She'd come up with the slightly believable story on the ride in the uncomfortable hackney. "I believe he's staying here."

The man hesitated, unsure how to treat her. She

clearly wasn't a whore, but no lady would arrive at an inn by herself in search of a gentleman.

In the end he decided to err on the side of a slightly sullen courtesy. "Right behind you, miss."

It was all she could do not to burst into noisy tears of relief. "Miss Kempton? What are you doing here? Has something happened to Hetty?"

"Cousin William!" she said loudly, taking his arm. "Is there someplace where we may speak privately?"

"There's my room, but that would be improper…"

"Lead on. Oh, but wait! First I need some money."

He was staring at her in mystified disbelief, but fortunately he was a reasonable soul, so he simply pulled out his purse. "What do you need?"

"Actually I need you to go out there and pay that hackney driver. I forgot that I would need money when I left the house."

"Something's happened to Hetty. Please, Miss Kempton, you must tell me!"

"Pay the driver first, and then we may talk in private."

Annelise had had more than her share of uncomfortable moments in her life, but standing in the middle of the well-populated tavern of the Albion Inn with seemingly a hundred pairs of eyes upon her had to rank with the most difficult. Fortunately, Will moved quickly, returning from the street, catching her arm with more haste than politeness, and led her up the stairs.

"I wonder who's paying who?" some bright wag commented, loudly enough for them to hear, and Will halted, about to turn around.

"Ignore them," Annelise whispered. "We have more important things to worry about."

The room was small, the bed unmade, and Annelise plopped herself down in the middle of it, unconcerned about appearances. "Christian Montcalm has run off with Hetty," she announced the moment he closed the door. "As far as I can tell, they've been gone all night."

"He's kidnapped her?" William said, turning pale.

Annelise needed quick action, but she didn't want to lie. "At the very least he beguiled and misled her. And she was heartbroken when I gave her your letter—I'm certain she wasn't thinking clearly."

She should have known William would be a reasonable man. "If she went with him it was only because he took unfair advantage of her. And I don't care how many nights she's been with him—when we find them I'll kill him and take Hetty with me. We can get married and no one will have to know the truth—I can no longer worry about Chipple's villainy when Hetty's honor is at stake."

"If you kill Christian Montcalm it might look a bit suspicious," Annelise pointed out, ever practical. She was wise enough not to add that the likelihood of a young boy like William being able to defeat a practiced duelist was not good. "Our wisest course is to rescue her, convince Montcalm to keep silent, either by threat or bribe, and you two can elope to Scotland. Preferably before Mr. Chipple returns from wherever he's disappeared to and can put a stop to it."

"You're certain she didn't accompany her father?"

"Quite certain," Annelise said, the mocking note crumpled in her pocket. "Our only problem is discovering where he's taken her."

"I doubt they're still in London—the farther away he gets her the more difficult it would be to mount a rescue. But I have no idea where he might go. I don't believe he has a country house—"

Annelise let out a cry of relief. "Yes, he does! In Devon. I'm not certain I remember the name of the town, but his house is called Wynche End."

"Devon's a big county, Miss Kempton," William said doubtfully.

Annelise bounced off the bed. "I know that, William. My elder sister lives there. If you're so ready to admit defeat then I'll go after her myself..." she began, but William put firm hands on her arms and settled her back on the bed.

"I'm not going to admit defeat. I was unwise even to consider it. I just think we should find out what part of Devon..."

"It's on the coast. If I weren't so upset I'd be able to think more clearly, but once we're on our way it should come back to me." After all, she remembered just about everything he had ever said to her, done to her, every expression and touch. The rat bastard.

"All right," William said. "I'll arrange for horses—"

"No!" Annelise said, unable to hide her panic. "I can't ride. Besides, when we find her we'd either need to find another horse or some form of conveyance. You need to hire a carriage. A fast one."

"Perhaps I should go on my own. I can ride faster than any carriage, and go places that you couldn't…"

"She'll need the presence of a respectable woman if we're to rescue her from this folly," Annelise said.

"Then what are we waiting for?"

She suddenly realized that she'd left her valise in the hired cab, with only her embroidered bag of pearls still tucked in her pocket. It was too late to find the driver, too late to do anything. She would manage. She always did.

She rose from the bed. "I'm ready," she said as calmly as she could manage. And she held out her hand for his arm.

15

Christian Richard Benedict de Crecy Montcalm had never hurt a woman in his life, unless she'd specifically agreed to it, but right now he was on the verge of murdering one. He could throttle Miss Hetty, he thought absently, and it would silence her whines and sobs and constant prattle. He could simply gag her, but she'd already managed to connect one of her surprisingly hard fists with his cheekbone and he wasn't in the mood for a wrestling match. Particularly since he had no sexual interest in the outcome. Some things came with too high a price, and Miss Hetty Chipple was most definitely one of those things.

The journey hadn't started out well. In an elopement, speed was of the essence, and it necessitated hiring a small carriage, devoid of some of the comforts the spoiled Miss Chipple was so accustomed to. Her initial excitement had disappeared, and she'd complained about each bump in the road, and there were many: the quality of the leather squabs, the meager light, her rushed departure, and worst of all, to his surprise she complained that she hadn't been able to say goodbye to the dragon.

"Don't you think she would have tried to stop you?" he'd drawled, thinking of the note he'd sent her. A bit too provocative, but he never could resist his wicked inner promptings, particularly where the Honorable Miss Annelise Kempton was concerned.

"Oh, I wouldn't have told her the truth. I would have said I was running off with Will." The mention of his name suddenly seemed to suck the life out of her, and her eyes filled with tears. Thank God, Christian thought wearily. Anything to shut her up.

Then he was fool enough to respond. "I gather Miss Kempton approved of your childhood sweetheart."

"She said anybody was better than you," she replied with perfect frankness.

"Probably true," he said.

The little idiot had lapsed into a blessed silence, most likely mourning her lost love rather than reconsidering her reckless choice. The silence eventually settled into sleep, and they drove through the night-shrouded roads at dangerous speeds.

She'd curled up on the seat, somehow managed to adjust to the jolts of the carriage, and he could see the streaks of tears on her pretty cheeks. She was annoying and pathetic, but she was very, very pretty. And he suddenly had the most horrifying realization: She brought out his paternal side. She made him feel old, and wise, and even slightly protective. And not the slightest bit desirous.

She was fifteen years younger than he was—hardly

young enough to be his daughter. She was of marriageable age—most young ladies became attached during their first season, at seventeen, and most men waited until later, to his age, thirty-two, to marry. They would suit very well.

And yet he still wanted to spank her, not kiss her.

Of course, he wanted to spank the Honorable Miss Annelise Kempton, but that was a far different matter and she would likely be shocked at his randy thoughts.

Except that she hadn't seemed easily shocked. Embarrassed, perhaps, as he'd forced her to examine good old Priapus, one of his favorite Greek gods, but not shocked. Not when he'd kissed her, either, though she'd been startled. He really would have liked the chance to have shocked her.

Hetty slept on, thank God—the sleep of the innocent, he supposed.

And he closed his eyes and slept, as well, the divinely untroubled sleep of the wicked.

He awoke to complaints. By morning light she had begun to rethink her rash decision, and she looked at him accusingly, demanding they stop for a rest.

"We changed horses while you were asleep, darling," he said. "I didn't want to wake you."

"We need to stop now."

"The horses are fresh, and we need to make as fast a time as we can. You certainly don't want your father to catch up with us, do you?"

She turned pale, something Christian noted with surprise. She was frightened of the man, which shouldn't have been that unusual. Most children were afraid of their parents. But Hetty was a doted-upon only child, and the fear in her lovely blue eyes wasn't that of a naughty child caught doing mischief. It was a deep, mindless terror.

Perhaps he wasn't doing her such a disservice after all, running off with her. If her father caused such a reaction then even a rogue like him was preferable.

Annelise would be left to face that wrath. Not a happy thought, and not one he'd considered before. It wouldn't have changed his mind, of course. A man in his circumstances couldn't afford to be sentimental. And Chipple would never dare touch the Honorable Miss Kempton— he had enough sense for that. Any verbal abuse she could easily match, as he knew only too well.

"What are you smiling about?" Hetty said in a cranky voice. *Oh, God, was he going to hear that whiny little voice every morning for the rest of his life?*

"The thought of our happy life together," he said.

"We won't have a happy life together if you don't find me a necessary," she snapped. "I'm going to explode."

"I doubt it," he said. But he turned around and tapped twice on the glass. He'd relieved himself at the first stop, but right now what he needed most was a respite from her annoying voice.

After they had stopped he was afraid he was going to have to lift her up bodily and throw her back into the carriage, but at the last moment she climbed back in, glaring at him as they started forward again. "You need to be shaved," she said.

"Are you saying I'm not as pretty as you'd like?" he murmured with mock offense.

"No. You're always pretty, even when you look disreputable. That's why I picked you."

He didn't bother to dispute it. If she thought she'd had any choice in the matter once he knew the size of her fortune, then she was mistaken.

The only blessing to the wretched journey was that they made excellent time. It was near dusk when they reached the tiny town of Hydesfield, and mercifully dark once they arrived at Wynche End. She wasn't going to like the condition of her future home, and until she was thoroughly bedded she could still balk.

The servants were waiting, and he could see that Mrs. Browne did an excellent job at trying to clean up the place. There was no broken furniture in sight, fires were blazing—no doubt fed by the missing furniture—and the place smelled pleasantly of lemon polish and dried roses. He stood in the front hallway and felt an uncommon peace slip around him. He hadn't realized he'd missed it so.

"You didn't carry me across the threshold," the tiny harpy said.

His smile was effortless—he'd spent many years charming people he despised. "We aren't married yet."

She was so transparent. She was regretting her hasty exit more and more, and the large front hall of Wynche End had done little to reassure her. She probably had the foolish notion that until they were married she could always change her mind, return to her comfortable home in London.

But she'd been gone with him for one night, soon to be two, and it didn't matter whether he'd bedded her or not. She was effectively ruined, and marriage was the only option.

"I'm certain you must be tired, my darling," he said smoothly. "Let Mrs. Browne take you upstairs to our rooms. She's an excellent cook and I imagine you must be famished."

"Our rooms?" Hetty echoed suspiciously.

"Aren't you planning on sharing rooms with your husband? Perhaps even a bed?" He was mocking her, but she was oblivious, and inwardly he sighed. Her dragon would have fought back, deliciously.

"We're not married yet." She turned his own words on him. She gave Mrs. Browne her most regal look, quite ridiculous coming from such a dab of a thing. "You may show me to my room."

Bessie Browne gave him a questioning look, but Christian simply nodded. Anything to get rid of her. He didn't even wait to watch her shapely ascent up the ancient oak stairs. He went straight to the library.

As he'd expected, the Brownes had done their best in there, as well. A fire was blazing, a bottle of port was set out, and he sank into the old leather chair with a sigh of relief. A few moments of peace and quiet while he talked himself into going to his virgin bride.

He had no intention of raping her. Rape was distasteful to him, though that was not the case among some of his friends. He preferred his women willing, and he had yet to find a woman he couldn't eventually convince.

Hetty would eventually be convinced, too, but he'd have to put up with her pouts, her complaints, her incessant whining—and he doubted the sex would be worth it. If he shocked her she might balk at a wedding anyway, and while he wouldn't force sex, he'd definitely force marriage.

No, he needed to deflower her with utmost care and politeness, plant his seed if possible, which would be a novel experience. He always made certain to withdraw—he wanted no unknown bastards of his wandering around the countryside. There was no need for such a protective act with his fertile young wife, whether she was yet a wife or not.

He still wasn't interested in going to her, though. He'd barely slept during their breakneck pace, he'd barely eaten, and he was in a strange, melancholy mood that he refused to examine too closely. And Miss Hetty could wait.

He stretched his long legs out in front of him, kicking off his boots. Most of his friends wore boots that required help in removing, but since he preferred to be self-reliant he wore his looser.

He took a sip of the port. Mrs. Browne had informed him that she'd put Hetty into the only inhabitable bedroom among the seventeen in the rambling old house, and he'd be hard put to find an alternative bed. It didn't matter. The fire was warm, the chair was cozy, and the port didn't come from the benighted country of his birth but from Portugal. For the time being he was well content.

* * *

It was pouring rain. The horses were having a hard time in the mud, their pace was better suited to a snail, and Annelise was cold and wet and miserable. When they'd stopped to change horses and ask for directions she'd gotten her cloak soaked, and the cheap conveyance William had been able to hire didn't come equipped with anything to provide warmth or light. They'd gotten off to a late start—Christian would have abducted Hetty almost a day earlier, and they didn't dare hesitate. The sooner they found them the better chance they had of salvaging the matter.

At least luck had been on their side when they'd reached Montcalm's apartments. He was long gone, but the servant cleaning the stoop outside was quite talkative, and it was easily ascertained that the formerly impoverished Mr. Montcalm had hired a carriage and taken off for his home in the tiny town of Hydesfield, Devon. And, the young man added, had been most generous with his tips when he left.

It was a bloody long way, Annelise thought, but there was no way out of it. At least she was old enough that her own reputation wouldn't be in any danger. She was already going to be under a cloud when it got out that Hetty had eloped while Annelise had been visiting. At least she would make certain that Hetty married the right man, not the degenerate scoundrel who'd kidnapped her.

William had only balked at one moment, and that was when she asked him if he had a pistol.

"Of course not!" he'd replied huffily. "What do you take me for, a highwayman?"

"Then we're going to need to obtain one," she said. "Someone like Christian Montcalm is not going to give up such a juicy plum without a fight."

"Perhaps she wants to be with him." William's face was a mask of gloom.

"She wants to be with you, William. The only reason he was able to persuade her to go with him, if it wasn't outright kidnapping, was that she was heartbroken at your desertion."

"I had no choice!" Will cried. "Chipple threatened my family! He threatened Hetty herself!"

Annelise wasn't going to argue with such a preposterous notion. "Whether you simply misunderstood him or not, it no longer matters. We need a pistol, and we need to rescue her, and then you can leave me to deal with the odious Mr. Chipple."

William looked at her as if she'd lost her mind, but it was not an unfamiliar reaction. "I don't know how to shoot a pistol," he said finally.

"I do."

Getting one had proved more difficult, particularly since she didn't want to waste any time. In the end she had no choice—they had stopped at Chipple House on their way out of town and she headed straight for Josiah Chipple's library.

The under-footman who was taking the missing Jameson's place seemed uninterested in her doings, simply letting her in the front door and then disappearing, and Annelise breathed a sigh of relief until she saw that the hidden shelf was once again hidden.

The naked male statue smirked at her, and she averted her eyes hastily as she went to the wall, pushing and yanking at everything she could think of in hopes of discovering the hiding place. She was ready to start tearing the wall with her nails when instinct caught her—there was a large book on Greek mythology prominently placed a couple of shelves above where she remembered the opening. She reached for it, and the door swung open, revealing the cubbyhole.

For a moment she was afraid the pistol had disappeared. But then she saw the dull metal gleaming in the darkness, and she grabbed it, along with the accoutrements needed to reload if one bullet didn't kill the bastard. And then she ran, leaving the door open, and several books littering the floor. Maybe someone would come and clean up the mess she'd made, maybe they wouldn't. It was the least of her worries.

She set the gun down carefully on the seat beside her. William was looking at it as if it were a poisonous snake about to bite, but he said nothing, his jaw set in grim determination as they made their way through the crowded London streets with maddening slowness.

The rain had started by nightfall, first a light drizzle, then a downpour. Hetty had already been in the blasted satyr's company for one full night, and it appeared as if it was going to be another, as well. Difficult to redeem, but if anyone could do it, Annelise could. The best course would probably be to send Hetty off with William to Gretna Green directly. With Annelise as chaperon no one could do more than disapprove, but at least the child wouldn't be cut dead. And then the two of them could have their honeymoon, preferably as far away from England as possible, while Annelise dealt with the presumably volatile Mr. Chipple.

She dozed off and on, but the carriage was cheaply made and small, and every bump and jolt knocked her awake. The devoted swain seemed to have no trouble sleeping through the wretched drive, and she sat there in misery and cursed all men, particularly young, lovelorn ones who still managed to snore quite loudly when the object of their adoration was in danger.

She was uncertain when dawn arrived—the rain and gloom was so intense that there was barely any perceptible change in the light coming through the cheap windows. She checked and rechecked the pistol, making sure it was clean and loaded. It would have helped if she'd had a chance to fire it—most firearms were unreliable and were likely to pull to the right or to the left. If she wanted to blow a hole in Montcalm, she wanted to make sure it was where she'd placed it. She might feel like killing him, but in her heart she only wanted him to feel a very great deal of pain. Any stray romantic longing for him had vanished in a righteous rage.

Shooting him in the foot would probably be the best choice. It would hobble him, but there was no way it could kill him, and it would hurt like the fires of hell, something that would give her great satisfaction as she sailed out of his mansion with the two lovebirds at her side, leaving him to gnash his teeth and ponder the folly of his evil ways.

And she was getting too tired to think clearly. He wasn't a villain in one of the novels she adored... No, he was far worse. No one would push him over a cliff, much as he deserved it. No one would set his secret dungeon lair on fire to have him burn up inside it.

Which in reality was a sobering thought. She didn't want him dead, God help her. She just wanted him gone, forgotten, out of their lives.

But he had been out of her life. He'd said goodbye, and she'd been foolishly devastated. She was an idiot— it was doubtless some ailment spinsters were prone to. A solitary life and an unhealthy taste in literature were bound to produce fantasies that were quite improper.

The town of Hydesfield was dark and dreary, but she expected no less on such a miserable day, and it had been a simple enough matter to acquire directions to Wynche End. Getting through the increasingly rutted roads that led to Montcalm's estate was a different matter—it was as good as any gothic novel she'd ever read—and she held on for dear life as the coach lurched its way through the mud.

She heard the ominous crack first, and she was able to grip the side of the door and her precious pistol as the carriage collapsed on one side, tossing them heavily against the door. "Wheel's broken!" the benighted driver shouted through the rain. "I think I see a house up ahead. I can—"

Annelise was already gone, picking up her skirts and sliding through the dangerously slanted door. She landed in the mud, and it was only sheer providence that she didn't end up accidentally shooting herself. She was a wet, cold, muddy mess, and she didn't care. She could see the outlines of a huge, dark house up ahead, and she didn't hesitate, making her way through the mire at lightning speed.

She lost a shoe somewhere along the way. Her hood provided little protection from the pelting rain and her drenched hair had fallen down her shoulders, and she imagined she looked like the wrath of God. She certainly hoped so.

She pushed the huge front door open into the dark, cold hallway, but from a distance she could see candlelight and feel just the faintest trace of warmth penetrating her bones. She shoved her hood back, cocked the pistol and slowly limped toward the light.

He was sound asleep, his long legs stretched out in front of him, the blessed fire blazing, an empty bottle of wine by his side. He hadn't been shaved recently, and he looked rumpled, dissolute and beautiful. Like a fallen angel. She moved to stand in front of him and pointed the pistol directly at his heart.

"I wouldn't do that if I were you," he murmured, and then he opened his extraordinary eyes. "It's always unwise to shoot the man you're in love with."

16

He wondered whether she was going to pull the trigger in reaction to his taunt. Sooner or later he was going to provoke someone enough that they'd actually kill him, and it was no more than he deserved. But he didn't want it to be his dragon.

"Put the pistol on the table and sit down, my pet," he said, not moving. "You're shaking so hard it might go off by accident, and you wouldn't want that. If you truly want to shoot me then have at it, but if you're undecided I wouldn't want you to do it by mistake. Think of the guilt!"

"I'd get over it," she said through chattering teeth. But she set the pistol down on a table, out of his reach but well within hers, and glared at him.

She looked enchanting, like a drowned rabbit. Her wet hair was hanging down her shoulders, her spectacles were steaming up. She was muddy, shivering with cold or perhaps fury, and he wondered what she'd do if he tried to kiss her. Probably shoot him.

"Sit down, Annelise," he said gently. "I'd ring for a

servant to bring you a blanket but I'm afraid this house is very poorly staffed, and the Brownes are probably in bed. What time is it, anyway?"

"Past dawn." There was a chair just behind her, a little closer to the fire, but she wasn't moving.

"I must have drifted off."

"Where's Hetty?"

"Upstairs, presumably asleep. Or did you think I'd strangled her and tossed her in the Thames? Come to think of it, that might have been a good idea." He heard the slam of the door and the clumping of boots with resignation. Of course she hadn't come alone.

The young man stormed into the room, spied Christian sitting in his chair and started toward him with a murderous expression on his face.

Fortunately Annelise stood in the way. "Wait, William," she said, putting a hand on the boy's arm to stop him. It was a firm hand and she used a lot of force, or Christian expected the young man might have attempted to pound him mercilessly. Not that he'd be able to do it—not only had Christian whiled away a number of leisure hours studying the noble science of boxing, but he fought dirty when the occasion called for it.

"I'm going to kill him!" William said fiercely, pulling his arm from her grip but too much a gentleman to yank himself entirely free. Silly child. Then again, the Honorable Miss Kempton was surprisingly persuasive. "What have you done with Hetty?" he demanded.

"Listened to her incessant prattle, complaints, tears, demands, artless conversation and recriminations for more than twenty-four hours. You will be pleased to know I didn't touch her—if I had I would have throttled her. Take her away, if you please. I'd rather spend the rest of my life a pauper than have to spend even another day with the divine Miss Chipple."

William glared at him in clear disbelief. "Where is she?"

"Upstairs in bed, sound asleep, if I'm not mistaken. Go and find her—I expect she'll welcome you with open arms. Up the stairs, turn left, four doors down at the end of the first section of hallway. Go along, there's a good lad. Miss Kempton is safe with me."

That managed to startle an unladylike snort from Annelise, but after a moment's hesitation William fled, leaving the dragon to his wicked lures.

"Sit down, Annelise," he said again in a bored voice. "If you don't then manners decree I should probably rise, and I don't feel like doing so."

"I've been sitting for hours," she snapped.

"And is your backside in a delicate state? Trust me, my chairs are a great deal more comfortable than the jouncing seats of a hired carriage, even a good one."

Her eyes opened wide in outrage that he would mention such an indiscreet part of her anatomy. He tilted his head to get a look at that particular area, and she sat quickly, denying him his curious gaze.

"You've ruined Hetty," she said. "And now you no longer want her? Do you realize how truly despicable that is?"

"Did you want me to marry her? If you say so I expect I will—I do have an interest in pleasing you, but I really don't think the marriage would last terribly long. If I didn't strangle her I'd bludgeon her with a candlestick. And if you wanted me to marry her, that was my original plan. Why did you bring Saint George with you on your noble quest?"

"Stop trying to confuse me. Saint George and the dragon were dire enemies. If anyone is Saint George—" She halted.

His smile widened. "Were you about to suggest I might fit the role? I know this comes as a shock to you, but I am far from saintly."

Perhaps her fury would warm her, he thought absently as he watched her grit her teeth. She was no longer trembling, but she really did need to get out of those wet clothes and preferably into a warm bed. He doubted he was going to manage that much, but he was ever hopeful. He might as well salvage something from this debacle, and a romp with the Honorable Miss Kempton was well worth it. If he were frugal he could live quite comfortably on the money Chipple used to bribe him. Of course, he had never been particularly frugal.

And Chipple would probably keep trying to kill him until he succeeded. He would have shrugged, but it was too damned French. He smiled at the mortal enemy still glaring at him. She was exhausted, poor thing. And yet she wasn't complaining or whining or demanding. Well, she was demanding Hetty, and perhaps Christian's head on a platter, but apart from that, her own personal discomfort seemed the least of her worries.

"William will marry her. And if there is any premature issue you will simply have to keep your mouth shut and—"

"Didn't you listen to me, wench? I said I didn't touch her. Miss Chipple is still as pure and virginal as the day she was born. Unless someone else got to her first. I have been nothing but a perfect gentleman."

"A gentleman who abducts young ladies—"

"In truth she's the only young lady I've ever abducted, and she came with me quite willingly. I was surprised I didn't have to persuade her, but she simply got up from her dressing table and said yes."

"You were in her bedroom?" Annelise was scandalized.

"My sweet, I have been in a great many bedrooms. And I was merely standing in the doorway like the gentleman you doubt that I am, asking if she wanted to run away with me. She said yes and that was that."

Annelise was tired. He could see the shadows under her eyes, despite the spectacles, and she was paler than usual. She wanted to keep arguing, berating him, but she was running out of energy.

"How did you get here, the two of you? On horseback, I presume? In this downpour?"

"No," she said, and this time her shudder was from something entirely new. "I don't ride."

"So you came by carriage? Where is your driver?"

"The wheel broke. Or perhaps the axle. I don't know. I didn't pay attention—I just came ahead."

He rose languidly, towering over her. She stifled a yawn, and she didn't bother to move—she just looked up at him with a delightfully disgruntled expression. Interesting—he found her distemper enchanting. Hetty's was merely tiresome.

"Then I'd best see what I can do to help. Harry Browne and a lad from the village take care of the stables when I'm here, and I imagine they can help your poor driver. I expect you'll be wanting to take your little princess and escape from the ogre as soon as possible."

She was falling asleep, a fact that astonished him. Women didn't fall asleep on him, particularly when he was baiting them. At least, not at this stage in the proceedings. "Stop living in a fairy tale," she murmured, leaning back against the chair. "I'm not a dragon, Hetty's not a princess, and you're closer to a troll than an ogre."

Christian laughed. "Trolls are very ugly, dear heart. I may be conscienceless, degenerate, selfish and shallow, but I'm actually quite pretty by all accounts."

"Go find our driver," she muttered. "The sooner we get out of here the less likely it is that I'll kill you. I can still reach the gun."

"And you can actually use it?"

"My father taught me."

"Ah, yes, your father," he murmured, about to provoke her further. But she'd closed her eyes for a moment, just a moment, and he realized she was sound asleep.

He stared at her thoughtfully. And then he stripped off his rumpled coat and placed it carefully over her. It still retained some of his body heat, and he found he liked the idea of warming her, even vicariously. But that would have to wait for another time, another day.

He strolled into the hallway, following the trail of wet, muddy footprints, and opened the front door. It was very old and quite heavy, but Annelise had clearly managed it without difficulty. He liked that.

He could barely make out the shape of the overturned carriage through the murk of early dawn and the heavy rain. The last thing he was about to do was wander out into the downpour and offer help, no matter how much he wanted to get rid of Hetty, but he could go find Browne and his wife, since none of the bellpulls were working. Besides, he found he was starving—kidnapping heiresses and battling dragons worked up an appetite.

Browne was sitting in his wife's kitchen, drinking his morning ale, but he was ready in less than a minute, while Mrs. Browne looked at him with her usual motherly expression. He'd bribed them away from his grandfather—when he was growing up, Browne had been a stable lad and one of the few servants willing to ignore orders and be kind to a lonely boy. And Mrs. Brown had been a scullery maid, always willing to sneak extra food to him. The moment he became of age and inherited his mother's house he asked them to come with him, making the uncertainties of his fortune clear. And they'd come without question.

He'd always had enough to at least keep them going, but he'd been counting on the heiress to improve matters, hire some help for Bessie.

She looked at him worriedly. "None of these guests are staying, are they, Master Christian? I might be able to fix up one more bedroom, but beyond that it's hopeless. Though I suppose we could move our mattress…"

"Don't be ridiculous, Bessie," he chided her, reaching for a piece of the gammon she was frying. She slapped his hand as usual. "Your comfort comes before a pair of interlopers. In fact, once they leave we'll have fewer people in the house, because they'll take Miss Chipple with them."

Mrs. Browne nodded. "That's a good thing, then, sir," she said. Bessie had no qualms about giving him advice, calling him on his failings. "The girl wasn't right for you. She would have driven you mad in less than a year."

"She almost drove me mad in a couple of days," he said. "But her fortune was really quite well suited."

Bessie shrugged her plump shoulders. "You can't have everything, sir. I'll pray for you."

"I wish you wouldn't," he said, uncomfortable with the notion. "I'm not worth it."

Bessie gave him her maternal smile, something that should have amused him since she was only two years older than he was. But she was probably his favorite person in the universe for just that motherly air. "You're worth it, Master Christian. You just haven't figured it out yourself yet." She turned back to her cooking. "So how many for breakfast then?"

"I doubt they'll stay to eat, but there are two new visitors, plus their coachman."

"At least there's plenty of food," Bessie said, her main worry comforted. She hadn't wasted any time in spending some of the large amount of money he'd deposited in their hands.

"And as soon as they can manage it they'll all be gone, and I expect I'll be returning to the city." He could feel Bessie's silent disapproval, but she said nothing, merely nodded.

"I'm going to change. Don't wake the lady in the library—she needs a little rest before she has to climb back into a carriage." He allowed himself a small smile at the thought of Annelise's rump. Too bad she wore such awful clothes—he would have been interested in trying to discern just how she was shaped. Flat and boylike or plump and rounded? He was never to find out. But he could always ask.

"A lady, sir?" Bessie knew him far too well.

"No one of any importance," he said airily.

He made only the lightest of noise as he climbed the ancient oak staircase in his stocking feet. He'd had Harry Browne put his clothes in the Monk's Cell, or so he thought of it. It was decorated in dark, gothic splendor, and the narrow bed was better suited to a penitent than a rogue like him. It was in the opposite wing from the rooms where Hetty was ensconced, and he was suddenly curious, wondering whether she was that querulous with everyone or if young William was immune. He walked silently down the hallway, pausing outside the door, and then a slow smile crept across his face when he heard the sounds...

Miss Hetty might have arrived at Wynche End a virgin, but she wasn't leaving as one, through no fault of his.

He wondered how she'd managed it. He had no doubt at all that this noisy consummation had been initiated by his bratty abductee—young William looked far too stalwart to take advantage of a young girl, particularly one he was so clearly, desperately in love with. He was probably much more likely to lay down his life for her than deflower the little baggage.

He looked at the doorknob. He had no particular interest in watching them, though he could easily enough. The door had no lock, and they were so involved they wouldn't even notice.

But he'd had more than enough chances to watch other couples copulate, and the initial excitement had worn off quite quickly. He seldom joined in the communal revels of Crosby and his friends, preferring to concentrate on his own pleasure rather than someone else's.

Then again, he'd never seen anyone actually making love, and that would be a novelty. There was no love, affection or even much past initial acquaintance among the couples he'd watched. Not just couples, in truth, but threesomes, even foursomes. It would be interesting to see if it was any different between two young innocents who cared for each other.

No. He would simply count his blessings—with Hetty deflowered by her true love, he was no longer the chief villain in the piece. Or at least, no longer the one held responsible. Hetty had sealed her fate by seducing young William, and he had little doubt that she'd done it for that very reason. He wished them joy of each other.

The Monk's Cell had been dusted and aired, though the mattress was gone from the narrow bed, presumably too mouse-eaten to remain. He washed and changed quickly, choosing something somber and particularly flattering. Bastard that he was, he wanted Annelise to pine for him as she drove off with the young lovers.

He met a rain-soaked Harry Browne as he came downstairs. Harry shook his head, spraying water like a large dog. "That carriage is going nowhere, Master Christian. I had young Jeremy help the coachman take the horses into town, but the carriage is pretty well banged up. Cheap thing it was, and old. From the looks of it, it can't be easily fixed."

"How unfortunate," Christian said. "Good thing that the coach I hired hasn't been returned—though I'm afraid it's built for speed but not for crowds. It will only hold two besides the driver. And we have three guests."

"You'll get rid of the two newcomers?" Harry asked.

A slow smile spread across Christian's face. Wickedness shouldn't be rewarded but his was about to be. "No, I'll send Miss Hetty off with her fiancé. The Honorable Miss Kempton will simply have to remain until we can make other arrangements."

"What other arrangements? If the hired one can be repaired it will take days, even weeks. Perhaps Dickon at the Royal Oak would be willing to hire his out. It's not much but it would serve as transportation if someone wasn't too choosy."

"Oh, he wouldn't want to do that," he murmured. "You needn't bother to ask. Have your good wife make something substantial to eat and I'll rouse our guests and explain the unwelcome situation. I'm sure they'll be practical enough to accept it. Miss Hetty's chaperon will simply have to content herself with a week or two in the remote countryside until the coach is mended."

"We've got extra horses, Master Christian. The young man could ride beside the carriage..." He looked at Christian as realization began to dawn. "Ah, but then, I forgot—only the carriage horses are in any condition. The others are lame. All of them."

"I rather thought so," Christian said. "Such an unfortunate situation, we'll have no choice but to make the best of it. You might put the two...er...lame horses in a separate area of the stables in case someone decides to snoop. They need peace and quiet for recovery."

"Understood, sir. I'll see to everything."

Christian was humming under his breath as he walked back into the library. The fire had died down a bit, but Annelise slept on, the pistol still by her side. It was tempting to leave it, and see whether she'd actually try to use it, but in the end he simply scooped it up. Strange-looking pistol for a lady to carry. He wondered how she'd managed to acquire it on such short notice. It couldn't have belonged to her late father—it was far too serviceable and lethal a weapon. In truth, this was a firearm made to kill a man with no prettiness about it. It must belong to Josiah Chipple.

The old man was going to be very angry, Christian thought, hiding the gun under the cushions of one of the sofas. His daughter would be married to a country bumpkin, his houseguest had failed him and run off at the same time. Annelise was smart enough to wonder why Josiah would have such a menacing-looking pistol in his house, though she might reasonably assume it was due to his less-than-stellar ancestry. Or she might begin to realize that Josiah Chipple wasn't a benevolent, nouveau riche shipping magnate but someone very nasty indeed.

Just as well she wasn't going anywhere. Otherwise she would probably deem it her duty, once she got the two lovebirds safely married, to go back and face the old man. Not a good idea.

When he was through with her, which might be a few days or even up to a few weeks, she probably wouldn't want to look Chipple in the eye. He meant it with no malice—Christian simply wanted her, and he wasn't going to stop until she wanted it as much as he did.

He didn't expect it to have any other deleterious effect. She was facing an empty life of visits and spinsterhood, and he could show her the kind of pleasure she probably had no idea even existed. Give her something to look back on as she declined into old age.

Or perhaps she'd marry some solid widower, one who would look the other way at slightly soiled goods, and raise his children and even some of her own, and when she lay beneath the old man's sweating body she'd close her eyes and imagine it was Christian.

No, that fantasy was somehow far from pleasing. He didn't want her marrying, didn't want her lying beneath, or on top of, anyone else. Selfish bastard that he was, he wanted her to pine for him the rest of her life.

Well, he'd never made the mistake of thinking he was in any way a decent human being. And he'd take care not to impregnate her—it would be too cruel an act. But as his mind danced over the sudden image of her with a rounded belly it was absurdly enchanting.

He took the seat opposite her again. He was going to have to handle this very delicately—if he was indiscreet she'd probably try to walk back to London, soaked, muddy and with one shoe.

No, she needed to have no idea what delights he had in store for her. Until it was too late for her to run.

17

When Annelise awoke it was full daylight, with the rain settling down to a light mist, and she ached in every part of her body, first from the jolting carriage ride, second from falling asleep in a chair. In front of Christian Montcalm, no less, she thought with horror. She was blissfully warm, and she glanced down at the blanket that was covering her. Not a blanket at all, but the coat he'd been wearing, now streaked with the mud she'd brought in with her.

She looked up, but she was alone in the room. The fire was still burning brightly—someone must have built it up while she slept. And the pistol was gone.

Not that it mattered particularly. She wasn't going to shoot him—she'd had every chance, and every incitement to do so, but she hadn't. It was just as well it was out of her reach. He'd been right about one thing—if she shot him accidentally she would have felt miserable.

He was wrong about everything else. *The man you're in love with!* Totally untrue and bad grammar, as well. It should have been the man with whom you're in love, and so she ought to tell him when next she saw him, but perhaps it would be wiser not to bring up the subject at all during the few short hours they would be there.

She rose, setting the coat down carefully on the table where the gun once was, and stretched. She would have given anything for a long soak in a hot tub of water, but that was going to be denied her until they reached William's home. She could only hope the Dickinsons had a fondness for bathing.

And that William had been correct in their approval of his bride. She'd never considered that their eventual arrival at William's home might not be a welcome one, and she wasn't going to worry about it now. Escape from this place was of the utmost importance—they would deal with their arrival later. She could only hope William was not mistaken in his parents' support.

She glanced around the library. It was tidy, well dusted and shabby. The curtains hung in tatters, the fabric on the furniture was shredded, the carpet a danger to unwary feet. This was a house badly in need of a vast infusion of money, and she'd just stopped it. If an innocent young woman hadn't been at stake, she'd feel a bit of regret. It really was a lovely room.

But that reminded her—she needed to find Hetty and make certain she was in good shape after her ordeal. What had Christian told Will? Up the stairs, four doors on the left at the end of the wing? It should be easy enough to find. William was probably comforting her— they might be holding hands, talking in low whispers of the future. She needed to put a stop to that, of course.

With Hetty's reputation so compromised she must make certain that there was no appearance of impropriety.

She'd already come up with a relatively believable story. Mr. Chipple had gone on a business trip, Hetty had become so desperately homesick she'd been unable to eat and William and Annelise had deemed it a good idea if she went back to Kent for a visit. On their way they visited an old friend of the family's before ending up in the comfortable family home in Kent.

Of course, Kent was in the opposite direction of Devon. And there was a chance even a country squire would have heard of the notorious Christian Montcalm. But William had assured her during their journey together, at monotonous length, that his parents approved the match as much as they disliked Josiah Chipple. They would welcome the three of them with open arms. After that, Annelise was unsure quite what she would do. There was little doubt that Josiah Chipple would be just as displeased with her as he was with Hetty, untempered by any parental affection. Her wisest course would be to send a letter to Lady Prentice, to see if she could arrange an alternative visit for her errant godchild, preferably far away from the temptations of London and beautiful, charming villains who could confuse even the most practical of souls.

The hallway was a gloomy reflection of a rainy day, and Annelise started down it, only to be stopped by a too-familiar voice.

"I wouldn't go in there if I were you."

She turned and saw Christian, looking clean and

beautiful while she felt like a mud-soaked troll. She resisted the impulse to snarl at him. "Don't be ridiculous!" she snapped. "I need to make certain poor Hetty has survived her ordeal in decent spirits, and tell her and Will that we need to make ready to leave. We'll want to travel as much time in the daylight hours as we can."

He sauntered—there was no other word for it—toward her, tall and lean and graceful. "I expect Miss Hetty is in very decent spirits, but perhaps a bit of privacy?"

She resisted the impulse to use one of her precious curses. She limped over to the door, knocked once, and then turned the handle.

As soon as she peered inside, Annelise jumped back with a shriek, slamming the door, her face flaming. "I warned you," Christian said mildly, coming up beside her. He rapped on the door in a peremptory manner, waited a moment, and then pushed it open again, waiting for Annelise to precede him into the room.

Not that she wanted to, but she had never been one to shirk her duty. At least Hetty and Will were sitting side by side now, covers up to their bare shoulders, looking as shamed as they ought to. She turned to Christian. "This is all your fault! If you hadn't molested her she wouldn't have felt it necessary to give in to Will's importunities, and…"

"I didn't molest her. I didn't touch the tiresome chit, did I, Hetty? And I don't think the importunities were on Will's part."

The part of Will that was exposed, far too much of him in Annelise's opinion, was bright red, but Hetty tossed her head defiantly. "I wouldn't let you touch me," she said loftily. "I'm in love with William, and besides, you're too old for me."

Christian laughed. "A wound straight to the heart, dear Hetty. Indeed, when I'm around you I feel very ancient indeed. But I'm afraid it's time to rouse yourself from your bed of sin and find your way back to civilization. Were you planning a quick trip over the border, or will you chance a more formal wedding? I'm not sure that it would be wise to wait—Chipple is a vindictive man when his plans are thwarted, and apart from that you wouldn't want any premature issue from this unfortunate slip."

"I've already figured out what to do," Annelise said, her voice still a bit strained from shock. "My brother-in-law is a vicar and his parish is not too far to the north from here. We'll go there first, see if there's any way to circumvent the marriage laws and join them without Mr. Chipple's permission, and if not, we'll continue up to Scotland have them married there. Once Hetty's safely married, Mr. Chipple won't dare interfere."

"You're trying to contravene the laws, Miss Kempton?" Christian said, lightly mocking. "I'm astonished and admiring. You've thought of everything. I only hope you are right about Chipple. At least his wrath will be directed at someone other than me for the time being."

"Until I inform him of what you did," Annelise said.

He turned his head to look at her. "Would you do that, my sweet? How unkind of you, when no harm's been done and young Romeo and Juliet will live happily ever after. Indeed, you ought to thank me. If I hadn't intervened, forcing the two of you to come after me, it's very likely that Hetty would be engaged to some old windbag with a title and young…William, is it?…would be marrying a local beauty. Instead we have a revoltingly happy ending for all. I get to live without Miss Chipple but still with an impressive inflow of cash, the young lovers are united, and Miss Kempton…well, I'm not certain what her happy ending is. At least an escape from Chipple's household?"

"What impressive inflow of cash?" Annelise asked suspiciously.

"Hetty's so-generous father gave me fifty thousand pounds to leave the girl alone. Very thoughtful of him."

"And you abducted her anyway?" she said, scandalized.

"Don't look at me like that, dragon," he said mildly. "A man who'd take a bribe wouldn't hesitate to go back on it. But in the end I'm holding true to my word. I will leave the future Mrs.…whatever to her bucolic future."

"Mrs. Dickinson," Hetty said.

"Better than Chipple," Christian said. "Now, why don't we see about how we're going to get you safely on the road. The rain has halted, and it's only late morning. I imagine we can get you out of here within the next few hours."

"Thank God," said Annelise, ignoring the little twinge of sadness she felt. It was simply reluctance to climb back into a carriage, she told herself. And for the boon of never having to see him again, then she'd willingly climb back into the hideously sprung equipage that had brought them there.

"But we have a bit of a problem," he added.

"Could we at least get dressed before we discuss this?" William asked.

"No!" Annelise said, thoroughly annoyed with them. "You've literally made your bed and now you must lie in it until we discover what we can do. And don't give me that look, Hetty Chipple. Your eyes should be downcast in shame at your behavior."

"I'm not ashamed! And if you weren't a bloodless old maid you'd understand!" she shot back.

It wasn't so much that she minded being called a bloodless old maid. She just would have rather not had Christian there to hear it.

He seemed merely amused by it all, which wasn't the least bit gratifying.

"Behave yourself, Hetty," he said. "I resisted the temptation to spank your overindulged little backside, but I can always change my mind."

"You won't dare touch her!" William declared, starting to throw back the covers while Annelise shrieked and closed her eyes. Observing Chipple's indecent statues was bad enough—she really didn't want a full view of William Dickinson.

"Behave yourself, William," Christian said. "If you think I couldn't thrash you soundly you're mistaken, and I doubt Miss Kempton would object."

She opened her eyes, deciding she was safe. William had sat back down again, pulling the covers up to his waist. He was a nicely made young man, she supposed, as hairless as the statues. At least above the waist.

She could feel her face flaming at the thought, but fortunately no one was looking at her. "If anyone deserves a thrashing it's you, Mr. Montcalm," Annelise said. "You're a disgrace."

He smiled at her, that sweet, beguiling smile that always had the ability to disturb her cool and rational mind. "Indeed I am," he said. "It's a shame I never had someone like you to show me the error of my ways when I was younger. I'm afraid by now I'm a lost cause."

"And totally unrepentant."

"Oh, I repent. I'm sorry I ever thought I could tolerate Hetty's incessant yapping for the sake of her lovely fortune and her equally lovely face. But I'm afraid she's not worth it. And stop trying to jump out of bed to hit me, William. You'd embarrass Miss Kempton more than you have already. You need to concentrate on getting your betrothed out of here before another storm hits. This time of year the roads get near impassible, and you definitely would not want to be trapped here."

"Definitely not! We'll leave as soon as our carriage can be made ready," Annelise answered for him.

"Ah, but there's the problem. The cheap carriage you hired has a broken axle as well as a broken wheel, and it's uncertain whether it can even be repaired. At the least it will take several weeks to get the work done, and I'm not prepared to have company for that long."

"Then we'll hire a new one."

"There are no carriages for hire in a tiny town such as Hydesfield."

William looked momentarily daunted, but Annelise was undeterred. "Then we will simply have to take your carriage," she said. "I'm certain you were just about to offer it—it's the least a good host could do if his unexpected guests are stranded. Particularly since it's his fault they're there."

"Indeed, that was my very thought," Christian said, affable as ever. "Except there's still a minor problem."

"And that is?"

"It's a hired carriage, not exactly what you're used to, and I doubt the driver can be persuaded to abandon it. He will, I'm certain, be happy to transport you wherever you wish to go, for a price. And the carriage isn't bad—it's fast and light and surprisingly comfortable."

Annelise felt a sudden foreboding. She wasn't sure why—he just seemed way too smug for the problem to be answered that easily. William was looking none too happy, and even Hetty seemed to realize the mysterious problem.

"And?" Annelise demanded.

"It only carries two passengers."

She refused to panic. "Then I'm sure William could sit up with the driver…"

"There's no room, Miss Kempton," Christian said blandly. "And there's no way William could manage to drive it—they're tricky things to manage and not easily mastered. No, I'm afraid you have no choice but to go with the coachman."

"I see no problem. The driver can drive and William can simply ride beside the coach. Dreadfully uncomfortable for you, William, but probably for the best, seeing what proximity with Hetty has led to."

"Again, another problem," Christian said. "Carriage horses, as you know, are unridable, and I have only two other horses in my stable, due to my straitened circumstances. One is lame, and the other far too small to carry William's weight. She might possibly support a woman of your stature, Miss Kempton, if you care to try."

She was going to disgrace herself and cry, Annelise thought. Either that, or hit him. There was no way she could climb on the back of a horse, even to escape him. No way out. And the devil knew it.

"I don't see what everyone's so concerned about," Hetty piped up. "William and I will depart for her sister's house, and the moment we get there we'll send a carriage for Miss Kempton. There's no reason why she can't stay here for a few days."

"But she's an unmarried lady..." William began.

"Pish! She's on the shelf and we all know it. If Christian was able to resist me then someone like Annelise is perfectly safe."

This was certainly a perfectly miserable conversation, Annelise thought, unsure how to stop it. Christian Montcalm was leaning against the door, faintly amused by the whole thing.

"Well, of course she'd be safe," William replied, totally without tact. "She's hardly the sort of woman who tempts a man to misbehave. There is still the question of her reputation."

"If she were young enough and eligible enough it would already be in tatters," Hetty pointed out. "After all, she's spent the night with you—she'd be ruined. Fortunately people are unlikely to see anything improper when a well-bred female of her advanced age is in the company of a man. After all, if spinster chaperons required their own spinster chaperons there simply wouldn't be enough to go around."

"Charmingly put, Hetty," Christian said.

Annelise had reached her limit. "I'm not yet thirty, for heaven's sake!" she snapped. "Hardly tottering by anyone's standards. And I'm not staying here!"

"But Annelise, no one would ever think someone like Christian would be interested in you," Hetty kindly explained. "He's known as a connoisseur of beauty. Your reputation would be perfectly safe. Whereas he's right—I need to get out of here and under the care of respectable people as soon as possible. You wouldn't mind staying. You have no home of your own—and visiting one person's house is not different from another's, even if this place is remarkably shabby. And it won't be for long—we'll send someone after you as soon as we reach your sister's house."

"I won't—"

"You have no choice, Miss Kempton," Christian said in bored tones. "It shouldn't be more than a few days, and I give you my solemn word that I will do nothing to impinge on your sterling reputation."

"You already have," she said, knowing she was trapped, still fighting.

"Hetty's right, you know," William said helpfully. "No one would ever think a philanderer such as Montcalm would have any interest in one such as yourself."

And indeed, Montcalm was looking totally bored by the entire conversation. "I leave it up to the three of you," he said. "You have my word as a gentleman that Miss Kempton is perfectly safe with me. Argue amongst yourselves—in the meantime I have some work to do. I have neglected this place for far too long, and the charming nest egg needs to be wisely spent. At least some of it does, before I return to London. I've ordered the carriage put to and informed the driver, and Mrs. Browne will have packed a meal for you to carry you the first stage of the journey. Just let me know how many guests I'll be having for dinner."

"If I stay I'll eat in my room," Annelise said, and then bit her tongue. She shouldn't have even entertained the notion that she might stay under the profligate's roof.

But he seemed to have lost interest in her. In fact, ever since her arrival he'd seemed far more interested in getting rid of Hetty than in Annelise's presence. Most likely his flirtation was nothing more than a way to annoy and distract her, and now that he had decided Hetty wasn't worth the price, then her interfering companion was negligible. As Hetty and William had discussed what a total antidote she was, he'd made only a token effort to object, to defend her. She'd been a game that he had now tired of.

It should have been a relief. In fact, it was a relief. Just a deeply depressing one.

"As you wish," he said, clearly dismissing her. "I can count on Mrs. Browne to see to your comfort, and this is a big house and I keep odd hours. Besides, I'll be extremely busy taking care of things I've been neglecting. I doubt you'll even see me during your reluctant stay."

She would have come up with a disparaging insult except that it appeared he meant exactly what he said. And to have expressed disbelief would have sounded both conceited and deluded. Despite his recent wicked behavior, he was no longer any threat to her at all.

"Very well," she said, because if she said anything else she might cry, stupid sentimental female that she was. "I'm sure I'm making a fuss for nothing. I'll stay until you can arrange transportation for me. Though I dislike the thought of you two being unchaperoned."

"I think that particular milk has already been spilt," Christian said. "I'll have Mrs. Browne see to a room for you, Miss Kempton."

She was about to insist that it be as far away from his rooms as possible, but he'd already left. And such a request would have sounded absurd, given that she had been put so firmly in her place. On the shelf, unwanted.

There were no tears in her eyes when she turned back to the two miscreants, only determination. "William, wrap something around yourself, take your clothes and depart. You can wait for Hetty downstairs. I may have only a few hours left with her as my charge but I intend to make a few things clear."

Hetty didn't look any too pleased at the lecture she knew was coming, but William had the good sense not to trifle with a dragon. He pulled the coverlet from the bed, wrapped it around his body and scooped up his clothes. "I'll be right back—" he began, but Annelise interrupted him.

"You'll see to the carriage and the horses and that there are enough blankets to keep Miss Chipple warm, and good food to eat. And you will not touch anything but her hand or arm from now until you are decently wed. Do you understand?"

"Yes, Miss Kempton," he stammered, looking like a schoolboy. And she a stern schoolteacher. She sighed for what was and couldn't be changed.

"Then go," she said. And turned her steely gaze on the newly deflowered Hetty Chipple.

18

Christian wasn't lying when he said he had work to do. Not that he wouldn't lie when it suited him, but with no money he'd had no choice but to ignore the rapidly deteriorating state of Wynche End, and now that he was back, at least for a while, he realized how much he loved the old place.

His fondness for the house was ridiculous—it was full of dark wood and gothic trim and spiderwebs. It wasn't as if he'd ever lived here with his family—he'd spent the first twelve years of his life with them in France, and estates left behind in England held little interest for them. They'd lived well in France—in an old château with many servants and everything they needed, and they'd been a large, happy family. His mother had been a great beauty at the French court, but by then she'd lost interest in anything but her husband and growing family.

His grandfather had told him with great contempt that he looked like her, but it had been a strange sort of comfort. He could look in the mirror and see his mother's beautiful eyes, her high cheekbones and her full, mobile mouth. Most people thought he was uncommonly vain, and deservedly so. But in fact, there was no vanity in him at all. His devotion to mirrors was simply a chance to see his mother once more.

Wynche End was all he had left of her and his family. He'd never understood why his father had left England for good to live with his wife in shabby luxury on the Normandy coast. Once he met his grandfather all was made clear.

He hadn't understood politics at that point. All he knew was that he was being sent away to England for schooling, and that the rest of the family would soon follow to settle into Wynche End. It was astonishing to him—they had never traveled farther than Paris, but he went without argument, knowing they would soon follow.

But they didn't. Couldn't. They'd been slaughtered during the early uprising of the Terror, the château burned, every one of them murdered, and he'd been left in the merciless care of his grandfather, who hated everything about him, including the father who'd married against his will and left England for France.

The only thing he'd shared with his grandfather, apart from the bloodline, was a hatred of everything French. He couldn't change his name, but he could avoid anything that reminded him of that benighted country. His grandfather had unwittingly assisted—having his French clothes destroyed and replaced by good English cloth. Every bit of cruelty had been a blessing—when he'd beaten the French accent out of him it had only made him stronger and more English. Until no one knew he had any French blood in him.

The French had spilled it all.

He was being pathetic, he mocked himself. He was about to have a most enjoyable interlude, once he got rid of the annoying young lovers. He wondered how long it would take him. Annelise would put up an impressive defense, he was counting on it. But he knew women far too well not to recognize her vulnerabilities. Not that she was like any other woman he'd known so far, which was part of her appeal. Or rather, all of her appeal, he told himself. It was the sheer novelty of an overtall, overdignified old maid that fascinated him.

Too bad Crosby wasn't around to place a wager on it. He could always place a bet with himself. If he set his mind to it he had little doubt he could have her in his bed by nightfall. But he didn't want to rush it. The hunt was half the pleasure. The feint and attack, the thrust and retreat. And he was becoming aroused just thinking about it.

He doubted he would be able to lull her into a false security—she had too much good sense for that. But she was also ridiculously innocent for a woman almost thirty, and when he feigned disinterest her low opinion of her attractions surely tempted her to believe it.

Foolish dragon. He hoped he wouldn't hurt her. He didn't particularly want to break her heart. Not that he believed in broken hearts, except in those too weak and too sentimental to face the practicalities of life. His dragon was made of sterner stuff than that.

No, she wouldn't fancy herself in love, despite his teasing, and she wouldn't pine after him like a schoolgirl. She was much too practical. But he had little doubt he could make her experience a pleasure she had never even imagined, and he was anticipating it with great delight. When he left her she would have learned a great deal, and he suspected the Honorable Miss Kempton could become a dedicated student.

In the meantime he was going to have to see about the classroom. There were no more beds in the house, and he didn't fancy deflowering her where Hetty and William had been. Harry Browne and his wife could be counted on to come up with something. He'd put her in his great-aunt's room—it was still in reasonable condition despite the sun-shredded curtains. He could never understand how the sun could do that much damage in such a dark, rainy country. But then, it had taken decades to rot through the silk.

He strolled down the long hallways to the kitchen. The bellpulls no longer worked, and the Brownes had more than enough to do without having to run to him for orders. They were friends as well as employees, and he would often end up in Bessie's kitchen, stealing trifles and teasing her until she turned bright pink. The drawback to that was that Bessie Browne knew him far too well, and she would disapprove of the plans he had for Miss Kempton. And she wouldn't hesitate to tell him so.

He didn't particularly mind. He knew he was a consummate bastard and hearing someone who loved him like a mother tell him so was oddly comforting. She knew what he was and she still cared about his worthless soul.

Miss Kempton's lectures were just as entertaining. He'd give her full rein—she could feel free to scourge him for the heartless, selfish, dishonorable rogue that he was. She could do it as she lay beneath him, between gasps of pleasure.

He did a swift turnaround. He had to stop thinking about Annelise, or he was going to be in no condition to be facing anyone. He was as randy as a schoolboy with his first taste of sex. And he found himself smiling, really smiling, for the first time in what seemed like years.

Hetty responded surprisingly well to Annelise's lecture on proper behavior. She was still a bit dazzled by her experience, and Annelise couldn't help but feel an unbecoming jealousy. Not that she had any interest in the young Mr. Dickinson. But Hetty had clearly moved well beyond Annelise in experience, and there was no doubt it had been absolutely splendid.

Which was a surprise. Neither of her sisters had expressed much enthusiasm for the marriage bed, and her acquaintance did not generally include the sort of women who did. She understood the mechanics, at least to some extent, having been raised around stock animals, but as far as she could tell, when it came to humans the act was for the male's pleasure and the female's fertility. Hetty seemed more like a newly mounted she-cat than a proper young woman—she was practically purring.

But Annelise helped her wash and dress with brisk efficiency, ignoring the bloody smear on the sheets that had once been Hetty's virginity. She would have killed for a basin of hot water herself, but by now the mud was caked and dry, and Hetty needed the water more than she did. Once Hetty left, perhaps she could talk someone into bringing her at least an ewer of lukewarm water.

There was no sign of Christian as they made their way downstairs. The rain had stopped, though by now it was midday, late to start out on a long journey. William looked exhausted, as well he should, the wicked boy, and far too pleased with himself, and Hetty was stifling a yawn. Annelise could content herself with the assurance that they were both much too exhausted to get into trouble in the confining carriage that would take them to her brother-in-law's vicarage up north.

She had a lingering hope that the carriage might prove larger than Christian had said, in which case she would have forced herself between the two of them and endured another endless trip. But he hadn't exaggerated—there was barely enough room for the two of them and the driver.

Not to mention the hamper of food, the hot bricks and the blankets. By the time she had the two of them bundled into the small interior of the carriage there was scarcely room for them to breathe. There was no question but that she was well and truly trapped here for the time being.

And no question that any fears she had about her own chastity were entirely wishful thinking. "Are you certain you don't mind us abandoning you?" Will asked anxiously, ever the gentleman. Hetty had settled comfortably into the carriage and seemed to have no qualms about deserting her chaperon, the ungrateful wretch.

"Of course not," Annelise lied through her teeth. "It's not as if I am a young woman of marriageable age."

"True," said William, totally without tact. "And no one is likely to even imagine a man like Christian Montcalm would offer you any importunities. The very idea is absurd."

"Absurd," Annelise echoed unhappily.

"I'm sure your sister will send transport for you as soon as we reach there. I wouldn't recommend you returning to Chipple House—Josiah Chipple is not a man to be crossed. We would welcome you in Kent once we return."

Hetty looked so displeased at this option that Annelise almost laughed. "Thank you, William, but I'll be returning to stay with my godmother, Lady Prentice. I'm certain we can arrange to get my things from Chipple House without too much difficulty."

"Perhaps," Hetty spoke up. "My father has a vindictive nature. Anything I didn't want to lose I took with me."

"You didn't look particularly well packed," Annelise pointed out.

"Yes, but I have my jewels. They're extraordinarily fine—if we have any difficulties they should keep us quite nicely."

"We're not living off your money!" William said, scandalized.

"Of course we are, if we have no other choice," Hetty shot back, but her words were lost as the driver snapped his whip, bringing the horses to attention, and the goodbyes were swallowed up in a spray of mud as they drove off, leaving Annelise standing very still, fresh mud on her already bedraggled face, thinking of the false pearls that were supposed to be her eventual redemption.

You're beyond redemption, old girl, she told herself, wiping some of the mud from her face and limping back inside. She supposed she ought to go out and look for her lost shoe while the sun still shone, but she couldn't bring herself to care. It was only going to be a few days, and with luck she wouldn't even see her reluctant host the entire time. She was no longer an entertainment, thank God, but a burden, and the sooner he got rid of her the happier he'd be. She was certain of it.

In the hours she'd already been at Wynche End she had yet to see a servant, but a plump, motherly woman was waiting for her in the hallway, a concerned expression on her face. "I'm Mrs. Browne, the housekeeper, Miss Kempton," she said, curtsying deeply. An absurd act, given Annelise's mud-worn appearance, but nice nonetheless. "I'll show you to your room if you'd like."

"I would like that very much."

"Master Christian has gone out, and I'm not certain when he's expected home, but he said you shouldn't expect to see much of him during your stay." Mrs. Browne sounded a bit doubtful.

"Yes," Annelise said, telling herself that the sinking

feeling in her stomach was a flood of relief sweeping over her, and not disappointment. It was, it truly was.

"I'll be happy to bring a tray to your room if you'd like. The dining room is a bit...well, Master Christian usually eats in the library, but I could have my husband see if he could do something about the ceiling..."

"A tray in my room would be lovely," she said. Right now, she added mentally. She couldn't remember the last time she ate.

But blessed Mrs. Browne was ahead of her. "I've already brought up a tray of cold chicken, cheese and apples just to tide you over until dinner. If there's anything else you want you have only to ask. Except I'm sorry to say none of the bellpulls are working. You'll need to come find me, but I'll do my best to check at regular intervals in case you need something. It's just Browne and me and young Jeremy, the stable lad, so I'm afraid you won't be as comfortable as I might have liked."

"I'm certain I'll be fine." Food was coming, but there went her hope of at least a partial bath if they were that short-staffed. It had started to rain again—maybe she'd just strip off her clothes and go outside. Then again, maybe not.

But she'd underestimated the divine Mrs. Browne. Not only was a tray of food waiting for her in the huge, shabby bedroom, but a full tub of steaming water. Annelise almost hugged her.

"I gather you didn't bring much in the way of clothing, so I was bold enough to see what was on hand and came up with a few serviceable pieces belonging to

Master Christian's great-aunt. She was a tall woman, and though the clothes are out of date I think they should fit. At least you'll be dry and comfortable."

"You are a saint, Mrs. Browne."

Mrs. Browne's plump face beamed. "We're glad to have you here, miss. We don't often get company. And rest assured you'll be treated with nothing but respect from everyone in this house," she added darkly.

If anyone could make Christian behave it would be the sturdy Mrs. Browne. "I don't think that's going to be a problem," Annelise said, pleased at how calm she sounded.

But Mrs. Browne looked doubtful. "Let's hope not," she said. "Dinner's usually at eight. I'll check on you in a few hours and see if you want something sooner, but in the meantime I thought you'd probably like a rest. Just leave your clothes and I'll see what I can do to salvage them."

"I'd be most grateful." That was almost a lie. If she never had to wear the shapeless brown wool dress again it would be too soon, but then she couldn't very well leave this place in someone else's clothing. She could only hope that Christian's aunt shared her sober tastes.

Once Mrs. Browne closed the door Annelise kicked off her only shoe and attacked the meal left for her. She hadn't realized quite how hungry she was, and she finished everything, including the pleasant glass of canary wine. It surprised her that it wasn't a French wine—she had some vague knowledge that part of Christian's ancestry was French, and she would have thought he preferred that country's vintage. Like all good Englishwomen she considered the French essentially despicable, particularly when it came to the recent revolution, but they did manage to produce some very fine wines.

But the canary was good enough.

She began stripping off her clothes, wincing as the caked mud fell on the worn carpet beneath her feet. She didn't want to make more work for the beleaguered Mrs. Browne, but she could hardly sweep it up herself. In the end she stripped off everything, down to her chemise, and approached the still-steaming tub.

It smelled of roses, a faint, soothing scent, and there were towels nearby that carried the same pleasing odor. What Mrs. Browne was capable of doing in such a wreckage she did very well indeed.

At the last minute she stripped off the chemise, as well, stepping into the tub stark naked, not wanting anything to get in the way of that warm, wonderful water. It wasn't as if anyone was around, and she'd always preferred bathing in the nude. In the more crowded households, with maids likely to walk in and out with little warning, she always bathed in her chemise, but right now it was a small, wicked indulgence she had every intention of taking.

She set her glasses down on the floor beside the tub, then ducked her head under the water. It felt so blissful she almost didn't want to come up for air. The soap carried the same rose scent, and she scrubbed every part of her body, from her scalp to her toes, then stood up and rinsed with the jug of fresh warm water on the table beside the tub. She stepped out of the tub, directly onto her spectacles, feeling them crush beneath her foot.

She let out a yelp of pain, barely managing to keep her balance as she hopped over to the table and wrapped one of the towels around her. Her wet hair was streaming down her back, her foot was bleeding from the broken glass, and her temporary sense of well-being evaporated. She collapsed in a chair, grabbing another towel to wrap around her foot to soak up the blood, using her most colorful curses under her breath.

"Bloody damn rutting pig cock," she muttered. The last one she seldom used, but in these circumstances it was called for. What was she going to do without her spectacles? What was she going to do with a lacerated foot?

Fortunately the cut wasn't as bad or as deep as she feared. Her discarded chemise was free from mud, and the cotton was old and worn, quite easy to tear a strip off the bottom without destroying it completely. She wrapped her foot up, quite handily, and then breathed a sigh of relief. One crisis averted. She'd worry about being able to see later.

She hobbled over to the bed and the clothes laid out for her inspection. The undergarments were wonderful—the softest silk, the finest lace, beautiful bits of needlework such as she had never worn. The dressing gown was of white lawn, of the sort that used to be known as a powdering gown, Annelise thought. Back when the older generation would powder their hair, they would wear these to protect their clothing.

She dressed quickly, wrapping the lacy gown around

her, and climbed up onto the bed. It was freshly made up, the velvet coverlet worn in some places, and she knew if she lay down with her hair still wet it would dry in ridiculous curls. If she got up to search, she could probably find a comb or brush of some sort, and she could braid her hair into a tight knot of submission, but her foot was throbbing, her energy had fled, and in the end it didn't matter. No one would see her but Mrs. Browne, and she could always wet her hair again and set it to rights.

She leaned back against the pillows, staring up at the ceiling above her. And let out a gasp.

Josiah Chipple wasn't the only person who enjoyed mythology. The ceiling above the bed was painted with a charming fresco in the Italianate style, and the painting itself was particularly unfortunate.

At first she thought it might portray the rape of the Sabine women, but as she focused on the details the reality was even worse. It depicted Persephone, drawn down to the dark and dangerous depths of hell, lured by Pluto, the god of Hell, who was both terrifying and beautiful. And looked far too much like Christian Montcalm.

Persephone herself bore an uncomfortable resemblance to Annelise herself. Her long, milky limbs were well exposed by the filmy piece of cloth she was wearing, and she was much more slender than the style of painting usually called for. It took Annelise only a moment to realize that the two main characters of the ceiling fresco must have been patterned after the previous occupants of the room. The Persephone could only be

Christian's overtall aunt, and the demonic Pluto could only be his ancestor, as well.

She rolled over on her stomach and moaned. If only her long-distance vision had suffered—the ceiling would then be merely a blur. But in truth she only needed her spectacles for minute details—she simply wore them because they suited her.

She could ask for another room, but wouldn't put that much work on the good Mrs. Browne. Perhaps later she could express her discomfort. While the god of hell was more decently covered, she had a very strong suspicion that he was in the same state of Priapus, and having such a creature leering down at her while she tried to sleep was unbearable.

Except that she would bear it. And he wasn't exactly leering. And not at her. He was staring at the woman in his arms with a look of inexplicable longing, despite the fact that he clearly had her captive. She'd never stopped to think about the Greek god's thoughts in the matter, sympathizing more with Persephone's plight and her mother's loss than the villain's desires. But it was more than clear, in this painting at least, that Persephone's surrender was of all-consuming importance to the dark god.

If worst came to worst she could have someone help her drag the bed from under the indecent ceiling fresco. If she could stand up to Christian Montcalm in the flesh, she was hardly going to let a hundred-year-old painting disturb her.

At least, not while she was awake.

19

The problem with falling asleep at odd hours, Annelise thought, was that you woke at odd hours. Ever since she'd set off on this ridiculous rescue mission her sleep had been fitful and uncomfortable, and it was no wonder she managed to drift off in the strangest of circumstances, including sitting right in front of her direst enemy.

She woke briefly when Mrs. Browne came to check on her and bring her a tray of food. She clucked over the cut foot and rebandaged it for her, had the men remove the tub and generally fussed around her in the most delightfully maternal way. Annelise had never known a mother, and her older sister, Eugenia, was somewhat lacking a nurturing streak, at least where her siblings were concerned. Wrapped in comfort and a full stomach, she fell back into a deep sleep only to wake up at some godless hour, and lie staring at the dying embers of the fire.

She lay there wondering what time it was, when, as if in answer to her unspoken question, a clock chimed somewhere in the bowels of the house. Three times. At least something in this place was still in decent order.

The main disadvantage to lying in bed, sleepless, is that all one's worries came flooding back to haunt one, and were magnified a thousand times. At three o'clock in the morning Josiah Chipple was a deranged murderer, Hetty and William certain to die in a carriage crash, and Christian Montcalm was the devil incarnate.

It was the damned ceiling fresco, she thought, rolling over and punching the pillow. Even in the darkness she knew it—she didn't have to see it to remember each lascivious detail. As long as Christian's ancestor looked down at her in the darkness it was no wonder she couldn't sleep.

When the clock struck four she gave up, lighting the candle beside her bed, and started looking for something, anything to read.

Mrs. Browne had cleaned and dusted the room well, but its state of disrepair was impossible to disguise. If she had needle and thread she could mend some of the tears in the cushions, but there was nothing, and if she didn't find something to occupy her mind she'd go mad with worry.

The house was silent, and she knew where there were books, hundreds of them. She could find her way there quite easily, snatch one or two, and be safely back in her bed before anyone in this sleeping house realized it. She had no idea where Christian's bedroom lay, and she didn't wish to. Besides which, he'd probably drunk himself to sleep, the profligate wretch. Just a short little foray through the silent house and she'd be set.

She stepped into the hallway, the candle flame doing

precious little to pierce the inky darkness. Her foot caused her little trouble—just a slight tenderness protected by Mrs. Browne's more efficient bandage, and she only limped slightly as she made her way down the broad oak stairs.

The library was to her left, easy enough to find, and though the floors were cold beneath her feet, she moved slowly, afraid she'd bump into something unexpected.

There was still just the trace of a fire burning in the fireplace, adding a touch of light that was needed. She went first to the shelves on that side of the room, lifting her candle high, squinting in the darkness at the titles.

"The novels are on the other side of the fireplace." His voice came out of the darkness, and she let out a little shriek, dropping the candle, plunging the room into darkness. She froze, terrified that he was somewhere around her like a shapeless monster, about to pounce, her imagination going wild, when she saw his shadow move in front of her, and a moment later he'd lit a candle from the dying fire.

He didn't even glance at her—simply turned around and began to light the tapers in an elaborate candelabrum, bringing too much light into the room, illuminating him far too clearly. His hair was loose—much longer than she'd realized, and he wore nothing but breeches and a white shirt that was unfastened at lacy cuffs and collar. And halfway down his chest. He looked rumpled and faintly grumpy—as if he'd been roused from sleep.

"To what do I owe the honor of this midnight visit, dragon?" he inquired mildly enough.

"I would think it would be obvious enough," she replied nervously. "I was looking for something to read."

"You came to the right place. You also woke me up and I always have trouble falling back asleep. You'll have to entertain me." He dropped into a chair with languid grace, looking up at her out of his extraordinary eyes. The eyes of a devil.

Annelise jumped. "Certainly not!"

"You have a very suspicious mind, Miss Kempton. I meant conversation, nothing more. Clearly you're having trouble sleeping, as well. So sit down and tell me what you think of my decrepit gothic manse."

She was torn. On the one hand, she wanted to bolt for the stairs, secure in the belief that he'd make no effort to stop her. On the other hand, his very lack of interest ensured her safety. She hesitated.

He sighed, as if he found the whole thing very tiresome. "Miss Kempton, I promised on my honor that I will manage to behave myself. I'd hardly take advantage of a defenseless young woman under my own roof."

"Of course you would," she said, moving toward the chair. "But since I'm not a defenseless young woman I have little doubt that I'm safe."

He smiled. It was an unnerving smile, as if he found her amusing. He didn't bother to contradict her, the swine. "Even so," he said. "You're still safe. Why are you limping?"

"I cut my foot."

He frowned. "Was something left lying about? That's unlike Mrs. Browne, but—"

"It was my spectacles," she said, sinking into the chair. The same one she'd fallen asleep in before, but this time sleep was far too elusive.

"Ah, I wondered what had happened to them." Apart from curiosity he seemed unmoved. She was marginally prettier without her spectacles—her gray eyes were her best feature. But he seemed uninclined to tell her so. "How do you manage to see?"

She didn't even consider not lying. He would know far too well what she was lying beneath in that grand bedroom, and she wouldn't give him that satisfaction. Unless, of course, she was attaching far too much importance to herself, and he wasn't even vaguely interested in where she slept. "I can manage a few feet in front of me," she said. "After that everything is a blur."

Now, why did she think he didn't believe her? "Pity," he murmured. "Piquet?"

"I'm not playing cards with you. And what are you doing down here anyway? Shouldn't you be in bed?"

"Ah, but someone else is already sleeping in my bed," he replied, shuffling the cards as he disregarded her protest. "And for some reason I doubted you'd feel like sharing."

"I'm in your bed?" Annelise shrieked.

"Exactly where you belong." His smile was devilish. "When I sent Hetty and her champion off I told you I didn't have the beds for you all. The rest are mouse-eaten and mildewed—Harry dragged them outside to burn them."

"I can't sleep in your bed—it's…it's indecent!"

"Not without me. Don't worry—the sheets are clean."

"But what about the bed where Hetty and William… that is…"

"Where they what? You never struck me as someone who'd shy away from plain speaking. What did they do in that bed?" His voice was lazy.

"Stop goading me, or I won't play cards with you," she said.

"Blackmail," he said. "It always works. And their mattress went the way of the bonfire too. You're sleeping on the second best—Bessie did some quick work to make it usable, but the rest were beyond her talents."

"That's a relief at least."

"You mean you feel better lying in my bed than Hetty's? I'm charmed!"

"Be quiet and deal."

"I should warn you," Christian murmured. "I'm very lucky at cards, and I intend to win."

"Why would you care? It's not as if we're wagering any money on the outcome. I have none."

"True enough. But playing cards without wagering is a waste of time and no fun at all. There are things to wager besides money—you suggest the stakes."

She didn't hesitate. "If I win you send your man as far as he needs to go to hire a carriage for me. I don't care if it's all the way to Bath."

"Agreed, though I rather hate to put a lame horse on the road. As for what I want…" He let his voice trail off as his eyes swept over her.

"Don't even think it."

"Now, how can I help what I think?" he replied. "What is that thing you're wearing, by the way? It's surprisingly…diaphanous."

"Behave yourself. It belonged to your esteemed aunt."

"And looking at you in it makes me feel positively incestuous." He dealt the cards with swift, casual grace, the lace on his unfastened sleeves dripping down over the cards. Making it far too easy for him to cheat.

"Why don't you roll up your sleeves," she said. "I'd prefer to get a clear look at your hands."

He held them out. They were a gentlemanly white, long fingered and elegant. Hands not suited for hard labor. Hands suited for playing cards and drinking wine and touching a woman….

"They're very graceful, aren't they?" he said with pride, admiring them. "I've been told my hands and my eyes are particularly pleasing. Though there are other parts of my anatomy that are equally gifted…."

"Stop it! Do you accept my wager?"

"Of course, my pet. And if I win, I want a kiss. No more, no less."

"No."

"But yes," he said, giving her his devilish smile. "I think my terms are very reasonable. I could have asked for far more, and instead I'm content with one little kiss from the lady. What do you have to lose?"

He was far too amused by all this. "I thought you made it clear that you no longer had any use for me."

"Now, what gave you that impression?"

"Perhaps the fact that you abducted my charge."

"Such provincial thinking, dragon. I'm perfectly capable of juggling two women or even three."

"You promised you wouldn't touch me."

"And I won't. Unless I win the hand."

She stared at him, full of mute frustration. She told herself she had nothing to worry about. He was teasing her, simply because he could. She was the best entertainment the place could offer, and annoying her clearly amused him. Not that he'd mind kissing her—he seemed to find a level of enjoyment in it. But his main goal was to irritate her, which kept her relatively safe. And the chance that she might win, and escape this uncomfortable situation sooner, made it worth the risk.

Because she didn't really want him to kiss her. Did she?

"Done," she said. "Deal the cards. And roll up your sleeves."

"You think I'd cheat?"

"Without question."

He laughed. "My love, if you were a man I'd have to kill you for that."

"But I'm not. And I don't trust you."

"Very wise," he said, rolling his sleeves up. Not necessarily the best idea—his forearms were strong, formidably attractive. She seldom saw men's arms beyond the lace cuffs, any more than men saw women's legs above their ankles. It made things uncomfortably intimate.

He scooped up the cards and dealt them again, still too quickly for her peace of mind. The first hand went well, with Annelise winning by a few points. The second hand went to him, overwhelmingly so, and she was feeling less and less secure.

"Best two out of three?" he suggested.

She had been an idiot to agree to this in the first place. Her father had taught her to play cards as well as swear, but she was in the presence of a master. She realized that the first win he'd simply been toying with her.

The sooner she got away from him the better. "Agreed," she said, wondering if she could figure out how to cheat. He'd never suspect it of her, and dishonorable as it was, fudging the cards might prove her only chance.

But even if she were an accomplished cheat she would have gotten nowhere. Despite his lazy attitude his eyes were alarmingly intent, and he watched every move, every expression with the attention of an avid gambler, not a lustful lover. At least she could calm herself with that notion. He didn't want to win so he could kiss her, he wanted to win for the sake of winning alone. He'd only picked the prize to embarrass her.

She'd been embarrassed before in her life and survived—she'd survive this, she thought as she let her losing cards drop onto the table.

"Best three out of five?" she suggested helplessly.

"I don't think so. Time to pay your debts."

She wasn't going to argue, or plead. She had too much dignity for that. She rose, feeling like a French aristocrat about to face the guillotine. She almost said as much, but something stopped her. Blind instinct, or some hidden memory or whispered gossip, but she kept silent, her back straight, waiting for him.

He rose, strolling around the card table with casual grace. "You needn't look so martyred, dragon," he whispered. "It's not going to hurt."

"I believe it's a dragon's victims who tend to be the martyrs," she pointed out, trying to stand her ground.

He came up to her, far too close, and once again she was conscious of his height. No one ever made her feel small, helpless, but if anyone had that effect on her it would be Montcalm. There was no question that next to his impressive height she actually felt delicate. There was something ridiculously protective about his sheer size. And she had to stop thinking things like that just as he was about to kiss her.

She reached behind his head, caught his long hair in her hand, and offered her cheek to him, closing her eyes.

He laughed. "I don't think so, my love." And he swept her into his arms, pulling her tight against his strong body, and put his hungry mouth on hers.

He tasted like wine and hot sweet sin. She let go of his hair, needing to hold on to something more solid, and his body was the only thing in reach. She clutched his shoulders, just for support, and let him kiss her, trying to remain very still.

He lifted his head and looked down at her, and she had no choice but to look up into his laughing eyes. "We'd already gotten to lesson two, dragon. You can do better than that." And this time she let him press her mouth open as his hands cupped her face, holding her in place as he slowly, leisurely kissed her, a lazy seduction that left her heart pounding, her pulses racing, her stomach knotting in inexplicable longing.

When he drew back this time there was a self-satisfied expression on his face that she wanted to slap off. She yanked herself out of his arms. "We wagered one kiss," she said. "That was two."

"Was it?" he said innocently. "Then I'd better give it back." And before she realized what he was doing he'd pulled her back against him, into a tight embrace, and kissed her again.

She wasn't expecting it, wasn't prepared for it. This was no lazy seduction, no charming flirtation. This was carnal, deep and shattering, and before she realized it he'd pushed her up against the wall, holding her there as he kissed her, and the feeling was so powerful she felt as if she might explode. His hand covered her breast, barely restrained by the antique chemise, and she could feel her nipples tighten against him, feel a wash of something totally foreign and good sweep over her body, until she was both hot and cold, trembling, wanting to weep, wanting to slap him, wanting to rip the white lace from her body and place his mouth where his hand was.

When he drew back this time he was breathless, and his usually laughing eyes were dark and troubled. "That was more dangerous than I'd expected, dragon."

She couldn't catch her breath. She wasn't going to cry in front of him—indeed, what reason did she have to cry? It was nothing more than a kiss. Or three kisses, to be exact.

She shoved him back hard as anger swept over her. "You bastard," she said, furious.

The confused expression in his eyes had already vanished, and he was laughing at her again. "Such language, my pet," he said. "No need to get overset by a simple kiss or two. It means nothing."

It was bad enough already. That mild dismissal was the last straw. If she had shoes she would have kicked him. As it was, she slapped him so hard that it made her hand numb, whipping his head to one side, and all laughter was gone from his face. Her violent reaction startled her and she wondered whether he'd hurt her in retaliation.

"I suppose I deserved that," he said after a moment. "But I wouldn't make a habit of it if I were you. Some men hit back."

She tried to say something arch and dismissing. She even had the words in her head, something along the lines of a mocking, "They're not gentlemen like you," but her voice, her resolve failed her. She opened her mouth to speak, shut it again, and then ran like a coward, knowing ridiculous tears were beginning to spill over. It wasn't until she reached the bedroom and slammed the door behind her that she remembered she'd left the books behind.

She looked at the bed. His bed. And pulling the heavy covers from it, she dragged them over to the fire and wrapped them around herself, lying down on the threadbare rug, away from the disturbing painting that loomed over the bed, to stare, hollow-eyed, into the fire.

* * *

Hell and damnation, Christian thought, staring after her. He didn't think dragons could cry. It was a good thing she'd run—if he'd actually seen the tears he would have had to comfort her, and if he'd comforted her he would have kissed her, and this time there would be no stopping him.

She really had the most astonishingly arousing effect on him. He couldn't remember having that powerful a reaction to a simple kiss before. Well, in truth there'd been nothing simple about the kisses or the…feelings lurking beneath. He'd wanted to shock her.

He'd managed to shock himself.

He really ought to get rid of her. She was more complicated than a simple game to amuse him while he was rusticating. She was dangerous, and he was a man who knew to avoid unnecessary peril.

She had no idea how lovely she was in that flowing lace that had been delightfully transparent. Her long mane of thick, wavy hair was a complete surprise—it was a crime to keep such lustrous beauty tied back in a tight little knot. And while some sentimental part of him missed her spectacles, he could bless the fact that they were no longer able to obscure her huge gray eyes. Or the emotions that stormed through them that she tried so hard to hide.

No, she was a greater danger than he'd realized. In the end, she'd won her wager after all. In the morning he'd have Harry send Jeremy the stable lad out to hire a decent carriage for her, and once she was safely gone he could concentrate on Wynche End. He still had a sizable amount of money from Chipple's payoff, and if he was careful it could go quite a ways toward restoring this place a bit. Even make it self-supporting if he managed to get the place working again. The breeding stables had once been very fine, in the time of his great-uncle, and the surrounding land, currently untended, had always been fertile. All it required was a concentrated effort.

He didn't expect any trouble from Josiah Chipple. He'd be too busy chasing down his daughter, trying to stop her marriage, blustering and yelling. Wynche End was too far away for him to bother and Christian planned to keep that nice safe distance. At least until the old man's wrath had cooled.

In the meantime, he was perfectly fine here. As soon as he got rid of the Honorable, far too distracting, Miss Kempton.

Josiah Chipple was not a happy man. He'd lost an entire cargo—once an uprising began and blood had been spilled it was a waste trying to save anything for future profit. Better to simply obliterate the rest of the holding into the sea than deal with the kind of problems restive slaves could provide. He hired the right kind of men who kept them chained, passive and so beaten down that they'd cause no trouble for any prospective buyer. But once they began to fight back there was no salvaging it.

He'd lost half his crew, including his captain, a vicious brute who'd served him well and shared his profits for the last twenty years. He'd have a hard time replacing him, and in the meantime one less ship was running, one less cargo was being harvested and delivered. He'd arrived back at Chipple House in a foul mood, only to be greeted with the news that his daughter had run off with the man who'd dared to blackmail him.

If it hadn't been for business, Christian Montcalm would have been dealt with promptly. But things hadn't been going Chipple's way, and the morning after he returned home he was ready for blood, any blood. It mattered not if it was related to him—his daughter had betrayed his wishes, and no punishment was harsh enough. He'd been foolish to think she was the only way to fulfill his dreams. He was still a young man, just this side of fifty. He was wealthy and could marry again, perhaps a titled widow who was still fertile enough to give him sons. He had no more need for Hetty than he'd had for her mother once she'd proved unable to give him any more children.

First, he had to find where Christian Montcalm had taken his daughter. And discover where that snotty bitch Miss Kempton had gone, as well. Betrayal was on every side, and Josiah Chipple did not take well to betrayal.

He would use every means at his disposal to ensure his vengeance, and one of the most valuable was information. By the end of the day he knew more about Christian Montcalm and his forebears than the man did himself. The possibilities were endless. He only had to choose one and set it into play. And watch his revenge flower.

20

It was a gloomy, gray day, matching Annelise's mood. There was still no sign of her brown dress, and the only thing sedate enough in Christian's great-aunt's wardrobe was a forest-green riding habit. Even putting it on made her feel edgy, but it was either that, or a dress with far too low a décolletage, or the powdering gown, and the habit was the least of all the evils.

No shoes, of course, and the elegantly clocked silk stockings were slippery on the floor. At least the cut on her foot was healing. She bundled her hair into a tight knot at the back of her neck, pulled a chair close to the fire, and sat, determined not to move until she absolutely had to. She wasn't going to face Christian Montcalm again unless she was forced to.

When Mrs. Browne brought her a tray of food, she had taken one look at her expression and backed out quickly, with the muttered promise that she'd work on her dress. Annelise had nibbled on the cheese and bread, then ignored the rest. There had to be some way out of

Wynche End. And fast. She was far more susceptible than she'd ever realized.

The sound of horses' hooves drew her out of her gloom and she went to the window, peering out through the light mist, just in time to see Christian disappear down the overgrown drive on what looked to be a perfectly healthy horse. One that could have carried William while Annelise rode safely with Hetty. It was the final straw. She was going to find wherever Christian had hidden Chipple's heavy gun and shoot him. She was going to walk twenty miles in stocking feet just to get away from him. She was going to do just about anything to ensure she never had to be near that lying, rutting bastard again.

She found the kitchen with no difficulty, and stormed into the room to find Harry Browne sitting at the table, drinking a mug of tea, and Bessie busy making bread. Sensing that what was about to follow such an entrance was women's talk, Harry excused himself and left as quickly as he could.

"Your husband's a wise man," Annelise said in a tight voice, taking the seat he'd vacated.

Mrs. Browne laughed. "You'd scare the bejesus out of the devil himself, miss," she said. "Though I'm thinking it's not my Harry you're wanting to kill."

"You'd be right. Where has Mr. Montcalm disappeared to, and where did he find that horse?"

"He told you he had no horses?" Mrs. Browne asked incredulously. "Well, I shouldn't be surprised—he'll do just about anything to get his way. You shouldn't let him bother you, miss."

"I'm not going to let him bother me. I'm just not going to let him keep me here. What I need are a pair of boots or shoes that would fit me. I intend to walk and keep walking until I find some form of civilization where they'll help me."

Mrs. Browne looked hurt. "Now, miss, I'll help you if that's what you want. Master Christian led me to believe you wanted to be here."

"Master Christian is a bald-faced liar."

"He is, indeed," Bessie agreed in a comforting voice. "He needs someone to teach him a lesson."

"He's past being taught," Annelise said.

"There's another horse in the stable, as well, and I know Harry would saddle her for you…"

"I don't ride," Annelise interrupted. "Walking will do me just fine."

"It's more than three miles to the village, the roads are a sea of mud, and another storm is coming in. I'll talk to Master Christian, see to it that you have decent transportation…"

"He can go to hell."

"Aye, there are times when he's sure that's his only choice. The poor lad's had a rough time of it, and it's little wonder he is what he is. Not that it's any excuse, mind you."

Annelise wasn't going to ask. She had no interest in Christian Montcalm's "rough time" and nothing under the sun would induce her to respond to Mrs. Browne's careful hint to probe deeper.

And then she sighed. "Why has he had a rough time?" she asked wearily.

"Lost his entire family to those bloodthirsty Frenchies," she said. "Mother, father, brothers and a sister. Murdered in cold blood, while Master Christian was here visiting his grandfather. He's always blamed himself that he wasn't there with them. Not that he could have helped—he'd simply be dead, as well. But guilt is a funny thing."

"His family was killed during the Terror? But he's not French."

"Half-French," Mrs. Browne corrected. "But you won't find him admitting to it. He wiped every trace of that country out of his life, out of his voice and his clothes. With the help of his grandfather's beatings, I might add. He was left an orphan at the mercy of an evil old man, and he learned to survive as best he could. But he won't drink French wine, won't wear French clothes, pretends he doesn't understand the language. Pretends his poor lost family never even existed."

"And that gives him an excuse to lie? To use other people as he sees fit?"

"No," Bessie said. "But there's still a decent man inside worth saving. Harry and I wouldn't be here if we didn't believe it."

"Well, I'm not saving him," she said crossly. "And he wouldn't want me to."

"Of course not, miss," Bessie said, a little too quickly. "I wasn't even thinking such a thing. I just didn't want you to judge him too harshly for his selfish ways."

"All I want is to escape from his selfish ways," Annelise said flatly. "And I'll need my clothes and a pair of shoes to do so."

"I can see to it. Promise me one thing, miss. I'll find you a decent pair of shoes, I'll finish fixing your dress and I'll make sure Harry has transportation for you tomorrow morning. It might only be a farm cart, but he'll have that much or he'll hear from me."

"All right," she said, waiting to hear the rest.

"In the meantime there's a pair of riding boots in the scullery that might fit. Nothing fancy, of course, but at least they'd be something."

Annelise plastered her best smile on her face. "That would be lovely," she said in a dulcet tone.

Then came the Annelise's part of the bargain.

"And you'll wait until tomorrow?"

"Of course," she said without blinking. "I'll just go for a little walk. I need some fresh air."

Mrs. Browne looked at her doubtfully, but in truth there was nothing she could say. She could only watch as Annelise found the oversized boots, slipped her feet inside, and stepped out into the damp spring air.

It was time to face the harsh facts of life, Annelise thought. If she didn't want to stay here, at the mercy of Christian Montcalm and her own foolish fancies, then the alternative was to leave. Just because she hadn't ridden in five years didn't mean she didn't know how—she'd always been a natural horsewoman, and that innate talent didn't vanish from lack of use. She was wearing a riding habit, and apparently the Montcalm stables had another suitable horse. All she had to do was saddle and bridle it, no difficult task for her, and then ride away. So simple, and yet so complicated.

But hiding in her room didn't fix anything. As far as she knew Christian was still out for the afternoon, and while she was running the risk of meeting him in the stables when he returned, at least there'd be other people there. The stable lad, and maybe Harry Browne. He wouldn't dare do anything with an audience.

But there was no sign of anyone as she made her way through the old house. The afternoon sun slanted in the western windows, penetrating the gloom just a bit. If this were her house she'd rip away the tattered curtains, pull up the shredded rugs, wash the windows and toss all the broken furniture. The place could be made habitable, with a small army of servants to clean it and a thoughtful touch. Flowers from the overrun gardens would be a start.

But not for her. She skirted the flower beds with their riotous growth, resisting their beckoning colors as she made her way to the stables. She saw with approval that at least this outbuilding was in reasonable shape— no leaking roof, no broken windows to let in the damp spring weather. Her father had been the same— neglectful of his own dwelling while making sure that his horses were well tended to—but in this case Annelise couldn't object. People could fend for themselves. Horses needed proper care. She could overlook carelessness toward humans more easily than she could toward animals, which was a strangely irrational attitude. But one that held firm. The state of Christian Montcalm's stable was the first genuinely good thing she could say about him.

She walked into the outer building, but all the stalls were empty. It smelled of fresh hay and manure and all the lovely horse smells that she'd missed so much. It smelled like her childhood, when she had been happy, and she almost turned around and ran back into the house rather than face all the painful memories that had come flooding back. There wasn't a day when she didn't miss her father, his feckless charm, his casual affection, his boundless optimism in the face of total disaster. She never knew for certain whether the fall had been an accident or not. Her father was too good a horseman, even in his cups, to make the kind of mistake that sent him sailing over the hurdle ahead of his horse, to a broken neck that killed him instantly. But then, he wouldn't endanger a horse if he were bent on killing himself. He'd have taken one of the dueling pistols and put a gentlemanly end to himself.

Although he wouldn't have wanted his daughter to find him. He'd always been absurdly fond of Annelise, a fact that her sisters found annoying. She understood him, weaknesses and all, and loved him anyway. To her sisters he was simply a disappointment and an embarrassment.

There were times she was even glad he'd died the way he did. The last thing he would have remembered would be riding hell bent for that jump, his favorite gelding, Bartleby, beneath him, the wind rushing through his overlong, grizzled hair, the light of joy in his blood-shot eyes. When they'd found him he was smiling, his lifeless eyes staring upward into the sky.

She hadn't let them shoot Bartleby—it hadn't been his fault that his master had been thrown. There were times when she thought the horse grieved as much as she did. But there was no money left, the estate was entailed to a second cousin from America, and the horses had to be sold to pay off her father's massive debts. Even her own beloved mare, Gertie, had gone, the most wrenching blow of all. At least she could content herself with the fact that wherever Gertie ended up, she'd be loved and ridden, and if there'd been any way for Annelise to keep her she still wouldn't have ridden her.

All these memories were far too painful, but Annelise stiffened her shoulders, dismissing them from her mind, and walked forward. She couldn't afford to shirk from anything, no matter how difficult. The least she could do was face Christian's horses, see if she could even contemplate riding one.

Annelise instantly regretted her resolve, as Christian came through the door from the adjoining stable area, still dressed for riding. Bad timing all around, Annelise thought, but she wasn't going to run.

He didn't look particularly pleased to see her, which was a relief. Wasn't it? "What in the world are you doing here? And what's that you're wearing?"

"Good afternoon to you, too," she responded tartly. "It's a riding habit, a bit out of date but still perfectly serviceable. I believe it belonged to your great aunt. And what else would I be looking for in the stables but the horses?"

"You're afraid of horses."

"No, I'm not."

"You simply don't like them?"

"I love horses." She wasn't going to give him any more information than she could, a tiny bit of revenge that didn't go very far in assuaging her own sense of emptiness.

"You love horses, you're not afraid of them, but you don't know how to ride?"

"I never said that. I know how to ride. I choose not to."

He looked at her for a long moment. His hair was loose and wild from his ride, his high cheekbones flushed from the wind. He'd make some unsuspecting heiress a most attractive husband, she thought grimly. But he was not for her, and he seemed to have suddenly remembered that.

"And are you changing your mind?" he asked.

She might have asked the same of him, but she didn't. "I thought I would merely check out your stable and see whether there might be a suitable mount. The sooner I leave Wynche End the better for both of us."

"Agreed," he said coolly, and she didn't flinch. Her father would have been proud of her. "I intend to do some entertaining and your presence would be a bit difficult to explain."

"Indeed." Entertaining? He'd already found a new heiress, she surmised. She should have known—when there was no other female around he whiled away his time flirting with her, kissing her, teasing her. Give him an alternative and she was quickly forgotten. She'd always despised self-pity and here she was, falling prey to that very same emotion.

He was watching her closely, but she knew that her calm expression gave nothing away. "My neighbors have a couple of marriageable daughters," he continued in an affable tone. "Very pretty, the both of them, and the parents seem inclined to overlook my less than stellar reputation in return for the joining of our two estates. They wouldn't be too pleased to think I had a mistress in keeping."

"Mistress? Oh, for heaven's sake!" she snapped. "All they would have to do is see me to know how ridiculous that is."

"I think you underestimate the world's capacity for gossip and salacious thoughts," he murmured. "And I think you underestimate your ..." A sudden noise from the far room stopped him, before he could finish his sentence.

It was a horse, making a huge racket, whinnying with great urgency and kicking at the sides of the stall. "What the hell?" Christian said, turning.

The young stable boy, Jeremy, rushed through the door. "Something's wrong with the chestnut mare, sir. She's having some kind of fit."

"Don't be ridiculous—she's the sweetest tempered horse we have. Did she get into something? Eat something that's upset her stomach?"

"No, sir, I've been very careful. Once the two of you started talking she began kicking up a storm."

The horse let out a distant bugle of sound, and Annelise felt prickles rush over her body. It couldn't be. It was too unlikely, too wrong, too incomprehensible. One horse sounded much like another from that distance, through thick walls, and how could something like that happen, in all of England, that Gertie could...

"Excuse me," Christian said with ill grace, turning toward the door.

But Annelise was already ahead of him, practically pushing him out of the way, picking up her skirts and racing into the inner stable.

Jeremy tried to bar her way. "Miss, she might be dangerous," he said nervously, but she ignored him, staring straight at the horse making such a racket.

She was a rich chestnut color, with a blaze on her forehead that reached one eye, and two front stockings that were in evidence as she kicked at the door of the stall, trying to free herself.

"I don't believe it," Annelise breathed in a hushed tone. "My sweet girl."

Christian had come up behind her, and he laid a restraining hand on her shoulder, but for once his touch was barely noticeable. She shook it off and ran for the stall, opening the gate, ignoring the horrified protests of Jeremy and his master.

And then all was silent as Gertie lowered her head to rest against Annelise, at peace. She was crying, and she didn't care who saw her, as she stroked her mare's long neck, whispering love and reassurances that no one else could hear. Gertie pushed her nose against Annelise's shoulder, seeking comfort and memory and probably long-remembered treats.

She didn't know how long they stayed like that, in the stall, with Christian and Jeremy a safe distance away. Nothing mattered but that the one creature left on this earth who loved her unconditionally was suddenly there once more.

Gertie lifted her head, looking over at the two men. "Now that's more like Gertrude," Jeremy said. "I don't know what got into the creature. You shouldn't have ought to run in there, miss. Horses can be dangerous creatures when they're upset, and something must have upset her real bad…"

"Miss Kempton is just fine," Christian said. "It's her horse. Isn't it?"

Annelise stepped back, wiping the tears from her face surreptitiously. Where were her spectacles when she most needed them? "Long ago. When my father died they were all sold."

"Your father…he must have been Lord McArthur," Christian said.

"Yes."

"Wild man McArthur. You're a far cry from him."

She turned on Christian, suddenly furious, and left the stall, leaving Jeremy to finish calming the horse. "I am not," she said in a low, dangerous voice. "I don't care what nasty gossip you heard, but my father was a good man, a decent man."

"Who had a bit of trouble with gambling and drink. Who died and left his daughter homeless and penniless."

"Damn you," she said, forgetting where she was, forgetting everything but the pain his words brought back. She went for him, wanting to hit him, but he was prepared, and he caught her wrists before she could connect, and pulled her against his warm wool jacket so that she could cry while he held her. She didn't want to, she didn't want his comfort, but there didn't seem to be any choice in the matter. And as unlikely as it was, he did provide solace. The strength and warmth of his body reaching into hers, the arms that held her, the hands that stroked her hair and her back, the voice that murmured soft, comforting things. She stopped fighting it, at least for the moment, and simply cried.

And then Mrs. Browne was there, taking her from Christian into her warm, motherly embrace. It seemed for a moment as if Christian didn't want to let her go, but a moment later he released her, and Mrs. Browne guided her back into the main house, soft and comforting, smelling like cookies and lemon oil and all the safe things in life.

She took her to the kitchen, sat her down and gave her a cup of hot tea with honey and a plateful of ginger biscuits, and she clucked over her like a mother hen and patted her every now and then in a reassuring manner. Finally Annelise's tears stopped and she drank her tea, managing a watery smile.

"Are you feeling better now, dearie?"

"I've made a fool of myself," she said dismally.

"Now, now, sometimes we just have to cry. It's all very good to be strong all the time, but every now and then things just get to the point where there's nothing to do but weep. And then you dry your eyes, straighten your shoulders and get on with life. Don't you?"

"Yes," Annelise said wryly. Her shoulders were already straight, no longer slumped in defeat, and she wanted more ginger biscuits.

"I'm going to have a talk with Master Christian. His little games are all well and good, but he needs to have a care for other people. I don't know what he did to upset you, but I'm going to give him a piece of my mind...."

"It wasn't him. It was Gertie. My horse."

"I thought you didn't ride?" Mrs. Browne said blankly.

Annelise was so tired of explaining. She should have kept her mouth shut in the first place. "I used to ride," she said. "Before my father died."

"Ah, I see," the housekeeper said. "I think you need to go home."

"I do." Annelise wasn't going to cry again—there weren't any tears left. "But I don't have a home any more." She swallowed a hiccup. "Do you have any more biscuits?"

"All the ginger biscuits in the world for you, sweeting," Mrs. Browne said. "It will all work out in the end. It always does."

Annelise managed a smile. "If you say so," she said. Not believing it for a moment.

* * *

Annelise stared out at the rain as it lashed against the leaded glass windows. They needed fixing, like everything else in this old, decaying house, and the wind rattled against the casement like a hungry ghost. But there were no ghosts in Annelise's life—those whom she loved stayed dead once they died. She would have liked the chance to see her father again. Liked the chance to tell him she loved him. To tell him...

She was back in her serviceable brown dress and her plain cotton underthings. She still had only one of her shoes, though Mrs. Browne had cleaned it as best she could. Still Cinderella, except that she was already on her way back into the shadows.

A good thing too, she told herself with a sniff that was nowhere near the tears that had overwhelmed her earlier. She was a level-headed woman, and she knew better than to have airs above her station.

In fact, her station in life was far too tenuous. Her name, her pedigree, the Honorable Miss Annelise Kempton, guaranteed her a certain standing and privilege. Her impoverished state tore most of that away, leaving only her impeccable reputation to sustain her. And by now it was sorely tarnished.

She should have known the moment she set eyes on the beautiful Christian Montcalm that he would be her undoing. And the wretched, damnable part of it was that he hadn't undone anything about her. Except, perhaps, her resolve. And that wasn't enough to make it worthwhile.

Her elder sister Eugenia would lecture her, telling her she'd always thought too highly of herself. It wasn't true, though. She just thought she'd known who and what she was, who and what she wanted after almost thirty years of living in this body. All it had taken was the touch of Christian Montcalm's mouth to realize she knew nothing at all about herself.

She rose from the window seat to fetch the velvet bag carrying the false pearls, as false as her belief in her own power. In defiance she put them on, letting them rest against her chastely covered bosom. She moved back to the window seat to stare into the darkness. She had to leave, had to make some kind of plan, but her mind was blank. The thought of abandoning Gertie once more was unbearably painful. The thought of never seeing Christian Montcalm again was far, far worse. And the only thing she could sanely hope for.

She didn't hear him coming—his step was stealthy, like a cat or a sneak thief. And he didn't bother to knock on her door—he simply opened it and walked into her room as if he owned it. As he did, she supposed. But he didn't own her.

"Mrs. Browne said you didn't touch your dinner," he said abruptly. There were only a few candles lit in the room, and she couldn't see his face clearly. A small blessing, she reminded herself.

"I wasn't hungry," she said in a tight voice.

"And you're back to wearing your nun's robes. I must say I like you better in my great aunt's dishabille. Though the riding habit wasn't bad."

She ignored his jibe. "I need to leave here."

He hadn't closed the door behind him, a small reassurance, and the hall was better lit than her bedroom, silhouetting him. He seemed restless, uneasy, as he prowled around her room. "They haven't sent a carriage back for you yet," he said, pausing by the rumpled bed. Staring down at it.

"But we both know that if you wanted to you could find a carriage. It was a lie, wasn't it? I could have always left?"

"You needn't be so harsh. It was never impossible—nothing is, if you have the money and right now I'm quite awash with it. It was just very difficult, and would have necessitated having that wretched brat in my house for hours, perhaps even a day, longer. When it was a choice between my sanity and your reputation my sanity won. I'm a very selfish man."

In better times she could have raised an eyebrow, but right then she was too weary and defeated to bother.

"I need to leave here," she said again, her voice listless.

He frowned—she could see him by the light of her bedside candle. "There's a horse you know well, and I could send Harry with you for protection. You wouldn't even have to be in any rush to return her—she's livelier today than I've ever known her to be."

"Don't be ridiculous. I haven't the means nor the place to keep her. Besides, I've told you, I don't ride."

"But you did. When did you stop? On the day your father died?"

Even that couldn't goad her into anything more

than a numb response. Of course he'd know that. He was a devil—he knew everything he wanted to know about her. Knew just how vulnerable she was to him, despite her protests. Knew that more than anything she just wanted him to touch her, kiss her, take her. It didn't matter how much it hurt or how unpleasant it was; it didn't matter that it would leave her totally ruined and bereft with no future whatsoever. She still wanted it.

"Since the day my father died," she echoed.

He was still edgy. In another man she might have thought he was nervous, but Christian Montcalm wasn't prey to such petty emotions. Particularly around her.

"I've decided to be noble," he said abruptly.

His words were enough to startle Annelise out of her malaise. If he was thinking of being noble then he had every reason to be nervous—it would be a novel experience for him.

"Indeed?" she said, turning to face him.

But he wasn't looking at her—he was still prowling. "I'm going to let you go."

"Was there ever any doubt of it?"

"No," he said. "The only question was what shape you were going to be in when you left, and I've changed my mind. You get to leave here just as virginal as the day you arrived. Two or three more stolen kisses shouldn't make much difference, and you're such an upstanding, starchy dragon that no one would dare believe you capable of licentious romping."

"Licentious romping? I think not. But you already

swore to Will Dickinson that I was perfectly safe. Swore to me, as well, I believe."

He didn't even blink. "I lied," he said simply. "I do that, you know, when it suits me. I would have thought you'd realized that by now."

It was enough to rouse her. She swiveled around on the window seat, putting her stockinged feet on the floor. "What are you talking about?"

Somehow during his edgy perambulations he'd come dangerously close. She'd seen the wild animals at Astley's Circus, had been mesmerized by the beauty and inherent danger. She should have realized the resemblance sooner.

"I was going to ruin you, dragon," he said softly. "Quite thoroughly, quite deliciously. I had every intention of going well beyond lesson three until you were a bona fide expert. I was going to teach you everything I know and could think of, until there wasn't the tiniest bit of starch left in you." His voice was soft, regretful and still utterly beguiling.

"But why? For the sheer sport?" she demanded. "For a wager? Out of malice? Why would you want to ruin my life? Why would you be so cruel? What have I ever done to you?"

His smile was the definition of rueful. "Such a silly dragon. Malice, sport and cruelty had absolutely nothing to do with it. I wanted you. And when I want something I tend to take it, without considering the consequences."

His voice was detached, distant, almost as if he were

talking about another man. As indeed he seemed to be. The Christian Montcalm standing in her bedroom had little resemblance to the man who had once planned her seduction. Except that he was fully as beautiful.

She couldn't even begin to sort through the reactions that flooded her, wouldn't even consider why it felt so much like pain. Her voice was cool when she spoke. "I'm pleased to know you've seen the error of your ways," she said, as starchy as he'd ever accused her of being. "When can I expect transport out of here?"

"Browne should be able to come up with a decent carriage by tomorrow, and I'll have Mrs. Browne find one of the village girls to provide you company during the trip. I expect you'll pass my returning carriage on the way, but that is of little import. The most important thing is to get you out of my wicked clutches, is it not?"

"Yes," she said.

He stood there, unmoving, clearly at a loss. "You should eat something. I'll have Mrs. Browne send up another tray."

"I'm not hungry."

"Damn it, I don't care," he shot back, shoving his long hair away from his hollow, beautiful face. "You need to eat something."

"Damn it, I don't," she replied deliberately. "I don't have to do a blasted thing I don't want, and there's nothing you can do to make me."

She'd managed to surprise him, and a faint smile played around his mouth. "Such language, dragon!" he scolded. "Where did you learn that—in your father's stables?"

"Yes."

"There's always been something irresistible about a starchy virgin who curses like a stable hand," he murmured.

"But you are nobly resisting my siren lures anyway," she shot back. She recognized the faintly aggrieved note in her voice and should have bitten back the words, but with any luck at all he wouldn't notice the slip.

But then, she had no luck at all. He stared at her for a long moment, tilting his head to one side, and his smile widened, reaching his dark, unreadable eyes.

"Perhaps not," he said.

And he reached out for her.

21

She flinched, as if she expected him to hurt her, but Christian simply picked up the strand of false pearls she'd put around her neck, and she held very still. He thought he knew women—he'd spent more than his fair share of time with them, loved them, and he took great pleasure out of knowing what they wanted and giving it to them, especially when they didn't even know it themselves.

But the Honorable Miss Annelise Kempton was a mystery to him. A delicious, starchy, fire-breathing mystery, like a present waiting to be unwrapped, layer by layer, so that he could fully enjoy the secrets that would be revealed.

But he'd told himself no. She was simply a woman, when it came right down to it, no more, no less, and there were a great deal of interesting women in the world. Women with more beauty, more money, more experience. And it was hardly the challenge she presented—there were just as many women who didn't want anything to do with him, whom he could just as easily convince otherwise.

So why was he so fascinated by his dragon? Enamored? No, that was surely the wrong word—enamored suggested love had something to do with it, and that was one thing he was absolutely certain of. His feelings for Annelise Kempton had nothing to do with love, and everything to do with simple, uncomplicated lust.

So why was he letting her go?

Because she had cried in his arms? Because she'd been betrayed by everyone in her life, particularly the son-of-a-bitch drunken father who'd taken her pearls, her love, and then died a selfish death leaving her nothing, not even the horse she'd loved or the ability to ride? He knew that she had no brothers—presumably her father was the only man she had ever loved, and he'd betrayed her cruelly. It was little wonder she breathed fire to scare everyone away.

At least he'd known love, a lifetime ago. The love of his parents, so vast and encompassing it had surrounded him and his four siblings, keeping them safe, protected and unaware of the storm that was coming. His parents had loved each other deeply—he and his brothers and sisters had teased them about it, but it had only added to their enormous sense of safety and happiness. His warm family had been replaced by his monstrous grandfather, but at least he'd once known selfless love. He suspected that Annelise never had.

He looked at the pearls as they rested in his long fingers. He could see the nervous pulse beating in her slender neck, could sense the panicked flutter of her heart. She stood very still, frozen, and he wondered why she was so afraid of him.

"Why are you wearing these?" His voice was not much more than a whisper.

"To remind me."

"Of what?" A strange stillness had settled over him, as well, a waiting. The earth was shifting beneath him, and he had the hideous suspicion that his entire life was about to change if he didn't get out of there, now. Away from the unexpected, undeniable lure of the dowdy young woman in front of him.

"Of my father," she said, and her lower lip trembled slightly. She had delicious lips, and he wanted to still that tremor, but he didn't move.

"They're fake," he said.

"I know. I loved him without reservation, and he took everything from me, including the one thing of value my mother had given me. He killed himself in a drunken fall, not even caring what happened to the horse he was riding, not to mention what happened to his daughter. All he cared about was his own selfish desires and I'm wearing these to remind me that men are thieves and liars who eventually betray you."

Christian gave the strand one yank and they spilled onto the floor, rolling across the dusty wood planks. Pulling on them had brought her closer before they snapped, so close that he could feel her grief and panic, so close that he should have reassured her, kissed her on the forehead, and left her.

She looked down at the false pearls scattered across the floor. "They weren't even very good fakes," she observed in an empty voice. "If I'd looked closer I would have noticed they weren't properly tied. But then, I thought my father loved me."

"I can't imagine that he didn't—" *Move away,* his inner voice ordered him. *Step back from her.* She was a siren in sackcloth who was going to lead him to certain doom if he didn't run away. "But like most men, he couldn't resist what tempted him most. Not all men are drunkards."

"I don't care."

He slid his hand up her neck. There was a faint red mark where he'd pulled the pearls from her, and his fingers gently stroked it. He could feel the shiver that ran down her body, and it was almost his undoing. He knew that shiver, of fear and delight, and knew where it could lead.

He wanted to yank the dress off her, the ugly, shapeless thing that shielded her like armor. No, like a dragon's scales. He was the knight in armor, a slightly tarnished one. As for his dragon, he had the totally unnerving feeling that she'd swallowed a princess, and all it needed was his touch to release her.

He stroked the back of her neck lightly. She hadn't been able to subdue her hair properly ever since she'd arrived at Wynche End and a few stray curls were escaping from the tight bun she'd attempted. She had a row of buttons down her back, tiny ones, and he wondered how she managed without a maid to help her dress.

He decided to ask her.

She was standing still beneath his soft touch, like a nervous filly ready to be gentled. "I usually can avail myself of the services of one of the household maids when I make my visits. Otherwise I simply do it myself."

His fingers brushed the top button at the nape of her neck, and slipped it free. "That seems impossible."

"You said nothing is impossible if you have the money. Let me assure you that nothing is impossible if you have the will."

"And you are a very willful creature, aren't you?" he murmured, unfastening the second button. She made no sign that she knew what he was doing.

"My clothes are made with deliberate room, so that if necessary I can pull them on backward, fasten the buttons and then slip them around the right way, finishing with the last few."

He undid the third button. "Fascinating," he said breathlessly. "Quite ingenious."

She was looking up at him, and even in the shadows he could see her expression quite clearly. He'd never realized how much he liked tall women—ones who could meet his gaze with unflinching steadiness. But then, Annelise was the only one he'd met. And he was far too aware of how much he liked her.

Her reputation was already ruined by her stay at Wynche End, his conscience argued. What harm could be done? He was adept at making certain there were no unwanted children from any of his liaisons, either short or long term, and no one would have to know. They'd guess and gossip, but then, they would anyway. If her reputation was already in tatters then what was to stop him? His guilty conscience was no match for his need for her, which had grown to such a powerful level that he could barely restrain himself.

"You really do have the most deleterious effect on my resolve, Miss Kempton," he whispered, his fingers reaching the fourth button and stopping. "I keep telling myself no, and my body keeps telling me yes."

The saucy wench looked downward and a dark blush stained her cheeks. "Not quite Priapus," he said, deliberately goading her, "but getting that way."

It was enough to make her pull away from him, to harangue him in her acid tongue as he fully deserved. But she still didn't move.

He undid the fourth button. "I really find it quite mystifying," he said. He could feel her skin now beneath the slowly parting dress. She was cold, and he wanted to warm her.

She had an ounce of fight left. "I think you're making things far too complicated," she said, and another man wouldn't have heard the strain in her voice. "It's simply that you've never shown any restraint in your wicked life. If you didn't tell yourself no you'd quickly lose interest. But as long as you try to convince yourself that you shouldn't...shouldn't..." Her words trailed off as her cheeks reddened and the fifth button went.

"Shouldn't? Shouldn't what, dragon? Shouldn't touch you? Shouldn't want you?"

She was still fighting. "It's simply because you're denying yourself that it becomes irresistible. It's human nature, quite an ordinary reaction, and you're not the type of man to be controlled by ordinary impulses. The only reason you want me is because you told yourself you can't have me, and that's scarcely a reason at all."

He smiled then. His dragon was beginning to breathe fire, just a bit, the way he liked her. When she was woebegone and bedraggled he wanted to comfort her. When she was fighting back he wanted to…

"I came here to tell you I was letting you go. That I changed my mind about your total ruination and decided to leave you in peace."

"So you said. And I appreciate your generosity." Her voice was getting frostier, but her eyes were grieving. What a strange, enigmatic creature she was, he thought. And it was definitely going to be a case of damned if he did and damned if he didn't.

In truth, he was already twice damned, and he knew it. "Unfortunately I've changed my mind again," he said, unfastening the next button. The dress was loose enough that it was beginning to drop down a bit, exposing her pale, beautiful shoulders. "I think I'll ruin you after all."

She was very still, the only sign of life the nervous flutter of her heart against the pale skin above her drooping dress. And the rise and fall of her rapid breathing, aiding in the descent of the hideous brown cloth.

He had two hands, and he could unbutton a woman's dress with only one. Hell, he could do it with his teeth if necessary—he had more than enough practice. He took one hand from her back and pressed it between her breasts, over the plain white cotton of her chemise, to feel her heart hammering against his long fingers. He had the pale hands required of a gentleman, but his hand looked dark against her perfect white skin.

The buttons were giving way with surprising ease, probably due to her original way of fastening them in the first place. And the dress was lamentably old as well as ugly—if burning wool didn't smell so awful he'd throw it on the fire. He put his mouth close to hers, just a moment away from kissing her, and her impossibly fast heartbeat raced ever stronger against his fingers.

"Shall I ruin you, dragon?" he whispered, aching for her. "Or shall I send you on your way?"

Her eyes were dark and steady, at odds with her flying pulses and rapid breathing. "Why?"

He didn't bother to pretend to misunderstand. Their mouths were so close it was as if their breath was kissing, dancing, copulating between them, and Christian began to wonder if he was going to give Priapus a run for his money.

"Silly dragon," he whispered. "Because I want you. And it has nothing to do with whether you want me or not—of course you do. And if you didn't, I could make you want me. I'm very good at it."

She didn't bother to deny it. "If I say no will you leave me be?"

"I could try. I've never been terribly good at resisting my dark side. And making love to beautiful, starchy spinsters with no possible future to it is a very dark, bad thing to do."

Her faint smile was almost his undoing. "You mean you're not going to carry me off to Gretna Green immediately afterward and make an honest woman of me?"

"Alas, no. While my need to marry money is no longer as pressing, thanks to Mr. Chipple's generosity and Hetty leaving behind several of her tackiest, most valuable pieces of jewelry, I still know that I'm incapable of being faithful to one woman. And you really wouldn't want that. If you had a husband you'd insist on someone who was sober, devoted, hardworking and totally tiresome."

"If I had a husband I'd insist he was you."

His hand stilled at the base of her back, almost at the last button. The dress was only kept up by her arms. If they dropped, the ugly dress would drop, as well, into a puddle of brown mud on the floor between them.

"Then it's lucky for you that I would never marry you," he said. Odd, his own heart was racing. "All I'd do is disappoint you."

"Extremely lucky," she said. "As you pointed out, I deserve far better than the likes of you."

"You do indeed," he whispered. It seemed she had surprisingly lovely breasts hidden beneath the plain cotton chemise, and he wanted to move his hand just a fraction, to cup the soft skin. "So I presume that taking you to bed would be a very bad idea?"

"Very bad," she said, and she closed her eyes for a moment in thought. And then she opened them again, looking into his quite clearly. "But then, we've already established that you are a very bad man, haven't we?"

It was permission, of a sort, when he would have staked half of Hetty's jewels that he'd never have any such thing. He barely hesitated. "Then shall I ruin you, dragon?"

"Yes, please," she said. And she let the brown dress drop on the floor between them, closing her eyes once more.

He put his hand behind her neck then, drawing her against him and he kissed her with long, slow, drugging kisses that made certain she wouldn't abruptly panic and that her calm good sense wouldn't return at an unfortunate moment. His fingers slid through the ugly bun, pulling out hairpins and letting them litter the floor as her hair fell loose, almost to her hips. He slid his arm around her waist and lifted her out of the ugly dress that lay rumpled at her feet, and carried her over to the bed. She was an armful, and he found her strength arousing. As if he needed to find anything else about her arousing. He lay her down on the bed, and noticed that the snowy-white chemise that reached from her collarbone to her ankles was just as plain and ugly as the brown dress that covered it. Its only good point was that it was thin from wear, and he could see her body quite clearly underneath, the plump roundness of her breasts, the darker nipples. No, the other good point was that it would tear quite easily, and he didn't even hesitate, ripping it open from neck to hem, shocking her.

She could still change her mind, he told himself, and he would give her every chance. He knelt on one knee, beside her on the bed, and slowly pushed the torn chemise away from her body, taking in a deep, painful breath.

She could have been one of Chipple's statues—a marble-toned goddess of curves and shadows and astonishing grace. But she was no statue—she was a living, breathing woman lying in his bed. A virgin, when he hadn't had one in years. A fire-breathing dragon who lay ready for the ritual slaughter of the most delicious kind.

The candlelight by the bed cast dark shadows on the wall and he couldn't appreciate the creamy wonder of her skin as much as he wanted to. He'd have to take her outside, in the warm daylight, so he could savor every inch of her against a soft green bed of grass. But it wouldn't be summer for months, and by then she'd be gone. He'd have sent her away, finished with her. Wouldn't he?

He tugged at his loosely tied cravat, sending it sailing. He ripped at his own buttons, opening his shirt and reaching for his breeches, when he stopped. "One last warning, love. This is no fairy-tale business, no pretty dream. It's real. It's dark and messy and for you, painful. In the beginning, at least. You'll end up hating me."

"Don't worry about it, Christian," she said. "I already hate you."

Her calm words were an unexpected shock. And then she smiled at him. "That's why I'm lying naked in your bed, waiting for you to get on with it and stop trying to scare me. Besides, your reputation is legendary. If you can't make it enjoyable then I expect no one could, and I know for a fact that women do enjoy it. Hetty was *aux anges,* and I doubt William had anywhere near your expertise."

"Hetty was in love with the oaf. It makes a difference." She was right—why was he doing it? he wondered. Why was he trying to warn her off, when, if he didn't release the buttons on his breeches, he might suffer a permanent injury. He'd never had a conscience before and he refused to have one now.

She smiled up at him with a sweetness he might not have known she possessed, if he hadn't known her so well. "We established that you are a very bad man," she said. "And I thought we already established that I'm in love with you. You told me that the first night I arrived."

"I was trying to annoy you."

"Your presence on this earth is annoyance enough," she said with a trace of her usual asperity. "But in this case you were right."

He should have been horrified. "You said you hated me."

"I've been struggling between the two for far too long. Why don't you do something to make up my mind? Aren't I overdue for a lesson?"

He laughed then, the last, unlikely strands of his conscience disappearing into the shadows. "And you are such a fast learner," he said, pulling her up so that her torn chemise fell completely away from her.

She twined her bare arms around his neck and kissed him, all of her own volition, her full, ripe mouth against his, and he felt the faint tug of her teeth against his lower lip, the touch of her tongue. He pulled back in shock and a shadow crossed her face. "Didn't I do it right?"

"A very fast learner indeed," he muttered, pushing her back down on the bed and cradling her head with one hand as they kissed each other in a glorious blending of mouth and tongue and teeth. They kissed until they couldn't breathe, stopped and then kissed again, and he stretched out beside her, pulling her over against him, reveling in the feel of her soft, warm skin.

No one had ever had such beautiful, creamy skin, such firm, ripe curves. She still had the strong body of a horsewoman, even though she'd refused to ride for countless years. She would ride him. She would do everything he wanted her to do, and more, and the night, the days would be endless, a sea of dark pleasure, until he was ready to let her go.

If that day ever came.

22

There was the faintest, sullen hint of daylight in the room. Annelise lay facedown on the bed that had been torn apart during the last few hours, so that the sheet bunched up beneath her, the pillows were long gone and the only thing covering her naked body was some kind of heavy woven coverlet. She ached in every part of her body, including places she'd never ached before, and she felt as if she'd gone for a long, hard ride that she hadn't been prepared for.

It was the truth. Nothing had prepared her for the endless night that had just passed, despite her smug certainty that she was conversant with the mechanics of sexual congress. Nothing had prepared her for the bone-shaking power of her response.

He'd pulled her on top of his body, pushing the tattered chemise from her, and it had been skin to skin. He was so warm in the dark, cool room, and she could feel muscle and bone beneath his smooth flesh, feel his heart beating beneath her own, feel his hand on her neck as he moved her head to kiss her. She was learning the very taste and texture of his mouth, learning to delight in it, wanting it more than breath, more than life itself.

Her arms were trapped between them, and she didn't like it. "Let go of me," she whispered against his mouth.

He did so, immediately, so quickly that she might have been offended if she didn't know him so well. She slid off his body, onto her side, and he sat up, almost as if he was going to desert her.

She put her hand out to stop him, and the tensile strength of his shoulder shocked her. "I want to touch you," she said in barely more than a whisper.

But he heard her. He shrugged out of his shirt, and in the darkness she didn't even see where he dropped it. The whole room must be littered with their clothes. He lay back down, and she could see the gleam in his beautiful, exotic eyes. She leaned over him, and put a tentative, trembling hand on his chest.

His heart was racing, as fast as hers, and yet she knew he was afraid of nothing. His skin was silky smooth, elegantly muscled, and on sheer instinct she leaned down and pressed her mouth against his heart, kissing him.

This time she didn't mistake the groan for anything other than approval. Her hair had gotten loose—she couldn't remember when, and it spilled over their bodies. It fell around them as she moved her mouth, kissing him lightly, taking pleasure in the small, delicious taste of him.

He took one of her hands in his, holding it, stroking her fingers with his. He placed it on his stomach, his own hand covering hers, and then, to her shock, slid it downward, until she encountered the unfastened front of his breeches. She tried to resist, to pull away, but he wouldn't let her, though he didn't force her farther. "I hate to tell you, dragon, but that's an integral part of the whole business," he whispered. "If you're afraid to touch me then we're not going to get very far."

She lifted her head to look at him. "I thought I could lie back and let you ravish me," she said with complete honesty.

He shook his head, the smile hovering around his lips, his eyes intent. "This is a cooperative effort, my love. You have to do your part." And he exerted just the slightest amount of pressure, to move her hand downward.

There was the fine doeskin of his breeches between his skin and hers. And no reason to be missish when she was lying naked in his bed, she told herself. And let him slide her hand down over him.

She let out a little squeak of dismay—she couldn't help it. All her memories of Chipple's naked statues were nothing compared to the hard ridge of flesh beneath Christian's breeches, beneath her trembling fingers. But she didn't pull away. Beneath her natural panic she was curious—this surely wouldn't work. There was too much disparity in the parts that were supposed to fit together. He didn't seem concerned, but then, he'd warned her it would be painful for her.

It was long past the point of no return, even if she wanted to escape. If it hurt, so be it. She wanted it anyway. She wanted Christian Montcalm inside her body, belonging to her, if only for one night, and she wanted it with the wild determination of the most shameless of courtesans.

He did nothing when she lifted her hand off his hard flesh. Until she began unbuttoning the bone buttons of his breeches, until she could push her hands under the fabric to touch his body, touch the part that would soon be a part of her. She felt him quiver and then he lifted his hips and shoved the breeches off, so that he was as naked as she was.

"Do this," he whispered, covering her hand with his and wrapping her fingers around him. "Just for a moment." And he moved her hand up and down, gently, and impossible as it seemed, he seemed to grow larger, harder with her grip.

Odd, but the muffled sound of pleasure he made caused her own insides to flutter in response. This must be why it worked, she thought. It was logical—even though women couldn't enjoy it, they enjoyed the pleasure they gave a man they cared about. That must have accounted for Hetty's blissful expression. And there was no question that she wanted to give Christian pleasure…

"That's enough, or I'll spill in your hand," Christian said.

She released him, startled. "But I thought you liked it…"

"You're thinking too much," he said. "Dragons aren't supposed to think—they're supposed to act on instinct."

"But what if I'm not really a dragon?"

He leaned over her in the darkness and she could see

his wicked smile. "I know you're not, sweetheart. I'm the dragon, and I'm about to devour a princess."

"I don't think..."

"Good. Don't think. Let's get this over with."

It wasn't particularly what she wanted to hear, as he pushed her down on the bed and moved to kneel between her legs, and it was too late to change her mind. He made it sound like an unpleasant task to be done with, but if he didn't want to do it why would he bother? She steeled herself, expecting pain, but the first touch of his hand on her hip was incredibly gentle.

"Don't look so worried," he said with a soft laugh. "It's not going to be that bad." And he leaned over and kissed her, slowly, kissed her mouth and her eyelids and the side of her face, kissed her neck and the pulse beating wildly there. He moved down and startled her by kissing her breasts, and letting his tongue run over them, then sucking at her for a brief moment like a babe, so that her hips rose off the bed involuntarily and she let out a little cry. He wasn't touching her between her legs, not yet, but she could feel it, feel the sensations run straight from the tight knot of her breast down the center of her to pool between her legs, and she reached up her hand to touch him, to push his long, loose hair out of his face, to caress him.

He gave both of her breasts equal, lavish attention, then moved down, to the softness of her stomach, and she suddenly knew what he was planning. No wonder they called him a degenerate—she knew of such practices because of her wide reading, but that someone would actually do such a thing was beyond shocking.

She tried to push him away, but she'd forgotten how strong he was. "Sweetness, don't fight me," he murmured. "You're going to like this. And I did warn you you were about to be devoured."

And he put his mouth between her legs. She tried to close her thighs but his hands caught her hips and held them open. She attempted to pull him away but he ignored her. The touch of his tongue was a shock, a disgrace, an act of moral perversion and a sensation of such melting pleasure that she wanted to weep with it. She had told him yes, he could do as he willed, and she already knew that if she truly said no he would pull away and leave her. And she would die of the pain.

She loosened her grip on him, reaching down her other hand to touch him, caress him as he used his mouth on her, and she let the strange, wicked sensations wash over her body.

It was like nothing she had ever felt before, heat and cold, longing and fulfillment, pleasure so intense that there was a grace note of pain within, and she could no longer think, could only feel as the tension spread throughout her body.

He slipped his fingers inside her and she arched off the bed, wanting to tell him to stop, when a small shiver swept over her, followed by another, followed by a fierce, brief convulsion that left her startled and breathless and gasping.

And then he was above her again, wiping his mouth on the rumpled sheets, and she could feel him against her, the hard, impossible part of him, and she wanted to brace herself but her bones were strangely liquid.

He kissed her, and she could taste herself on his mouth. "Good girl," he whispered. "Now you're ready."

In her dazed state she felt oddly gratified, even as he began to push inside her. After such unexpected pleasure she could withstand anything, even the shock of him filling her. She closed her eyes, letting the sensation fill her just as he did, when he stopped, and she opened her eyes to look up into his dark, intense ones.

The laughing rogue was nowhere in sight. "Why did you stop?" she whispered. "It's actually almost pleasant."

For a moment there was a flash of amusement in his eyes, and then it was gone. "Almost pleasant," he muttered. "Give me your hands."

"What?"

He didn't bother to repeat the request—or was it an order? Her hands were lying by her sides, and he took them, twining his own fingers through hers. "Just hold on," he whispered. And pushed the rest of the way.

There was no way she could bite back the tiny cry of pain, and she clutched his hands so tightly she thought her fingers would break. She took a deep breath, and then another, resisting the impulse to try to throw him off her. He would be done in a moment, and he would leave, and she could curl up in a ball and remember the strange, wonderful feeling that had coursed through her body for a few brief moments.

But he wasn't moving, and she slowly loosened her grip on his fingers, then opened her eyes. He was absolutely still, above her, inside her, like a statue: a warm, living breathing version of that wicked marble in Chipple's garden. He started to pull away and her sigh of relief was cut short when he pushed inside her again. She should have known from watching animals that it would probably take more than one thrust. She'd just hold still and bear it…

"Don't look so martyred, dragon," he whispered in her ear. "It only gets better from here."

She didn't believe him, so she said nothing, lying still beneath him as he moved, telling herself it would be done soon, but her body seemed to arch up against his instinctively, and when he kissed her she kissed him back, and when he released her hands entirely she slid her arms around his strong back, holding on to him. His hands slid down her legs, pulling them up around his thighs, pushing in deeper still, but instead of pain she felt a surprising flutter of response, a slow, steady ebb and flow as his body ebbed and flowed with hers. His entire body was tight in her arms, rigid with self-control, and she wondered why he didn't just finish it. Why was he holding back, at such great effort?

And then the same little convulsion shook her, coming out of nowhere. But this time, with him inside her, it was even more powerful, and she let out a surprised cry.

"That's better," he murmured, his rhythm as slow and measured as his body was tense. His heart was slamming against his chest, but he kept himself in check as his hips moved against hers.

She could feel tears forming in the back of her eyes,

and she had no idea where they came from. Her breasts were burning, and between her legs was a kind of restless aching that she needed to calm, but he was there, and she didn't know what to do, as another little shiver ran through her body, moments longer than the last one, everything in her body tightening for a minute, and Christian let out a muffled cry.

"*Chérie*, I am going to die if I don't finish," he whispered in a hoarse groan. And the words, as if by instinct, were in French.

"Then finish me," she whispered in the same language.

It was like unleashing a storm. She'd had no idea what kind of power he'd been holding in check, but at her words of permission he moved, harder and faster, in some kind of hurtling race toward God knew what, and she clung to him, because she could do nothing else, holding on as tightly as she could, when he reached between their bodies and touched her, just above where he was so ruthlessly thrusting, slamming into her, touching her hard, and it was as if the night exploded.

Her body convulsed and she tried to cry out, but nothing came from her throat but a strangled cry. She was out of control, lost, gone somewhere that she hadn't known existed, and the only thing with her was Christian, his arms around her, shaking as hard as she was as he spilled himself deep inside her.

She didn't know when she'd be able to breathe again. When she'd be able to think again. It was as if she drifted down from the darkness, back onto the tumbled bed, with his body sprawled across hers, powerful and hot and sweaty, and yet tiny tremors kept rippling across her skin, and she wanted to clutch him to her, drawing him in tighter, deeper, closer.

After a long moment he lifted his head, looking down at her. The strange, unbidden tears were flowing down her face, and his smile was wry, almost loving. He kissed her, whispering against her mouth, her ear, her cheek, soft, delicious words of praise and love, all in French, and she had no choice but to reply, to tell him what she'd already told him in English, half facetiously, but now, in French, with his body still inside hers, what felt like an eternal pledge. "I love you," she whispered. *"Je t'aime."*

"Encore," he said. And began to move again.

She wouldn't have guessed she had the capacity for that night. He made love to her, bathed her, kissed her, and started all over again, and each time her response came faster, stronger, until she thought she could bear no more and he proved to her that she could. He had her do things she'd never imagined, taking him into her mouth with wicked pleasure, moving into any position he wished, beneath him, above him, on her knees with her back to him like some kind of slave. And she would think he had done all he wanted, and she could rest, and then he would touch her again, and she would come alive once more.

She must have slept. Or fainted. She didn't remember him leaving the bed, leaving her, but as she slowly opened her eyes to the murky predawn light she knew she was alone among the tangled sheets.

Someone had built up the fire. She moved her head, carefully, since everything felt weak and fragile, and she could see him, sitting on the bench beneath the window, staring into the flames.

He was dressed, or at least halfway there. He had his breeches on, and his shirt was half-buttoned. He must have finally run out of things to do with her, she thought dazedly. So why, when she looked at him, did her body still shiver in longing?

He must have known she was awake, though he kept his gaze averted. "Where do you wish to go?" His voice was flat, emotionless, a shock. He was speaking English once more, and those long, dark, indecent hours might never have existed.

"Go?" she said stupidly, forcing herself to sit up, pulling the coverlet around her. Of course, he was sending her away—hadn't he made it abundantly clear that he had no feelings for her? At least, not when he spoke English.

He still didn't look at her, but he was as casual as if he were discussing a wager. No, even more casual. Wagers involved money, and that was of a great deal more importance than one deflowered spinster.

At her continued silence he turned to look at her. He'd pulled his long hair back and tied it, but one shorter strand still hung down the side of his narrow, beautiful face. If she were closer she'd lovingly push that strand back behind his ear—or slap his face, she wasn't sure which.

"You aren't going to be tedious and cry, are you, dragon?" he drawled. But something didn't seem quite right in his lazy tone. Not after the hours they'd just spent.

"I'm not going to cry," she said steadily.

His smile was brief. "Of course you're not. You're ever a practical creature. I'll make arrangements for you to go wherever you want. Back to Lady Prentice? Perhaps a short visit to a member of your family? Anywhere but Josiah Chipple's." He sounded no more than vaguely interested in her destination. He was sending her away, and there was nothing she could do about it.

Except debase herself still further. "I love you," she said in her perfect French. "I can't live without you. I'll do anything you want if you let me stay with you."

He didn't even blink. "I'm sorry, my dear, but I don't speak French." And he strolled out of the room without a backward glance.

23

She hadn't made a sound when he walked out the door. If she had, he might have stopped, might have turned back to her like the idiot he was. But she was absolutely silent, and he closed the door behind him, closed her away from him, and slowly walked down the stairs.

It was a waste of time telling himself what a fool he'd been, what a selfish bastard—none of that was news. He'd known the first time he'd looked directly into the Honorable Miss Annelise Kempton's clear gray eyes that he'd have her, and despite his occasional attempts at restraint he'd done just that.

And the sooner she got away from him the better.

He couldn't believe that he hadn't pulled out in time. That he'd spilled his seed inside her, something he took great pains never to do. The chances of her actually conceiving would be slight, but it wasn't impossible. What would she do about it? How could he have ruined her even further?

She was a practical woman, he reminded himself, walking into the darkened library. The rain had finally come to a stop, and the fitful sunrise was spreading slowly over the tangled countryside. He would send her safely out of his reach, hating him enough to never want to see him again, and he could get on with his life without any unwanted responsibilities.

If she was pregnant she would probably be smart enough to find someone to get rid of it for her before she began to show. It was the levelheaded, practical thing to do, but knowing his fire-breathing dragon, he doubted she'd make that choice. No, she would do what most ladies did when caught in an embarrassing condition. She'd go for a long, edifying journey, and when she returned she'd appear just as she was, and some farm couple would have a new child to raise.

He'd always tried to avoid that. He didn't want any bastard of his at the mercy of someone paid to take care of him. He'd known both sides—what it was like to grow up loved and to grow up with no one giving a damn about him. He wouldn't let the latter happen to anyone of his blood, not if he could help it.

He threw himself down on the sofa, groaning. He was certain of one thing—she'd be all right. Once she was away from his pernicious influence she'd be back to her usual starchy self and no one would ever guess she'd spent an endless, and yet far too brief night in the arms of one of the wickedest men in England. In the end it might even do her some good. Assuming there was no unfortunate result from the night's work, she might be more open-minded when it came to courtship. In truth he couldn't imagine that dozens of men wouldn't want her. She could take her pick of them and end up with children and a husband and a happy life.

All thanks to him, he mocked himself. What a noble fellow he was, to kindly enlighten Annelise about the pleasures of the flesh. One might almost consider it to be one of his finer moments. If one was as deluded as he dearly wished he was.

He could still see the look in her eyes, the expressions that danced across her face when he touched her in a certain way, moved her just so, cajoled her into doing things the very thought of which would have turned her creamy skin red with embarrassment. He'd convinced her, and she'd reveled in it. And he was growing hard again just thinking about it, when any sane man would be sound asleep after such an energetic night.

He had to let her go. She might escape censure if she got away quickly, but time was of the essence. She'd already stayed dangerously long, and if he didn't get her away from him…

The slam of crockery was enough to make him jump. He hadn't even noticed that Bessie Browne had marched into the room with a tea tray and the expression of an avenging angel on her broad, plain face.

He sat up, looking at the jumbled tea things, the broken dishes, and then lifted his eyes to meet Bessie's stormy gaze. "We don't really have much of the good china left to spare," he said mildly.

"You're lucky I didn't dump it on your head, Master Christian," she snapped. "How could you do that to that poor girl?"

He stalled for time. There were few things that chastened him in this life, but Bessie Browne's fierce temper was one of them. "What do you mean?"

"You left the door open, you shameless man! I saw the two of you sound asleep without a stitch of clothing on. You're just lucky I didn't come in and give you a piece of my mind, but I thought to spare the lady—something you clearly didn't care about."

"Oh," he said blankly, at a loss for words.

"You promised her she'd be safe here! You swore on your honor that you wouldn't touch her. She trusted you!"

"She never trusted me, Bessie. She's much too smart for that. And she should have known I could never just let her go."

"Do you have to bed every single woman you meet? Is no one safe from your wickedness? I've a good mind to find a horsewhip and teach you a lesson. Harry refused, though he's sorely disappointed in you, but it's not beyond my capabilities or your desserts."

He glanced up at Bessie's sturdy, work-honed frame, and half wished she would. "I don't bed every woman I meet. I left that infant I eloped with entirely alone."

"Then why Miss Annelise? It was a cruel, heartless thing to do, Master Christian. Not like you. To be sure, you're feckless and selfish and irresponsible, but I've never known you to be cruel."

He felt an unaccustomed warmth hit his cheekbones. It was nothing he hadn't said to himself, but seeing Bessie's stern condemnation made it even worse. She and Harry had given up everything to come work for him, and they seldom saw a farthing for it, but they'd always had an odd, classless friendship, and her good opinion mattered.

But it was too late. He shrugged. "I couldn't resist her," he said simply.

"Are you going to marry her?"

"Good God, no!" he said. "If I marry at all I should marry money. Besides, I doubt she'd have me. She's much too smart for that."

"True enough," Annelise spoke from the doorway. "Mrs. Browne, I need to leave here as soon as possible. Is there any possibility your husband could see to some sort of hired conveyance for me, to take me at least as far as the next coaching stop? A farm cart would do."

Bessie's ire was forgotten as she rushed to Annelise's side. "Don't you worry about a thing, miss. My Harry will see to your well-being, if he has to steal a carriage himself. Ten years of living with Master Christian has taught us to disregard the law when necessary."

She managed a tight smile, not looking at him. "That would be very kind. I'd need some sort of shoes..."

The three of them looked at her feet. They were bare, and she had surprisingly pretty toes. He'd never considered feet to be erotic before, but he was fast changing his mind.

She was wearing that hideous brown dress. He should have ripped it off her, as he had the chemise. What was she wearing underneath the scratchy wool, then? And why couldn't he stop thinking about such things, when he should have clearly had his fill of her?

"We'll take care of it, miss. Come along and I'll make you some breakfast, and I'll make certain you won't have to see that miserable excuse for a man again."

At that Annelise glanced at him, and to his shock she managed the very ghost of a smile. "Oh, he's quite manly enough in certain ways, Mrs. Browne," she said. "But I think he's taught me enough by now."

There was no sign of tears in her clear gray eyes. She must have found at least some of her discarded hairpins, for she'd managed to tuck her hair into a disordered bun at the back of her neck. The sort of thing that would come undone with just one deft pull.

He wanted to say something, to stop her, but there were no words. She gazed at him for a long, thoughtful moment and then turned and followed Bessie, out of his sight and his life forever.

To his astonishment he slept, stretched out on the sofa, the broken crockery still in front of him as a stern reminder of his infamy. When he awoke it was bright daylight, and there was no sign of either Annelise or Bessie. He found Harry, but one look at his stern, disapproving face convinced him not to ask. Besides, he really shouldn't care what happened to her once he'd left her in Bessie's capable hands. They'd take far better care of her than he ever had.

He managed to get the grudging Harry to carry bathwater for him, though he barely brought enough and it was cold. He didn't argue—the need to bathe was paramount. He smelled like her—sex and flowers, and until he could wash away the scent and the feel of her he wouldn't be able to put her out of his mind.

He was dressing himself, ignoring his empty stomach, when he glanced at his reflection in the mirror and halted as he was buttoning his snow-white shirt. There was a bite mark at the side of his neck, and he remembered all too well when she'd done it, when he was goading her past bearing, prolonging her climax until she'd bit down on him rather than scream. He pulled his shirt free and looked at his chest, at the tiny marks and scratchings that had driven him over the edge. And he pushed back the foaming lace cuff to look at his forearm, at the bruises left by her fingers when he'd taken her from the back and she hadn't been able to keep from making all the pleasure-filled sounds he'd been wanting from her.

Damn her. And damn him. He couldn't, wouldn't let her go, not so quickly, he had to…

Harry had opened one of the windows facing out to the front of the house—probably in the hopes of having him contract a fatal ague, he thought to himself—and the sound of the rider was unmistakable, even on the muddy drive. He felt a sudden panic—she couldn't have gone so quickly—and when he looked out he saw to his utter astonishment that Crosby Pennington was dismounting a bay mare that had clearly been hired at no slight expense.

Crosby never rode when he could help it—he loathed the exertion and hated the countryside even more. He'd been known to turn down offers for the most amiable of house parties if they were too far away from London. And now he'd suddenly shown up at Wynche End without warning? How very curious. Maybe his visit was just the thing to distract him from his foolish infatuation.

He finished dressing as quickly as he could, cursing the boots that would have gone on much more easily with Harry's help, then sauntered down the oaken stairs just as Crosby was removing his dusty greatcoat.

"What brings you to the back end of beyond?" he greeted him as he reached the landing.

"Montcalm, thank God you're here!" Crosby cried. Since Crosby did his best never to show any emotion other than ennui, Christian was becoming ever more curious.

"I'm here," he said briefly. "What astonishes me is that you're here as well. Not that you aren't welcome, dear boy, but you never leave London."

"I've the most astonishing news and I felt it couldn't wait until you returned. I cajoled your direction from Henry and took off immediately."

Every trace of charming sloth had been stripped from his voice, and Christian was instantly wary. "Come into the library and I'll have Mrs. Browne bring us a bottle and we'll discuss—"

"There's no time for that!" Crosby cried, frustrated.

Now Christian was totally baffled. "There's always time for a glass of wine—"

"Christian!" Crosby interrupted. "Your brother is alive!"

He froze. There was no other word for it—he could feel ice flow through his veins, rendering him as incapable of moving as Chipple's damned statues. "What are you talking about?" he said finally, his voice strained. "My family died more than twenty years ago in the Terror."

"One of them survived. Your youngest brother was taken by loyal servants and has spent the last fifteen years in hiding. He was finally able to arrange passage from France when someone informed on him. He'd been in hiding in a small coastal village, but he managed to get word out, begging for your help."

The words were incomprehensible. Christian stared at him blankly. "How is this possible?"

"You know I have my sources. Freetraders brought the message—they were looking for you. Apparently they were promised a large sum of money if they found you. With such incentive they managed to find me, and of course I came racing after you as any true friend would after suitably rewarding them. By the way, you owe me fifty pounds for the bribe."

"I don't believe you."

"I beg your pardon?" Crosby said, clearly affronted. "You accuse me of lying?"

"Of course not. It's just…I can't comprehend…"

"I've got passage waiting for us on the coast. Rough quarters, I'm afraid. The best possible passage is by smugglers' craft, but I thought you wouldn't object."

Christian stumbled backward, sitting down on the landing. "Of course not," he said, trying to take it all in.

Charles-Louis, his laughing infant brother, still alive after all these years? There was still one member of his family he could save, and he'd damn well swim to France if he had to. "How soon do we go?"

"As soon as you're ready."

He didn't argue. "Give me five minutes."

"Be certain to bring as much cash as you have on hand," Crosby called after him. "You never know when we might need it."

"You're coming with me?"

"What are friends for?" Crosby replied with a wry smile. "You know you can count on me."

"Five minutes," Christian said again. And went off in search of weapons.

The small sitting room was warm, relatively dust free, and the love seat was surprisingly comfortable beneath the tattered coverings. The tea tray lay on the table next to a small marble statue of Diana that reminded Annelise of the Chipple household, and looking at it made her feel worse. She turned her back to it rather than have to stare and remember how she'd gotten into this mess in the first place. She was clean, dressed and well fed, and all she had to do was wait.

She'd had no choice but to put on the riding habit once more, along with some of the plainest of undergarments from the lavender-scented chest. Mrs. Browne had seen to a warm, calming bath and fresh clothes, though she had no choice but to keep the riding boots. There was no other option—they would serve her well enough while she traveled. All she had to do was wait for Mr. Browne to return with some kind of conveyance, and she would be gone from this place and the man who didn't want her.

She refused to feel sorry for herself. She'd known what she was getting into, she'd fallen in love like a mooncalf when she was old enough and wise enough to know better. She ought to regret the night, and sooner or later she would, but right now she was defiantly glad she had done it. She had tasted a joy she hadn't even dreamed existed, and for a few brief hours she had been beautiful and loved. It would have to last her a lifetime.

There would be no child from her precious night of debauchery. She knew enough about animal husbandry and human bodies to realize the chance of conceiving so soon after her menses was highly unlikely. He'd made no effort to protect her, something that surprised her in the calmer light of day. He'd claimed that he had no illegitimate offspring. If he'd spent many nights like the last one he was certain to have half a dozen littering the countryside.

The thought of him spending similar nights with other women was ridiculously painful, so she dismissed it firmly. It was time to look forward, not into the past, and Christian Montcalm had made it very clear that her future had nothing to do with him.

She ought to be ashamed of herself. In the end she had begged him and he'd walked away. She could save her pride by knowing that at least her pitiful words hadn't been in English, but he'd known exactly what she was saying, what she was asking. And for that she'd always feel a stab of shame. She shouldn't have begged. And she wouldn't again—she'd drive away from this place without giving him another thought.

Annelise had been dozing fitfully when Mrs. Browne came into the room, a troubled expression on her face. "My husband's back from town and he's had some luck, though not as much as I could have wished," she said. "The Royal Oak has a carriage to let, but it needs mending, and it won't be ready to go until tomorrow. It's nothing elegant, but it should get you where you need to go, and my Harry's an excellent driver. You'll have me for company, just to keep your reputation in good shape, and we'll take you to London or wherever you want to go."

"I think it's a little late for my reputation," Annelise said softly. "And I shouldn't take you away from your duties…"

"Cleaning up after Master Christian's selfish messes is my duty," Mrs. Browne said firmly. "And I don't care how much he's inconvenienced. Serves him right."

Annelise didn't bother to argue. "But I really can't stay beneath the same roof…"

"Oh, you won't be," the housekeeper said airily. "He's gone."

It shouldn't have felt like a stab to the heart—he'd already walked out of her life, and she'd accepted that fact. That he'd left the house should have been a relief.

"Gone?" she echoed. "Where? Back to London?" Not that she had any intention of returning to the city—

her sister Eugenia was relatively close, and she would provide her shelter as long as she needed it. Accompanied by improving lectures, of course, but in this case Annelise deserved them.

"Master Christian's friend Mr. Pennington showed up and dragged him off without barely a moment's notice. He didn't say where he was going and I didn't ask."

Did he say anything about me? She wouldn't ask the question out loud—she already knew the answer. He hadn't even thought of her as he went on his way to new and sordid pleasures.

But Bessie seemed to read her mind. "He said one thing when he left," she started. "He told me to make certain you were taken care of, no matter what happened."

Annelise sat bolt upright. "What does that mean?"

"I have no idea. But I've never seen the lad look so grim. And I don't trust that Mr. Pennington—I've heard bad things about him. But that isn't your worry, Miss Annelise, nor mine at the moment. He's a grown man—he can take care of himself. I just wish he hadn't taken the pistols. In the meantime you're safe enough here. I promise you he won't touch you again."

She managed to hide her total lack of gratification at such a notion. "You've been so kind, Mrs. Browne," she said.

"Nonsense. I told you, he's a good lad at heart, just a little wild. I'd say he was spoiled but no one's spoiled him since he came to England. He learned to make his own way and care for no one, and it's little wonder that beneath it all he tries to be very hard. He's not, really, but you deserve far better than the likes of him."

"I don't believe he was ever a possibility."

Mrs. Browne sighed. "No, probably not. But you would have been the making of the lad. I'll bring some nice hot tea, how would that be?"

"That would be lovely," she replied, her voice only slightly hoarse. She leaned her head against the chair and stared out into the bright afternoon and closed her eyes, drifting off.

The strange noises woke her up. The slamming of a door, the sound of heavy footsteps, a scuffle and a few muffled oaths. She jumped up in sudden hope—Christian must have returned—and as she started for the door it slammed open, nearly hitting her.

Someone filled the entry, someone large and bulky, and in the afternoon shadows she couldn't quite believe her eyes. "The Honorable Miss Annelise Kempton," Josiah Chipple's big voice boomed forth, sounding sinister. "I've been looking for you."

24

"Mr. Chipple," she said, suddenly nervous. "I had no idea you were expected."

He pushed his way into the room, closing the door behind him. He was a very large man—not as tall as Christian but far bulkier, and his air of bonhomie had vanished. "I don't believe I was," he said. "But when a bleedin' bastard the likes of Christian Montcalm blackmails me and then goes back on his word then there's no doubt what Josiah Chipple will do about it. To him and to those who helped him." He glanced around the shabby little room and sneered before turning his attention back to Annelise. "Sit down, Miss Kempton."

"I'd rather not."

"Sit down before I make you." He didn't wait. He pushed her so hard she fell back into the chair, and it almost toppled over beneath her. Shock spurred her reaction and she bounced right back out of it again, slapping him across the face.

A mistake, she realized in retrospect. Josiah Chipple was not the demi-gentleman she'd thought him to be, and as her father had warned her, one should never hit someone who's likely to hit you back. His fist slammed against her cheekbone and she fell back against the oak casement, tumbling to the floor as she held her face in shock.

"And there's more where that came from, missy," he sneered. "You should never underestimate Josiah Chipple—I figured such a starched-up spinster would have the sense to know that. But you have no sense, have you? You let that bastard Montcalm carry off my daughter, and then you stayed to spread your legs for him, as well. You're as great a whore as m'daughter, Miss Kempton, for all your fine ways. And I'll be teaching you a lesson."

Annelise didn't move. Her face throbbed, and she'd caught her hip on the hard wood, but she knew if she rose he'd either hit her again, or she'd try to kill him. Since the only weapon in sight was a silver knife and fork from the abandoned tea tray, and he was wearing a heavy leather coat across his impressive paunch, she decided her chances were not good. She stayed where she was.

"I have no idea what you're talking about, Mr. Chipple," she said in a frosty voice, trying to ignore the fact that her mouth hurt from where he'd hit her. She had come up with so many varied stories to explain her sudden departure from London that she couldn't remember which one they'd settled on as the least destructive. "Your daughter isn't here."

"Of course she's not. She's off with that Dickinson

boy, and it's your family who's hiding them. It took me long enough to track them down but I know they're somewhere north of here. My men are searching for them, and they'll be bringing them here before much more time passes. I'm not sure what will happen to your family—my men aren't noted for their gentlemanly restraint, but you can tell yourself it was all your fault in the first place for interfering in my plans."

"I didn't interfere," she said, close enough to the truth. "Hetty was miserably unhappy and she gave in to Mr. Montcalm's blandishments and went off with him. Knowing that you'd never approve of such a match, I enlisted Mr. Dickinson's aid and went after them and we were able to arrive before Montcalm had even attempted to molest her." Of course, then Will and Hetty had gone at it, but she certainly didn't need to apprise this dangerous bully of that fact.

"My daughter's happiness is of no concern to me. She had a duty to perform, to marry well, and she's both failed me and shamed me in the face of society. She'll learn her lesson since clearly I haven't taught her well enough in the past."

The man sounded positively evil. "You wouldn't hurt her!" she protested inanely, given that he'd already slammed his fist against her face. If he'd hit a stranger, a well-bred member of society, then he'd have no qualms about beating his own.

His laugh was mirthless. "If I were you I'd be more concerned about your family and your own safety. You have a pretty young niece of no more than fifteen, do you not? There's a lot of damage a rough man can do to an untried girl."

Annelise stared at him in disbelief. She wanted to throw up. He couldn't mean the horrible things he was saying—he was just trying to scare her.

"How did you know I have a niece?"

"Oh, I know all about you, Miss Kempton. I had you thoroughly vetted, even before I brought you into my house. I have ways of finding out everything, including that your drunken father deliberately killed himself and made it look like a riding accident, leaving you penniless and at the mercy of strangers. I'm sure he had no idea you were going to end up being at the mercy of *me*."

She slowly rose to her feet, watching those hamlike fists warily. Her head was still spinning and her entire body hurt, but she wasn't going to cower in a corner. "Where are the Brownes?" she demanded.

"They've been taken care of. Tied up and locked away. Put up quite a fight, they did."

"But Christian isn't even here!"

"Of course he's not. He's exactly where I want him to be. About to meet a knife across the throat and a watery grave."

Annelise sank down on the window seat, trying to catch her breath. "What are you talking about?"

"He's off on a wild-goose chase, thinking he's going to find a long-lost brother. He's fool enough to grasp at straws, and his friend was easy enough to bribe. By now he'll be at the coast, meeting up with what he assumes to be friendly smugglers. I expect they'll wait until they're out to sea before they kill him, but the deed may already be done."

"But why?" she demanded. "He didn't hurt your daughter!"

"I'm past worrying about my daughter's feckless choices. The man knows far too much about me to return to society and start wagging his tongue. Any man who crosses Josiah Chipple and then threatens to expose him has signed his own death warrant."

"You think I'm not going to tell people what you've done?" she demanded. "That you struck me?" The moment the words were out of her mouth she realized how unwise they were. Particularly with Chipple's unpleasant smile.

"You're not going to be telling anyone anything," he said. He cocked his head to look at her with a judgmental eye. "You won't fetch much, but if I cut out your tongue it should improve your price."

"My price?"

"I traffic in human goods, Miss Kempton. Something that wouldn't go over too well in the society that still accepts the money that comes from it. Not just Africans, but young women from the poorer ports of Europe and North Africa. There's a large market for women with pale skin in the brothels of Arabia, and even with your drawbacks you should still bring in a pretty penny."

"You're mad."

"Not at all, Miss Kempton. I'm a businessman. I haven't made up my mind whether you'll have my daughter for company in the hold of the ship. Now that I've decided to cut my losses there are still a great many ways to make up her value to me."

She hid the shiver that swept over her at his cold words. "No man would pay money for me, Mr. Chipple," she said. "And I would ensure my behavior would make me even less appealing than my physical defects."

"Oh, you're not half-bad when it comes down to it. A little old, and much too tall, but you could still fetch a decent price. And we make certain the women are well broken in before they land on the auction block. It's surprisingly easy to break a woman's spirit if you know how to do it. I might just take over that little task myself."

She believed him. She would rather be hit again with those brutal hands than have them on her for any other reason, and she'd kill him before she'd let him. If she had anything to kill him with.

She rose, slowly, so as not to alarm him into another cruel action. "What if I tell you I won't fight?"

He nodded. "It would be the smart thing to do. If I know my men there's not much left of your family, and Montcalm will be dead before dawn. Putting up a fight will just make things more unpleasant for you. Someone will still be cutting out that infernal, nagging tongue of yours, however. Probably me."

She tried for a seductive smile. It felt stiff and wooden on her face, and she expected the side of her mouth was swelling, but she was a desperate woman. Who had just spent a very instructive night. "If I'm to be a slave I would think there'd be reasons a man might want my tongue intact," she said in a silken voice, moving toward him. "Particularly if I'm well trained in certain arts."

She'd managed to surprise him. His laugh was unpleasant. "You've been having a good time with Montcalm, haven't you? Filthy lecher. But your point is well taken. We'll just make certain you're sold into a place where no one speaks English, and it'll be up to them whether they want to limit your value as a whore. I expect someone will kill you before the year is out, but that's of no consequence to me. Well-bred women seldom survive long."

She hid her horrified reaction. "You've done this before?"

"A number of times. M'poor wife didn't even make it off the ship."

"I don't understand why you hate me so much, Mr. Chipple. I've never done you any harm."

His laugh was humorless. "You're just like all of them. Thinking you're better than me, just because you were born to a drunken lord who killed himself and left you without a farthing."

She took a deep breath, thinking of the marble bust that was just out of reach. "I am better than you, Mr. Chipple. Not because of my birth, but because you're a loathsome, evil man who traffics in human misery. You're a revolting little toad whose ill breeding would have shown itself even more flagrantly than it already has with your ostentatious, tasteless house and your appalling manners. Sooner or later you'll be caught, and you'll be hanged like the baseborn monster that you are."

He leaped for her, as she expected, but she was fully prepared and whirled to one side as he crashed down against the chair. By the time he caught his footing and started to turn on her she'd picked up the marble bust of Diana, and brought it down squarely on his head.

He dropped like a stone. Her hands were shaking, and she looked down at the marble, now marred with blood and hair. There was no mistaking the horrifying crunch of bone when she'd hit him, and he lay perfectly still, blood seeping from beneath his head.

She'd killed him, and she was glad. She was half tempted to lean over and bash him one more time, just to make certain, but she resisted the impulse, setting the statue down on the table once more. She skirted his body and crept to the door, putting her ear against it. There were men in the hallway, not that far away, and from the tone of their conversation their morals and intentions were not an improvement on the late Mr. Chipple. She couldn't escape that way.

Annelise moved back, stepping over the body and lifting her skirts so they wouldn't drag in the blood, and went to the window. It opened easily enough, letting in the cool fresh air of late afternoon. It wasn't a particularly large window, and it was a good eight feet off the ground, but she had little choice. She climbed through, banging her head against the window frame, and jumped.

She landed on her backside in mud, of course. Even though the rain had finally stopped, the mud was everywhere, and she dragged herself to her feet, ignoring the

pain that coursed through her body. At least she still had
the boots on.

She had no idea how many of Chipple's henchmen
were there, how long it would take them to decide to
check on their nefarious employer. She could only assume that her time was limited, and meeting up with one
of the men who were waiting outside the door seemed
even less desirable than being trapped with Chipple
himself.

Annelise had no idea where to start looking for the
Brownes, and she didn't dare take the time. She had to
warn her sister, if it wasn't already too late.

She had to warn Christian.

To her relief the stables were empty of Chipple's co-
horts, but in the front corral were at least half a dozen
new horses patiently waiting. They hadn't been unsad-
dled or properly cared for, and it took all Annelise's res-
olution not to stop and tend to the poor creatures. They
were ill treated and ill nourished, but she didn't dare
waste any time. She could only hope that at least one of
Chipple's men had some sense of responsibility for the
animals, or at the very least a practical consideration that
their mode of transportation needed to be protected.

Gertie raised her head when Annelise slipped into the
inner room, instantly alert. She made a soft, welcoming noise, and Annelise breathed a sigh of relief only
slightly tempered by nervousness. She had sworn never
to ride again, and it had been almost five years since her
last turn. And now she was planning to go haring off into
the sunset in rescue of the ones she loved.

She was mad, but there was no choice. It was easy enough to saddle and bridle Gertie—she took to Annelise's familiar touch with preening satisfaction. She had to drag a mounting block over to Gertie's side—in the best of times she would have been able to simply leap on her back. One advantage of her unusual height.

But the unaccustomed ache in her hips and thighs precluded such energy, though she wasn't about to consider what had caused such discomfort. Christian didn't have a lady's saddle, and she had no choice but to climb astride, bunching the skirts up around her long legs. The moment she landed in the saddle she panicked, and her fear immediately spread to Gertie, who backed up with a nervous whinny.

Annelise took a deep breath, leaning down to touch Gertie's neck, whispering calming words that were meant more for her than for her horse. She was about to urge the horse forward when a small movement caught her eye.

Her first instinct was to get out of there. But if whoever or whatever hid in the shadows was any danger to her he would have attacked already.

"Who's there?" she demanded in a sharp whisper.

A rumpled head of hair appeared over a bale of straw, followed by the stable lad's woebegone face. Jeremy, she remembered. "I'm sorry, miss. I was afraid," he cried.

He was probably not much more than fifteen. The age of her niece, the one Chipple had threatened. "Do you know where the Brownes are being kept?"

He shook his head. "Mebbe in the cellars—you can

lock them easily enough, and I don't think anyone would dare mess with Mrs. Browne if they had any choice."

"Do you think you can help them?"

He shook his head again, frankly terrified. "I'm not sure where they are, miss. And I'm afraid of those men."

He truly did look petrified. "But you could ride for help, couldn't you? Take one of those horses and go find someone?"

"Yes, miss," he said, nodding, still not looking too eager.

Now that Jeremy would help, she had a decision to make. Should she go down to the coast, to warn Christian before it was too late? Or north to rescue her sister? Annelise knew where her duty lay. She knew where her heart lay. And she knew her sister was twice as formidable as Bessie Browne and Annelise put together.

"I want you to ride north to Marymede," she said to him. "My sister and her family need to be warned that Chipple is sending men after them, as well. It should be easy enough to find—my brother-in-law is the vicar, and their house is next to the church."

"Are more of those men there?" Jeremy questioned, looking less than resolved.

"Not if you get there first." The boy was panicked and witless. Christian was a grown man, more than able to take care of himself, while the vicar's household consisted of her sharp-tongued sister, her gentle husband, her niece and possibly the two lovebirds, Will and Hetty.

And somehow she doubted Will would be much defense against Chipple's marauders.

There was no question what she *should* do. And no question about what she was going to do anyway.

"Go," she said. "Head north and with any luck you should be there by daylight. Lives may depend on you."

Probably the wrong thing to say to a trembling boy, but he straightened his shoulders and suddenly looked very brave. "Yes, miss. Are you coming with me?"

"No," she said firmly. "I'm going to save your master."

25

Even riding hell-bent didn't stop Christian's fertile mind from working. As far as he knew, Crosby had never done an unselfish thing in his life. That was one of the advantages of having him as a friend and companion—he was possibly even more unsentimental than Christian himself. Only the promise of money would send him haring off into the countryside, and it would have to be a very large sum of money indeed. Not the simple repayment of a bribe to a simple freetrader.

Perhaps his baby brother had somehow managed to survive all these years. If there was even one chance in a hundred he'd risk everything, walk into a trap, in order to try to save him. And he had little doubt that was exactly what was happening. He just didn't know how Crosby had gotten mixed up with a roller like Chipple.

The sun was setting when they reached the bluff overlooking the rocky coast of Devon. They stopped at the top of the narrow path. There was no sign of anyone on the beach, not even footprints, but the tide was going out, taking everything with it.

"Where are your smugglers, Crosby?" he asked.

Crosby looked as innocent as a lamb, and it appeared a little too forced, an act. "Where do you think they are, old man? Hiding down there by the caves. Smugglers don't usually advertise their presence in broad daylight."

"Can our horses make it down the path?"

"You're not suggesting I walk?" Crosby said in horror. "Of course they can. But we'd best move along before it's fully dark."

"Indeed," Christian said in an even voice, one hand touching the pistol tucked beneath his waistcoat. If Crosby had lied to him, betrayed him, he'd shoot him. It would be that simple. He expected treachery from his friend. But not treachery that involved his lost family.

He let Crosby lead the way, noting that he seemed far too familiar with the stony path. It was almost full dark by the time they reached the pebbled beach, and there was still no sign of the smugglers that were supposed to lead him to France and rescue.

"Where are your smugglers, Crosby?" he asked again. Crosby had dismounted, and he was looking around him in the dusk with a fair amount of nervousness.

"They should be here. I was told they'd be waiting."

"By whom, Crosby?" He dismounted as well, his voice even. He could see movement in the shadows, over by the edge of the cliffs. Presumably from the caves Crosby had talked about, and he expected he was about to get his answer. The pistol wasn't primed and ready, and in defense it would provide little more than a club. But he'd been taught to fight by the best and the worst, and he had more weapons than Crosby would even begin to suspect, including the jeweled blade his mother had given him, strapped to his ankle.

"What do you mean, old man?" Crosby was sounding nervous now, and the shadows were separating into the shapes of men, moving toward them.

"Who paid you to bring me here, Crosby?" he asked in a calm voice. "What was your price to sell me out?"

A rueful smile touched Crosby's thin lips. "You've always been a smart one, Christian. And I have to tell you that it pained me, deeply, to do this to you. But it's very costly to live a gentleman's life and my expenses were crushing. You would hardly expect me to turn down such a magnificent offer."

"Hardly," he echoed. There were at least twenty of them, scum of the earth, if he was any judge. "What was my Judas price? I'm just curious what I'm worth on the open market."

"Oh, quite a bit, old man, if the one who wants you dead is determined enough. Five hundred pounds for me, plus the expense of all these good men. They really are smugglers, you know."

"I imagined so. Only five hundred pounds? I'm offended, Crosby. You should have held out for more. I'm certain Chipple would have met your price."

"There's not much one can put past you," Crosby said in admiring tones. "When did you figure it out?"

"At least an hour ago."

"And you still came along?" he said, astonished. Christian shrugged, no longer caring that it was such a Gallic gesture. He had more important things to attend to at that moment. "There was always the slight chance that you weren't lying."

"Worth your life?"

"I'm not going to die, Crosby."

Crosby looked at the ring of men who'd surrounded him. "I'm afraid you are, Christian. A pity, because I've always admired you, but—"

"Will you shut yer bleedin' trap?" One of the smugglers stepped forward, clearly the leader. "We have our orders, and we'll follow them, but that doesn't mean we have to listen to the likes of you jawing on and on."

Crosby looked affronted. "I beg your pardon? I brought him here, and—"

"And your part is done. You're expendable." He turned to the other men. "Isn't he, lads?"

The response was far from heartening. Crosby began to back away, looking nervous. "Then I'll just leave you with him," he said. "I'm certain you're more than capable of doing your job."

"I don't think so," the leader said. "I like your horse."

"You're a smuggler—you can't put a horse in a boat!" Crosby cried.

"True enough. But we have places to store things— that pretty little horse will be just fine for a few days while we go to France."

"You really are taking Christian to France?"

"Hell, no. We'll drop him overboard halfway between—that way there'll be no trace of him."

"Oh," Crosby said blankly, still backing away. "But

I'm certain you wouldn't leave me here without a proper mount. When the tide comes in this place is flooded."

"True enough," said the leader. "And we can't take you to France with us—the boats will be crowded enough with his nibs along. I think we'll just have to finish you right now."

"You wouldn't—"

The pistol flashed in the gathering darkness, bright enough to expose the expression of outraged shock on Crosby's face before he crumpled onto the rocky beach, blood streaming from the hole in his forehead.

"Good shot," Christian said coolly. Crosby's one drawback was that he'd always been more greedy than wise, and he had just paid the price. And Christian had no inclination to feel regret.

The leader sized him up. "Don't waste your breath with compliments, m'boy. You'll be just as dead as he is before long."

"I expect so. Why not now?" He was merely curious. Not that he had any intention of dying, but the logic behind the smuggler's actions was interesting.

"I was told to take you out to sea and cut your throat, and Dick Parsons is a man of his word."

One of the smugglers snickered, and Parsons whirled around with a snarl. "Don't you be trying yer luck, Hoskins! The sea will take yer body as well as that toff's without any trouble."

All trace of amusement vanished from the assembled men. There was no way Christian could fight his way past the lot of them—he'd simply have to take them one at a time. If worst came to worst, he was a very strong swimmer, and he could simply dive overboard when they weren't expecting it.

"It's an honor to be dealing with a man of his word," Christian said politely. "When are we planning to leave?"

"What's it to you?"

He shrugged. "I'd like a chance to clear my conscience."

"What are you, some bloody Frenchie? We don't have no priests here!" the man snapped.

"You astonish me. But I have no interest in popish rites. I'd simply like a quiet moment or two to go over my sins in private and come to terms with my demise."

"Fair enough," the chief smuggler replied. "We're waiting to be paid, and I don't do nothing for free. Unless you annoy me. I expect our employer will want to see us cut yer throat for himself, but I'm hoping we can reason with him. If he expects us to drag a bloody corpse into the boat he'll have to pay us more than he has already. I expect we'll be leaving at high tide. Take him into one of the caves and tie him up until we're ready." He glanced over at Crosby's corpse. "And you can toss that one into the water."

"Won't the tide wash him ashore?" Christian said.

The smuggler looked at him with new respect. "You're a cool one, aren't you? There's a strong current in these parts that'll carry him halfway down the coast before he's found. By then there won't be much to recognize."

Merci beaucoup, Christian thought. That information could be very useful if he ended up swimming for it. "You've thought of everything," he said with tones just admiring enough to be believable.

"I'm a careful man. Don't ever forget it."

"I don't expect I'll have a chance to," Christian replied.

The cave was cold and damp, not unexpectedly, and they tied him tightly, not bothering with a gag, then left him. He closed his eyes and bowed his head, looking repentant, and they wandered off, chuckling.

It would take him less than five minutes to free himself, he reasoned. They'd deprived him of his pistols, the small sword and the jeweled dagger, but they'd never considered that a gentleman would be conversant with back-alley tricks, and the knife tucked behind his back remained hidden there.

He had two choices. He could free himself immediately and make his escape before they even knew he was gone. Or he could wait until Chipple arrived. The latter was infinitely more risky, but undeniably appealing. He owed Chipple; not for the kidnapping and the murder plot but for the cruelly false hope about his brother that he'd given him for a precious hour or so.

Yes, he would wait. Long enough to finish Chipple, and then he'd fight his way out of there. And if he failed, so be it. There wasn't anything particularly inspiring to live for.

Would the dragon mourn him? he wondered. Probably not. He'd left her with a solid hatred of him—the best thing he could have done—and if she was the sensible creature he hoped, she'd rejoice at the news of his disappearance and probable demise.

But she wasn't the sensible creature she appeared to be. Beneath that starchy surface was a soft, melting woman, one who was foolish enough to think he was worth loving. She'd mourn him, and he hated to think he'd cause her more tears.

The answer was simple. He wouldn't die. If only to let her keep on hating him.

He leaned his head back against the damp wall of the cave and closed his eyes. It was early evening and high tide wouldn't come till after midnight. He had no idea when Chipple was expected, but he imagined it wouldn't be for a few hours. In the meantime he could conserve his energy for when he needed it. And stop thinking about the maddening Miss Kempton.

The noise and shouts came sooner than he expected, startling him into full alertness. The moon was only partway across the sky—and yet someone had clearly arrived. It didn't sound as if it was a particularly welcome guest, and he wondered if Harry Browne had come to his rescue. It would be the foolish sort of thing he'd do, but he would have no idea where Christian had disappeared to. By the time he found him, Christian would be long gone.

Maybe it was just some poor sailor who happened onto the wrong section of the coast. In which case the shouting would be done, the sailor would have joined poor old Crosby, and he could go back to sleep.

He could hear them approaching the cave, and he

quickly closed his eyes in prayerful repose. He doubted it was Chipple himself—the men were making obscene comments that would hardly befit the man who was paying them. And then he felt a sudden horror shoot through his body, opening his eyes just as they dumped a bedraggled package of humanity a few feet away from him.

"This your lady friend?" Hoskins, the one who'd dragged her and dumped her unceremoniously, questioned. "You should be able to do better than this." He prodded her huddled form with his foot. "Cap'n Parsons ain't too happy to have another one, but he's thinking Chipple might pay double for her. Otherwise we'll just cut her throat."

"I don't know what you're talking about—" he said in a bored voice. She was no more than a bundle of wet rags and he wondered what they'd done to her. At the thought, he felt a rage sweep over him, so powerful that it took all his self-control to feign disinterest.

"The ladybird. Came looking for you, she did, carrying a pistol and everything. Too bad she didn't know how to shoot." Hoskins leaned over and grabbed her hair, dragging her to a sitting position. She didn't make a sound.

"We'll leave you two together. Shouldn't be long now, and if she's one of your sins you can always ask her forgiveness." He chuckled, dropping her back against the wall. She lay unmoving, her eyes closed as the man left them, still laughing.

If she was dead he would kill every one of them. And then she opened her eyes, and he decided he'd kill her instead.

"What the bloody hell are you doing here?" he demanded in a sharp whisper.

She looked terrible. Her hair was a loose tangle, her clothes torn and muddy. Her mouth was swollen on one side, she had a black eye on the other, and she was the most pathetic thing he'd ever seen. Damn her.

"Rescuing you," she said in a rusty voice.

If his hands were free he would have strangled her. "Did it ever occur to you that I might not need rescuing?"

"Chipple arrived at Wynche End. He said they were going to cut your throat and toss you into the sea. I sent Jeremy off to warn Hetty and my sister, and I came here. Stupid, I suppose."

"Extremely stupid. How did you get here?"

She swallowed. "I rode."

He was silent for a moment. "How did you know where to find me?"

"Chipple told me. He was…threatening me, and he told me you were going to be murdered by smugglers."

"Chipple told you?" he repeated. "I doubt it was an accidental slip of the tongue. And then he just let you go?"

"No, he didn't. He's dead. I killed him."

Maybe he wouldn't strangle her after all. He took a deep breath. "How did you manage that?"

"I bashed him on the head with the statue of Diana."

"Very fitting," he murmured. "But that still doesn't solve the problem."

She turned her head slightly. She looked exhausted, which was no wonder. Had it only been the night before when they'd been entwined in the one bed at Wynche End? "What problem?"

"I can escape easily enough. Trying to get you out as well makes it a great deal more difficult. You really are the most tiresome creature."

He was hoping to goad her formidable temper, but she simply closed her eyes again. "Then leave me. When Chipple fails to show up they'll probably just head out to sea and forget about me."

"When Chipple fails to show up they'll rape and murder you, my pet."

"Better than Chipple's plans. He was going to sell me to a brothel and that would have lasted a great deal longer. I warned him I wouldn't fetch much of a price, but he said he didn't care."

"True enough. Is that when you killed him?"

She opened her eyes to glare at him, her first sign of life. "If escape is such an easy matter, why don't you go ahead? Just leave me. I'm capable to taking care of myself."

His laugh was without humor. "Of course you are. And if you think I'm going to endanger myself because of your half-brained notion of rescuing me then you are deluded."

"I have no delusions about you," she said wearily. "If you're leaving, go."

"Who hit you?"

"Does it matter?"

He'd managed to slide the thin blade from behind his back, and he began sawing away at the ropes. "Not particularly. I was just curious."

"The man who dragged me in here. I gather I'm to be his reward if things go well. Not that he seemed particularly gratified at such a boon, but I guess I'm better than nothing."

"Stop feeling sorry for yourself. It's tedious."

She jerked her head up to glare at him. "I have every right to feel sorry for myself!" she snapped. "I'm about to die in a very unpleasant manner, and you're not even grateful that I was fool enough to come to try to warn you. I made the colossal mistake of falling in love, and not only that, I destroyed my reputation for no other reason than wanton lust."

He didn't smile, much as he wanted to. He wasn't in the mood to make her feel better. He kicked free of the ropes, tucking the knife into his boot, and rose, towering over her.

"Are you just going to leave me here?" she said, trying not to sound pathetic.

"It's the practical thing to do. If I try and take you with me they'll catch up with us, and I can't risk that. This is your fault—you'll just have to live with the consequences. When I reach the nearest town I'll send help. They might make it here in time."

"Lovely," she murmured. "You worthless, donkey-loving whoreson," she added in French.

At another time he might have laughed—or kissed her. Instead, he simply shrugged, stepped past her and out of the mouth of the cave.

The moon had risen, and he could see them all quite clearly while he remained in the shadows. They had two longboats, and even on such a still night it would be rough going on the open channel.

He could escape quite easily, scrambling up the side of the cliff before they even noticed he was gone. As long as he didn't have the substantial weight of a tall woman dragging him down.

She didn't make a sound behind him in the cave. "Son of a bitch," he muttered, and turned back to where Annelise was huddled, yanking her upright and slicing through her bonds with a little less care than he should have used.

As he suspected, she was none too steady on her feet, and she swayed for a moment, looking at him through dazed eyes. "What are you doing?" she asked.

"Saving your goddamned life," he muttered. "Though I have no earthly idea why. I'll probably die doing it."

"Because you care about me?"

He managed a totally derisive laugh before slinging her over his shoulder. Why the hell did he have to get saddled with such a tall woman? he thought. Why couldn't he have fallen in love with a—

He almost dumped her over the side of the path as that unwarranted thought popped into his brain. As if he needed more irrational complications at that moment. He growled, low in his throat, and started up the narrow pathway.

He'd waited too long, of course. The moon moved from behind a cloud, illuminating them far too clearly, and he heard a shout from the shoreline, followed by the crack of a rifle. "He's getting away!" someone shouted. "Damn you, get after them."

There was no mistaking Josiah Chipple's booming voice. "Killed him, did you?" Christian muttered, dumping Annelise onto the ground without ceremony. She let out a muffled *oof*. "He seems to have survived quite handily!"

"I did my best," she said in a sulky voice.

"You can't get away, Montcalm!" Josiah shouted from the shoreline. "If you come down without any trouble we'll let the girl go."

Not bloody likely, he thought, glancing down at Annelise. She was pale and silent and he cursed again, wishing he still had at least one of his pistols.

"Stay here," he whispered.

"No! Don't believe him!" she cried desperately, clutching his boot.

He helped her into the undergrowth with the vain hope of hiding her, when all hell broke loose from the beach below them. There were suddenly three times as many men on the beach, and it was all-out war.

"Don't move or I'll come back and strangle you," he said, half wishing he meant it, and then he raced down the twisted path to the beach, charging into the midst of the fray, allowing himself only a brief moment to wonder whether he'd ever have a chance to threaten the dragon again.

26

The Honorable Annelise Kempton couldn't believe the situation she was in. She'd been shoved, punched, slapped, tied up, had filthy inappropriate hands all over her. Riding astride on Gertie's broad back hadn't helped the general achiness between her legs, and remembering why hadn't helped her state of mind. She'd pounded through the countryside on the back of a horse for the first time in years, clinging for dear life, terrified that she'd be too late only to realize that she was worthless against a gang of smugglers and simply an inconvenience for Christian.

Stupid, stupid, stupid, she told herself, crawling out of the underbrush. And even now, amidst the noise and gunfire, he might be killed. It would serve him right, and she would go down and pick up his limp body and tell him so, just before she walked into the sea.

Damn him, anyway. She shouldn't have bothered—after all, she was never going to see him again anyway. Whether he was dead or alive shouldn't have made any difference.

But it did. Because no matter how cruel he was, Christian Montcalm couldn't make her stop loving him. Idiot that she was.

She struggled to her knees, looking down at the carnage below. In the bright moonlight she could see Christian quite clearly. He was astride some man, beating him, and for a moment Annelise assumed it was Josiah Chipple. But Chipple was standing to one side, between two uniformed soldiers, and most of the fighting had stopped. A few bodies littered the beach, a familiar-looking carriage waited off to the side, and as Annelise stumbled to her feet she recognized who had come to the rescue.

Her sister, brother-in-law and William Dickinson, accompanied by a troop of soldiers, one of whom was pulling Christian off the unconscious man he'd seemed determined to kill.

And then it was very still, only the sound of the surf breaking the silence. They were talking down there, and she called out, but her voice was cracked and dry and no one seemed to hear her. She started down the path, slipped and went down on her rump, letting out a cry of protest. As if her poor body hadn't been through enough. At this rate she wasn't going to sit down for days.

By the time she reached the end of the trail she was ready to cry from sheer frustration. The sight that met her at the bottom was far from reassuring—instead of carting Chipple off, the soldiers were standing by while the smugglers climbed into their boats, with the addition of the man Christian had beaten and Mr. Chipple.

"What in the name of God are you doing?" she called out in a cross voice. It came out as little more than a croak, but at least someone heard her. Eugenia turned her head, a disapproving expression on her face, and strode across the sand.

"You've made quite the mess of it this time, my girl," she scolded. Eugenia was the bossiest female on the face of the earth, and Annelise hadn't the slightest expectation of sympathy. "At least you managed to have the good sense to send someone to warn us while you went haring off like an absolute hoyden, nearly getting yourself killed. And a good thing we were already coming after you to rescue you from that den of iniquity. Not that I blame you entirely. Mr. Montcalm has a great deal to answer for, and so I told him, and shall elucidate more clearly once we get off this dreadful beach and—"

"Why are they letting them go?" Annelise broke through her sister's diatribe. Eugenia was several inches shorter than she was and a great deal stouter, but she still managed to make Annelise feel like a naughty child.

"Because there's no way of seeing Mr. Chipple brought to justice without ruining both his daughter and you, my dear. He's off to France with those disreputable smugglers with the stern warning not to return. In my opinion he probably won't make it as far as the coast. The smugglers don't seem to have a very high opinion of him, and he's done nothing to endear himself to them."

"They killed a man," Annelise said. "They shot a man in cold blood, and they were going to kill Christian and me. How can they let them get away with it?"

"Mr. Montcalm," Eugenia corrected primly. "The fact is, both you and Mr. Montcalm are perfectly all right, except for those horrid bruises on your face, and it sounds as if the late Mr. Crosby Pennington was no great loss to society. One must be practical about such things, Annelise. I thought I taught you to be practical above all things."

"I try," she muttered.

"Joseph and William are taking care of any details. Right now I want you to accompany me back to the carriage, and you are not to speak to Mr. Montcalm or even glance his way. Do you understand?"

She'd been glancing his way intently since she'd reached the bottom of the path, but he seemed totally oblivious to her. "I need to—"

"You don't need to do anything at all but come back to Marymede and keep me company while we attempt to repair your good name. Clearly the man has no proper interest in you, and all you have of value is your reputation, thanks to our father's fecklessness. We can repair it, but you'll have to do exactly as I say."

Eugenia always wanted people to do exactly as she said, and there were very few brave souls who attempted to defy her. Perhaps when she felt stronger Annelise would put up a fight. Right now she was too weary. And there was nowhere else to go—Christian's back was to her now, as he looked out to sea and the boats disappearing on the glassy surface. She could almost imagine he had gone, as well—out of her life, across the clear blue sea.

Eugenia took her silence for assent—she could imagine no other response to her orders. "Come along now, Annelise. The sooner we get you away from this place the better."

"What about Gertie?"

"Your old horse? What about her? She was sold along with the rest of the property."

"She's mine now. I tied her up at the top of the bluff, and I'm not leaving without her."

"But where did she come from?"

"She's mine," Annelise said stubbornly. If Christian wouldn't give her up then he'd have to face her and talk to her. Otherwise Gertie was coming back with her, where she belonged.

Eugenia let out a long-suffering sigh. "You are the most uncooperative of females. I'll see what Joseph has to say." She turned her back on her bedraggled sister and made her way across the pebbled beach with all the aplomb of a duchess.

This left Annelise with two choices. To run across the beach to Christian and to force him to face her. Or to head straight back up the cliff to Gertie and wait for them to reach her. In one direction was disdain and rejection and in the other was the unquestioning love of an animal. The cliff wasn't that steep.

She started up it. Her feet in the unaccustomed boots were killing her, her thigh muscles ached, her head throbbed and her throat was tight with unshed tears. She climbed higher and higher, holding on to wind-warped branches as she made her way. Staying with Eugenia was the best thing possible, she told herself. She deserved her improving lectures, and Eugenia was so firmly above reproach that her exceptional reputation would hopefully spread a bit to her wayward sister.

She found she could smile. The very thought of the Honorable Miss Annelise Kempton being wayward was curiously cheering. Within a short time she would settle back into her cool, disapproving spinsterhood. She'd replace her spectacles, order a new set of lace caps and prepare for a quiet life in the country.

But for this last day she could revel in being the wanton who lived in her heart. The wanton who belonged only to Christian.

She was out of breath when she reached the top of the bluff where Gertie was patiently waiting. She sank down on the ground, looking out over the moonlit ocean. The boats were almost out of sight now, and she thought she saw a splash to one side, as if something large and unpleasant was being thrown overboard. Or perhaps it was just wishful thinking.

The wind had picked up. Her hair was a tangled mess, blowing in her eyes, and as she pushed it out of the way she ran her hand over her damp face. She had no idea why it was wet—the climb hadn't been that strenuous. Perhaps it was simply a reaction to all the high drama. After all, she'd nearly been killed tonight. It was understandable that she'd feel a bit overwrought.

She sat for a long time, the wind whipping her hair. The moon set, the boats had long disappeared across the horizon, and the first rays of sunlight appeared in the east. A new day, she thought wearily. A new life.

She'd drawn her knees up, her arms clasped around them, and she put her face down against the soft torn wool of the ancient riding habit, wishing she could sleep, wishing she could cry, wishing a thousand things that she couldn't have. And when she lifted her head he was standing there in front of her. Alone.

She looked at him. His hair was loose, blowing in the wind, as well. His shirt had been torn open, he had a bruise across his cheekbone, and his hands...

"There's blood on your hands," she said in a hollow voice.

"I didn't kill him."

"Who?" Chipple had seemed remarkably intact as he'd climbed into the boat. She wondered if he'd been so when he'd gone over the side.

"Our friend Hoskins. He hurt you."

She blinked. Why he should care one way or another was beyond her comprehension. "Chipple hit me, too. I'm afraid it's too late to go after him but I appreciate the thought."

The ghost of a smile danced across his mouth. "There's my dragon. Though I may have to revise my opinion of you. Your sister is enough to put the fear of God into any man."

"She's a real corker, isn't she?" Annelise said wistfully. "I wish I had half her strength of character."

"You have far too much already."

"Flattering as always, Mr. Montcalm."

"They live too close to Wynche End."

"They're at least two days away! The only reason

they got here so quickly is they'd come to rescue me. And I'm sure they won't be any trouble to you—they'd have no reason to try to pursue the acquaintance, given the circumstances."

He ignored her little speech. "Your brother-in-law seems like a decent enough man, however. Long-suffering, poor soul, to put with a creature like his wife, but then, I can understand that kind of torment. He's probably not any worse off than me."

"What in the world are you talking about?"

He stared at her in silence for a moment, as if he was at a loss for words. But the charming Christian Montcalm had never been at a loss for words in his life—not for long.

"In truth their proximity is a fortunate thing. No one will have any idea you spent the night at Wynche End. People will believe the worst, of course, but in the end most everyone will accept that you spent a chaste week at your sister's house, spending a great deal of time in bed getting over an unpleasant illness."

"I did spend far too much time in bed," she snapped. "And 'unpleasant' is too mild a word."

He laughed, when she thought she would never hear him laugh again. "So you're free and clear and I owe you nothing."

"Indeed," she said in an acid voice. "You may rejoice at your lucky escape. As may I."

He shook his head. "I'm afraid not," he said. He reached down for her hand, but she had no intention of giving it to him. He had no intention of not taking it, and a moment later she found herself hauled to her feet in front of him.

"It's a good thing you're an aging orphan," he murmured, gently pushing the hair away from her face. "I don't have to wait around to get anyone's permission."

"Permission for what, you rat bastard?" she said.

"Such language, dragon. I'm afraid you're going to have to marry me."

Her eyes widened in outrage. "You just told me that my reputation is intact. My sister will ensure it. And if you're worried about any issue from that night of total debauchery you can set your mind at ease. I had just completed my menses and the likelihood of becoming pregnant is almost nil. If by any chance I'm mistaken I'll be certain to let you know."

He put his other hand on her cheek, cupping her face gently, careful not to touch the bruises. "I *am* a rat bastard," he acknowledged genially. "I deserve a lifetime of torment and repentance. You're the most qualified person I know to deliver such a punishment."

"You have no right to mock me!" she said. "I've had a very difficult few days."

"As have I. Don't be tiresome. I've already abducted one bride, I would have no qualms about abducting another. And we wouldn't have as far to travel."

"You don't have to marry me!" she cried. "Did someone hit you on the head and knock you senseless? If so, I'd be more than happy to administer another blow to see if it might cure you. My reputation is safe. There is no need for you to make a decent woman out of me."

"Ah, my sweet, I already have," he said. He was going to kiss her, and if she had any pride at all she'd kick him in the shins with her heavy boots, shove him away, over the cliff if she could....

The touch of his mouth on hers was so soft it was like a benediction, and she felt the embarrassing tears fill her eyes once more. He had the most deleterious effect on her strength of mind, damn him.

"You'll marry me, my dragon, and you'll bear my children, and you'll drive me mad and live in that ramshackle old house with me and I'll even put up with the occasional visit from your sister if I must. But you'll marry me. Not because you have to. But because I won't let you go."

She was crying, damn it, and there was nothing she could do about it. "Why?" she demanded.

And he answered the only way he could, in French. *"Je t'aime,"* he said. "I love you."

She must have been holding her breath for days. She released it, melting in his arms. *"Je t'aime aussi,"* she said. "And I will make your life a living hell," she added in the same language.

He smiled down at her. "I'm counting on it."

EPILOGUE

10 years later

Christian Montcalm ambled across the field in the direction of the old mansion, two spaniels at his heels. He was in shirtsleeves, but it was a warm day, and he was in no particular need of a coat.

Wynche End was looking better, though nothing would disguise the gothic eccentricities of the place. The new roof had just been completed, and he was pleased that he would no longer be distracted by importunate leaks when he was in the midst of his marital duties. Though he was broad-minded enough to appreciate a few surprises and Annelise had responded with appropriate enthusiasm, sleeping in damp sheets had never been a pleasant experience.

He heard the screams of rage from a distance, but he made no effort to quicken his pace. It was far too nice a day to rush, and he had little doubt where the noise came from. By the time he reached the stable yard the battle seemed to have been concluded. His six-year-old son, Christopher Hercules, was on the ground in the dirt, howling with rage, as his eight-year-old daughter, Minerva Elizabeth, sat atop him, keeping him down. In the meantime, the Browne twins, both seven, were trying to reason with his termagant daughter.

He paused long enough to pluck his daughter off her brother and set her on the ground. She immediately charged back toward her furious sibling, but he simply caught her and held her for a moment, dangling in mid-air. "Behave yourself, Minnie, or I'll tell your mother," he said. Enough to put the fear of God into most people, but Minnie was more than a match for the dragon.

She knew better than to protest. He set her back down on the ground, and she glared at her brother as he scrambled to his feet. He looked as if he was about to leap on her, and Christian cast a warning glance in his direction. "That goes for you, as well, my boy."

Hercules was wise enough to fear his mother's formidable temper, and he retreated with a muttered curse, one that Christian wisely overlooked. They knew to harness their language in the presence of their starchy aunt and uncle, and in the meantime it was an improvement over fighting. Hercules was sporting a black eye from the last go-round, and Christian was sorely tempted to pick them both up and toss them in the pond to cool their tempers. It was a pity neither of them took after him, but at least it kept things lively.

A moment later all was sunshine as the four children

took off for the fields, chatting amiably, some new plan forming. Christian shook his head, trying to dispel the sudden feeling of dread as he considered just what those four fertile minds could come up with, and walked the rest of the way to the house.

He found his wife in the library, her spectacles at the end of her nose as she perused some improving text full of high-flown romance. Her taste in literature had always amused him, a sure sign that her taste in husbands was equally impractical.

She looked up and gave him a quick smile as she closed the book, shoving it behind her in an effort to hide it. He leaned over and kissed her. "Your children are killing each other," he said mildly.

"Again?"

"I expect the twins will keep them alive. After all, their parents did the same for me."

She gave him a fond glance. "I expect Minnie was just pointing out the error of Hercules's ways."

"I expect she was." He wanted her beside him, and not in that spindly chair, so he simply reached down and picked her up. She let out a shriek of surprised laughter before he dropped down on the shabby sofa, holding her in his lap.

She let him distract her for a few moments, then emerged from his attentions with a stern expression on her face. "You haven't told me about the horses."

"Mother and foal are doing very well." He let her pull her dress up with great reluctance. The Brownes were used to his indiscretions, but some of the underservants expected a more traditional household, and he did his best not to rattle them.

"Good," she said, her voice a bit absent, which wasn't like her. Annelise took the breeding program very seriously indeed, and the horses produced by their small stable were becoming legendary.

He tugged at her dress again, just enough to give him access to a few inches of her shoulder, and he kissed her. He could feel her nervousness, which always amused him. Even after ten years he had the ability to unsettle her.

"I think you look tired," he murmured against her skin. "You need a nap. A few hours of rest—I'll make certain none of the servants are anywhere around to bother us."

"Behave yourself," she said in much the same tones he'd used on his children. "I need to tell you something."

He set her beside him on the sofa, watching her warily. "Am I going to like it?" he asked cautiously.

"Yes and no," she said. "My sister Eugenia is coming to stay again."

"Oh, God, no!" he groaned. "She nearly killed me last time! You'd think all her energy would have been spent on you and the new baby, but no, she had more than enough advice to spare for her poor brother-in-law."

"She's good for you. Makes you behave."

"I don't like to behave."

"I know, my darling. But you will while she's here. You'll be on your best behavior."

He didn't bother to argue—it would be a waste. "And when are we expecting the boon of such a visit?"

"In approximately eight months." Her smile was dulcet, almost shy, and if he'd ever forgotten why he loved her that furtive smile would have reminded him.

He put his hand on her still-flat belly, leaned down and kissed her, quite indecently. She laughed, drew him up and kissed him on the mouth. "So what are we going to name this one?"

"Aphrodite if it's a girl," she said.

"Priapus if it's a boy?"

She gave him a tiny shove. "That's reserved for his father. It's no wonder I'm in this condition again."

"No wonder," he said, brushing his mouth against her temple. "Why don't we call him Tom or John or Dick or something?"

"Ares," she said. "That'll give him a fighting chance against his sister."

"It won't do any good. We breed powerful she-dragons—the poor males are no match for them."

"Oh, I think you're a very good match indeed," Annelise murmured. "And you're right—an expectant mother does need to nap more often."

"I knew there was something to make up for your sister's imminent visit," he said, rising and taking her hand. "I'll see to it that you get lots of rest."

"Of course you will," the Honorable Annelise Kempton Montcalm teased, letting him lead her up the stairs. "You are, after all, such a gentleman."

And the very wicked Christian Montcalm simply smiled.

Please turn the page for a sneak peek at Anne Stuart's next book, COLD AS ICE, a riveting contemporary romantic-suspense novel, on sale in November 2006.

1

Genevieve Spencer adjusted her four-hundred-dollar sunglasses, smoothed her sleek, perfect chignon and stepped aboard the powerboat beneath the bright Caribbean sun. It was early April, and after a long, cold, wet winter in New York City she should have been ready for the brilliant sunshine dancing off the greeny blue waters. Unfortunately she wasn't in the mood to appreciate it. For one thing, she didn't want to be there. She had a six-week sabbatical from her job as junior partner in the law firm of Roper, Hyde, Camui and Fredericks, and she'd been looking forward to something a great deal different. In two days' time she'd be in the rain forests of Costa Rica with no makeup, no contact lenses, no high heels and no expectations to live up to. She'd been so ready to shed her protective skin that this final task seemed like an enormous burden instead of the simple thing it was.

Grand Cayman Island was on her way to Central America. Sort of. And one extra day wouldn't make any difference, Walter Fredericks had told her. Besides, what red-blooded, single, thirty-year-old female would object to spending even a short amount of time with *People* magazine's Sexiest Man of the Year, billionaire division? Harry Van Dorn was gorgeous, charming and currently between wives, and the law firm that represented the Van Dorn Trust Foundation needed some papers signed. This was perfect for everyone—serendipity.

Genevieve didn't think so, but she kept her mouth shut. She'd learned diplomacy and tact in the past few years since Walt Fredericks had taken her under his wing, and she knew that for now going along was in her best interest. She'd have time to think about things once she got to Costa Rica and shed all the trappings that had become a suit of armor.

So she'd pulled out her pale gray Armani suit, put on seven-hundred-dollar Manolo Blahnik shoes she hadn't even blinked at buying, the shoes that hurt her feet, made her tower over most men and matched the Armani and nothing else. When she first brought them home she'd emerged from her corporate daze enough to look at the price tag and burst into tears. What had happened to the idealistic young woman who was determined to spend her life helping people? The rescuer, who spent her money on the oppressed, not on designer clothing?

Unfortunately she knew the answer, and she didn't want to dwell on it. In her tightly controlled life she'd learned to look forward rather than back, and the shoes were beautiful and she told herself she deserved them. And she'd brought them to see Harry Van Dorn, as part of her protective armor.

They didn't make climbing down into the launch any easier, but she managed with a modicum of grace. She hated boats. She rarely got seasick, but she always felt vaguely trapped. She could see the massive white shape of the Van Dorn yacht against the brilliant horizon—it looked more like a mansion than a boat, and maybe she could simply ignore the sea surrounding them and pretend they were in a fancy restaurant. She was good at ignoring unpleasant facts—she'd learned the hard way that that was what you had to do to survive.

And it was going to be only a few hours. She'd let Harry Van Dorn feed her, get him to sign the papers she'd brought with her in her slim leather briefcase and once she'd arranged to have them couriered back to New York she'd be free. Only a matter of hours—she was silly to feel so edgy. It was far too beautiful a day to have this sense of impending doom. There could be no doom under the bright Caribbean sun.

Her tranquilizers were in her tiny purse. Harry Van Dorn's crew had gotten her comfortably seated with a glass of iced tea in one hand. It was a simple enough matter to sneak out one yellow pill and take it. She'd almost planned to leave them behind in New York—she didn't expect to need tranquilizers in the rain forest, but fortunately she'd changed her mind at the last minute. It was going to take a few minutes for it to kick in, but she could get by on sheer determination until then.

She'd been on yachts before—Roper and company specialized in handling the legal concerns for a myriad of charitable foundations, and money was no object.

She'd gone from her job as public defender to private law practice, and she'd hoped specializing in charitable foundations was still close enough to honorable work to assuage the remnants of her liberal conscience. She'd been quickly disillusioned—the foundations set up as tax shelters by the wealthy tended to spend as much money glorifying the donors' names and providing cushy jobs and benefits for their friends as they did on charity, but by then it was too late, and Genevieve was committed. Harry Van Dorn's floating palace, SS *Seven Sins,* was on a grander scale than she'd seen so far, and she knew for a fact it was owned by the Van Dorn Trust Foundation, not Harry himself, a nice little tax write-off. She stepped aboard, her three-and-a-half-inch heels balancing perfectly beneath her, and surveyed the deck, keeping her expression impassive. The boat barely moved beneath her feet—a blessing—and with luck Harry Van Dorn would bee too busy on the putting green she could see up at the front of the ship to want to waste much time on a lawyer who was nothing more than Roper, Hyde, Camui and Frederick's perfectly groomed messenger. Damn, she wasn't in the mood for this.

She plastered her practiced, professional smile on her Chanel-tinted lips and stepped inside the cool confines of what must be the living room, if you even called it that on a boat. It was massive, beautifully furnished in black and white, with mirrors everywhere to make it appear even larger. She could see her reflection in at least three different directions, but there was nothing interesting to show her. She'd already checked her appearance before she'd left that morning. A young woman, just past thirty, with her long blond hair neatly arranged, her pale gray suit hanging perfectly on her shoulders and disguising the fifteen pounds that Roper et al. didn't approve of. Genevieve didn't approve of it, either, but all the dieting and exercise in the world couldn't seem to budge it. In the end Roper et al. had stopped pressuring her, a sure sign of their high expectations for her, Walt had said in his genial voice. At the time Genevieve had felt flattered. Now she was rethinking everything.

"Ms. Spencer?" It took her a moment for her eyesight to adjust from the bright glare of the sun on the water to the dimmer light in the large room, and she couldn't see anyone but the indistinct shape of a man across the room. One voice held a faint, upper class British accent, so she knew it wasn't Harry. Harry Van Dorn was from Texas, with a voice and a character to match. The man took a step toward her, coming into focus. "I'm Peter Jensen, Mr. Van Dorn's personal assistant. He'll be with you in a short while. In the meantime is there anything I can do to make you comfortable? Something to drink, perhaps? The newspaper?"

She hadn't thought of the word *unctuous* in a long time, probably not since she'd been forced to read Charles Dickens, but the word suited Peter Jensen perfectly. He was bland and self-effacing to a fault, and even the British accent, usually an attention grabber, seemed just part of the perfect personal assistant. His face was nondescript, he had combed-back very dark hair and wire-rimmed glasses, and if she'd passed him on the street she wouldn't have looked twice at him. She barely did now.

"Iced tea and the *New York Times,* if you have it," she said, taking a seat on the leather banquette and setting the briefcase beside her. She crossed her legs and looked at her shoes. They were definitely worth every penny when you considered what they did for her long legs. She looked up, and Peter Jensen was looking at them, too, though she suspected it was the shoes, not the legs. He didn't seem to be the type to be interested in a woman's legs, no matter how attractive they were, and she quickly uncrossed them, tucking her feet out of the way.

"It will only take a moment, Ms. Spenser," he said. "In the meantime make yourself comfortable."

He disappeared, silent as a ghost, and Genevieve shook off the uneasy feeling. She'd been working too hard—she was imagining things. She'd sensed disapproval from Harry Van Dorn's cipherlike assistant—he'd probably taken one look at her shoes and known what she'd spent. Normally people in Jensen's position were impressed—she'd walked into a particularly snooty shop on Park Avenue in them and it seemed as if the entire staff had converged on her, knowing that a woman who spent that kind of money on shoes wouldn't hesitate to spend an equally egregious amount in their overpriced boutique.

And she had.

She steeled herself for Peter Jensen's reappearance, but she should have known better. A uniformed steward appeared, with a tall glass of icy-cold Earl Gray and a fresh copy of the *New York Times*. There was a slender gold pen on the tray, as well, and she picked it up, looking at it.

"What's this for?" she inquired. Didn't they expect her to be professional enough to have brought her own pen?

"Mr. Jensen thought you might want to do the crossword puzzle. Mr. Van Dorn is taking a shower, and he might be a while."

Now, how did that gray ghost of a man know she'd do crossword puzzles? In pen? It was the Saturday paper, with the hardest of the week's puzzles, and she didn't hesitate. For some irrational reason she felt as if Peter Jensen had challenged her, and she was tired and edgy and wanted to be anywhere but on Harry Van Dorn's extremely oversize, pretentious yacht. At least the puzzle would keep her mind off the water that was trapping her.

She was just finishing when one of the doors to the salon opened and a tall figure filled the doorway. It had been a particularly trying puzzle—in the end she'd been cursing Will Went, Margaret Farrar and Will Shortz with generalized cool abandon, but she set the paper down and rose with serene dignity.

Only to have it vanish when the man stepped forward and she realized it was simply Peter Jensen again. He glanced at the folded paper and she just knew his bland eyes would focus on the empty squares of the one word she couldn't get. "Mr. Van Dorn is ready to see you now, Ms. Spenser."

And about frigging time, she thought. He moved to

one side to let her precede him, and it was a momentary shock to realize how tall he was. She was a good six feet in her ridiculous heels, and he was quite a bit taller than she. He should have dwarfed the cabin, and yet he barely seemed to be there.

"*Enigma*," he murmured as she passed him.

"I beg your pardon?" she said, rattled.

"The word you couldn't get. It's *enigma*."

Of course it was. She controlled her instinctive irritation—the man got on her nerves for no discernable reason. She didn't have to play this role for very much longer, she reminded herself. Get Harry Van Dorn to sign the papers, flirt a little bit if she must, and then get back to the tiny airport and see if she could catch an earlier flight.

The bright sun was blinding when she stepped out on deck, and there was no more pretending she was back on the island with all the water shimmering around them. She looked up at the huge boat—not a mansion, an ocean liner—and followed Peter Jensen's precise walk halfway down the length of the ship until he stopped. She moved past him, and then the cipherlike executive assistant was dismissed from her mind as she took in the full glory of Harry Van Dorn, the world's sexiest billionaire.

"Miz Spenser," he said, rising from his seat on the couch, his Texas accent rich and charming. "I'm so sorry to have kept you waiting! You came all this way out here just for me and I leave you cooling your heels while I'm busy with paperwork. Peter, why didn't you tell me Miz Spenser was here?"

"I'm sorry, sir. It must have slipped my mind." Jensen's voice was neutral, expressionless, but she turned back to glance at him anyway. Why in the world wouldn't he have told Van Dorn she was there? Just to be a pissant? Or was Van Dorn simply dumping the blame on his assistant as he knew he could? She'd seen that done often enough to know that it was par for the course.

"No harm done," Van Dorn said, moving forward, taking Genevieve's hand with the most natural of gestures and bringing her into the cabin. He was clearly a physical man, one who liked to touch when he talked to people. It was part and parcel of his charisma.

Unfortunately Genevieve didn't like to be touched.

But she'd done worse things for Roper, Hyde, Camui and Fredericks, so she simply upped the wattage of her smile and let him pull her over to the white leather banquette, dismissing the unpleasant little man who'd brought her here. Except that, in fact, he wasn't that little. It didn't matter—he'd already made himself scarce.

"Now don't you mind Peter," Harry said, sitting just a bit too close to her. "He tends to be very protective of me, and he thinks every woman is after my money."

"All I'm after is your signature on a few papers, Mr. Van Dorn. I certainly wouldn't want to take up any more of your time...."

"If I don't have time for a beautiful young woman, then I'm in a pretty pitiful condition," Harry said. "Peter just wants to keep my nose to the grindstone, while I believe in having fun. He doesn't have much use for women,

I'm afraid. Whereas I have far too much. And you're such a pretty little thing. Tell me, what sign are you?"

He'd managed to throw her completely off guard. "Sign?"

"Astrology. I'm a man who likes my superstitions. That's why I named the boat *Seven Sins*. Seven's my lucky number and always has been. I know that put together all that New Age crap don't mean squat, but I enjoy playing around with it. So indulge me. I'm guessing you're a Libra. Libras make the best lawyers—always judging and balancing."

In fact, she was a Taurus with Scorpio rising—her teenage friend Sally had had her chart done for an eighteenth birthday present, and that was one of the few details that had stuck. But she had no intention of disillusioning her wealthy employer.

"How did you guess?" she said, keeping the admiration in her voice at a believable level.

Harry's laugh was warm and appealing, and Genevieve was beginning to see why people found him so charming.

People magazine hadn't lied—he was gorgeous. Deeply tanned skin, clear blue eyes with laugh lines etched deep around them, a shock of sun-streaked blond hair that made him look like a slightly seedy Brad Pitt. He radiated warmth, charm and sexuality, from his broad, boyish grin to his flirting eyes to his rangy, well-muscled body. He was handsome and charming, and any intelligent woman would have been interested. Right then, Genevieve couldn't have cared less.

But she had a job to do, and she knew that one of her unspoken orders was to give this very important client anything he wanted. It wouldn't be the first time she'd considered sleeping with someone for business reasons. She knew perfectly well what that made her—a pragmatist. She'd avoided it so far, but sooner or later she was going to have to be less fastidious and more practical. If it turned out that she had to sleep with Harry Van Dorn just to get some papers signed and get out of there—well, there were plenty of more onerous duties she'd had to perform while at Roper et al.

But she knew the drill. They weren't going to get to the business she'd brought until the social amenities were covered, and with Texans that could take hours, and nothing would hurry them.

"You mustn't mind Peter," he continued. "He's an Aries, with a very auspicious birth chart, or I wouldn't keep him around. April 20, as a matter of fact. He's too damned gloomy by half, but he gets the job done."

"Has he worked for you a long time?" she asked, wondering when Harry was going to take his hand off her knee. Good hands—big, tanned, perfectly manicured. There could be worse hands touching her. Like the slimy Peter Jensen.

"Oh, it seems like forever, though in fact he's only been with me for a few months. I don't know how I did without him before—he knows more about me and my life than I do. But you know how men like that are— they get a little possessive of their bosses. But I don't want to spend the afternoon talking about Peter—he's

about as interesting as watching grass grow. Let's talk
about you, pretty lady, and what brought you here."

She started to reach for her briefcase, but he covered
her hand with his big one and gave an easy laugh. "Oh,
to hell with business. We have plenty of time for that. I
mean what brought you to an old fart law firm like
Roper and company? Tell me about your life, your loves
and hates, and most of all tell me what you want my chef
to prepare for dinner."

"Oh, I can't possibly stay. I have a plane to catch to
Costa Rica."

"Oh, but you can't possibly leave." Harry mimicked
her. "I'm bored, and I know your associates would want
you to make me happy. I won't be happy unless I have
someone to flirt with over dinner and something pretty
to look at. Those oil wells aren't going to dry up overnight—nothing will happen if I don't sign the deeds of
transference till later. I promise, I'll sign your papers, and
I'll even see that you get to Costa Rica, though why you'd
want to go to that pesthole is beyond me. But in the meantime, forget about business and tell me about you."

The latest historical romance from

Nan Ryan

Kate Quinn arrives in Fortune, California, with little but a deed to a run-down Victorian mansion and a claim to an abandoned gold mine. But a beautiful woman on her own in a town of lonely, lusty miners also brings trouble.

Sheriff Travis McLoud has enough to handle in Fortune, where fast fists and faster guns keep the peace, without the stubbornly independent Miss Kate to look after. But when a dapper, sweet-talking stranger shows a suspicious interest in Kate, Travis feels it's his duty to protect her. And he's about to discover that there are no laws when it comes to love.

The Sheriff

ANNE STUART

32171	BLACK ICE	___ $6.99 U.S.	___ $8.50 CAN.
66908	STILL LAKE	___ $6.50 U.S.	___ $7.99 CAN.
66813	THE WIDOW	___ $6.50 U.S.	___ $7.99 CAN.
66571	SHADOWS AT SUNSET	___ $6.50 U.S.	___ $7.99 CAN.

(limited quantities available)

TOTAL AMOUNT $ _____
POSTAGE & HANDLING $ _____
($1.00 FOR 1 BOOK, 50¢ for each additional)
APPLICABLE TAXES* $ _____
TOTAL PAYABLE $ _____

(check or money order—please do not send cash)

To order, complete this form and send it, along with a check or money order for the total above, payable to MIRA Books, to: **In the U.S.:** 3010 Walden Avenue, P.O. Box 9077, Buffalo, NY 14269-9077; **In Canada:** P.O. Box 636, Fort Erie, Ontario, L2A 5X3.

Name: _____
Address: _____ City: _____
State/Prov.: _____ Zip/Postal Code: _____
Account Number (if applicable): _____

075 CSAS

*New York residents remit applicable sales taxes.
*Canadian residents remit applicable GST and provincial taxes.

MIRA®

www.MIRABooks.com

MAS0206BL